BETRAYING DESTINY

THE OMEGA PROPHECY III

NORA ASH

Illustrated by
NATASHA SNOW DESIGNS

ABOUT THE AUTHOR

Nora Ash writes thrilling romance and sexy paranormal fantasy.

Visit her website to learn more about her upcoming books.

WWW.NORA-ASH.COM

Stalk Nora

Newsletter
Facebook Group
Instagram

Goodreads
Bookbub
Website

Facebook Page
Pinterest
Twitter

1
ANNABEL

"Why?"

The word hung in the nothingness between us, expanding until it pounded in my temples and throbbed in my blood moving sluggishly through my veins.

"Why?" I repeated. The ice in my gut crawled through my body, numbing my arms, my fingertips... my chest. "Why, why, *why?*"

The last word came out as a wail, and Grim sighed, his lips parting slightly to expel his breath—the only movement on his granite features as he stared down at me.

Even in this place void of color, his eyes were mismatched—one light, one dark—and as bereft of emotion as the rest of his face.

"Grim!" Through the ice, through the agony pulsating in my chest where my matebonds hooked like

barbed wire, fury rose. He had tricked me. He had taken me from my mates.

He had *betrayed* us.

My magic rose from deep in my body like a firestorm, and I shot to my feet as golden light blasted out of me and into him. "*Why?*" I roared.

Dark magic flickered like flames around Grim, absorbing my energy and leaving the god before me untouched.

I balled my hands into fists, narrowing my eyes as I reached for my magic deliberately this time. "*Tell. Me. Why*. Or I swear, I will blast you into next Sunday! Tell me right goddamn *now.*"

"You shouldn't spend your magic needlessly," he said, his voice soft even if the blank expression on his pale face didn't change. "Hel is not a place to find yourself weakened."

I lifted my arms and shot another blast of golden energy directly into his chest with a scream of rage.

Grim's magic rose around him again, once more warding off my attack. With a wave of his hand, the air shifted around me, knocking me off my feet. I landed on the mossy ground with a grunt and found myself locked in place by invisible hands.

"Enough," he said. "You will hurt yourself."

"*Why?*" I ground out through clenched teeth. "Why do you care if I hurt myself? You *killed* me. I'm in *hell,* and you brought me here!"

"Hel," he corrected. "You're in Hel."

"Really? You're going to argue semantics with me now?" I hissed, squirming against my invisible ties. It did nothing, and I screamed with impotent frustration.

"It's a bit more than semantics," Mimir muttered from his place on the tree stump to my right.

I turned my head to glare at him. "And you! Are you in on this? Did you lure me here like some sort of grotesque bait?" Something dawned on me and I cussed, twisting back to face Grim.

"Loki! Loki sent me to you. He... He knew? He's behind this? *He's* the... Betrayer? Oh, God, he fucking *tricked* me! I can't believe I trusted him!"

"It will do you no good to fret about what is done, Annabel," Grim said.

"Are you fucking serious?" I snarled. "You *killed* me. You've doomed the entire world—your own brothers—and you're telling me not to *fret?*"

Grim crouched in front of me, and something that could have been regret flickered across his features for the briefest of moments. "I have not doomed my brothers. Because of me, they will make it through Ragnarök. This prophecy of yours..." He gave Mimir a less than respectful glance. "They were foolish to place so much faith in you. Reckless to risk everything on a mortal's strength, even if she has been touched by Fate. You ask me why? The answer is simple, Annabel: I will sacrifice anything and everything for my brothers. And so I did."

I bared my teeth at him in another snarl. "You killed

their mate! Do you not understand how a mateclaim works? They will die!"

"No, they will not. I took you through to the Realm of Death with your body intact. They will hurt, and they will suffer, but they will not die. Once Ragnarök has swallowed the nine realms, once the end has come and gone, I will be able to break their matebonds to you.

"They will be free, Annabel. And alive. Find comfort in that."

"But I will still be dead," I whispered, and finally the ice and fury seeped from my body like melting snow, leaving only the torment of my four bonds and an aching hollowness surrounding them. Tears pricked at my eyes, overflowing as the truth of what I'd lost finally set in. "I will never see them again. I will... be here? Alone? For eternity?"

"Yes," he said softly. A chilly touch ghosted against my cheek, making me recoil before he pulled his hand back to look at the wetness coating his fingertips like the physical display of my grief was puzzling to him. "There was a time you would have done anything to be free of your Fate. Given anything—maybe even your life. Perhaps with time, you will come to see your new existence as freedom. Perhaps not. But it is your reality, Annabel. The sooner you come to accept it, the less you will suffer."

I screamed in his face. It came out as a hollow wail—a sound as devoid of power as I felt, bound and trapped in Hel.

Dead. I was dead.

There was supposed to be peace after you died. I hadn't thought much about any afterlife before I was kidnapped by Viking gods and sucked into living myth, but I'd had this hazy knowledge that once I took my last breath on Earth, there would be peace.

But this? This was anything but peaceful. This was agony, despair—rage and sorrow. I felt too much, *hurt* too much. How could this be *death?* How could this be the end when my body and soul still reverberated with emotion as powerfully as when I'd been alive?

Flashes of last night blazed through my mind, of the waves of lust and love I'd felt in the arms of my mates. So strong. So... unbreakable. At least, that was what it had felt like. Unending. Unyielding.

But I'd been wrong. Verdandi had been wrong when she wove my thread with my mates'. One of the men destined to claim me had chosen another path, and this was the result.

At least the Norn had been right about that part. Any diversion from our Fate and there would be nothing but misery for me.

"I don't understand," I whispered, my voice breaking with the grief still thick in my throat. "Why not let us try? Fate chose us for a reason. If you'd felt what it was like when we faced Loki and Nidhug... the strength of our combined power... That is why Verdandi believed in us, Grim. We... We could have won. We could have saved the world, but you chose...

this. You've chosen death. Destruction. *Ragnarök!* You think your brothers want this? That they'll be happy in a world of nothingness? Matebond or not, you've doomed them. *You* did that."

Grim rose to his full height. Even through this world's lack of colors, I could see his eyes glowing as he stared down at me. "You are wrong. You did not have the power to withstand what is to come, and you did not have the power to protect my brothers. You may rage against me if you wish, Omega. You may curse me, and you may refuse to accept your fate. It changes nothing.

"Once Ragnarök has eaten the world, I will break your bonds to my kin and the ties to your old life will be gone. Eventually you will succumb to the numbness of death. You won't yearn any longer. You will just... be. Here. For eternity.

"There is no point in arguing. There is no point in asking me why. You are never leaving Hel, Annabel. Never. And your so-called mates are better for it."

2

MAGNI

Pain.

I cried out as my chest cavity split in two, and my eyes flew open while I desperately tried to fill my collapsed lungs with air. I expected to see an enemy above me and a blade in my chest, but there was nothing but the ceiling slashed with ribbons of light.

Roars of agony mixed with my own, and through the haze of torment I sensed *them*—my brothers in soul.

I tried to reach for them, to come to their aid, but I only managed to roll onto my side before the hole in my chest sent me sprawling with another agonized sob. I reached for my ribs, some half-coherent instinct urging me to stem the bleeding, but my fingers met nothing but my skin. There was no gaping wound, no blood, and no weapon embedded in my flesh.

"Anna!" Modi's broken cry sliced through my confusion and rendered me ice-cold. *Annabel.*

I searched inward through the painful hole to that place where my bond to my mate had anchored me since I clamped my teeth on her neck during her first heat. *Nothing.*

"Annabel!" My roar mixed with my brethren's as I forced my body to move and my eyes to focus. I let my panicked gaze sweep the room, but all I saw was Modi, Saga, and Bjarni on the floor, grasping their own chests and crying out for our mate.

She was gone.

"No. No, no, *no!*" She couldn't be. She was just *there.* Finally, after so many weeks apart, she had returned to me. She couldn't be gone. She couldn't.

I fell to my knees on the skins where she'd slept, my hands skimming over them as if I would somehow find her there. There was still an indent of her small body, and they smelled like her, and us, and sex.

But this didn't feel like when she had left for Midgard and I'd been a walking zombie waiting for her return. I'd still been able to feel her bond, painful as it had been. Now... Now there was nothing.

My Annabel was gone.

I DON'T KNOW how long I was out for. I had a faint memory of passing out and assuming I was dying the way an Alpha should have when his mate was ripped from him. I'd been so relieved.

But when I opened my eyes, I was still staring up into the same blasted ceiling as before, and my chest throbbed with dull, consistent agony.

Someone grasped my shoulder. Saga. He leaned over me to search my eyes, gray gaze bloodshot and dull.

"What is this nightmare?" I rasped. "We should be with her. We should be dead."

"We should be," he agreed. "Which is why she can't be gone, Magni."

I scoffed. It came out as a pained wheeze. "This is what death feels like."

"But we are not," he insisted. "So she can't be. There has to be... some way to bring her back from wherever she's been taken."

I wanted to tell him that he was grasping at straws, but I couldn't get the words out. If he was right—if there was even a sliver of a chance that she wasn't dead—then I would rather tear myself to shreds with my bare hands than give up on her.

So long as my painful clump of a heart still beat, I would never give up searching.

I nodded feebly. "If there is, we will... we will find it. We will find her. The others—?"

"Still passed out." Saga grimaced and pressed a hand to his chest for several breaths before he managed to steel himself and turn to the room. "You get Modi up.

I'll get Bjarni."

I grunted an agreement, though it took me several minutes to regain enough strength to get to my feet.

My brother was sagged on the stone floor a few feet from the skins we had slept in. It looked like he had tried to go for the door before the agony of our loss had rendered him unconscious. I knelt by his side and placed a hand on his shoulder.

"Modi," I rasped, shaking him with what strength I could muster. "Modi. We need you. Annabel needs you."

He jerked on the floor, a long whimper escaping him before his consciousness floated back into his reluctant body. "Anna?" he croaked. "*Anna!*"

"Shh." It was the first time I regretted what I had done to my brother. Somewhere behind my own misery, I knew that if I had not brought Annabel to Trudheim—if I had not introduced her to him—he would not be in this much pain.

At that moment, I couldn't give less of a shit about prophecies and Norns and the godsdamn end of the world. All I knew was agony, and that if I had chosen differently, my proud brother would not be sobbing on the floor, calling for his mate like a lost child.

"We'll get her, baby brother. I promise. We'll find her and we'll bring her back." I spoke the words with more confidence than I could feel through the hole in my chest, but as I watched Modi struggle for breath, I knew we had to. There was no other choice. If she had been dead, so would we. There were no ifs, and, or buts about it, so *she* had to be alive. And if my mate still breathed, if even a shred of my beloved still existed, then we would reunite with her no matter the cost.

I rubbed Modi's shoulder and back with long, calming strokes until he could breathe steadily again. A few feet away, Saga embraced his blond bear of a brother. Bjarni's face was pale and drawn with lines of grief as he processed the sensation of loss still tearing at us.

"Who took her?" Bjarni finally rasped.

"We don't know," Saga said, his mouth drawing into a grim line. "Nor how. How did someone steal her from our *bed?*"

"She got up just around dawn," Modi said with a frown. "Said she had to relieve herself. I... fell back asleep before she came back. In fact... I fell back asleep within seconds. It was impossible to keep my eyes open."

"You think someone drugged us to get to her?" I asked, my own brows locking into a matching frown.

"More likely used magic," Saga said.

"Son of a bitch!" Bjarni snarled, grief turning to fury in the blink of an eye. "She promised Loki she'd free him. If she did and he repaid her by snatching her, so help me—"

"But if he was the Betrayer, why not allow Níðhöggr to eat us alive?" Modi asked. "It would have been much easier than.... this."

"Loki does whatever will gain him the most," I said, not quite managing to keep the disdain for my new brothers' father from my voice. "He could have taken her for reasons we have no understanding of."

"Where is Grim?" Bjarni asked.

It wasn't until then I realized we were short one Lokisson.

"He left while we were with her last night," Saga said. "He has no way of knowing she's gone, so likely he's somewhere in Valhalla, sulking."

"Perhaps he has seen something," Bjarni said, the hope in his voice infectious enough to make my heart pick up speed.

"Then let us find him," Modi said. He pushed off the floor and got to his feet. "And after, we will find whoever thought it wise to steal our mate, and we will make him *pay.*"

3

ANNABEL

The sky was as gray as the rest of the world when the nothingness of dreamless sleep released its grip on me.

I didn't know when I'd fallen asleep. All I remembered from before I'd lost consciousness was crying and screaming at Grim, and his granite features as he took in my despair. Possibly he'd magicked me to sleep when he got tired of listening to me curse his miserable name into the ground.

I stared blankly into the colorless swirl high above. Even in Jotunheim and Asgard, the sky had seemed familiar, as though those realms still inhabited the same plane of existence as Earth, despite all that set them apart. Hel? Hel was very clearly another thing entirely. The gray sky above should have been filled with clouds, but instead it looked like swirls of mist scored through with lines of inky blackness. It turned into an enormous funnel cloud of some sort, its touchdown disappearing far out of my field of vision.

Every muscle in my body hurt, and my eyes were swollen and sore from crying. Behind my ribs there was nothing but pain and visceral anguish. I couldn't sense so much as a ghost of my mates' awareness, and I didn't dare prod at where the connections should have been out of fear that the resulting agony would rend my mind.

So this was death.

So far, I wasn't a fan.

A deep, continuous rattle finally made its way through my misery to my conscience. It took me several minutes of staring into the swirling celestial sphere to care enough to investigate.

I turned my head to the right and was greeted by the disturbing sight of Mimir's severed head still propped on the tree stump. His eyes were closed, his mouth hanging slightly open. The grinding sound was coming from him.

Snoring. The animated head was snoring.

They did say sleep apnea occurred somewhere between the sinuses and the throat, unluckily for Mimir.

The thought made me snort. I grimaced at the raw feeling crawling through my throat in response. Water would have been nice. And a pee.

To my surprise, I had full use of my limbs again.

Grim must have unbound me after he'd knocked me out.

Small favors, I guess. I sat up, groaning at the stiffness in my body after a night on the bare ground, and took in my surroundings.

My eyebrows hit my hairline when I spotted the darkhaired Lokisson seemingly fast asleep on his side at the edge of the small clearing.

He'd... stayed? But why? My mates would have no way of knowing he was behind my disappearance. Why not just drop me off and then return, pretending like he knew nothing of my whereabouts while Ragnarök tore our worlds apart?

I was half-tempted to kick him awake and ask him. Or just kick him. But as I clumsily got to my feet and stretched my sore body, I decided against it. I didn't particularly want to spend another sixteen to twenty-four hours bound on the ground and forced to wet myself, so I resorted to giving him a death glare before I left the clearing to find some water.

After half an hour's searching, I hadn't managed to find anything but trees—lots and lots of pine trees stretching high toward the sky, their gray needles reaching for the swirling fog.

"Stupid, useless death-realm," I growled to no one in particular. Only then did I realize that my throat wasn't really sore anymore. And I wasn't thirsty, either.

Odd.

However, my bladder was still functioning and making its unhappiness with my delay known.

Great. More squatting behind a bush. An eternity of it, in fact. Peeing outdoors had been one of the many sucky things about my trek through Washington and Oregon with Modi and Bjarni, and I'd intensely looked forward to the luxury of indoor bathrooms for the entire journey. Only now it seemed like that was yet another comfort I would never experience again.

My hatred toward Grim was at a boiling point as I squatted next to a pine tree to relieve myself.

There was a bright red streak in my underwear. I stared at it, dumbfounded by the almost obscenely rich color in the midst of all the gray. It took me several moments to realize I'd gotten my period.

I'd... actually gotten my period. In Hel. I was dead, yet I was still menstruating. Fuck. My. Life. Or death, as it were. Fuck my death. *So* hard.

It was only while I was looking for moss on the forest floor to stuff into my panties that I realized this was the first time since I'd left my home that I'd bled. I'd been too swept up in Fate and myth and saving the world to track the dates, but now that I came to think about it, I should definitely have had at least one more period between arriving in Iceland and now.

Had I gotten pregnant during my last heat? Was this...? I swallowed thickly and pressed a hand to my abdomen. *Oh, God. No. Please, please, no.*

I didn't have any more tears left. Didn't have the capacity for anymore sorrow. I'd lost everything already, and if this was more than a delayed period, then...

Mechanically, I gathered the rest of the moss and placed it as best I could in my underwear.

For a moment I just stood there, staring blindly ahead into the gray forest. I didn't have anywhere to go. I thought about continuing into the woods and letting them swallow me up, but the thought of being all alone in Hel was even more awful than having to see Grim's face again.

In the end, I walked back toward the clearing. I hadn't paid much attention to which direction it lay when I went out to search for water, but as I made my way back through the pine trees, the path seemed clear, almost as if I had a homing beacon to guide me through.

When I broke through the tree line some twenty minutes later, both Grim and Mimir were awake.

The darkhaired alpha seemed to have been pacing. He stopped when he spotted me, angular features pulling into a frown. "Don't wander off on your own. This is dangerous territory."

I snorted in disbelief. "Dangerous territory? I'm dead, remember? How much worse can it get than dead?"

"Decently bad," Mimir said, his voice mild and irritatingly cheerful. His eyes flicked to the funnel cloud in the distance. "There are stages of death, my pretty plum. All things considered, we're lucky."

I eyed the bodiless man for a long moment, but decided against pointing out that he'd probably feel luckier with legs. Instead I glared at Grim. "I don't see why you'd care if I extra-died, seeing as you were the one to kill me in the first place."

Grim's full lips pulled up in a sneer, but instead of replying, he stiffened, nostrils flaring.

"What?" I asked, shifting uneasily. He was staring intently at me—or rather, at my crotch. He crossed the distance between us, eyes wide and locked on my lady bits.

Grim had never struck me as interested in... well, *me.* I still recalled that asshole Surtr's comment that he'd assumed Grim's kind reproduced asexually, and frankly, I wouldn't have been surprised if it turned out to be true. His sudden interest in my nether parts was wholly disturbing.

"Is that...?" Mimir said behind me, shock in his voice. "Is she truly...?"

"What?" I repeated, taking a step back from Grim to escape from his personal space.

It brought me closer to Mimir, who gasped and said, "She is!"

"I'm *what?"* I spun around to face him, partly to avoid Grim's continued stare.

"Your moonblood!" Mimir said, his mouth twisting

up into a wide grin. "You have been blessed with your monthly bleeding!"

So many emotions went through me at once, though complete mortification came out on top. "You... How do you know that?"

"It's a very distinctive smell." Mimir's eyes flickered to my crotch, then back up to my eyes. "My dear girl... do you know what this means?"

Smell it. They could *smell* it. Just... great.

"I don't know—probably that my brother-in-law murdered my unborn child?" I said, the words spilling out though I hadn't meant for them to, laced with bitterness and a pain I couldn't begin to process. "I haven't had a period since my first heat, and I suspect passing into the death realm isn't the healthiest thing for a fetus."

"No." Grim's voice was almost a growl. Almost, but not quite. "You were not with child. I made sure."

"He's right," Mimir said, his voice still way too happy. "It would have smelled differently. This is fresh, healthy moonblood."

Relief I hadn't been expecting washed through me. At least that was one loss I'd been spared.

Behind me, Grim breathed in deeply, clearly scenting me. "How are you doing this?"

Embarrassment reignited in my gut and traveled up to my face as the awkwardness of having the disembodied head of a prophet and my coldblooded murderer discuss my period set back in.

"I'm not *doing* anything. Pick up a biology book." I turned away from both of them to retreat to the other side of the clearing.

"You are dead! This is impossible," he growled, apparent frustration finally breaking his composure.

"I guess I'm just lucky," I snarked. "And may I take this opportunity to thank you for killing me in such a way that I apparently get to keep my period for the rest of eternity? Really. *Thank you.* Nothing like scavenging for fucking *death moss* to stuff into your panties to really brighten your non-existence."

"You don't understand, plum," Mimir said. "This is Hel. This is the realm of death."

"I'm aware," I bit, turning to shoot him a withering stare. "Everyone's been quite clear on that."

"Life doesn't touch this place," he continued, ignoring my sarcasm. "But *you*... Your body is preparing to bear a soul. It's capable of birthing life. *Here.*"

"How?" Grim asked, voice twisted with darkness, but the irony of having him ask me the exact question I'd screamed at him over and over yesterday didn't escape me.

I snorted, partly from disbelief. *"How?* You think *I* know how any of this bullshit works? *You're* the magically gifted god. And *you,"* I pointed at Mimir, "are a literal prophet. You work it out."

"In the well of eternity, this has never happened before," Mimir said, his gaze turning distant as if he was searching a vast expanse for an answer. "Only mortals are gifted with monthly bleeds, but the instant a human crosses the border to Hel, there is no turning back. They are lost for eternity, and so is their ability to bring life into the world."

"Maybe's it's a fate side-effect-thing," I said, shrugging. "Does it really matter? I'm still dead, aren't I?"

"You are," Mimir said. "But—"

"But the second they smell you, every wretched creature in this place will either hunt you down to make you carry their spawn, or shred you apart to prevent you from birthing such a monstrosity," Grim interrupted. When I turned to look at him, he was pinching the bridge of his nose in a very human gesture. "Gods damn you, why are you always such a pain in my ass?"

I opened my mouth to suggest what he could shove up said ass, but the realization of what he'd just said made the words die on my suddenly too-dry tongue. Seemed Mimir had been right—things could indeed get much, much worse.

Grim drew in a deep breath and lowered his hand. "Stay here. Mimir's presence will offer you some protection. I will search the area—make sure nothing dangerous resides in the vicinity."

Without waiting for my response, the darkhaired Alpha walked off to the edge of the clearing, letting the thick forest swallow him up.

"Something dangerous? Besides him?" I muttered.

"Come here, plum," Mimir said.

I turned to him. "Why?"

He gave me a small smile. "No need for suspicion, young one. I am merely a head. I won't be among the creatures attempting to impregnate you."

I stared at him. "And yet you managed to lure me to Hel. Excuse me if I'm less than trusting."

"I was not a willing participant in that ploy," he said, the amusement in his voice finally dying.

"Oh? So you just happen to be hanging out in the death realm for no real reason? Chilling in the woods, waiting for someone to stroll past?"

"The manner of how I came to be here I cannot discuss with you, but my choice it was not. Even for a man whose home is a well, this place is... unpleasant."

I put my hands on my hips, no less suspicious. "You can't? Or won't?"

"I cannot." His bushy eyebrows pulled into a frown. "And for now, it is not important. What is important is that I learn the truth of your ability to sustain life in this place before your cold companion returns. Come. Pick me up."

"He's not so much a companion as he is my killer. You get that, right?" I said, hesitantly returning to Mimir's tree stump. I wasn't sure exactly what the prophet wanted from me, but if he wished to do it before Grim came back, it might mean that he was... well, at least not on the same side as the asshole who'd betrayed me.

"He was the tool that brought you here. I understand," Mimir agreed. "Now lift me."

I hesitated for another moment, the thought of touching a severed head making my stomach twist.

Mimir arched his eyebrows at my reluctance. "I don't drip. The spell that sustains my life has me perfectly preserved. Come now—the woman prophesied to save the world can't be squeamish."

I grimaced, reaching down to gently grab him under the ears. He maybe had a *small* point. "I thought me dying kind of ended that prophecy. Can't I be as squeamish as I want now?"

"Ah, but *did* you die, plum?" he said, eyes sliding from mine to my throat. "That is the only question worth asking now. Hold me against your neck. I need to smell you."

Awkwardly, I did as he commanded. His beard and eyebrows tickled me as he inhaled deeply at the hollow of my throat, and I gritted my teeth to resist the urge to toss his head like a ball.

"Interesting," he murmured. "*Very* interesting."

"So? Am I not dead after all?" I asked, wild hope blooming through the bizarreness of this whole encounter. I pulled him out at arm's length to look at him again, willing him to confirm that this had all been some horrible misunderstanding.

"Oh, no, you're dead," he said, and my moment's worth of elation withered into dust. "But... there is... *something.* Some... *shred* of immortality lingering in your essence where there should be nothing but humanity. Tell me, little omega, has anyone gifted you an item of divinity?"

An item of divinity? I frowned. "What, like a necklace that grants nine lives?"

"A necklace, a trinket... an apple, perhaps?" His dark eyes bored into mine, and those bushy eyebrows quirked knowingly.

An apple. I blinked, the memory of Bjarni feeding me a golden fruit as we crossed Bifrost flickering in my mind, as well as his matter-of-fact attitude as he told me what eating it had done.

Immortal. He had made me immortal. Somewhere along the journey to find Loki and fighting Nidhug, I'd forgotten the magnitude of that gift.

I gasped, eyes going wide as I stared at Mimir. "Idun's apples! Bjarni... he stole one for me!"

"Bjarni Lokisson! That boy isn't half as dumb as his reputation would have you believe. Oh, my pretty plum, *that* is why your womb is still fruitful." Mimir cracked a wide, toothy grin. "And that is how we are going to escape this miserable place."

I blinked, my brain taking a while to process his words even as my heart picked up speed. "Escape? There's... There's a way out of here?"

"There are..." He looked up toward the sky. "...two ways out of Hel for the omega still carrying a spark of life where nothing but death should exist. But, I suspect, only for as long as the apple's effect is still within you. Once a year, the gods must eat from Idun's tree. If you are still here after that time, there will be no stopping death's final ravishment. And should you be killed while still in this realm..."

"Then no more second chances, either," I said, but despite the grimness of his warnings, excitement pounded in my veins. "So I'll be careful, and I'll be out before a year's passed. Tell me, how do I escape?"

He quirked his eyebrows at me. "I will tell you in due time, plum."

"And *now* isn't 'due time'? Grim's going to come back at some point, and I doubt he'll be on board with this plan of yours."

"For now, I will tell you which direction to go," he said mildly.

I arched an eyebrow at him. "You don't trust that I won't leave you behind if you tell me now? Really? Didn't you prophesize a whole thing about me saving the world? You'd think that would make me, ya know, pretty trustworthy."

He gave me a small smile. "You might be surprised how many heroes touched by Fate are scoundrels at heart. The Norns care little for a person's character when they weave their threads, only the end goal. Now let us get going. You have a world to save, after all."

4

GRIM

Huldra blood still dripped from my knives as I breeched the clearing where we'd found Mimir. Normally I'd have taken the time to care for my weapons, but the second my blade had plunged into the monster's heart and the adrenaline of battle eased, a sense of urgency that still hadn't released its hold gripped my lungs and pulled me back. Back to Annabel.

I quickly took in the space, prepared to sling my magic out if something had crept up on the omega while I was away—but nothing but gray grass met my eyes. Gray grass and an empty tree stump where Mimir should have been.

Despite the urgency still clawing at my lungs, I lowered my weapons with a curse. I knew exactly what had happened. No beast had taken the prophet, nor savaged the omega I'd ordered to stay put. She'd simply... *left.*

"Curse that woman," I growled into the silence. She may have hated me for what I'd done, but I had hoped she would be smart enough to realize that she needed to stay close unless she wanted to experience much, *much* worse parts of Hel.

But apparently not.

Despite Saga, Modi, and Magni doing their best to tame the willful omega, it would seem they'd all failed spectacularly, like I'd always known they would. And the result? The result was that I got to hunt a girl capable of bearing life through the Realm of Death. Hopefully I'd find her before she was raped or torn to pieces.

The way Saga and Magni had been acting while she was off finding Loki, I very much doubted my brothers would survive it if she got herself hurt in this place. And if they died...?

Teeth clenched, I jogged off in the direction the pull from her called.

I'D MOVED through the forest for nearly an hour when an unmistakable roar rang through the trees.

"Odin's beard," I hissed just as bright light flashed between the tree trunks a few hundred yards up ahead. Another roar, angrier this time, had me sprinting toward where Annabel's unmistakable magic ripped through the forest once again.

I arrived at the flat-bedded creek just in time to see Annabel standing in ankle-deep water as she lifted her right hand to fire another blast of magic into the body of a humongous troll on the other bank. Mimir's head was tucked tight underneath her left arm.

The monster bellowed as her power struck his already singed chest, making the smoldering bald patch around his nipple wider. His face contracted in fury as he patted at the embers in his fur, froth dripping from his tusks.

"Dammit! Why isn't this working?" Annabel's voice was shrill with fear.

"Because troll skin is impenetrable to magic, you ignorant fool," I growled, leaping forward just as the troll lunged off the bank toward the omega. My dark magic wrapped tight around its enormous body, yanking it off its trajectory and into the creek. The forest shuddered around us as it landed with a thud and a splash that sent a good amount of water cascading over both banks. It soaked me, but I didn't pay the wetness of my clothes any mind; my focus was purely on the troll.

Abandoning one dagger, I clutched both hands around the handle of the remaining one and used all my strength and the weight of my body to thrust it between the troll's ribs. But just as I impacted, the monster jerked and my blade dug into bone.

The troll roared, its pain granting it enough strength to shake free of my magic's hold. Before I could reorient, a hand the size of a small boulder struck me in the side. I heard a distinct *crack,* followed by a lancing pain that seemed to bloom all the way through my left side. I stumbled on the slippery river rocks with a groaned curse.

The troll swung again, and I only narrowly managed to dodge out of the way before its fist connected with my head. It hit me in the left shoulder instead, shattering the joint with another crack.

I managed to bite back on the dark fissures threatening to take away my consciousness, pulling strength from the pain as it fueled my battle rage. Before the troll got another chance to hit me, I tightened my magic around it like a fishnet. The beast struggled against my bindings, but I kept my focus ironclad.

A gleam of metal from the stream revealed the location of my discarded blade. I did my best to protect my injured left side as I rolled up on my knees with a grimace, reaching for my weapon with my right hand. Only when I was once again armed did I force myself to my feet and turn to face the troll.

It was lying on its back in the creek again, muscles straining against the dark ribbons of my magic. Living in Midgard for all those years had dulled my senses, had made me forget the lessons I'd learned in my youth. It wouldn't happen again.

Baring my teeth at the creature, I straddled its chest

and pushed the tip of my blade against its thick skin, this time using the tendrils of my magic not binding the troll to help me push down. My broken ribs and shoulder made me hiss with agony, but I kept my focus, and the knife slowly slid through its flesh and into its heart.

Beneath me, its great body lurched a final time with a shout that shook the trees lining the stream. Then, finally, it stilled.

Breathing heavily, I sagged against the troll's chest, hand still wrapped around the knife. For every rapid pulse of my heart, the adrenaline left my system, allowing the pain from my broken bones to overshadow my relief at bringing down the monster.

"Why did you follow me?"

Annabel's sharp voice pulled my thoughts halfway from my misery, and I looked at her over my uninjured shoulder. She still had Mimir tucked under one arm. The other she had raised out in front of her. Light glowed around her palm.

I barked a laugh, instantly regretting it when my ribs were forced to expand around my lungs. "Are you going to kill me, omega?"

She could, I realized. I was too weak to shield myself from an attack for long, thanks to the troll's fists, and inexperienced as she may have been, I wasn't a fool. She'd taken down Loki. She was powerful. And very, *very* angry.

"I'm thinking about it," she said, a snarl on her delicate features that made her look more savage than any omega had any right to. "Fair's fair—you killed *me,* after all. So, I'd like to know why you saved me from that... thing."

I blinked slowly. She was trying to weigh whether my reasons for saving her were noble enough to spare my life. I wheezed out another laugh.

"I'm afraid I have to disappoint you. I have not turned *honorable*, and I do not have regrets. I saved you from the troll because you are still tied to my brothers. If you are hurt, if you die here... they will feel it. And their lives will be forfeit. So I will remain by your side, and I will protect you until Ragnarök has shattered the nine realms and I can break your bond to them."

She stared at me, her dark eyes hard. I remembered their chocolate-brown color from the world of the living, the eager shine in them as she'd looked over my horse, Draugr. She'd been a different person then. Softer. Innocent.

"You won't make it here on your own," I reminded her. "Even with your magic, you're nothing but a lamb in this world, ripe for slaughter. You can hate me as much as you like, but I know how tight those mate-bonds bind you. Just the thought of the agony they'd go through at your death... You won't risk it, even if it means sparing my life."

Annabel narrowed her eyes at me, and for a moment the light in her palm flared brighter. With a scoff, she closed her hand into a fist, the light dying down. She spared me another hard look before she turned on her heel and stalked off into the woods.

Grimacing, I forced my aching body upright and followed her.

SHE WALKED UNTIL NIGHTFALL, only occasionally exchanging a few words with Mimir. When the gray light faded into darkness and it became impossible for her to see with her human vision, she finally stopped below a small hill.

It wasn't a bad place to make camp—the overhang from the hill provided some shelter from wandering night terrors, and the thick layer of pine needles littering the ground would make for a somewhat soft bed.

Not waiting to be asked, I gathered up a few sticks and fallen branches and set about making a fire to keep away the worst monsters that prowled in the darkness. When I came back to the hill with a collection of tinder, I saw her huddled next to Mimir, speaking low but urgently at the severed head.

"How much longer until we're there?" I caught her whispering.

Mimir cleared his throat and shot a look in my direction, bushy eyebrows raised. Annabel looked over her shoulder and clammed up, lips pinched with irritation.

So there was a point to this trek through Hel's

woods? A destination? I didn't say anything as I pulled the flint from my pocket and lit the fire. She didn't need to know I'd heard her, and neither did that tricky prick of a prophet. What scheming had he pulled her into? Something that had given her a sense of purpose, clearly. A harebrained plan to escape, perhaps?

Once the fire was going, I slumped back against a large rock and closed my eyes against the pain still radiating through my body. If something did cross the barrier into our little camp, I'd be hard-pressed to protect Annabel like this, or from whatever folly Mimir had roped her into. Broken bones took me a few days to heal, even in the human world. In Hel? Nothing healed here.

"Why am I not hungry?" Annabel's voice made me open my eyes again. She was looking at Mimir, brows pulled into a frown. "We've walked all day, and I'm not even thirsty."

"You're dead," I reminded her, the constant pain in my shoulder and ribs making me less patient than usual—which, according to my brothers, was already not one of my virtues.

She shot me an ungrateful look.

"Your body does not need nourishment here," Mimir explained.

"That makes no sense. I'm tired, and I had to pee this morning," she said, frowning deeper.

"Your body still carried some leftover processes

from when you were alive. As for the urge to sleep—even Hel cannot quell your spirit's need for rest," Mimir said.

"Don't go drinking from Hel's rivers or eat any berries you come across," I said, irritated with myself that I hadn't told her sooner. "It is not nourishment you will find in either."

"I guess that makes sense," she mumbled. "Why would the Realm of Death sustain life, eh?"

"Precisely," Mimir said. He smiled broadly, looking very much like a satisfied teacher whose pupil has finally clocked on to the finer points of his tutelage. Gods, how I wanted to kick his head like a ball, an urge I'd had to repress whenever I'd been reminded of his idiotic prophecy.

"So... what exactly happens if you die again in this place?" Annabel asked. I didn't miss how she eyed me as I winced and cradled my ribs. "How can you be extra-dead?"

"Better you don't worry about that, plum," Mimir said mildly. He yawned wide. "We should all get some rest before the light returns. Or what constitutes as light in this dreadful place."

Annabel flattened her lips, clearly frustrated at getting brushed off, but before she could snap at the prophet, I said, "You have your body still. Once it dies, only your soul will remain. And it too can die. It can be shredded into pieces, torn asunder, or eaten by the nightmares wandering these lands. What remains, Hel herself will enslave.

"You have seen the great siphon in the sky? It is made up of her army—broken souls having met their final death here, funneled into her palace where they will await her command to descend upon the lands of the living in the final days of Ragnarök. They are said to be aware, even in that state. No one can really tell for sure."

Annabel shuddered, wrapping her arms around her midriff. "This doesn't sound much better than the Christian version of Hell."

I shrugged. "My sister has made of her realm what she saw fit."

The omega blinked, straightening as she stared at me. "Your sister? The Queen of Death is your sister?"

"A daughter of Loki," I said, poking a stick at the fire before throwing it onto the burning logs.

"Of course," she muttered. "Man, that guy has fathered a lot of bullshit."

I didn't miss her look in my direction.

"How on Earth have Saga and Bjarni turned out so well? Their mother must have been a literal angel," she continued.

I stiffened at the mention of my stepmother, muscles tensing from memory alone before I could quell my body's reaction. When I glanced up at Annabel, it was clear I hadn't managed to hide it.

She stared at me, mouth partway open and eyes wide as if she'd just remembered something important.

"What?" I snapped.

"Bjarni told me... she used to beat you. When you were a kid." Her voice was... not gentle, but less hateful than it had been.

I glanced at the prophet, who was looking from Annabel to me with eyebrows raised in apparent interest.

"So?" I arched a brow at her, feigning disinterest. "Jotunns are not known for their nurturing spirits."

"You didn't want to see her when we were in Jotunheim. Your brothers made fun of you for it. They never understood, did they? Saga... During that trial to get into Asgard, he had to face his worst fears. One of them was not being able to protect you and Bjarni. But he never protected you from her, did he? He never saw the need." She was staring intently at me, as if my answer was somehow important to her.

I narrowed my eyes. "There *was* no need. I don't know what your obsession with one Jotunn bitch is, but it will do you no good. My stepmother was a vile woman, but she did as Loki tasked her to do—she raised me into adulthood along with her own sons, and that is all there is to say about the miserable cow."

"Hmm," Annabel hummed, narrowing her eyes too. I didn't like the shrewd look sliding over her face. When she got to her feet, I followed her movements as she walked around the fire and sat down next to me.

Without a word, she poked me in my shattered shoulder.

I hissed in pain and bared my teeth at her. "*Careful.* I need you alive, not necessarily conscious. Injured or not, my magic is still far stronger than yours."

"And yet my magic can heal. Yours can't." She tilted her head as she took in what damage she could make out through my clothes. "I have a proposition for you, Lokisson."

"I am not helping you get back to Asgard," I said flatly.

"I know." She prodded at my shoulder again, gentler this time, but it still hurt like a bitch. I caught her wrist with my uninjured hand, growling a warning.

Her attention slipped down to where I touched her. "You're still cold," she murmured, surprise in her voice. "I can't feel the warmth of the fire, but you're still... so cold."

"He's not dead," Mimir helpfully supplied.

I ignored him. "What proposition do you have for me, omega?"

She looked back up from my hand. "I can heal you. But... at a cost."

I wanted to tell her that I didn't need her healing, but while I certainly could be stubborn to a fault, I wasn't unaware of how precarious my situation was. So instead I gritted my teeth and ground out, "What *cost?*"

She gave me a sweet smile that held just an ounce of malice. "I want you to tell me truths. Let's keep the number classic and say three of them. No trickery, no half-truths, and I get to dictate what they are."

I arched another eyebrow at her. She'd definitely learned a lesson or two while in my father's company. "And how will you know if I am telling the truth?"

"You will do a spell. Swear a blood-oath. Whatever hocus pocus ensures you can't lie." She glanced at Mimir. "I'm assuming such a thing exists?"

"Indeed," the bodiless prophet agreed. "It is pretty simple magic."

I glared at him before returning my focus to her. Her eyes gleamed in the firelight, and I once more remembered how beautifully, earthily brown and full of life they'd been before I took her here. "Why? What possible good could that do you?"

"I'd just like to know a bit more about my killer. And you're not the most forthcoming of people, ya know." She smiled at me again, just a small tilt of her lips. She was definitely planning something. But... magic or no, she was a mortal stuck in Hel. Dead. Nothing she could do would ever endanger me or my plans. If she wanted to dig around in old wounds and exact some small revenge for what I had done to her, it was a price I'd pay without a second thought to make sure I could protect her if need be, thus keeping my brothers safe.

"Fine. You can have whatever truths I can provide—*after* you've healed my injuries."

I slid my hand up her wrist, twining my fingers with hers. My magic came willingly, almost eagerly, wrapping around our combined hands, tugging at me to drape my very essence around her—that same nauseating urge I'd felt since she was nothing but a newborn spawnling.

I gritted my teeth, pushing down instincts I wanted no part of, and focused on the spell. "Three truths I shall give you. Three answers you may request. Set my bones and strengthen my body, and your questions shall be answered."

My power sparked in my blood, flaring between us before snuffing into nothing but a leftover hum in my hand.

Annabel glanced to Mimir, who nodded—always an interesting movement for a bodiless man.

"Yes. That should do it, my pretty plum," he said. "But please do keep in mind that your magic resources are somewhat low after that nasty troll encounter."

A look passed between them, and I narrowed my eyes at the confirmation that they definitely had some sort of plans which required Annabel's magic to function. Bjarni and Modi had told us what it took to *refuel* her powers. No doubt she still had plenty of strength left to heal my injuries after that depraved reunion she and her mates had indulged in the night before I lured her away.

But if healing me would drain her just enough to weaken any attempts at escape? Well, that was just a bonus.

I released my grip on her hand and straightened up. "Well? Do you want your truths, omega?"

"Of course." She let her gaze slide over my shoulder and down to my ribs, attempting to evaluate the injuries. "I need to be able to touch your skin."

I reached for the hem of my tunic, but the movement sent jolts of anguish through both my shoulder and ribs. Grunting, I clutched my hands around the fabric, trying to anchor my swimming vision. *Odin's beard,* that hurt.

"Let me," Annabel said. She got to her feet and grabbed for my tunic, carefully edging it up my torso and over first my good arm, then head before she eased it down my injured left side. I was somewhat surprised by her care—she could easily have made it hurt, but chose not to.

One glance at her face now focused on my damaged body, and it was clear she'd let those soft omega feelings sweep away some of her anger, at least for now. She worried her lip as she narrowed her eyes at my shoulder, her slim fingers dancing across my skin with featherlight touches.

I hated it. Hated every gentle brush of her palms and her small hum of concern when I hissed from pain. I'd *killed* her. I was going to break her matebonds and leave her in Hel for eternity—and still she was so achingly gentle as she handled my broken body. It was... *irritating.*

"Get on with it," I growled, shifting away from her

careful exploration. The movement made my shoulder pang, but it was better than Annabel's touch.

She pinched her lips and sent me an admonishing glare. Again she grabbed for my shoulder, firmer this time, and then her magic welled up and into me.

I wasn't prepared for the sensation of it, of *her,* rushing through me like a wave. Before my mind's eye, I saw the golden shine of her power, even if it was colorless in Hel, and I shuddered at its touch. It was balmy and pleasant, and it pulled a groan from my throat that nearly turned into something akin to a purr before I managed to stop it.

My own magic rose to meet her, more eager to wrap around her light than when I'd sworn my oath of truth. She allowed it to, prodding at it and sending shivers through my entire being.

No, no, *no.* With a force of will, I clamped my shields down, leaving her with nothing but an impenetrable ice barrier. I kept it in place as her magic slid across it, testing once before she returned her focus to my broken body. Her amusement echoed in my mind before her magic dove into my flesh and through my bones.

I kept my teeth gritted through the arduous healing process, my sole focus on my inner barriers. Just that briefest of touches of her essence, that single moment of feeling her within, and I knew what her plan was—why she'd proposed this trade.

She was looking for a weakness. Looking for a way

in, to twist me into compliance like she had her four mates.

"That's one down," Annabel said, pulling her hands from my shoulder. When she looked up at me, the strain of what she'd done was evident on her face. Exhaustion painted lines on her delicate features, and even in the darkness, the dullness of her eyes was clearly visible.

"If you continue, you will drain what's left of your magic," I said, my voice calm; emotionless. "Are you certain you wish to render yourself defenseless for whatever answers you seek?"

She jutted out her chin, a look of defiance I knew all too well from the years I'd seen her grow from a child into a woman replacing some of her exhaustion. "I won't be defenseless, Grim Lokisson. That I promise you."

She pressed her hands to my left side, forcing her magic into my body with a grunt of effort. Instantly the agony eased some, and I watched her as she slowly mended my shattered ribs.

She truly believed she would find a way to make me see the errors of my ways. She was banking every last drop of her strength on it. Once she'd healed me, she'd be as weak as a kitten, entirely reliant upon me for protection. As if finding whatever weaknesses she was searching for would somehow give her a path to my heart, like it had with my brothers and our enemies.

Perhaps if she'd known that my kind had nothing

but ice where she was hoping for warmth, she would have thought twice before she spared my life. I may have looked like a man to her, another god to be brought to his knees by Fate's siren call, but I was not.

Monsters birth monsters, and I was born from ice and mist and terror. To Annabel, I would be nothing but her destruction.

5
ANNABEL

I slept for a long time after healing Grim's injuries.

It was hard to judge the passage of time in Hel, but when I woke up, the gray light seemed dimmer, as if dusk was nearing.

"What's the time?" I mumbled groggily as I sat up. My head was still wrapped in the cobwebs of dreamless sleep, but I had the distinct sensation I'd been out for a while.

"Time is not a relevant concept in this place, plum," Mimir said. When I looked in his direction, I saw his head sitting on a turned over tree trunk, the same place I'd put him down when we made camp last night.

"You have slept for nearly a full day." Grim's voice was gruff and unfriendly, as usual. I turned to him and arched an eyebrow at his near-naked figure. He was sitting cross-legged with his back to a large rock, some form of breeches covering his private parts and one of his knives in one hand and some sort of whetstone in the other. It made a slick, slicing sound every time he ran it along the blade.

"Get too hot?" I asked, giving Grim a small smirk when he shot me a dark look from underneath the shock of charcoal hair covering one of his eyes. The blue one, if I remembered correctly.

"Troll blood is vile, even without its usual stench," he said, nodding to the large rock next to the one he was leaned against. His wet clothes hung over it, boots and belt at its foot.

"I suppose that is one plus about Hel—no bad smells," I sighed, then grimaced when I remembered how he could still smell one particular thing. It was as good a reminder as ever to go hunt down some fresh moss.

Grim looked up when I got to my feet and staggered a little as my knees threatened to buckle. *Shit.* I shouldn't have been so weak after sleeping for so long. I'd known healing him would drain most of my magic, but it seemed I'd pushed it too far.

"Don't leave my side," he said, his voice brusque as he paused the whetstone's rhythmic slide.

"I need more moss. Feel free to tag along if you have a period fetish, I guess," I said, walking off before he could voice another command.

I didn't hear any movement behind me, but before I'd taken more than a few steps into the woods, Grim fell into step by my side. He was wearing his boots and leather trousers, and he had a knife in each hand, but his torso was still bare.

"I didn't take you for the kinky type," I said, keeping my tone light as I continued walking.

"A mild-mannered gnome could kill you without breaking a sweat," he snarled, gaze searing the side of my skull. "Don't stray unless you wish to die—and, as a byproduct, cause your *beloved* mates unthinkable agony before their shredded spirits join us."

I pushed the pang in my soul away at the mention of my mates. I had to stay focused, and the hollowness in my chest whenever I thought about them threatened to take my ability to so much as think.

Mimir was guiding me to a way out of Hel, but even if I succeeded in escaping this cursed place, there was still Ragnarök to worry about. The prophecy was clear —Verdandi had been clear. I needed five mates. Not four.

Grim was my fifth. Grim, who'd murdered me. Grim, who hated me.

Grim, who for the briefest moment had shown me a shred of vulnerability—an inkling, a faint whisper that somewhere, behind the betrayal, behind his icy exterior, there was an actual person. Someone I could make see how awful, how incomprehensibly wrong his choice had been. A last ghostly thread of hope for humanity, for the nine worlds... and for myself.

And so I had to focus on the here and now, and lock away the agony of my tattered bonds to the four men who'd given everything for me. I had one goal now, and I could not afford distractions. I had to crack his icy heart, make him understand—and, however impossible it felt, find a way to forgive his betrayal.

I glanced at the brooding god out the corner of my eye. He was painfully beautiful. They all were, my fated mates, but Grim was... different.

I'd never seen him topless before, and the dimness of the gray forest around us did nothing to hide the width of his chest and every hard muscle flexing with every step he took. Like his brothers, he was so obviously an alpha, but that was where the similarities stopped. His bared skin was so pale it seemed to be made from pure frost, an ethereal glow to it that underlined his otherworldly heritage, and there was nothing warm or primitive about him.

Out of all three brothers, he was the one who looked most like Loki, with his black hair and high cheekbones. His features were so lean they were almost gaunt, but there was nothing sickly about him. Just haunting, icy beauty and a darkness that seemed to spill out from within.

"Why did he put you up to this, Grim?" I asked softly.

"Who put me up to what?" His voice was as gruff and unfriendly as ever, his focus on our surroundings rather than me.

"Killing me. Betraying us. I claim one of my truths—I want to know why Loki decided to welcome Ragnarök.

And why you would rather trust him than your brothers."

He snapped his head around to look at me then, the expression in his mismatched eyes inscrutable. His jaw clenched, his Adam's apple bobbing once, almost as if he'd tried to speak but *something* had stopped him.

A small growl slipped past his lips. "I am unable to answer that."

I frowned. "What? But you swore an oath."

Grim leveled me with a hard stare. "I *cannot* tell you anything concerning he who is responsible for Ragnarök's coming."

I blinked. "Is it... is it because he put some sort of silencing spell on you?"

The alpha didn't respond. I took that as a yes.

"Christ." I shook my head, then spotted what looked like a suitable patch of moss and crouched to pull some free.

"You do that a lot," he said, his voice somewhat softer.

"Hm? Do what?" I looked up from the moss and caught his haunting eyes. They were so intense I found it hard to hold his gaze.

"Invoke the Christian god, or his son. Even now, after everything you've seen. You don't call out for Thor, or Odin, or any of the other gods you have encountered—not even your own mates. It's always this Christian deity. Why?"

I shrugged. "It's how I was raised, I guess. It's mostly

an expression. Why do you ask?" Then something dawned on me. "Is it.... offensive to you guys?"

He chuffed a breath through his nose. I could almost have believed it was a laugh, if not for the darkly serious expression on his face. "Offensive? To a god who cares about mortal worship, perhaps. *I* was perfectly happy living in exiled oblivion. You can call to your desert god as much as you please. It's too late for regrets for your kind."

Something in his words, in his tone, made a memory niggle at the back of my mind—a passing comment from Loki on our way back to Valhalla, something about... forsaking our old gods? I shook my head, dismissing the hazy thought. It wasn't important, not now.

"Well, if you can't tell me anything about Loki's plans, then I have another truth I want from you," I said, pulling the last chunk of moss free before I stood back up. "Tell me what it was like for you growing up. Tell me about your mother, about why you were taken to Bjarni and Saga's childhood home to be raised. About your relationship with your brothers, your father, your stepmother. I want to know exactly what it felt like, every painful detail you would never tell anyone else, every moment of joy, every loss. All of it."

Grim bared his teeth at me, such a ferocious alpha threat it should have looked foreign on his cold features. It didn't—it just looked exceptionally scary. Enough for me to take a step back.

"You want my life story, Annabel?" Despite his obvious anger, his voice was still soft like black silk. "You think you'll find a way to manipulate me through my past? You will be sorely disappointed. Nothing I say will help you escape."

"Just tell me," I said, forcing more bravery into my voice than I felt.

He sucked in a deep breath through his nose, staring me down, and for a moment I thought he would refuse. Undoubtedly he would have, had he not been bound by the magic of his oath.

"I was birthed by one of the Jotunns of Niflheim," he began, and from the hesitance in his voice it seemed the words were being forced out of him. "They are... different than other Jotunns. And they have little maternal instinct. At six months, once their offspring no longer require their mother for nourishment, they will usually be left to fend for themselves.

"I am told my mother attempted the same with me, but I was a halfling. Had my father not come by to finally meet his youngest son, I would have perished in the mist. He bribed my mother with magical gifts to care for me past her natural inclinations. And she did, to the extent she was capable.

"I have few memories of my time in Niflheim. Of *her.* I do remember her attempts at making me stronger. I was... an embarrassment, I imagine. A squalling, weak little thing clinging to her teat. Had it not been for my father, I am sure she would have drowned me in the bogs."

"How did she try to make you stronger?" I prodded.

Darkness flashed in Grim's eyes. "She would beat me to get me to fight back. It never worked, of course. I would just cower and wail and plead for mercy.

"My father's next visit happened to come during one such lesson—on my fourth birthday, I believe. That's when he took me to Jotunheim to be raised alongside Saga and Bjarni. I suspect he recognized that there was too much of his blood in me to survive a childhood in Niflheim."

"Four? She did that to you when you were *four?"* Despite my anger with him, my heart gave a spasm at the thought of a helpless toddler in the hands of... of a *monster*. "And Loki let you stay with her for *four* years?"

"Ah. Does your soft heart betray you again, omega?" He gave me a small smile that held no warmth. "Perhaps I only killed you because my mother beat me as a child—is that what you're thinking? Does it make it easier to accept what I did to you now?"

I glared at him. "Continue."

"As you wish." He chuffed through his nose and leaned back against a tree trunk, seemingly unbothered by the rough bark against his skin. "My brothers' mother was about as thrilled to have Loki's mistborn bastard in her home as could be expected, but she fed and clothed me. And through my brothers, I learned the concept of loyalty. It took us a while to get along—I was a stranger in their house, younger than them, and... odd. Not entirely of their world.

"But I will always remember the autumn day I'd gone out to search for poisonous mushrooms in the woods surrounding our cabin. Bjarni had tied me up in the outhouse overnight, and I was planning revenge. But the mushrooms grew farther away than I'd anticipated—almost to the foothills of the mountain range.

"I didn't notice the troll until it was on me. My father had started my magical education at that point, but I was still too young and too inexperienced to fight back. I knew I was going to die. But..." His lips curved in a half-smile. "My brothers had followed me into the wilderness. When they heard me scream, they came bursting out of the underbrush, armed with nothing but sticks and stones. Saga was barely eight at the time, Bjarni only six. They attacked that troll with a fervor Tyr himself would be hard-pressed to match.

"To this day, I don't know how they managed to chase it off, but they did. They saved my life. After, Bjarni hugged me while I bawled my eyes out. It was my first experience with a kind touch. If he hadn't held my arms so tightly, I would have punched him.

"After that day, I swore I would always protect them, no matter the cost. We weren't *friends*, not for several more years, but we looked out for each other. They made life under their mother's roof tolerable for me."

"And your father?" I asked. "Where was he?"

Grim shrugged. "Who knows? Wherever his

schemes and plots took him. He would stop by from time to time to check on our progress and prepare us for our supposed Fate to save his bloodline."

"No kind words? No hugs?" I asked, even though I pretty much knew the answer already. The God of Mischief hadn't exactly come across as a warm and jovial father on our first meeting.

Grim's smile turned acrid. "From Loki? I'm sure the answer surprises you, but no. I never minded. My brothers did, for a while. He is our sire, and without his teachings, I would not have become as powerful as I am. But my loyalty is with my brothers. Not him."

I frowned. "Yet you betray them to help him? I don't understand."

He only gave me that dark stare of his, and I sighed.

"Right. You can't tell me. Fine. Continue. When did you, Bjarni, and Saga become friends, then?"

Grim's sensuous lips turned to a flat line. He hesitated for several breaths, before he finally said, "When I Presented as alpha. I… was not expecting it. My mother's kind is not subjected to base biology, not in the same way as the inhabitants of the other realms. I had no such… interests. I'd passed the age when both Bjarni and Saga Presented with no change, and so I assumed I took after her in that way.

"When my first rut struck, I thought I was dying." He stared straight ahead at some point above my shoulder. His voice was flat, emotionless as always, but something about him was… off. Different.

"Bjarni and Saga were out. I would have gone to them otherwise. But they weren't there. I was so out of my mind, I went to *her* instead—their mother. I came crashing through the door, wild and panicked and *hungering.* I didn't understand what was wrong with me, but I knew I needed help, no matter who it came from.

"She was in the kitchen when I saw her. And... something in my brain clicked into place. I *hated* that woman, but right then... she was female, and that was all that mattered. I fucked her against the kitchen counter first. Then on the dining table. And finally in her bed. It was sickening. In the few moments' respite between ruttings, I wanted to vomit. The sensation of being tied so intimately with *her*... But it didn't matter. She would make this... crooning sound, and my body ached for more."

"You... you raped Bjarni and Saga's mother?" I whispered, so stunned by his admission I didn't know what else to say.

"You would think so," he said softly. "You haven't met her. I would be hard-pressed to overcome her now. I was smaller then. When I came for her, she smiled and spread her legs for me and told me to, ah—*stick it in*, I believe were her words."

I blinked. Repeatedly. "What... the hell? You were her stepson!"

"Bjarni and Saga returned home when I was still tied with her after the final round," he continued, ignoring me. "I thought they were going to kill me. Part of me wanted them to. They took me out to the stables, but instead they sat me down and talked about what it'd been like for them when they Presented. How scared they'd been when they felt like they lost all control. They explained about the biology of it, about the urges, and how to sate them without going into a frenzy.

"After that, our bond became... different. Stronger. I have been by their sides ever since. Until you."

"And... their mom?" I asked, not quite capable of getting that disturbing image out of my head. "How old were you when this happened? Did you all leave her home to come to Iceland then?"

"I was... thirteen, I believe. We stayed for four more years before we left to explore Jotunheim and beyond. We didn't come to Iceland until centuries later."

Thirteen. Thirteen, and his stepmom had let him...

"You *stayed*? What... How did that go? Did you all just pretend like it never happened?"

"Bjarni and Saga did," he said, eyes finally flicking down, though he still avoided my gaze. "To them, it didn't matter. It happened during my first rut, and their mother told them she was fine. It was just an unfortunate event no one was responsible for. I think they've genuinely mostly forgotten."

"And with their mom?" I asked. "Were things... different?"

He paused, his throat bobbing once as if he was trying to hold the words back. But the magic in our oath forced him. "Yes. They were... different. The next week, she found me in the woods. She told me she wanted a child with the same magic that runs in my veins. It took me a moment to understand what she expected of me. My rut was over, and I informed her of how I'd rather fuck a mountain troll. She didn't take that too kindly.

"So she told me that if I didn't give her a child, she would make sure I never saw Bjarni and Saga again. She would poison their minds against me, and I would be returned to Niflheim."

He breathed in, pushing off the tree trunk to roll his shoulders. "I never did give her a child. Stars be thanked she didn't conceive during my first rut, or that time in the woods, and I made sure to put a mixture of belladonna and mandrake in her food every night after. It didn't stop her from trying until I finally persuaded my brothers to leave."

"Grim..." I'd had it so wrong. So, so wrong. *He* hadn't assaulted *her*. She had used his love for his brothers to make him submit against his will.

Thirteen. I didn't care if he'd been an alpha at the time, or the son of a god. He'd still been a child.

He finally looked at me, but there was nothing but cold indifference in his mismatched eyes. "Does your heart bleed for me, little omega?"

"Yes," I whispered, ignoring the sting of his sarcasm. "Bjarni and Saga—they don't know, do they?"

"Of course not," he sneered. "They love the woman."

And he would do anything to protect them, even from the horrible truth of their own mother.

I remembered how he'd stiffened at the prospect of stopping by her cabin, and how he had been reluctant to force a mating with me, going so far as to stop his brothers from taking me that first night in Iceland when my heat was about to break. I'd come to assume it was because he found the idea of bedding me repulsive, and I was sure that was at least part of the reason, but... perhaps there had been just an inkling of pity from a man who knew what it was like to be made to surrender his body.

"If you told Bjarni and Saga, they would believe you," I said softly. "And they would be on your side."

He scoffed. "Please. Unpleasant as it may have been, it was just sex—and it was a very, very long time ago. If I wanted them to know, I would have told them centuries past. Now, are you quite done—or are there still some deep, dark secrets you wish to pry from me?"

I had made my bargain in the hopes of finding a way to understand this dark alpha. And now... I did. He may keep an indifferent façade, but I wasn't fooled. Not anymore. Mistborn or no, any man with his upbringing would have encased his heart in ice to get through it alive. But behind it... just maybe... there was still a fragment of a soul.

"Yeah. I'm done. For now."

Hopefully by the time I had my two other truths, I would find a way through his defenses.

6

MODI

There was no trace of the Mistborn within Valhalla's walls, nor had anyone seen him or Anna. Not that the gods, servants, and Valkyries we'd asked had much mind for anything but the chaos left in the wake of Loki's escape.

"I think we have to consider that whoever took Annabel might have taken your brother as well." Magni looked at Saga and Bjarni. "We are wasting our time here. I understand that he will be her fifth mate, but without Annabel, there is no point in looking for him. There is no point in anything."

Saga only nodded. He was leaning against a wall in one of Valhalla's many internal courtyards, eyes closed and face pale. I didn't envy either of the Lokissons. I knew every one of us felt our mate's loss so deep into our souls that there wasn't room for anything else. If Magni had been missing, I wouldn't have had the capability to care, and the guilt of it would have eaten up whatever shreds were left of me without Anna.

"We have searched everywhere and found no trace of her," Bjarni said, despair thick in his throat. "Where do we go next?"

"Trud was searching for Mimir and Freya, was she not?" I said. The faintest thread of hope sparked somewhere behind the thick fog of misery. *My sister.* She was the cleverest person I knew. "She might have found something that will set us on the right path, either to our mate or the prophet. Or perhaps she will be able to scry for her."

Magni lit up. "Trud! Of course. She will know what to do."

"Your sister is a völve?" Saga asked.

"Yes, and a powerful one at that." I clasped a hand on his shoulder, willing some of my own buoying hope into him. "Have faith. Trud will send us down the right path, brother. We will see our Annabel soon."

TRUDHEIM'S SPIRE rose toward the sky as proudly as ever, but my usual sense of homecoming at the sight of it was gone. *Annabel* was my home now, and she was missing. I didn't greet the servants scurrying about the courtyard as I normally would have, my sense of purpose blotting out any capability of manners.

Inside, my childhood home was as frantic with life

as outside. Servants bustled around, most carrying armor and food, and the informal dining table I'd eaten most of my meals at as a young lad was laden with a mixture of platters, leather, and metal.

At its head, my father was on his feet, barking orders and rummaging through weaponry. He looked up at our entry, eyes narrowing at Bjarni and Saga for a long moment before he turned to point a finger at me.

"It is not on your head that the Traitor fled his punishment—you brought him back like I knew you would. But if you bring his spawn into my home, you'd better be ready to wager your own neck that their allegiance won't waver while we cut down their father."

He thought we had come to join him in battle—to fight alongside him as he hunted for Loki—like the obedient sons he had raised us to be. For glory and honor.

The band on my bicep seemed to constrict tightly around my muscles as I remembered that desperate moment in Midgard when I had called for him and he had not come.

"Loki is not the Betrayer. He saved my life. Without him, we never would have been able to defeat Níðhöggr. He could have run then, but he did not. If he were the Betrayer, I would be dead."

My father's eyes widened—and then his face broke into a huge grin. "You defeated *Níðhöggr*? Ha! That's my son!" He turned to the nearest servant and slapped him on the shoulder, nearly sending the poor man to his knees. "You hear that, Gorm? My son slew Níðhöggr! A chip off the old block, that one."

There was a time his boasting would have filled me with pride. Now I felt nothing but emptiness.

"No, Father. Bjarni, Annabel, Loki, and I slew Níðhöggr, and we very nearly did not make it back. I called for you. Why did you leave me there?"

My father frowned, his smile fading. Gorm had the good sense to scurry out of the kitchen, bringing along the other servants. Everyone in Trudheim had learned to anticipate one of Thor's infamous explosions.

"What do you mean you called for me?" my father asked, his voice clipped. "Are you suggesting I'd turn my back on my own son? In front of *them*?" He indicated Bjarni and Saga with a tilt of his chin.

"I am making no suggestions. I am merely asking why, when I captured Loki like you commanded and was stranded in Midgard with Magni's life on the line, did you dismiss the connection I forged through the band?"

I tapped my bicep to indicate the band hidden there, the one he had gifted me so that I might always reach him—except, as it turned out, when I needed him most.

A look of confusion passed over his face, deepening his scowl. "I have no idea what you're on about, son. I received no communication from you while you were in Midgard."

I clenched my jaw as Bjarni's and Annabel's speculations about him echoed in my head. There was no way he was the Betrayer. No way he could be. I had known that in the marrow of my bones, and I had defended him fiercely.

And yet… And yet I knew that I had used the band to contact him—and that it had connected.

"It doesn't matter," Magni interjected. "We're here for Trud. Finding our mate is more important than this discussion."

"You are right. Our mate is infinitely more important than a man whose honor is more valuable to him than his own blood, and certainly more important than fighting an unwinnable battle."

I turned to the stairs, intent on locating my sister, but before I could take more than two steps, Thor closed his hand around my arm.

"What do you mean *our* mate?" he growled. I was surprised he'd picked up on that tidbit in the midst of my other insult.

"I mean that Magni's mate is mine as well," I bit. My muscles twitched as instincts otherwise buried in sorrow reared up, ready to defend my woman. "I found my soul in Midgard—in her. I found two new brethren in her other mates. I found my purpose—my *true* purpose—and it is not to stand by your side as Ragnarök swallows all nine worlds.

"But she is missing, and I do not have time to argue with you, Father. I hope to see you on the other side of this madness, but if I do not, may your death be honorable."

I pulled free of his grasp before he had a chance to respond and headed up the stairs with the others behind me.

We found Trud in her room. She was perched on a chair facing the window, but instead of taking in the pretty views surrounding our home, she was staring intently at the pages of a large, worn book.

She jerked her head up at our entry, and I halfway expected her to scold us for not knocking like she had so many times when we were kids, but she just expelled a deep breath, relief crossing her face.

"You're here. Things have been... difficult while you were gone."

"Things are difficult now," I said.

A vague smile pulled at the corners of her lips, but as she swept her gaze over our group and our worn expressions, it withered. "Where is my sister-in-law?"

I grimaced at the pang from the hollow in my chest. "She is gone, Trud. We need your help."

My sister stood so abruptly the book in her lap flopped to the floor. "Gone? What do you mean *gone?*"

"Someone took her," Magni said, his voice raspy and pained. "We woke up, and she was... gone." He pressed a fist to his chest, against the hole. "It feels like she is dead, but we are still here, still alive, so she can't be. Right?"

Trud's face turned ashen. "Annabel is *gone?* No. No,

she can't be. You would be dead too." She swept her blue gaze over us, as if ensuring we weren't ghosts returned from Hel to haunt her. "What do you mean, it feels like she is dead?"

I breathed through another painful flare and stepped toward my sister. "It will be easier if you..."

She nodded and placed a hand against my chest. I felt the jolt of connection, reminding me of how it had felt to blend my magic with Annabel's, but where my mate had brought elation and warmth, Trud's magic was paltry by comparison.

The second her power touched where my hollow bond rooted, she gasped and jerked back, severing the connection between us.

"Stars above, Modi," she whispered.

"Can you find her?" I asked through gritted teeth, because I knew if I accepted the empathy radiating off my sister, I would break.

She hesitated for a moment, and Magni, croaked, "*Trud*. Tell us you can find her."

"I think... I think she is where Freya and Mimir are," she said quietly. There was regret in her voice now. "I have been scrying endlessly for the goddess and the prophet, and they are... somewhere dark. And lonely. So lonely. That touch of Annabel's essence still within you... it feels the same."

"Where *are* they, then?" Saga asked, impatience coloring each word. "Tell us where our mate is and we will retrieve her."

"I am not sure." Trud looked to the floor where her book lay. "It makes no sense."

"Woman, I don't care if it makes sense or not. All I care about—all any of us care about—is that you tell us where Annabel is," Bjarni rumbled, an uncharacteristic edge to his voice.

"Hel," she said softly, sending a shudder of icy horror through each and every one of us. "I think... I think they are in Hel. But it makes no sense; the Queen of Death bows to no one. Why would she agree to hold them captive? She is beyond our petty squabbles, beyond any power held by any other god. And Annabel... Annabel is mortal. If she were truly there, you would all be in Hel too. No human can cross the barrier without succumbing."

"And... And if she weren't... *entirely* mortal?" Bjarni asked.

"What do you mean?" Magni demanded.

"If she... ate one of Idunn's apples. Would she be capable of entering Hel without dying?" the blond Jotunn asked.

Idunn's apples! I remembered the golden fruit he had casually fed our cranky mate as we passed over Bifrost.

"Bjarni Lokisson, you magnificent god among gods!" I blurted as I jerked back around to Trud. "Would that explain it? Is that why she is still alive? She is in Hel—but immortal?"

Trud frowned, her lips pursing. "I... I don't know. Perhaps? I have never heard of such a thing—a mortal eating one of Idunn's apples. And it does not explain why Hel would agree to imprison the goddess and the prophet. Nor does it bring back your mate. If she is truly in Hel, then I do not know how to retrieve her."

"Then who does?" Saga demanded. "I don't care if we have to burn Hel to the ground to get her back. I don't care if we have to give our own lives. If that is where our mate is, then that is where we will go."

Trud hesitated. "You don't understand. If someone has made a bargain with Hel—"

"It does not matter," I interrupted her. "I do not care if it is Loki. I do not care if it is our own father. Nothing matters until Annabel is returned to us. If you know of someone who can help us, please, sister. Tell us."

She shook her head slowly before she looked at me —at all of us. "I know of one creature who might be capable of untangling the thread of an undead mortal stuck in the void between Fate and Death. Seek out the Norn Verdandi and plead for her aid. In the meantime, I will track down whoever is behind this. Few would have the power to negotiate with Hel herself. In banishing your mate, they may just have given us the clue we need to bring him into the open."

7

ANNABEL

We walked for more than a week. At least, I thought it was more than a week. Time didn't feel like it worked right in Hel, and I was so chronically exhausted from healing Grim it was hard to keep my bearings.

Thankfully we didn't come across any more undead trolls, or other nightmarish creatures looking to impregnate and/or murder me. I hadn't had the stomach to ask which option the troll had most likely been after.

I also hadn't asked Grim for any more truths.

He was as cold and indifferent toward me as ever, but I... I was less so. Still angry that he goddamn murdered me, obviously, but it was becoming clear he had some twisted idea that this was the only way he could protect his brothers. And after what he'd shared, it was obvious that he would do anything for them.

At least we had that in common.

I glanced at my dark companion as he strode a few steps ahead of me, scanning our surroundings for any hint of danger. I felt a *tiny* bit guilty for having forced him to share such private and painful details of his past, but in this case, I'd made my peace with the ends justifying the means. And I knew I would have to burrow deeper if I wanted any chance of making him understand how wrong he was for believing Ragnarök was the only way this could end.

"Hrm-hmm."

Mimir cleared his throat, and I glanced down at his head beneath my left arm. The bodiless man arched his bushy eyebrows at me before casting a meaningful look at Grim's back. "We are getting close, plum," he whispered. "Time to lose the broody one."

I frowned and cast a quick look at Grim to ensure he hadn't heard Mimir. Judging from his long strides, he wasn't paying attention to either of us.

"What do you mean? I can't exactly leave Hel without him."

Mimir huffed. "You'll have to. He won't let you escape this place so long as his allegiance is twisted."

"It's *your* prophecy," I reminded him. "It's supposed to be five gods' sons, not four. Grim's my fifth."

"He'll have to join up once we return to the world of the living. Much can be done to change a man's loyalty, but you will not be able to stop Ragnarök while you're trapped in Hel. Come morning, you will have to leave him behind." Mimir gave me a meaningful look.

"And how am I supposed to do that?" I asked. "He's so much stronger than me, and I'm… not in peak condition."

Which was putting it mildly. All I wanted to do was sleep, but every morning I woke as exhausted as I'd been when consciousness left me the night before. Sleep wasn't going to fix this—only one thing would. I'd drained my energy too much when I healed Grim, and courtesy of my omega nature, the only way of recovering was to let an alpha restore my reserves. With his dick. Because of course.

Unfortunately, the only available alpha was not exactly in the mood to offer his services, and frankly, I'd rather collapse from exhaustion than ask Grim for the magical equivalent of a pity fuck.

"Leave that to me, plum. Just make sure you go to sleep close by me tonight, and be ready to run once I wake you."

We stopped to make camp for the night by the side of a pond that could have been beautiful, if Hel hadn't left it devoid of color and life.

"Is it safe?" I asked as I gave the tranquil water a longing look. I wasn't dirty, per se—I didn't sweat in Hel, which was at least some sort of silver lining—but I still had soil and pine needles stuck to my hair and clothes from sleeping on the ground. Just the thought of a refreshing dip seemed to lift some of the heaviness weighing down my body.

"Nothing is *safe* in this realm," Grim growled.

I heaved a sigh and looked to the less *doom-and-gloom* of my companions. "Will some monster eat me if I go for a swim, Mimir?"

"Unlikely," he said. "The more nefarious of the water creatures tend to attack only when their prey is alone. But if you hear a violin, best come back to shore."

"A violin?" I asked as I stripped out of my feathery leathers, focus mostly on the still water ahead.

"The Nix can be a bit of a difficult spirit. Sometimes he'll teach you to play, sometimes he'll lure you underwater and drown you. Seeing as we're in Hel, it's probably best to assume the worst and keep a wide berth," the prophet explained.

"Oh, so he's like the freshwater version of a siren?" Finally naked, I walked to the water's edge and dipped my toe in. I'd expected it to be cold, but the water held no temperature at all.

"Similar," Mimir conceded. "Though his prey is always children or women, not men. The children he lures with his music, the women with his pretty face."

"How equal opportunity of him," I muttered as I took a full step into the lake, "making sure it's not just horny men trapped at sea for too long getting targeted."

A strong, cold hand closed around my upper arm,

halting me before I could take another step. I gasped as much out of shock at the chill against my flesh as the unexpectedness of the touch. I spun halfway around, only to be met by Grim's dark stare. He stood close, way into my personal sphere, his boots kissing the edges of the lake.

"Don't drink the water. Not so much as a mouthful," he said.

"I wasn't planning to," I said.

"If you do—"

"Yeah, yeah, I'll extra-die. I get it," I said. It was meant as a snarky bite, but his nearness sucked the air out of my lungs, leaving my voice breathy and hoarse.

Standing this close to Grim was like being in the presence of a glacier large enough to have its own gravitational pull, and his grip on my arm raised goosebumps along my skin and made my bared nipples harden into points.

I hadn't worried about stripping down in front of him—he'd been so abjectly uninterested in my body it seemed ludicrous to be bashful—but this close to him, his dark stare boring into me, I felt so utterly bared for him, so completely stripped of any and all protection. Despite the chill of his touch, something warm curled in my abdomen. I couldn't tell if it was arousal or embarrassment.

Quite probably it was fear.

"Don't think it will be a fast, easy death," he sneered. Before I could think of a response, he released me and took a step back, leaving me to stagger as my body readjusted to the absence of his magnetic pull.

I didn't look at him again; I was too tired to deal with the enigma that was Grim. That would have to wait until we were back among the living and I'd had my energy restored.

Unbidden, images of the last time my mates *restored my energy* came rushing back, and I bit my lip as the heat in my abdomen turned a lot less confusing. The aching sear that made my heart stutter as I remembered every kiss and caress was wholly less pleasant.

I missed them so much it felt like I was one gust of wind away from shattering. All that held me together was sheer determination and the knowledge that come tomorrow morning, I would finally have the means to return to them.

I sucked in a deep breath, forcing the memories back into the hollow pit in my chest before I refocused on the water. All I could do now was have a swim—so that was what I was going to do.

The water felt odd as it crawled up my legs with every step I took into the pond, like some unnatural mixture of silk and oil wrapping around my skin. It lacked the refreshment that usually came with being submerged, but it was still a soothing sensation.

I walked out until the water lapped at my navel, then sucked in a deep breath and dove fully under.

The gurgling sound of water rushing in my ears was more familiar, and the movement of it against my skin made it feel less alien. I opened my eyes—keeping my lips firmly shut—and took a couple of strokes out, following the silty bottom of the pond.

The greyness of Hel seemed less disturbing underwater. It was more like swimming at night under the moon. I reached out and touched the leaves of a trailing plant reaching toward the surface. It moved gently under my fingertips, its surface soft and pleasant, if a bit slimy.

I kicked, moving farther along the lake floor, and picked up a gleaming stone to inspect it. It too was smooth under my fingers, but the shell I picked up next had some texture. A crustacean poked out from the shell, probably in response to being hauled free of the sand, and clacked its miniscule claws threateningly at me.

I let out a bubble of surprised laughter, and it dawned on me that as scary as Hel was, it also had its beautiful sides, if you took the time to search for them —an odd thing for a realm that seemed so tightly twined with terror and misery.

The air in my lungs turned heavy, so I put the creature back on the bottom of the lake and kicked against the sand. The water caressed me as I shot up through it, parting as I broke the surface and gasped in a few deep breaths.

I swirled around to reorient myself, my eyes landing on the shore where we'd made camp. Mimir was still on the stone where I'd placed him, overlooking the lake, and Grim...

My heart skipped a beat as my gaze locked with his.

He was crouching on the shore by the water where I'd left him, staring at me. Even from this distance I could see the darkness in his eyes. *Hate?* Was it hate he felt when he looked at me like that?

Goosebumps crawled up my arms and down my back, and I turned my attention away from him, swimming farther out to the center of the pond. I was pretty sure he did, in fact, hate me. He seemed entirely unremorseful for killing me, and he acted like my presence was a barely tolerable burden. If not for his loyalty to his brothers and the knowledge that if I perished in Hel before he'd broken the connection between us, they would die too, I was certain he'd have ensured I joined the siphon of souls doomed to serve Hel herself.

And once he severed that connection, he would leave me to rot here. No regrets. No empathy.

I forced the shudder that followed that train of thought away and dove back underneath the surface.

The pond was deeper in the middle, and many more aquatic plants obscured the bottom than had closer to shore. I swam through them, enjoying their whispered caresses along my body. Even as I finally dove deep enough to spot the sandy floor, plenty of light still filtered through from the gray skies above. That was probably why, when I swam past a large rock formation, I had no trouble seeing the exact features of the creature lurking there.

I shrieked, but the water swallowed the sound and turned my scream into bubbles. The vaguely female-looking beast flicked her tail and rushed up toward me, slapping a scaly hand across my mouth and nose and another around the back of my head before I could do anything else.

"Mmmph!" I flailed wildly, trying to shove her off me, but despite her slim frame, she was freakishly strong. On instinct I reached for my magic, but found the place inside me where it usually resided barren.

The creature shook me hard by her grip on my head, snapping my focus back to her. When my frantic gaze connected with her glossy and freakishly large eyes, she shook her head at me.

"Mmph!" I protested behind her hand—a noise that became significantly higher-pitcher when she opened her mouth full of long, sharp teeth and moved it toward mine.

"Mmmmmm!"

A muted boom cut off my attempted scream, echoing through the water around us and sending ripples through the otherwise still water. The creature before me turned her head with a snap—and a second later an invisible force exploded between us, sending us flying in opposite directions.

My shoulder slammed into the rock she'd hidden

behind, and I yelled out in pain—and swallowed a mouthful of lake water as a result.

The effect was immediate. A leaden sensation crept down my esophagus and lungs like poisonous sludge. Grim's warning flashed belatedly before my mind's eye, and I tried to hack and spit, but it only resulted in more water rushing into my mouth.

Shit, shit, shit! I kicked desperately against the sand, blind to anything but getting to the surface to expel the poison from my body, but my muscles refused to obey. Slowly the unnatural weight spread to them, constricting my movements with every second that passed.

Before I could finish the thought of what would happen if I didn't get to the surface soon, the water rippled around me again, and suddenly Grim was there.

His dark hair floated around his pale face like black seaweed, but I didn't have time to appreciate what a handsome merman he made. Without pause he wrapped both arms around my waist and pushed off from the sand, sending us shooting upward with rocket speed.

The second my head was free of the surface, I tried to suck in a lungful of oxygen, but my airways were full of water, and all I managed was a desperate rattle.

Grim didn't pause to help me. Still with an arm around my torso, he buoyed me against his body and began swimming toward shore with long, sure strokes.

"Ghkkr!" I choked, trying desperately to alert him to my impending death.

"Hold your fucking breath!" he snarled without ever breaking his pace.

Easier said than done. My lungs burned and my vision swam, black dots dancing at the edges.

Before I could pass out, he threw me onto a hard surface and rolled me onto my stomach. Cold iron bands wrapped around my body, followed by something rock-hard punching right into my sternum.

My body reacted without my conscious choice—lake water sprayed out of my nose and mouth as I vomited violently. Another brutal punch had me retching again before I could so much as attempt to heave for breath.

Everything was agony and burning, desperate panic. I wanted to scream, or cry, or both, but I didn't have the air.

Another hard press against my sternum made me rattle, but it was less violent this time. No more water came out, but no air came in either.

The iron bands around my torso released me, and then I was tossed onto my back.

Through my streaming eyes I saw Grim fall to his knees by my side and bend over me, pinching my nose shut. Soft, cold lips pressed against mine, and then... sweet, cool air rushed into my lungs, raising my chest. And again. And again.

My airways opened, and I coughed into Grim's mouth.

He pulled back just enough to give me space to breathe, but left his hand resting against my breastbone.

I heaved in a deep lungful and groaned with relief when air filled them.

"Breathe, Annabel," he said, his voice raspy and deep as he too inhaled. "Breathe."

I stared up at him as my body obeyed his command, and that same sensation I'd had the first time I met him welled up—of *recognition* and a sucking undertow threatening to pull me under.

My dad had said those exact same words to me when he'd pulled me out of a frozen lake when I was a kid: *"Breathe, Annabel. Breathe."*

I'd seen Grim then too, when I plummeted through the ice and fought against the freezing water pulling me down. *Grim.* He'd been there, as vividly as anything. Or his eyes had been there, to be exact—an image of one amber and one icy blue eye, watching me.

I didn't know why the memory suddenly rushed back—perhaps it was the echo of my then-near-death experience now, the similarities in nearly drowning again—but I was sure.

"Grim—" I rasped, not sure what I was going to say, what I was going to ask.

The sound of my voice, weak as it was, made Grim jerk, his eyes moving from mine down to where his hand was resting against my chest. With another jerk, he pulled it away and sat all the way up on his knees to push his wet hair out of his eyes.

"I told you not to swallow any water," he growled. Angry. Curt.

"Am I going to die?" I croaked. "I swallowed... a lot."

"We got it all out. You're breathing. Talking. You wouldn't be if we didn't."

Only then did it dawn on me that he'd... Heimliched me? The rock that'd been punched against my sternum must have been his fists.

I rubbed my sore ribs. "Thank you. You... How did you know I was in trouble?"

"You let out a lot of bubbles, plum," Mimir said, distinctly unconcerned. "You were either in need of saving, or on cutting down on the cabbage. And since you haven't eaten since arriving in Hel..."

"Well... thank you," I repeated, ignoring the prophet.

"I told you there is no safe place here," Grim said, nostrils pulling up ever so slightly into his usual sneer. "Maybe now you'll listen?"

"What was that thing?" I asked, choosing not to make any promises I couldn't keep.

"A Sjörå, a type of Huldra who lives in lakes and ponds." Grim flattened his lips into a line as he looked back over his shoulder at the once-again still water. "They don't normally attack women."

"Remind me what a Huldra is again?" I forced my

muscles into action so I could sit up, grateful that they obeyed me this time, albeit with some protest.

"They dwell in the wilds and delight in luring men and boys into trouble," Mimir said mildly.

"Why are all these nature-lurkers so gender-biased? And what happened with this one? Was she just progressive for her kind?" I muttered, rubbing at my ribs again.

"I'm going to ask her when I find her," Grim said, the venom in his voice tensing my spine even though it wasn't aimed at me this time. He turned back to me, mouth open as if he were going to speak again, but his eyes landed on my still-peaked nipples and no sound came out.

Heat scorched my cheeks, my body's response to his attention as immediate as it was embarrassing.

If Grim noticed, he didn't show it. Without a word he got to his feet, turned to the lake, and shrugged out of his already soaked tunic before he waded into the water. He dove under the surface, and I sat there in silent shock over the fact that Grim Lokisson, despite all evidence to the contrary, might have at least a single drop of hot blood in his otherwise frosty body.

"Well, that was comforting," Mimir said from his perch on the rock. "I was beginning to worry that Verdandi chose the wrong life-thread to weave as your fifth. Don't ever tell her I said that, of course. She takes it personally when someone questions her work."

"Huh?" I turned my head to face him, finally managing to shake the shock of Grim's gaze.

"That grumpy godling was as alert as a guard dog while you were swimming. He came to your rescue the *second* he realized you were in trouble," Mimir said with a smile.

"So? He doesn't want his brothers to die—and if I kick it in Hel..." With a grimace, I pushed away the thought of my mates dying and rolled up on my knees to fumble for my clothes.

Mimir chuckled. "I'm sure that's what he wants you to think, plum. He might even have convinced himself of as much. I may have been relieved of the burdensome desires that come with having a body, but the Mistborn has not been so lucky. The heart doesn't always agree with the mind, hmm?"

"I'm not sure Grim has a heart," I said as I pulled my pants from the pile of clothes. Instant guilt gnawed at my gut and I bit my lip, my fingers hesitating around the waistband of my leather trousers. After what he'd shared with me, it was painfully obvious that Grim loved his brothers very much. No one capable of the devotion he had for them could be called heartless, even if he had no care for any other living creature in the nine worlds, me included.

"Ah, the drama of youthful romance," Mimir sighed.

"Drama of *romance?* I think you mean drama-of-getting-murdered-by-your-supposed-fated-mate," I bit.

"Besides, I don't think you can call Grim youthful. What is he, a thousand years old?"

Mimir only chuckled again at my irritation. "For a god, he is barely a babe. And you, dear one, you are so delightfully *human*. So full of emotions. Passion. It's all very dramatic."

"Well, I'm glad you're enjoying the show," I growled, refocusing on my pants. But when I went to put them on, my palms slid over something hard underneath the leather. Frowning, I dug into the pocket and stilled when my fingertips touched metal. A ring.

Or, more precisely, the ring I'd plucked off Loki's finger, freeing his powers from Odin's magic-suppressing trap. I'd forgotten all about it since landing in Hel.

Loki had been completely helpless until I'd removed it.

"Mimir... how are you going to stop Grim from following us to whatever is going to get us back to Asgard?" I asked. "His magic is... very strong."

"Best you don't ask too many questions," the prophet said, arcing a meaningful eyebrow at me. "You do not possess great control over your facial features, pretty plum. Nor that soft, human heart of yours."

"Are you going to hurt him?" I asked, frowning at the twinge in my chest at the thought. Determinedly, I pushed the idiotic emotion away. Perhaps Mimir was right about that stupid, soft heart of mine. It wasn't like

Grim had had any hesitance about killing *me*. Whatever had to be done to escape this place, I'd do.

"He'll survive," Mimir said mildly. "As you said, he's strong."

~

It felt like hours before Grim returned to our small camp. He was dripping wet, and judging by his drawn features, in a foul mood.

"Did you catch the sj... the water Huldra?" I asked, looking up at him from my seat by the fire.

"No." Without so much as looking at me, the alpha undid his weapons belt, letting it fall to the ground with a thud before he began working his trousers down his hips.

I quickly averted my gaze back to the flames, trying my best to fight the heat in my cheeks when a pair of linen breeches came into my field of vision draped over a couple of sticks.

He sat down with a grunt a few feet away from me, and from the sounds of it, began wiping down his blades. I had the idle realization that metal could rust in Hel, but pushed away the metaphysical implications of the concept.

"No? So... Maybe we shouldn't spend the night by her pond? I don't particularly want to be drowned again."

"She won't dare return. I will guard you while you sleep," he said.

"Oh. Okay. Thank you."

I wasn't really sure why I was thanking him—it was a purely selfish offer, like saving me from the troll and pulling me out of the lake had been. Me dying would ruin his plans. It didn't change the fact that he would leave me to fend for myself the second he thought he could sever my ties to my mates.

And yet, as I lay down next to the fire to let sleep whisk me away, a small thread of guilt wove through my wavering consciousness. Because I knew that while he would and had risked his life to keep me safe in Hel, I would leave him behind without a second through the moment I got the chance.

8

ANNABEL

"Wake up, plum."

The whisper threaded through my dreamless sleep and pulled me back from blissful oblivion. I forced my eyelids open and stared into a charcoal sky. Only the faintest trace of lighter gray suggested that dawn might only be a few hours away.

"Wake up. We need to leave now," Mimir whispered.

I rolled up on one hip and looked for him. He was still perched on his stone by the mostly dead embers of our makeshift fireplace. He raised his bushy eyebrows at me in what I assumed was his way of tilting his head, indicating for me to get a move on.

I got to my feet as quietly as I could and turned to see what had happened to Grim. I'd half-expected to find him missing, but he was on the other side of the fireplace sprawled on his back, seemingly lost in sleep.

I spun back around to grab Mimir, but before I could reach the prophet, my gaze locked on a shadowy figure among the line of trees bracketing our campsite.

I froze, my body going numb as naked fear crawled down my spine.

Long, tangled hair swayed as the figure moved toward us, its gait awkward and halting. It was a woman, I realized when she got close enough for the shape of her breasts to become obvious. A naked and rail-thin woman.

"Mimir?" I whispered, forcing the muscles in my throat to work.

"She's not here for us," he answered, his voice still soft and quiet. Whether it was to not disturb the woman or Grim, I didn't know. "I invited her here."

"You *invited* her?" I croaked, swallowing thickly when my voice carried across our camp. Thankfully, neither Grim nor the woman heard me. Her sole focus seemed to be on the alpha on the ground.

"In a manner, yes. She will give us the time we need to flee this place."

"So she's a good... creature? Person?" Even as I said the words, every cell in my body screamed in denial. Whatever she was, she wasn't *good.* I'd faced a lot of horrors since I'd left Iceland and the human world behind—Nidhug, the well creature, a humongous sea serpent, a troll, a murderous water nymph—but *this* woman? She set every instinct in my being alight with terror, as if my most primordial self recognized the danger she represented.

Possibly drawn by my panicked thoughts, the woman stopped her approach a few steps from Grim's unconscious body and looked up. At me.

Where her eyes should have been, only black, empty sockets stared at me. Her face was as thin as the rest of her body, her cheekbones as prominent as her ribs. Her skin was as icy pale as Grim's, but where his glowed softly, hers was dull. Like dead flesh made animate.

She tilted her head, thin lips drawing up in an unpleasant smile.

"It's time to go, Annabel," Mimir murmured. "Now."

His use of my name as much as the note of urgency in his voice finally snapped me out of my panic. I took a step back, scooped up Mimir, and continued backing along the shoreline and away from her, never taking my eyes off her. My throat was tight, and my fingertips frozen around the head in my grasp as I willed the monster not to take up pursuit.

She watched my retreat with her hollow eye sockets until I was several yards away. Only then did she snap her head back to look down on Grim.

"What's she going to do to him?" I whispered, the horror in my gut mixing with another thread of guilt.

Before Mimir could answer, the woman stepped over Grim and sank down on his chest, her bony hands weaving through his dark hair.

The alpha jerked underneath her, and she leaned forward to press her full weight down upon him.

That's when I saw her back. Or what should have been her back.

Instead of skin and muscle stretched over bone, the creature straddling Grim was *hollow.* I slapped my free hand across my mouth to quell my horror at the gaping, deep wound that let me see into the monster's body. No organs resided within, *thank God,* and no spine—just rotted, black flesh carved out like one would treat a holiday turkey.

"She will ride his chest, twist his mind, and suck his essence from his lips," Mimir said, his voice once again soft.

"What the hell is she?" I whispered, taking another involuntary step back.

"A Nightmare, a creature who feeds off our most private, most deeply buried fears. And one of the only things capable of weakening a god as powerful as Grim Lokisson long enough for us to get to where we need to go. Come, Annabel. We must make haste."

I cast one final look at the monster straddling the sleeping god. He was twitching underneath her, grunts escaping his lips until she lowered her mouth to his and swallowed them up.

Forcing myself to push the guilt down, I finally turned around and ran, leaving Grim behind with the Nightmare.

My legs ached as I passed through the thinning underbrush. I'd been running through dense woodland for what seemed like hours, every step seeming closer and closer to impossible. I was already so weakened from healing Grim's shoulder, and by the time open sky started to peak through the trees ahead, my vision was swimming.

"Keep going. We're almost there," Mimir urged from under my arm. "Just a little bit longer."

I bit back on a groan and pushed forward, my gait stumbling and uneven, but all that mattered was that it was forward. *Toward freedom. Toward my mates.*

I broke through the tree line and stumbled onto what turned out to be rocky cliffs. The swirling funnel cloud of souls on the horizon seemed so much clearer from here. We were much closer than we had been when we first set out, I realized.

"Toward the ocean," Mimir said, drawing my attention back from the sky. "Keep moving."

The ocean.

I could hear it: the rolling sound of waves just beyond the dunes. No scent of salt water or seaweed reached my nostrils, but nothing else in Hel had a scent. Why would the sea?

I dug deep and found the strength I needed to keep moving over the rocky ground. The aching hollow behind my ribs pulled me forward even as stones rolled underneath my feet, making each step harder.

"Hurry, Annabel," Mimir said, urgency coloring his voice. "Hurry!"

I forced my legs to push harder, throwing myself forward and up over yet another rocky hill, until finally —the sea.

Past a stony sliver of beach, a small rowboat was tethered to a rocky outcrop. Behind it, unfriendly waves rolled onto shore, frothy and dark.

And I… I had seen this place before.

I paused, dread and déjà vu flooding my body.

"To the boat, girl," Mimir said. "Across the sea lies Asgard."

The boat.

"Something's wrong," I croaked. "I've been here before."

"Wrong?" The prophet rolled his eyes up to mine. "This is our way out, plum. *Take it.* Before it's too late!"

Too late?

I had dreamed of this place. So many times I had dreamed of this beach, this boat. The shock of memory made me spin around on my heel.

And there he was.

Grim.

He came from the trees like dark vengeance, running across the rocks with the agile ease of a panther. Even from this distance, the rage on his pale face was palpable.

The dread turned leaden in my gut.

You're already dead, Annabel. You're already dead.

With a croak of horror, I turned back to face the ocean and threw myself onto the beach. The jagged rocks under my feet made me stumble with every step, but I kept pressing forward. The boat was my only hope.

Power knocked against my back, sending my forward with a scream. Mimir slipped from my grasp and tumbled to the side as my knees connected with the rocks. I bit my lip to try and contain the agony, focusing on the rowboat once more. Crawling on bleeding hands and knees, I pushed forward, knowing I had to get to it. *Had* to.

Another wave of power, this time grabbing me around the waist, flipped me to my back, pressing me into the ground until I was pinned, immobile.

I stared up at Grim as he approached, his charcoal hair spilling over his face, hiding his features. But I knew him. Like I'd known him those hundreds of times we'd been here before.

He lifted his hand to push his hair out of his eyes. *Rage.* He bared his teeth and snarled, "There is no point in fighting me. You're already dead. You *know* there's no point in fighting me!"

"I will fight you until the end!" I spat. "I will never stop fighting to save everyone from you!"

He stepped closer, looming right above me. There was such darkness in his eyes, it crushed against my sternum, making it hard to breathe. "No. You will not. We have been here so many times before, Annabel. So many nights. And every time, *I win.*" With that, he raised a hand. Darkness shot from it, followed by a splintering of wood.

Somewhere off to the side, Mimir cursed.

The boat. Our means of escape. Gone.

I screamed in impotent rage, fighting with what remaining strength I had left against the invisible bonds pinning me down. Only this time, the power constricting my limbs wavered.

I didn't pause to wonder why. Quicker than should have been possible for my weakened muscles, I kicked up, planting the bridge of my foot right between Grim's legs with all my strength.

He grunted, the fury etched on his pale face morphing into agony. And then, like timber, he fell to the ground.

An alpha god, conquered by his biology's greatest weakness.

I'm not going to lie, every part of me relished his pain as I pushed myself up to my knees, the vestiges of his power gone from my body.

The ring.

It was my one chance.

I threw myself forward on hands and knees. When I reached his side, I thrust my hand into my pocket, fumbling for the ring I'd taken from Loki's finger.

My fingertips brushed against the metal, and I yanked it up and grabbed for Grim's hand.

His muscles were stiff, resistant, but he was too weakened to fight me. With more force than finesse, I slipped the runed band over his thumb and wedged it down past the joint.

Grim groaned, a pained protest, but it was too late.

I sat back on my heels and looked down on the immobilized alpha.

Slowly he managed to open his eyes, locking his gaze on mine.

"What did you *do?*" he rasped. There was still anger in his voice, but it was not nearly as terrifying now that he was defenseless.

Perhaps I should have felt pity, but I didn't. He'd ruined my best chance at returning to my mates. I felt nothing but mild satisfaction that he got to experience what it was like being as helpless as I had been since we came to Hel.

"What did *I* do? What did *you* do?" I snarled, looking back over my shoulder toward the sea. Pieces of aged timber lay scattered in a semi-circle where the boat had been moments ago. "You ruined our way back!"

"For the last time, you are not going back!" He managed to roll up on his knees, fury once more overtaking his drawn features. "Never! Get it through your skull, Annabel. You are *never* leaving this place! No matter how many Nightmares you send at me, no matter how you kick and scream and play foul tricks. Never!"

"Er, the Nightmare may have been my doing," Mimir interjected, but if Grim heard, he ignored him.

"If you weren't such a coward, if you'd dared to accept Fates' plans for you, you would understand that nothing and no one is going to stop me from returning to my mates, Grim Lokisson!" I spat, turning back around to face him. My own temper eased the innate fear at his fury as he glared at me with hatred strong enough it could have made a flower wither and die. "I took away your magic, and I *will* escape this wretched place. You aren't nearly strong enough to stop me!"

Grim's eyes widened at my challenge, then narrowed into slits. Faster than I could follow, he wrapped his icy fingers around my throat, squeezing.

"I don't need magic to hurt you. Remember that, *omega*." He spat the last word out as if it were a curse.

I stared silently up at him, defiantly, willing him to follow through with the threat. After five long seconds, he pulled his lip up in a snarl and shoved me away, releasing my neck.

"You're not going to hurt me," I said, suppressing the need to swallow. I kept my eyes locked on his, refusing to submit. "You won't risk the harm it would cause your brothers."

"Even if I don't, others will," he growled. "You have seen the dangers here. You have drained your own powers. You *need* my protection—and I need my magic to protect you." Grim held his hand out toward me. The iron band on his thumb gleamed dully. "Remove it."

"No."

"Enough!" he barked. "You are not stupid enough to risk your mates' lives on this folly! You cannot best me in a game of wits, Annabel. I know you far too well to fall for this nonsense!"

I know you far too well.

Something he'd said before flickered in my mind. Something he'd said only moments before: *"We have been here so many times before, Annabel. So many nights. And every time, I win."*

Understanding yawned like a heaving chasm in the pit of my stomach.

He... knew me.

"I claim my second truth," I said, setting my jaw to steel my resolve.

"What?" The darkness in his eyes deepened.

"Now. I claim it right now."

He only glared at me, and I was fairly sure he was imagining my head exploding.

"You said we have been here before. So many nights," I said slowly, trying to find the right words to put the puzzle together from the multitude of pieces suddenly appearing for my mind's eye. "You say you know me, but how could you? We hadn't exchanged more than a few words before you killed me.

"I... *remember* you. I recognized you the first time I met you on your farm in Iceland. I have dreamed about you. Had nightmares of you. As a child and young girl, I saw your face in the shadows every time I was scared. And yet... I could never put my finger on it. I could never truly *remember.* Not until now. Until this place. The place you say we've been before.

"Tell me... Tell me why you were in my nightmares. Tell me what it means. Were you haunting me? Did you... Did you try to kill me then too? When I fell through the ice, was that you? Did you want to kill me before I could bond with your brothers?"

Grim sneered. "I am not a ghost. I don't *haunt* little girls."

"What, then? You don't deny you shared my dreams. Why?"

He breathed, deeply, finally moving his eyes from mine to stare at the angry sea beyond. "I should never have accepted your help to mend my bones."

"Grim. *Tell me.* You swore an oath."

"The day you fell through the ice, I felt your fear. It was... so intense. So painful. It pulled on me—yanked my soul across the distance to you. I saw you in the water, fighting like a lioness for survival even though you were so... *weak*. Small."

His words came slowly, reluctantly. "After that day, the connection to your magic must have been opened. Your visions of me would summon me to you. Your fears. When you were scared of the monsters under your bed, I was pulled across the ocean. I watched your father tell you no such things as monsters exist. I watched as you cowered under the sheets during thunderstorms. Watched you run from drunk groups of men shouting after you on the streets. But this place, this moment in time... this is where you brought me the most. I suppose I should have recognized it for what it is —perhaps then I wouldn't have lost enough strength to that Nightmare that you could put this cursed ring on me."

"I... I don't understand," I said. "Why would you *watch* me?"

Grim scoffed, finally turning his gaze from the ocean back to me. "It wasn't my choice. *You* called *me*."

"Me? I didn't even know you existed, let alone that I had any sort of magical powers!"

"You are so blinded by this supposedly sacred purpose some low-grade prophet spewed during a mead-induced stupor, you still don't understand," he said, the anger in his voice laced with a rare softness.

"Just who are you calling *low-grade?*" Mimir barked. Grim ignored him as he continued.

"Your birth was a curse, for me more so than my brothers. My father sired me to fulfill the prophecy. Verdandi claimed he would need a Mistborn son to claim this prophesized omega if he were to save his own skin once Ragnarök struck.

"I sometimes wondered if Verdandi tricked him. If she knew. If my bond to you is her creation, forged for her own devious schemes. Not that it matters. I care little for Fate's ties."

"Grim, I... I don't understand." My voice was hoarse, my throat tight. What he was saying... It was like staring into a kaleidoscope and desperately trying to hold on to some semblance of form, find some truth in the swirling myriad.

"I suppose you don't," he said, the softness waning for cold indifference. "You gave in to your supposed Fate without question. You accepted four mates for the sole purpose of fulfilling a prophecy that was doomed to fail from the start.

"The day you were born, Annabel Turner, I felt your arrival into the world. You call me to your dreams because your soul recognized mine long before we met in flesh. I know you because you are my soulmate."

9

GRIM

The dark-haired omega gaped up at me. Her mouth opened and closed repeatedly, the similarity to a fish not entirely flattering.

"S-Soulmate? What are you even...? *What?*" she finally managed to say.

I didn't respond. There was no point.

"I don't understand what that means!" Her eyes were wild, as if some part of her did understand, was murmuring the horrid truth to her even if she refused to listen.

"It means that were you not the one Fated to stop Ragnarök, had Verdandi not woven your thread with five godlings to save the nine worlds, you and he would still be twined together by the very essence of your souls," Mimir said, his tone thoughtful. "What an interesting twist. I never would have suspected. Yet you took her life? Whatever foul magic you have found to sever her ties with her other mates, you must know that nothing will ever break a soulmate bond."

"It is unimportant," I said, shrugging as I turned to look at the talking head. He had rolled a few yards when Annabel dropped him and was now upside-down atop some sharp-looking rocks. "My brothers' survival is the only thing that matters to me."

"But dear boy," Mimir said, his eyes widening. It could have been comical, but I felt nothing but vague dread—like I had since I realized what Annabel's second truth would force me to reveal. "If she stays here and you return—or worse, if she expires in this place—your own soul will be rent. You won't simply die, you'll—"

"I know," I interrupted him. "I have made my choice. Don't waste your breath attempting to sway me, prophet. I understand the consequences."

"*I* don't understand," Annabel said. "At all. You're... saying what, that I'm... That you're meant to *love* me, but you have chosen not to?"

I heaved another sigh and looked back to her. I should have let my bones stay broken. "*Love* has nothing to do with any of this. I am not a tool for Norns, or gods, or prophets to wield as they see fit. *That* is what I have chosen."

She blinked at me. Twice. "What happens to you if I die here?"

"His soul would be ripped apart," Mimir said softly when my silence made it clear I wasn't going to indulge her curiosity. "Your other mates would die painfully, but their souls would still be whole. *He* would be turned into... something lesser. Something dark and foul. A shadow who haunts the living, swallowing their souls in an eternal hunger to fill the void left by his other half."

Annabel blinked again, horror growing in her gaze. Horror, and *anger.* "You would rather become a literal monster than mate me? You'd rather turn into a grotesque *shell* than so much as *attempt* to stop Ragnarök? Are you mad? Are you entirely insane? Do you think, even for a second, that your brothers would want this—that they could live with the knowledge of what you'd become?"

I didn't answer her. She would never understand, and even if she did, it changed nothing.

"Grim!" Her voice cut through the crashing of waves behind us, and I glanced out at the rough sea. The forests of Hel weren't the only places monsters lurked. While I'd been trapped under the Nightmare, my dreams had been of serpents rising out of frozen water—horrible, coiling flesh and poison rendering me immobile as I watched Annabel drown under a thick layer of ice, forever dooming my brothers to Hel.

"Remove the ring, Annabel," I said, keeping my voice calm and reasonable. "I would rather save my brothers before I let you be eaten by whatever monster crosses our path. And so would you."

She gaped up at me, unshed tears making her eyes shine despite the dullness death had caused. For a brief, relief-inducing moment, I saw the first sliver of a crack in that iron will that lay behind.

But then she bared her teeth at me, lip curling as she shook her head. "No."

"No?"

"No," she repeated. Then she got to her feet, wobbling before she managed to straighten her knees. I stared at her as she walked over to where Mimir's head had fallen, bent, and picked him up.

Gently she brushed his cheeks free of sand and dirt, and skimmed over what looked like the start of a bruise forming on one temple with a featherlight touch. "I'm sorry I dropped you."

"Couldn't be helped," Mimir chirped. "Though I must say, even Hel looks better right-side up.

"Are you okay?"

He chuckled. "I'll be fine. It takes a lot more than a roll over some rocks to shake me. Now that time a pack of mountain trolls kicked my head around like a ball for a day..."

"Annabel. The ring," I snarled, my patience waning. Even a stubborn human couldn't be this thick-skulled. I knew her heart far better than I'd ever wanted to. It was weak and soft. She cared too much for her mates to risk their deaths.

"Where to now?" she asked, not taking her eyes off Mimir.

"West," he said. "But it won't be as easy as the boat."

"We don't really have a choice, do we?" she replied,

glancing at the remains of the rickety rowboat I'd destroyed.

"I suppose we don't," he agreed.

"West, then." She turned to the narrow path that had brought us down to the beach and began walking. Despite the surety in her steps, her exhaustion made her stumble.

And yet she kept walking. Away from me.

"Annabel," I growled. "You're being foolish. Whatever escape he has promised you, you won't find it. You will die out there without protection."

She stopped and finally looked at me. Her eyes were hard—and determined. "Fine. I will remove your ring, Grim Lokisson. On one condition."

I lifted my brows. "What do you want? More *truths?*"

"No. I want you to feel exactly what it is you're throwing away. I want you to truly know the pain you're inflicting on me, on your brothers, on Modi and Magni. You say you know me? I don't think you do. Whatever this *soulmate* connection you claim we have is, clearly it isn't worth a damn to you. But I know one thing that is. I know *one* way of showing you that I am strong enough to stop Ragnarök and save not only your brothers, but you as well.

"I will remove your ring and return your magic to you, Grim, after you claim me as your mate."

10

GRIM

"Claim you?" I stared at the clearly insane omega, the roar of blood in my ears almost making me believe I might have heard her wrong. But I hadn't. The anger on her face spoke the truth more clearly than her words ever could. She wanted me to suffer. She wanted revenge for what I'd done to her—what I would still do.

She was more devious than I'd given her credit for.

"Yes. If you want your powers back, if you want to *protect me,* you will claim me. So I guess the question is: How badly do you want to ensure your brothers live?"

I would give anything for my brothers' lives. I *had* given everything. But this? No.

Stars above, not this.

"Are you that desperate for a fuck?" I sneered.

Annabel laughed, a derisive sound that grated against my skin. "You can attempt to shame me all you want. I am not bargaining with you. This is not a negotiation. It is the *only* way I will remove the ring. Agree or don't. You have until my next heat to decide."

"You're bluffing," I said, wishing my throat wasn't dry with the knowledge that no, she wasn't.

"Watch me." Casting another dark look in my direction, she turned back around to the path leading back up the cliff and into the woods.

I bared my teeth at her back, a snarl forcing its way out of my throat, but Annabel simply kept walking. Away from me.

West.

I pushed myself to my feet, falling in behind her. I should have kept her bound with my powers. Should have hidden her away in some cave and sealed the entrance until I could return to my brothers and break their bonds to her. But I hadn't. There was no way out of Hel for the dead—*everyone* knew as much. Even Odin's wife Frigg, the god-queen herself, had been unable to save her son from my sister's clammy grip.

And yet Mimir had known of one.

I clenched my hands into fists at the memory of Annabel clawing her way across the stony beach toward the rickety old rowboat. The oceans surrounding Hel were vast and dangerous beyond measure, yet the prophet had wanted her to cross them in a wooden *rowboat*, though no doubt some ancient magic had been woven into its timber, allowing a dead woman and a bodiless fool to escape.

Wherever he was guiding her now, I would stop her. After the trick they'd played on me with the Nightmare, I would have had no qualms leashing Annabel in whatever cave we came across—and perhaps I'd find a nice, deep well for the talking head she was carrying.

But now? I could physically restrain the girl, easily even, but not continually—not for long enough. Eventually I would succumb to sleep, and knowing her, she'd take advantage the moment I closed my eyes.

So I followed her, waiting for my moment to stop whatever desperate plans Mimir had for this second attempt at escape. Annabel would never leave Hel, and I was not going to let down my guard again. All I had to do was stay alert—and make sure she didn't get herself killed—without the use of my magic.

Claim her.

I suppressed a shudder. There was a time I had accepted my father's plans for my brothers and me to mate the unborn omega he had bargained for. It would supposedly secure our survival, and I knew once my mark was on her neck, I would never have to interact with her again. Bjarni and Saga had been pleased enough at the prospect of a submissive omega mate that I knew I would be free of any obligations toward her.

Then *she* had been born. And my soul... my soul *ached.* My dark, twisted spirit tried to open, tried to welcome its other half into the world, but it was too cold, too dead.

I'd known then that claiming my promised mate

would be my destruction.

And still I'd followed my brothers' plans, helped them scheme and plot to get the girl to Iceland, because I would break myself apart a thousand times over to ensure my brothers' survival.

All the way up until *he* showed me the truth.

The dark spell that had been woven around my mind that day caressed the inside of my skull, talons digging in ever so slightly. *He* didn't like it when I thought about him.

It didn't matter; I'd known what I'd doomed myself to when I'd accepted his bargain—an eternity as a dark *thing*. A shell. It was nothing worse than what would happen to me if I claimed Annabel.

Claim her.

Even if *he* hadn't shown me the fruitlessness of stopping Ragnarök, I finally understood the impossibility of mating the girl when I saw her with her four mates that last night in Valhalla. She gave herself so willingly to them all, how she loved them so completely.

And instincts I thought I had buried centuries ago came roaring back, filling me until I thought they would shred through my skin, until all I wanted was to rip apart the four alphas who had taken parts of her soul, parts of *my* soul.

The sickness I'd felt as an adolescent while my body burned and hungered for the woman I hated most was nothing compared to the horror of knowing that if I claimed Annabel—if my sick, twisted soul reunited with its other half—I would *kill* my brothers to keep them from her.

"We need to find shelter."

Those were the first words I had spoken since we left the beach—the first any of us had spoken for several hours.

Annabel ignored me and kept walking. *Pride.* One of her many, many flaws. Her pace was slow, her feet unsteady against the forest floor. She was on the brink of collapsing from exhaustion, thanks in part to her attempt at running from me this morning and from healing my shoulder and ribs. She'd used every drop of her magic, and perhaps a touch of her own essence, to do so. And yet she pressed on, too stubborn to admit defeat. Or weakness.

"Annabel." I increased my pace for a few steps to catch up to her, halting her with a hand on her shoulder. She shivered at my touch, as if my innate coldness seeped through her leather armor. "We cannot stay out in the open once night falls. Not without my powers."

She hesitated for a moment, and I could practically sense her urge to argue. But then, by some miracle, her shoulders slumped.

"Fine," she said. "We'll rest."

If I had been able to feel anything but frustration and dread, I might have found some faint amusement in what my brothers always assumed would be a weak-willed omega woman taking the lead. Perhaps I might have felt regret too that a woman strong enough to bring four boisterous gods to heel would wither away in the darkness of Hel.

LIGHTING a fire without magic or flint was *difficult.* By the time a spark finally caught the tinder, my hands had blisters, and I was cursing the tricksy omega bitch under my breath every time my gaze caught the ring on my thumb. But we needed a fire to keep the night creatures at bay, and so I'd spent the better part of an hour rubbing a sharpened stick between my palms.

I shot a glare in Annabel's direction. She was leaning against one of the large rocks that made up our shelter for the night, head back and eyes closed while Mimir droned on about one of his old adventures with Odin, back when he still had legs.

She was barely conscious.

How much longer would she be able to keep going? She regained some of her strength while she slept, but every morning she seemed just a bit weaker than the day before.

Perhaps her reason for the bargain she'd suggested was not entirely to exact revenge on me. Maybe she realized she needed her magic back as well if she were to have any chance at escaping Hel—and me.

I bit the inside of my cheek as I weighed my options.

No doubt she would insist on her ludicrous terms until she was so weak, she would have to consider other options. If I waited her out, maybe she would restore my magic in return for her own.

Of course, that meant I would still have to lay with her.

A full body shudder traveled up the length of my spine as uninvited images of Annabel writhing naked echoed in my mind, and that hated, primitive heat curled in my pelvis.

Desire.

I forced it down and locked it up tight. Anger took its place as I stared at the half-sleeping girl, at her full, soft lips and the curve of her breasts. But my anger wasn't directed at her; this was my flaw, not hers. Another "gift" from Loki's side of my family tree.

True Mistborn never surrendered to baser instincts. Gods did.

But I had other gifts from my father—much more useful ones. Patience. Treachery. I could wait her out until even her impressive stubbornness would have to surrender to the reality of her situation. I needed my magic back more than I needed whatever shreds of dignity I had left.

Once she was weak enough to beg for it, I would trade my powers for hers. There was no need to claim her. She would have to bend on this long before I.

Annabel's stubbornness really *was* impressive.

Three days later, she was still stumbling west through the forest, tripping and falling over roots and stones because she was too tired to lift her feet properly.

I was starting to suspect she'd rather keel over dead than beg for my help, and I was running out of time. We'd come across several signs of trolls in the area, but had so far managed to avoid direct contact. However, I wasn't willing to gamble and see how much longer our luck might last.

"You know," I drawled when Annabel fought her way back to her feet after yet another tumble, "this whole escape plan you two have would probably be a lot easier if you weren't tripping over your own feet every five yards."

"You sound like you are about to sell me the cure to all that ails me." Despite her snarky tone, her breath came in small huffs, weakened by her exhaustion.

"I suppose that is one way to look at it," I hummed.

"What do you want, Grim? I'm too tired for games."

"You know what I want—my powers back so I can protect you. I suspect you might want your energy back. And, as a bonus, your own powers," I said, careful to keep my voice neutral.

Annabel jerked to a stop, her head snapping around to stare at me over her shoulder. "Wait—are you suggesting *sex?*"

The sheer shock on her features was somewhat... surprising. And possibly insulting.

"That is how you restore your magic, is it not?"

She stared at me for another moment, then guffawed and turned back around to the path ahead. "Now who's desperate for a fuck? The answer is no. I'm not removing your ring until you *claim* me. I told you, it's non-negotiable."

I gritted my teeth and forced my temper down. "I want you to imagine what's going to happen to your beloved mates if you die here, Annabel. Really, truly picture it. The agony they will suffer—the despair. The eternity they will spend down here without you, knowing your soul has been reduced to nothing but a husk for Hel's use. Who knows? Perhaps they will willingly give up their afterlife and join you in oblivion just to make the pain stop."

I saw her move her free hand to her chest, but she didn't respond. Without a word, she continued walking.

"Do they truly matter so little to you?" I asked. "I thought you *loved* them. Did the Norns make a mistake after all? Or is it that you truly see them as nothing more than a means to an end? Casualties in your arrogant belief that *you* can stop what has been foretold for eons?"

She whipped around so fast I thought she might fall, but she managed to keep her balance this time. "Don't you *dare* question my love for my mates, nor my devotion! You, of all people! Do *you* love your brothers? You say if I die, they will too—yet the one thing you can do to prevent this, you won't?

"You claim this is all some grand, sacrificial gesture to make sure your brothers survive Ragnarök, yet you refuse to bond with me so you can experience exactly what your plan will do to them. You're a coward, Grim—a pathetic *coward,* hiding behind martyrdom. You want your powers back? Then you will learn what true pain is. What it means to sacrifice."

Her words hung in the air between us, violent and raw. I stared at her, fury pounding in my temples, and took in her flared nostrils and the hate in her eyes, the way her fingertips dug into Mimir's cheeks, making the prophet wince though he—for once—stayed silent.

"You know nothing of sacrifice," I hissed. "You spoiled, impudent little girl."

I would have continued. Would have unleashed all my hatred and bile on the woman whose mere existence had brought about my destruction. But before I could let the words spill out of my burning throat, movement behind Annabel caught my attention—and my heart stilled.

What had looked like just another rock formation half-hidden behind trees and undergrowth rolled to one side and then rose, taking the shape of a great, lumbering mountain troll brandishing the snapped-off bottom half of a young fir tree as a club.

His beady eyes zeroed in on Annabel's small figure and a cruel grin spread on his ugly face.

Then he came for her.

11

ANNABEL

"Annabel! Run!"

The change in Grim's demeanor was so sudden and complete, it took me a second to process his command. One moment he'd looked like he wanted nothing more than to tear my head from my shoulders. The next, pure terror washed over his features—a look so alien on his pale face it made my heart skip a beat.

On instinct, I looked over my shoulder just as a *thud* rung through air and made the hillside shake.

A great, gray monster rose behind me, similar in appearance to the troll that'd nearly killed Grim in the creek: a huge, gray body, thickly muscled limbs, and a round face with small, black eyes and protruding fangs. Though where the other troll had been furry, this one's skin was bare and roughly textured, giving the impression it was made from rock.

It was also much, *much* bigger. And it was lumbering down the hill.

Toward *me.*

My stomach dropped, terror kicking through my veins. Clutching Mimir to my chest, I leapt forward, forcing my exhausted muscles to sprint. The second I passed him, Grim turned around and followed me.

"Faster, Annabel," he snarled behind me. *"Faster!"*

But I couldn't run any faster. Maybe if I hadn't been so drained, I would have been able to outrun it, but ten steps in and my muscles were already screaming, my vision blurring.

I didn't see the root in my path. One minute I was forcing myself forward, teeth gritted against the fatigue. The next, my face smacked against soil, and I slid a few feet on my stomach before coming to a halt. Mimir went flying out of my grasp, bumping a few times as he rolled down the path.

"Shit!" Grim skidded to a stop by my side, cool hands grabbing hold under my armpits—but before he could haul me to my feet, a great shadow fell over my prone body.

"Stars be *damned!"* Grim snarled, releasing me. For a dazed moment, I thought he was going to leave me behind, but then the metallic slide of his daggers being yanked out of their sheaths sang through the air.

I managed to roll around just in time to see the dark-haired alpha take up stance between me and the troll, weapons at the ready.

He was strong; powerful beyond any mortal, even without his magic. Yet seeing him before that huge monster made my gut clench with uninvited terror.

Alpha god or no, he was still one man with two slivers of metal against a beast who looked like it had been carved from the mountains themselves. And if he died, all I loved would die with him.

The troll paused, as if it couldn't quite comprehend that anyone would be dumb enough to get in the way of its intended prey. Then it roared, the trees around us shaking with the force of it, and raised its enormous club.

Grim dodged out of the way and leapt up, digging both daggers into the side of the beast and using them for leverage to pull himself up.

The troll roared again and swung its cudgel-free hand, smacking into Grim and ripping the daggers from its flesh. He crashed to the ground, rolling twice before he sprang back to his feet, but the troll was already moving toward me again.

"No, no, no!" I kicked against the ground, digging my heels into the soil to push away, but it was too little and too late. Thick fingers the size of tree branches closed around my torso and hauled me into the air.

I shrieked and clawed at its hand, but to my frail human fingers, its skin might as well have been truly hewn from rock. My nails broke against its rough hide, my feet impacting with nothing but air as I kicked.

The troll lifted me up, up, up until I was face to face with its boulder-like head.

It's going to eat *me!*

The thought came unbidden, the pure terror of it making me scream the first thing that came to me.

"Grim! Grim!"

The troll pulled me closer to its face, its breath hitting me fully in the face. The stench of rotting meat made me gag.

Not like this. Please, not like this!

A snarl ripped through the air, followed by the troll's angry growl. It dropped its club and swiveled around, grabbing for something over its shoulder.

Grim appeared on its other shoulder, teeth bared and eyes flaming with pure rage. I'd seen Bjarni succumb to battle lust before, had felt his berserker rage throb in our bond as he'd fought Nidhug. He was a warrior through and through, a true Viking god. I'd never imagined his icy younger brother possessed the same fire, but as Grim clung to the monster's neck with his knees and raised his daggers to strike, I finally saw it: the wild, primal power within him that was born not of mist and shadow, but blood and flesh and bone.

Quicker than the troll could readjust, Grim raised both daggers and dug them deep into the Troll's neck.

Gray blood sprayed out. The beast bellowed, furious now, and swung around again—this time releasing its grip on me to grab for Grim with both hands.

I flew through the air and crashed into the ground, my head smacking hard against the surface.

"Annabel!"

Blackness swallowed me whole.

My throbbing head was the first sensation that greeted me once my consciousness slowly returned.

"Eugh," I protested, squinting to protect my sore head from any sudden bursts of light. But the air above me was dark, only a faint flicker of light playing along the stony ceiling.

I was in a cave.

Muddy thoughts of the troll snapped back into my tender brain, and I gasped in a breath. Had it captured me? Was Grim—

As if summoned by the mere thought of his name, the dark-haired Lokisson appeared above me. He stared down at me, brows locked in a frown. "Can you see me?"

"Yeah, of course I can see you," I croaked. "What happened?"

He pressed his cool fingertips against my temples on both sides. The light pressure on the right side smarted, and I cringed. "Any nausea?"

"No," I said. "The troll? Are we safe?"

Grim exhaled a slow breath and leaned back on his

heels, seemingly content that I wasn't extra-dying. "Yes. For now."

"Is he still looking for us?" I whispered, the thought of being attacked by that monstrosity again sending shivers up my back.

"No. He is dead." Grim didn't take his eyes off mine. "But there are others like him in these parts. And worse. You could have died today."

I had an inkling where he was going, but I wasn't biting. "So could you."

Grim bared his teeth at me, but there was more irritation than anger in his eyes. "Are you truly *that* stubborn? You want revenge so bad you're willing to kill your mates? It's not a matter of if, Annabel—it's *when*, if you don't return my use of my powers."

My chest clenched like it always did when I thought of what I was gambling, but I forced my expression to remain calm. Without Grim, everything would be lost, regardless of mine and my mates' deaths. That was the reason for my bargain. In that awful moment of clarity when I'd seen my means of escape smashed to pieces on that beach and heard him tell me I was his *soulmate*—and that it meant nothing to him—that was when I'd realized that my only chance of saving the nine worlds and my mates was to chain Grim to my heart with a matebond.

I'd hated mine when they were first forced on me. Hated how tightly they bound me, how completely enslaved I was to them. It hadn't mattered. With each bite on my neck, I'd given myself completely to the alphas who'd claimed me.

But it worked both ways. As bound to them as I was, they were equally so to me—dedicated to protect me till their last breaths. Which is why, despite the aching bonds behind my ribs screaming at me to take Grim's offer and protect myself and the men I loved, I only raised an eyebrow at him.

"And you? Are you too much of a coward to see for yourself what kind of pain you're inflicting?"

His nostrils flared, mismatched eyes darkening. For the longest moment, we stared at each other in silence, each waiting for the other to break.

Finally he drew in a deep sigh and rose to his feet. "Fine. You win. I will claim you."

I blinked, not entirely sure I'd heard right. "You... You will?"

"If that is truly what it takes for you to remove this band, it is pointless to continue this argument." Considering how much of a fight he'd put up, he seemed... nearly indifferent now. He moved out of my field of vision and I sat up to follow him, leery of a trap.

A campfire burned in the middle of the cave. On the ground around us several animal hides were strewn, logs and rocks organized in piles.

He'd taken me to the troll's cave, I realized.

"Just like that?" I asked, narrowing my eyes at him.

"Just like that," he repeated, poking idly at the fire with a long stick.

"No tricks?"

He gave me a contemptuous look.

"All right, then. I'm glad. I guess I'll... let you know when my heat comes around." I hadn't really thought through what it'd be like—being claimed by Grim. The physicality of it.

Determinedly, I pushed those thoughts down until they were nothing but a murmur. I knew from experience that I would care way less about embarrassment and awkwardness once the urges to mate awoke in me. I'd worry about having to get naked and intimate with the cold god then.

"Where's Mimir?" I asked, partly to change the subject and partly because the memory of him bumping down the hill after my first fall came back to me, along with a wave of worry.

"Likely where you left him," Grim said without so much as looking up from the fire this time.

I gasped, outraged. "You *left* him? What if some other troll finds him?!"

"We should be so lucky," he mumbled.

Angrily I pushed up into a seated position, pausing for a moment as my head spun and throbbed. "I know you've gone all dark side, but leaving a defenseless man to be trampled or eaten by monsters is low, even for you."

Grim snorted. "Defenseless? He lured me to sleep and had a Nightmare attack me. He's far more powerful than he likes to pretend, *plum*. You shouldn't let your soft heart forget that."

I glared at him. "He's a *head.* You're really so vindictive you'd let a divine prophet die just because he had to use trickery to escape you? Do I have to remind you that *you're the bad guy?*"

Grim finally looked at me over his shoulder, resting his knuckles against his knees. A dark sheet of his hair fell over his face, concealing his lighter eye. "I know you think so."

I shook my head and forced myself to my feet. The world spun once, then stilled. "Grim, you're literally doing everything you can to bring about the end of *nine* worlds. It doesn't get much more bad guy than that."

"And yet you insist I claim you," he murmured softly, not taking his gaze off me. "An evil, vengeful god. The villain of your story. What does that make you, Annabel?"

"Desperate," I said, my voice as quiet as his. Without waiting for a reply, I turned toward the yawning mouth of the cave and headed for it.

"Where do you think you're going?" Grim's voice cracked like a whip, the softness gone.

"To find Mimir." I looked at him over my shoulder. "Chill out. I'm not attempting a grand escape. Even if I could make it more than half a mile before collapsing, it would be pretty counterproductive to leave you behind, now that you've agreed to my bargain."

"You're not leaving this cave until my powers are

restored," he said, getting to his feet. "There are far too many trolls in this area, and I won't be able to take down another. Not for a few days."

Only then did I notice that he was holding his left arm close to his body and carrying most of his weight on his right leg. He hadn't come out of that battle unscathed.

"I'm not leaving Mimir out there," I said. "Besides, who knows if one of that troll's friends won't stop by for a visit? I don't think this place is any safer than out there."

"Mountain trolls aren't social creatures—they usually don't cross into each other's territories if they can avoid it. This cave is the only place we won't risk another attack. And you are *staying,* Annabel." He took a step toward me, intent in every line of his face.

"Then you should have brought Mimir when you took me here," I said. "I'm not trying to be difficult—I'd rather avoid another monster encounter too—but I can't leave him in the mud in the middle of troll territory."

Grim stared at me for another long second before he pulled his nostrils up in a sneer. "*Fine.* I'll get him. But I swear, if you are not here when I return, I am cutting off his tongue, gouging out his eyes, and slicing off his ears. Do you understand?"

I swallowed thickly before nodding. "Got it."

He shot me another dark glare, pulled out his daggers, and then stalked out of the cave.

I stared after him for a long couple of seconds. For someone who seemed to take offense to being called a bad guy, he sure had a way of saying the most villainous things.

It didn't take long before Grim returned, this time with his daggers sheathed and Mimir's mud-dripping head dangling from one hand. He was carrying him by a fistful of hair, and from the angry sounds coming from the prophet, he was none too pleased about it.

"...spect for your elders!" Mimir barked. I didn't catch the first part, but I didn't need to.

"Grim! That's not okay!" I said, rushing over to grab the prophet from him.

Grim released his grip without protest and headed toward the fire.

"Are you okay?" I asked Mimir, making sure I cupped his head by the jaw as I lifted him up to inspect him for damage. Thankfully, apart from the mud and a few bruises, he seemed unharmed.

"Your mother should have drowned you before you could crawl," the prophet snarled in Grim's direction. Anger still flashed in his eyes when he turned his focus to me, but his tone turned somewhat milder. "I am, no thanks to that brute. I have a good mind to teach him what it's liked to be hauled around by the scalp."

"That would require hands," Grim shot back.

"Ignore him," I interjected when Mimir's eyes

widened with outrage and he opened his mouth, undoubtedly to retaliate. "He's just in a bad mood because he finally realized I'm not taking off his ring before he claims me."

Mimir's mouth slackened, his gaze flicking to me, to Grim, and then to me again. "He... agreed?" His voice was quiet now, almost a whisper.

I nodded. "Apparently we're camping out here until... my heat. He says it's safer."

"It is. But..." Mimir frowned. "If I were you, I'd be wary, plum. He must know a matebond will increase his urges to protect you exponentially. I'd bet a good horn of mead he's got something sinister planned."

"I'm sure he does. But it's the only chance I have at changing his mind. And we need him—you know we do," I whispered, glancing over my shoulder to make sure we hadn't caught Grim's attention. But the dark-haired alpha showed exactly zero interest in either of us.

"We do," Mimir agreed. "But we need you as well. You are the key, Annabel. If you are lost, there will be no more Asgard, no more Midgard—no more of anything. Don't put your faith in his better nature. He may not have one."

After a while, the offensive stench of mountain troll numbed my sense of smell. It made staying in the cave much more tolerable, but after four days, I was about to lose my mind.

At least I thought it had been four days—Grim refused to let me so much as look outside, and without hunger or thirst, it was difficult to gauge the passage of time. All I knew was that we had been there forever, twiddling our thumbs while Ragnarök proceeded as planned in the living realms.

I was beginning to suspect that this was why Grim had accepted my bargain. If I was stuck in a cave instead of searching for ways to escape Hel, he didn't need his magic to protect me, nor did he need to expend any energy in stopping me. He just had to wait until it was too late for me to do anything anyway.

I didn't know how long I'd have to wait for my heat to make an entrance. Supposedly it was a monthly thing for omegas, but I wasn't sure there had been a month between my two previous heats, nor exactly how long since my last one. And clearly my hormones were all kinds of fucked up anyway, given my singular period since I'd been pulled into this mythological clusterfuck. It could be weeks before my heat. Months, if I was really lucky.

Mimir seemed to be doing his best to distract me from my darkening thoughts. He told me stories of his many adventures before he lost his body, most of them about his and Odin's travels.

"Are you still good friends with the god-king?" I asked after he finished a tale of an old woman they came across while disguised as peddlers. She had bought a pretty comb from them, haggling with the two gods until they sold her the trinket well below its value just to get rid of her. But she had wished them "Odin's blessings" as they parted, and in return, Odin had indeed blessed her—with youth.

And later on that evening, he'd blessed her again, this time with a child, much to the dismay of his queen.

"He sounds kind of... vain and unfaithful, for a supposedly wise god. But I could be biased—I've not been a fan since he tried to have my mates killed."

Mimir chuffed through his nose. "Gods and men are much alike, in that aspect. We all have flaws. Odin has all days vied for recognition and worship from mortals."

"And your own flaws?" I pried.

Mimir gave me a half-smile. "Too numerous to count, plum, pride perhaps chiefly among them. No, Odin and I are no longer friends like we were."

"Is that why you lived in that well before you were taken here? Did Odin banish you there?" He seemed the type to banish people to wells.

"I chose the well of my own free will. Its waters bring wisdom. I did not, however, choose to leave."

I resisted the urge to suggest he might have decided to live *by* the well, rather than *in* it, but who was I to deny a bodiless god his quirks? "And the creature that took your place? Was it drawn by the water too?" I shuddered at the memory of the thing that had nearly killed Magni.

Mimir gave me a long look. "I suspect it was placed in my well after I was taken."

"You think someone deliberately set a trap for us? But who could have known we'd be going there? Verdandi wouldn't tell anyone—I think. I mean, I don't know her, but—"

"Verdandi would never betray you," Mimir interrupted. "Think, child. Who would gain from your death?"

"Loki," I said. "If he could have stopped me, then—"

"Loki was hiding in Midgard then," Grim broke in. I jolted at the sound of his voice—he'd ignored me ever since fetching Mimir, and I'd more or less gotten used to him being a silent shadow.

"He is right," Mimir said softly. "The trickster god had no access to my well."

I frowned. But who else would have gone to the lengths of planting some vicious monster in hopes it killed me? If Loki was behind the coming of Ragnarök, if he wanted me out of the way bad enough to have had Grim lure me to Hel—

I jerked upright, my spine straightening. If Loki had wanted me dead, why hadn't he left me to die along with Modi and Bjarni when we'd faced Nidhug? He could have run, saved his own skin, and gotten rid of us all in one fell sweep.

"Loki isn't behind this," I murmured, more to myself than anyone else. "I was wrong."

They were staring at me, Grim with darkness in his

eyes, Mimir with intent, but they were both silent—unable to tell me anything more, thanks to whatever spell had been put on them to keep them quiet.

How long had Grim been working for them? Before we arrived at Valhalla? Or had he been turned after?

I spent the next couple of hours in silence, working over what little information I had of who might be behind it all. It'd been a sort of comfort, really, when I was sure it was Loki. Not knowing was infinitely scarier, even if some small part of me was relieved we wouldn't have to kill Bjarni and Saga's father.

But would we have to kill Modi and Magni's? I remembered my concerns—concerns Bjarni had shared—when Magni's pleas for help to get us back from Seattle had gone ignored. And I remembered the power of the entity that had faced Saga and me during our trials to enter Asgard.

Wasn't Thor supposed to be the mightiest god of them all?

As far as evidence went, it was weak. I'd accused Loki too hastily, ignoring how easy it would have been for him to end my life without having his son kidnap me to Hel. Sure, before I knew he couldn't have been behind the well creature, I'd assumed he had some nefarious and magical reasons for not killing me the old-fashioned way, but I shouldn't have jumped to conclusions. I wasn't going to do that again. Even if Thor had proven to be a prime jerk and an awful father, it didn't necessarily mean that he was trying to bring about the end of everything that'd ever lived.

But who, then?

I rubbed irritably at my neck, the sweat on it making me itchy. I didn't know nearly enough about the intricacies of the gods to hazard a guess, and yet somehow it was *my* job to figure out not only who was behind this whole catastrophe, but also stop them. Because why not? It wasn't like Asgard was littered with literal gods who could maybe get off their collective asses and do something about it.

The feathers decorating my armor brushed against my throat, aggravating it, and the leather clung to my chest, overheating my body.

Growling, I pulled at the feathery piece, intent on freeing myself from its constrictive confines, when realization struck and my fingers stilled.

I was *sweating*.

Slowly I lowered my hands, my mind switching from trying to puzzle out the betrayer's identity to the here and now.

My blood felt too warm in my veins, and when I focused inward, my pulse drew me down to the heavy press low in my abdomen.

It was happening.

I bit my lip, anxiety flaring as I glanced over my shoulder at Grim. He was staring blankly into the fire, an unmoving sentinel, just like he had for the past four days. *Waiting.*

I should have felt relief; I'd been waiting for this. Once it was done, we could continue our search for a way out of Hel, and Grim.... Grim would learn that there was no choice but for us to fight against Ragnarök. Together.

But... I rubbed a hand against my chest, the leather still too tight on my skin, eying him again. This was... so very different than it had been with my four other mates. Saga, Magni, and Bjarni had all been keen to bed me, eager to put their marks on my neck. Even Modi, who'd been reluctant at first, was all heat and primal urges underneath.

Grim? Grim was ice and shadow and hate.

My supposed soulmate, who had killed me without hesitance.

Enough wallowing, Annabel. No amount of trepidation was going to change what had to happen now.

Trying to will my hands to stop shaking, I began to undo the straps tying my armor in place. First the plumed chest piece, then the wrist guards. My boots. I kneeled and undid my belt and leather trousers, sliding them and my panties off my thighs, until I was naked.

Still warmth licked along my veins, the momentary relief of being bare drowning as my temperature climbed. There was only one thing that would bring me true relief.

I walked on bare feet across the cave floor toward the fire. And Grim.

Only when I stopped by his side did he glance up at me.

"What—?" His smokey voice quieted as he took me in, eyes sweeping up the length of my body, pausing for a long second at the apex of my thighs. When he met my gaze again, dark determination shone in his.

Without another word, he rose to his feet and turned fully toward me.

He stood so close, his natural coldness leeching through the distance between us, pulling on me with the whispered promise of relief. His scent, though still dimmed by Hel, seemed stronger now. Delicious. *Alpha.*

Uninvited images of licking his throat popped into my head, and I swayed toward him, my body momentarily taking over.

His cool, strong hands closed around my forearms, stopping me. The shock of his chilled skin against mine pulled me out of it enough to draw my focus from his throat to his eyes.

"I'm sorry," I blurted. "I... I'm not sure how to do this."

It was true. The other times, I had been so deep in my heat my instincts had taken over, making me say and do things I wouldn't have if I'd still been in control of my mind.

Now? It was still early, and I still had the ability to feel shame. My body hummed with interest at Grim's presence, heat pulsing more heavily in my womb, but it wasn't strong enough to force me to my knees and beg for him to mount me.

I should have waited until it was.

"I'm sorry," I repeated, pulling away from his grip. I turned around before I could see the look on his face and retreated to my corner. Without looking back, I dropped down on the dried skin I'd used as a bed these past few nights, wrapped my arms around my knees, and pressed my face into them to wait for the sweet oblivion of my full heat.

Hours. It would be hours of increasing torture before it crested, if the past two times were anything to go by. I gritted my teeth and clasped my knees harder, trying to push down a sudden wave of despair. If my mates had been here, they would've seen me through this without shame or misery. They would've surrounded me with love and laughter, inflicted upon me guilt-free pleasure until every cell in my body was sated and my mind at peace.

Peace.

It had been mine for the briefest of moments, that night in the arms of the four men who loved me, before I'd been ripped from them again. I longed to be back there on the soft furs in that room in Valhalla, longed for it so much my heart ached.

A cold touch on my shoulder made me draw in a sharp breath, my sadness scattering. I hadn't heard Grim approach.

He wrapped his strong fingers around my braid,

then tugged, pulling my head back. He knelt down behind me, his body dwarfing mine as he bent his head to murmur into my ear, "Have you changed your mind, omega? Are you no longer interested in fucking me?"

I swallowed thickly, unsure how to respond. Was he toying with me? Mocking me? My blood pulsed, heating my thoughts until they were too hazy to grasp.

Grim leaned in closer, and I shivered as the chill of his body enveloped me from behind, making every hair stand on end and my nipples tighten. Still keeping his fist locked in my hair, he ran his nose up the side of my neck, a rough noise escaping his lips that woke my clit with a shudder.

"You smell almost like you did that night at our farm on the cusp of your first heat. So *needy*. Your scent nearly drove my brothers to force you up against the kitchen counter."

"I remember," I croaked. "You stopped them. Was it... Was it for their sake? Or mine?"

He only snarled in response and slipped his free arm around my midriff.

Even through his leather armor, it was such an intimate embrace from the alpha who had barely stomached my presence up until now. I drew in a shuddering breath, my mind reeling, but my body reacted on pure instinct, leaning into the man whose scent and touch promised blessed relief.

"Were you scared your first time underneath the

Thorsson bastard?" he asked, his quiet voice surprising me as much as the question itself.

I looked at him over my shoulder, tried to decipher his intentions, but his face revealed no emotion.

"Yes," I said. "I was. But the heat was... more insistent. I didn't register much else apart from the need."

He chuffed a breath through his nose, but it wasn't quite a laugh. "And now? Are you still afraid?"

"Yes," I admitted softly, because it was the truth. "But not of the sex—of what comes after."

"What comes after is your doing," he reminded me, a thread of anger in his voice. "Remember that."

He yanked my head back harder, making me arch my back and drop to my knees with a grunt of pain, before gliding his hand down my stomach and between my thighs.

I keened without meaning to, my knees spreading wide of their own accord. His fingers skimmed my still-hooded clit and I cried out again, a zing of pleasure tightening my spine. His skin was like ice against my molten flesh, heightening the sensation as he delicately traced the small fold hiding that bundle of nerves.

"Grim... touch me *there*," I gasped, all thoughts other than need fleeing my mind, all traces of embarrassment lost to the undertow of lust.

He breathed against my neck, the air on my skin as cool as his fingertips pulling back on my hood, exposing my clit.

"Yes," I hissed, pressing my back into him more fully. "Please, *yes."*

"So eager," he murmured. "One tiny little touch, and you've forgotten your shame of having to surrender to your enemy. I wonder—if I let you stew until your heat fully consumed your mind, would you force yourself upon me?"

Probably.

I whimpered. "Don't. Please, don't."

If I'd been fully with it, I wouldn't have begged him —wouldn't have shown him how desperate I was to avoid the agony of being without his touch. The second the words were out of my mouth, I cringed, expecting him to use them against me—to make me suffer for what I'd forced him to agree to do.

He breathed against my neck again, the shakiest note to it, and then brushed his fingertip up through my folds to ghost his touch over my bared clit.

I *quivered,* my breath exploding out of my chest at the blinding sensation of his featherlight caress. It was like fire, like ice—too strong, too much for me to contain. He brushed it again, and again, and I cried out and reached back, blindly digging my nails into his thighs bracketing my hips, needing to feel him under my palms to anchor me through the torrent of impressions.

How? The question echoed in my mind as I writhed in the alpha's grasp, my climax fast approaching despite

Grim giving my clitoris little more than featherlight attention.

"How are you doing this?" I gasped. "Oh, fuck, I'm... *I'm—!*"

I keened and *came,* the rising tension in my abdomen snapping as ecstasy danced along my spine.

Grim held me in place, fingers resting lightly against my pulsing bud of nerves until my orgasm ebbed. I groaned softly, and he released his hold on my hair and moved his hand from my pussy, letting me sag forward to support my weight on my knees. Despite still feeling light with the echoes of pleasure, my body was already heating up again, more insistently this time. Urgent.

Through hooded lids, I turned my head to look at Grim over my shoulder.

He was watching me intently, his expression still inscrutable—but his gaze was not. His eyes were dark with a hunger I recognized all too well, and relief flickered in my gut. Relief—and desire. He wanted me. Despite his anger, his plans, his hatred... he wanted me.

Slowly I bent forward until my cheek pressed against the dirty hide, arched my back, and spread my knees, submitting.

Grim snarled, the sound running through me like high voltage. I gasped as my body *clenched* in response.

"Alpha," I cooed. *"Please."*

"Alpha," he growled, the note of mockery not fully swallowed by the rumbling timbre of his own desire. He moved closer, and once again the chill of his

body brushed against my skin before he touched me. "Is that the game you wish to play, Annabel? A submissive little omega aching for her *alpha?* You don't need to pretend with me. I see your iron. Your fire."

"It's not a game," I said, grimacing as my abdomen clenched again, forcing slick to trickle down my thighs. "I need you. Please."

Silence followed. And then—cold, heavy pressure on the back of my neck as he rose up on his knees behind me, one hand keeping my head to the skins while the other...

"Yes! Please!" I whimpered as he traced my already sodden lower lips, teasing me open without ever truly touching me where I needed him most. And still, just the lightest brush of his skin against mine had every nerve in my body alight with sensation, as if I was somehow attuned to him. As if the icy magnetism of his presence had sucked me under, and every cell in my body now yearned to meld with his, until I was finally... *complete.*

"I need you," I croaked. "Inside me, Grim. *Please.*"

Air rushed from his lungs, his grip on my neck tightening and his featherlight fingers against my pussy flattening. I groaned incoherently at the firmer touch and rocked against his palm, icy fire licking up my spine.

It felt *so good.* I moaned again, pressing down hard to grind my clit on his fingers, but just as the first whispers of orgasm were within reach, he removed both hands from my aching body.

I hissed in protest. "No, please—"

The rustling of his belt buckle made me swallow, my plea dying on a gasp—a gasp that turned sharp when he grabbed my ass and spread me open.

The first brush of his cockhead was so cold against my molten flesh, it should have been soothing.

It was anything but.

Fire raced up my spine, my heat covering me in sweat even as I shivered at his touch. Inside, *inside!* He belonged in me, belonged *with* me—

Grim hissed when I bucked and tried to spear myself on him, his grip on my ass turning painful as he held me in place.

"Please, please—!" I begged, mindless for anything but the urgency pounding in my blood.

I needn't have.

Grim snarled, the sound rough and oh-so *alpha.* And then he took me.

Cool, unrelenting pressure caught in the mouth of my pussy for a brief second, but my slick, eager flesh opened for him, stretching to the point of delicious pain.

Grim made a choking sound I barely registered over the rushing in my ears and forced the head of his cock fully inside.

Yes!

I cried out, nails digging into the hide beneath me

as my entire body lit up from within, the sensation rooted in that burning, aching, throbbing part of me wrapped around him. I didn't get to revel in it, because Grim only paused for a moment. Sliding his hands up to my hips and grasping me hard enough to bruise, he pushed the full length of his cock inside me in one slow, smooth slide, forcing me wide all the way to my cervix.

"Nngh!" His cry mixed with my own as we both stilled. Everything was heat and ice, and I was so perfectly *full,* so entirely complete. My body thrummed with energy, a mixture of light and darkness swirling before my eyes, blinding me to the world. There was only *him,* inside of me. Where he belonged.

Grim slumped over me, his armor digging into my skin. His breath came in harsh, sharp gasps against my ear, the scent of alpha enveloping my senses.

"Grim," I murmured. *"Grim."*

His lips skimmed the shell of my ear—not quite a kiss, but the gentleness of his caress sent shivers down my spine. He groaned again, gliding his hands from my hips to my waist, bringing me with him when he sat back up.

The change in position brought me into his lap, straddling his cock still hard and unyielding inside me. With one hand, he released my waist, dragging his palm along my torso, over a breast, and up to my throat. His grasp was like iron, his hold on me unbreakable. I leaned my head back, resting it against his shoulder, reaching back to dig my fingers into his thighs.

Grim's first thrust was ecstasy made flesh. His cool, girthy cock filled me in a rough push, and I mewled at the brutal pleasure. He didn't pause when he met the bottom of my passage this time, instead giving me another harsh thrust. And another. And another.

I arched and spread my thighs as much as I could while he took me with rough, urgent groans, his previously light touches exchanged for bruising strength and dominance. It was exactly what I needed—what my body needed to ease the fires of my heat.

I cried out for him again and again, his name spilling from my lips to the tune of my pussy's syrupy smacks each time he drove home. He clutched me closer in response, held me so tight I struggled to breathe, but I didn't care. I just needed more of him, more of his cock, *more—!*

"Oh, *fuck!*" Without warning, every muscle in my body clamped down tight, my back tightening like a bowstring. My climax struck like a lightning bolt, pleasure seizing me as my pussy erupted in a series of flutters around his thickness.

Grim let out a strangled sound, his entire body freezing as his shaft thickened in my entrance.

I forced out a noise of protest through his grip on my throat, but Grim didn't draw out my torment. With a grunt of effort, he pressed his swelling knot home, the brutal bump hooking deep in my pelvis.

I wailed and clawed at my alpha's leather-clad thighs in retaliation, light exploding behind my eyes as equal parts pain and pleasure lanced up my abdomen and down my thighs. But his knot was immediately followed by cool, soothing liquid. It filled my pussy and bathed my cervix, alleviating the pain with each powerful spurt, and making my lover shudder and gasp against my ear.

"Grim," I rasped brokenly, his name the only word filling my mind. Grim, Grim, *Grim.* This was home. This was completion.

A deep growl rumbled through his chest and into my back in response.

And then he buried his sharp teeth in the back of my neck—and my soul.

12

GRIM

Annabel still shuddered periodically in my arms.

I'd stopped rubbing her clit some time ago, but small tremors of aftershock had her pussy tightening on me in uneven intervals. I buried my face in her sweat-soaked neck and clenched my eyes shut, reeling against the pleasure.

It was too much.

I'd never known anything could feel... this *much.* Everything was raw—my nerves, my soul... my heart, where something new and alien, yet achingly familiar hooked deep into the muscle. It bathed me in warmth and light too intense for my endorphin-addled brain to process, but I could do nothing to protect myself and there was no escaping it. I lay in dazed stupor as everything that was *Annabel* flooded me, filling up every dark recess, softening my icy flesh and forcing my organs to expand to the point of pain.

Mate.

The word throbbed in my brain in tune with her heartbeat drumming steadily under my palm where I was still clutching her against me. *Mate. Mate. Mate.*

I'd known claiming her would end me. But even as I'd accepted that, I hadn't been prepared for *this.* For how it felt.

"Grim," she mewled, thick and sweet. She'd been calling my name throughout, her voice drawing me in like a siren's song. Even now I shivered at the sound of it, another pulse of semen leaving my cock to bathe her womb.

"Mate." The word rumbled out of my chest before I could stop it, earning me a happy little chirp from the girl in my arms.

"Mate," she whispered, one hand coming up to prod at the fresh wound I'd given her. My mark was right in the center of her nape, gray in the dim light of Hel, but still visible, marking her as mine for the world to see.

"This feels... different than the other times," she mused, voice still soft and dreamy.

The others. I felt them in her—those dark, aching wounds near where our bond hooked on her end. Her other mates.

Cool rage stirred at the base of my skull, threatening to end my hazy bliss as I let the knowledge that my mate belonged to four other males wash over me. They had no right, she was *mine,* she was—

"Grim?" This time concern tinged Annabel's drowsy voice. "What—What's wrong?"

She felt me. Like her warmth and light filled me, my ice and darkness filled her in return.

I shook my head and pressed my forehead to the back of her skull, tempering the rage until it was a low, simmering ache in the pit of my gut. I'd known this would happen. There was nothing to be done about it, except accept it.

This—how I felt with Annabel in my arms—was biology, and Fate's slimy fingers pulling at the web in attempted manipulation.

At least the rush of anger at the memory of my mate writhing underneath four other males had managed to ease my knot.

I pulled my hips back, sliding out of Annabel despite her grunt of protest. The loss of her tight, wet heat was a gruesome mix of agony and relief, my cock already attempting to rise again to return to her hallowed depths, even as the severing of the pleasure gave my frayed nerves a much-needed respite.

Annabel rolled over to face me on the skin. Her eyes trailed up my body to my lips, lingering there for a moment as if she were contemplating kissing me.

"The ring," I reminded her. I raised my hand to hold it out to her, but without my approval, my fingers clasped onto her hip, stalling there, as if not touching her was impossible.

"Mmh," she hummed. She reached down to my hand, nudging the metal band with a fingertip. "If I remove it now, are you going to refuse seconds?"

I arched an eyebrow at her.

"My heat... It takes more than one time to sate it." She gave me a smile filled with the kind of promise that tightened my body with primal urgency.

I gripped her hip harder, enough that it would leave another set of bruises next to the ones already starting to bloom there. "I'll sate your heat. You know as much."

She did know—understood on a primitive level what her delicious scent did to my lizard brain. Even if I'd been inclined to fight the bond now tying me to her, I'd be unable to resist her body's call to mine.

A sliver of darkness pierced the now-warm place in my chest. I knew the futility in fighting the call to mate.

"Grim," she murmured, the softness in her tone pulling my focus back to her face. I saw it in her eyes then. The understanding. The empathy.

But this was nothing like then.

She was nothing like it.

I moved without thought, rolling her onto her back and pressing myself down over her, letting her pelvis bear my weight. She mewed and wrapped her legs around my hamstrings, desire sparking behind her hazy eyes. She submitted so readily for me. She may have been wrought from fire and steel, but beneath me, she was soft, yielding flesh; a warm, thornless embrace.

"Remove the ring and I'll give you *seconds,*" I purred.

She grinned up at me, and the shock of it struck deep. A glimmer of genuine happiness. Here, in this place. Despite everything that had happened to her—and still would. It resonated in my chest, the sensation alien, yet dangerously addictive.

Annabel didn't pay my dumbstruck expression any mind. She looked to my hand now resting next to her head and reached for it. I let her lift it and place it between her breasts, my fingers brushing the soft mounds. Heat rose from where my cock lay along her center, sparking images of my lips around one of those dusky pink nipples.

"I'd like you to," she said, her voice hoarse, and I realized my thoughts must have been written all over my face. "If you want."

Want.

I forced my gaze from her breasts to her face, staring at her, *into* her, until the bond between us thrummed.

Annabel didn't say anything more, but she held my gaze, chest rising and falling in rapid waves underneath my palm as she slowly wrapped her fingers around the ring on my thumb and pulled.

It slid off with ease, the void where my magic had been numbed springing to life. I groaned at the sensation, the darkness of it flooding through my veins and pouring straight through my bond into Annabel.

She gasped, her eyes going wide, and blind panic seized me by the throat. Hissing, I yanked it out of her and back into the place inside me where I kept it safely locked away—but where I expected agony to follow, only curiosity did.

"Do that again," she said.

"What?" was all I managed through gritted teeth still clenched with the remnants of terror.

Light flooded through our bond in response, rushing into me until it illuminated every dark corner of my mind. I gasped and jerked in reflex, but it wasn't painful. It was...

I groaned and squeezed my eyes shut as my magic rose to meet hers, whirling around her light in smoky tendrils, curiously examining the golden glow—her very essence.

Soulmate.

It throbbed in my mind, so similar to the word that'd filled me after I'd claimed her, yet... not the same. Her body was her own, a sacred space she allowed me to share, but this? Her soul? Feeling her very essence inside of me was like a soothing balm smeared over the ragged edges of my own conscience. As if long ago a piece of me had been broken off, and now it was finally being melded back into place.

Her lips skimmed mine, gentle and questioning. I didn't open my eyes, mindlessly pressing my mouth to hers in hungry demand, even as my focus remained on the wonderous sensation of her magic within me.

Annabel moaned softly, parting her lips in invitation. The touch of her soft tongue against mine made me shiver, and when I deepened my kiss, I let my dark power well through the bond and back into her.

She gasped into my mouth and clung to my shoulders, but this time I didn't pull back.

Happiness met me—wrapped around me like the most intimate embrace. She was... so pleased. So happy I was opening up to her, so relieved. Images met me—of every time she'd felt my presence or dreamed of me as she was growing up. Of our first meeting in the flesh back in Iceland, and that instant jerk of recognition. Of my face screwed up in rage as I shattered the boat that would have taken her back to Asgard and her mates, followed by relief that I would now help her, rather than stop her.

Gently I pulled back my magic, easing out of her consciousness before I could see any more of her excitement to be reunited with the four men who'd claimed her before me.

She gave me an unhappy moan as I lifted off her body a few inches, separating our lips as well, but withdrew her own, golden light from me.

"There is nothing to be jealous of," she said softly, moving one hand from my shoulder to cup my cheek. "They'll love you too."

"I don't need love," I said, moving to get off her completely, but she wrapped her legs around my waist, refusing to allow a full separation.

"It doesn't matter if you need it—you'll have it. The six of us—we belong together."

She genuinely believed that. She had accepted the Norns' schemes as her destiny so completely, she felt nothing but contentment at the violation of being so intimately tied to us. It hadn't always been like that. I remembered how wildly she'd fought against Saga and Magni when they'd first forced their claims on her, and briefly wondered if the bonds had lulled her into submission—or if this too was Verdandi's doing.

I didn't respond.

She gave me a lopsided smile and reached up to place a hand on my stomach. "So gloomy still."

I chuffed through my nose, not quite a laugh, but not quite derisive either.

"I'm still in heat," she reminded me, the curve of her lip turning slightly more feral. "And you promised seconds. You can brood later."

My gaze dropped to her breasts, and she hummed a happy little purr, clearly pleased at my instincts' easy surrender.

"Take off your clothes," she commanded.

I looked back up at her, eyebrow arched.

"I'm so hot—I want to feel your skin on mine," she said. "And your leathers chafe."

I hadn't given much thought to my clothes—the need to be inside her had overshadowed everything else. But I knew my cool temperature repulsed most hotblooded beings, especially in intimate situations.

My stepmother had demanded I keep my clothes on, that I touch her as little as possible—with one exception, of course.

"Please," Annabel added, her voice softer, as if she sensed where my thoughts had drifted. "Let me feel you."

I exhaled before I reached for the straps keeping my armor in place. Annabel watched me intently as I bared my body for her one piece at a time. When I was finally naked, she sat up and reached for me, hooking her arms around the back of my neck so she could haul herself onto the tops of my thighs.

I wrapped my arms around her back on instinct, pulling her close to secure her weigh, and she sighed with relief.

"Oh, that feels so good," she moaned, pressing her forehead against the side of my neck.

Her skin burned everywhere it touched mine, the heat of her making my blood hum and my cock rise between her thighs. I'd never been particularly bothered by temperature, but Annabel felt like embracing the dawn after a long winter's night.

I rubbed my cheek against her messy braid, shifting my hands to her plump ass as I rocked up against her. Her slick heat parted for my eager cock, and I rubbed through her wet cleft and up against her protruding clit.

Annabel mewled and rolled her hips down for more. "Yes," she whimpered. "Like that. Oh, Grim, *yes*, like *that*."

I let her grind on me for a few more breaths before I tightened my grip and lifted her up mid-rocking motion, just in time for the momentum to spear her opening on my dick and drive her halfway down it.

"Oh! Fuck!" Annabel arched in my arms, body stiffening and face screwing into a tight grimace as she took me in.

Heat enveloped me, radiating down my thighs and up my spine. I groaned unintelligibly, freezing for a long second as my nerves screamed with the intensity of our union.

Then instinct took over.

My mate cried out as I forced her all the way down on my cock, her channel fluttering around me, sucking me deeper still until there was nowhere left to go. I forced my eyes open then, as hungry to see her take me as I was to feel it. The look of near-pained ecstasy on her pretty features, of her teeth buried in her bottom lip and her breasts thrust out toward me, nearly summoned my orgasm.

I choked out a groan and bent forward, burying my mouth in her breasts as I pulled her against me by her ass, ensuring my cock stayed sealed deep inside of her.

One hard nipple popped into my mouth, and I latched onto it with a desperation I hadn't known I possessed.

"Grim," she crooned. Her slim fingers tightened in my hair, pulling me harder against her chest as she

peppered my scalp with kisses. "Suck me. Please, suck me."

Even if I'd wanted to, I would have been incapable of resisting such a sultry, needy command.

Moaning, I tightened my lips around the little bud and sucked.

Home.

This was *home.*

The pleasure burned bright, blinding me to anything but the sensation of *her,* throbbing and pulsing and so, so *hot.* But through the mind-numbing ecstasy of every physical impression, there was something else fluttering at the edges of my consciousness.

Safe. I felt safe in a way so wholly unfamiliar it would have scared me, had I the capacity to feel fear.

I flicked my tongue over her nipple, gasping as Annabel's responding shiver echoed through my own body, and tightened my seal on her breast.

She moaned again and clutched tighter at my hair, her pussy spasming on my cock still buried to the hilt inside of her.

"Oh, *Grim.*"

The yearning her soft coo sparked making me press my face into her breasts and rub at the softness enveloping me, my mouth popping off her now-glistening nipple.

Gods, she was... *everything.* A safe haven I hadn't known I craved. Hadn't known even existed.

An impatient roll of her hips had me kiss her soft

mounds still cradling my face, one hand slipping from her ass to her front. When I flicked my finger over her taut clit, Annabel groaned. The sound went through me like a lightning bolt, my focus turning carnal once more. When I turned my head to suck on her still unattended nipple, it was with intent.

"Grim," she cried, her pussy gripping me so tight it almost hurt. "Fuck, don't stop, baby. Don't stop!"

I pressed my thumb in harder on her clit and rubbed her, her hands in my hair ensuring I stayed latched on her breast for the duration. Only when her sheath erupted in spasms around me did I release her nipple in time to see her expression contort, her body stiffening against mine as her climax struck.

I rolled my hips up, giving her a deep thrust that had her crying out. And another. She still clung to my hair, yanking savagely at the roots, but the small hurt only fueled my need to *take.* With a snarl, I put her on her back, pressing my hips down hard between her thighs before she could reorient herself.

"Shit!"

I ignored her outburst at taking the full force of my cock and rolled my hips again, making her pelvis take my weight with every savage thrust. She came again, and I fucked her faster and harder through her pussy's desperate flutters, snarling every time I bottomed out against her cervix. Darkness mixed with brilliant, golden light behind my eyes, crackling through my every cell. There was nothing but *her*—nothing but her warm, sucking cunt and the certainty that if I ever stopped fucking her, I'd cease to exist.

She went lax underneath me, her molten flesh turning pliant and soft. My name still spilled from her lips, pleading now, her palms sliding to my abs in a weak attempt at slowing my assault. It only drove me harder, and soon her protests were replaced by soft moans, her sheath tightening around me once more. She came on my knot, hissing and spitting, my name a curse as she fought and surrendered.

When she asked me for *thirds* some twenty minutes later, I rolled her over to her stomach and allowed the instincts I'd hated for so long to swallow me whole.

13
ANNABEL

My nipples were as raw as my clit when I finally awoke without the haze of heat fogging my mind some days later.

Behind me, cool flesh pressed against my back, rising and falling with the rhythm of Grim's steady breaths. He'd slung an arm over my midriff, cocooning me with his chilly body, and I hummed a small sound of appreciation.

As far as heats went, having my mate regulate the awful, feverish temperature hike had been a godsend.

Mate.

I prodded gently at the new bond in my chest—the only one that wasn't a dark, festering wound. Grim murmured in response, tightening his grip on me, and I eased off our connection with a smile.

I'd not been prepared for how... *good* it'd feel.

My other four mating bonds had come with pain

and angst. I'd expected Grim, of all people, to give me a bond barbed with broken glass and darkness. I'd expected pain and misery, not… *this.*

I pressed a hand to my ribs and closed my eyes, focusing on the soft glow of it. Peaceful.

He'd fought it at first, but his surrender had been swift and complete. It still took my breath away to recall those moments when his magic had been within me and I'd felt whole in a way I hadn't expected to.

Soulmates, he'd called us. Was that why it felt like this? So… smooth. As if we were already carved from the same piece, so slotting together was friction-free.

Well. In spirit, at least.

I grimaced at the throbbing down below. Reluctant as he may have been, Grim had given in to his primal side as fully as any of my other mates. It still baffled me to know that the cold, withdrawn man, the dark god of mist and shadow, possessed a passion so fiery.

And that he had a proclivity for breasts.

"You've been awake for several minutes and no one's copulating. Am I to take it your brain is back in charge?"

Mimir's dry voice made me jolt—and wince, thanks to my sore abdominal muscles—and whip around. The prophet's head sat where I'd left him some time ago, on a skin on the floor. Staring right at me and Grim.

"You *watched?*" I hissed, heat that had nothing to do with desire and everything to do with mortification rising all the way from my toes to my cheeks.

He arched both bushy eyebrows. "Of course."

"What happened to having no such inclinations?" I snapped. I'd forgotten all about him. I'd forgotten all about everything, save Grim, but I really, *really* wished I'd at least had the wherewithal to turn Mimir's head in the opposite direction before surrendering to my heat.

"Ah. I find no personal pleasure in it, but I do admit the act is… fascinating to watch. Besides, it wasn't like there were a lot of other entertainment options these past three days."

"I told you you should have left him outside in the mud," Grim rumbled sleepily behind me. The cool arm around my midriff withdrew, followed by the comfortable pressure against my back as he sat up.

A jolt of… not anxiety, but nervous energy perhaps, flickered through my gut. He was awake. And no longer deep in rut.

Slowly I turned toward him, ignoring the pervert prophet.

"Hi," I said softly. I took in his sleepy expression, so unexpected on his ice-carved features. He still looked every inch the cold, dark god, but somehow… more human now. As if he was finally allowing me to see past the barriers.

Grim only tilted his head in response, his eyes sweeping over me, taking in my swollen nipples and lips before dipping to the many bruises on my hips and ribs where he'd gripped me so, so tight.

"My heat's over," I said, though I didn't need to. The

times I'd woken before him during my few fitful spurts of sleep these past days, I'd taken him inside of me before he was even awake.

"Are you all right?" he rumbled, reaching one hand out to trace a particularly dark set of bruises along my ribs.

The brush of his skin against mine made me shiver —not so much with desire now, but pure *awareness.* His nearness sparked something in me, made me lean toward his touch as if pulled by a magnetic force.

"Yeah. A bit sore. Nothing unusual." I bit my lip and looked up at him through my lashes, an odd sense of shyness setting in. The intimacy we'd shared had been so intense, but now, without the insanity of my heat, it felt… intimidating.

I forced myself to recall the sensation of it, of melding into one with him, and steeled myself. It wasn't just about us. I'd made the bargain with him because I needed this connection. Shying away from it now that I had it was folly.

Before I could change my mind, I leaned forward and planted my lips against Grim's.

The alpha started at my sudden assault, but when he raised his hand, it wasn't to push me away. He wove his strong fingers into my messy hair, cupping the back of my head as he parted his lips and kissed me back.

His cool breath mingled with mine, shivers shooting down my spine as our bond hummed. Grim rumbled an appreciative note and snaked his other hand around my back to pull me in closer.

So easy. This was... so easy. Like two streams of liquid metal pouring into the same mold, forming into one.

I don't know if I pulled or he pushed, but when Grim's tongue flicked over mine, I was on my back on the sleeping skin, my mate settling his hips between my spread thighs. Warmth fluttered in my core, the absence of my heat doing nothing to quell my desire for him. Judging from the cool, hard column of flesh pressing against my navel, it did nothing to quell his either.

"Much as I hate to interrupt two lovebirds, I do feel it prudent to remind you that we have places to be—and an ever-narrowing window of time to get there," Mimir said, shattering the cocoon of quiet wonder wrapped around me and my mate.

I froze, my fingers tightening on Grim's black locks enough to make him grimace. I'd forgotten we weren't alone. *Again.*

Grim lifted his head and gave the prophet a glare. "I find the concept of your use as a troll's ball increasingly fascinating."

"Mimir's right," I said, releasing my grip on his hair to pat at his shoulders. "We've already spent so much time. We don't know when it'll be too late to stop Ragnarök, nor how long it'll take to get back."

Grim shifted his gaze to mine. A flicker of darkness passed over his mismatched eyes, but it was gone before

I could fully register it. "You should rest for a few days. I sense your... fatigue."

I shot him a wry smile. "I don't think being worn out from a sex marathon is enough reason to leave the end of the world to do its thing. I do need a quick rinse, though. Do you think we can find a safe stream? I'm... sticky."

His eyes darted to the apex of my thighs where proof of our coupling clung to my skin. "I find my essence on you... appealing."

I snorted at his somewhat bemused tone. He seemed to not be entirely sure *why* he found his spent seed caked on my skin *appealing*.

"That's great, but I am not walking around like a bukkake fantasy to placate your instincts. C'mon, let's find somewhere troll-free to get washed up before we get moving."

GRIM WATCHED over me as I bathed in a shallow creek by the cave we'd spent the past few days in. I felt his eyes on my skin as a physical caress. It warmed my body like rays of sun, and I hummed with pleasure. Who knew? Who could have ever known that mating Grim would bring me such... pure joy?

I shot a grateful thought down the bond between us, but instead of a warm response, I was met with dark nothingness.

Frowning, I pulled my consciousness back. Okay, so it was probably too much to expect that the cool, complex man who'd only ever loved his brothers would open up completely so soon. My other bonds had taken some time to fall into sync too.

Sighing, I finished up in the creek and waded to shore, shooting my silent, brooding mate a gentle smile as I got dressed. He had scars. Bad enough he'd killed me rather than willingly surrender to our shared fate. But he was mine now, and that was all I needed. I could be patient with him.

Once I was dressed, I turned to Mimir—who'd also had a quick dip in the creek to get rid of the left-over mud from his tumble a few days ago. I'd washed him before I bathed myself, mostly because it'd seemed the right thing to do for a prophet. "Where are we going?"

"Farther inland," he said. "If we make good pace, we should be there in a day or two."

"How long until we're out of troll territory?" I asked, directed at Grim this time.

He shrugged. "I am not familiar with the area, but if the landscape turns less rocky, we should at least be free of mountain trolls. Not that there aren't plenty of other creatures to be wary of."

The surly note to his voice made my cheeks heat a bit. "I'm sorry about the Nightmare."

Mimir scoffed. "How quickly you forget why we had to call on her services. Your *mate* did everything in his power to keep you from escaping. We did what we had to."

"Yeah, well, I can still be sorry." I sighed and looked to Grim. He didn't meet my gaze, his attention focused up the path. "We have a tough journey ahead, but we will get there. Together."

Neither of them responded.

I TRIED to reach out through my new bond a few times while we hiked through the rocky hills and down into the deeper woodlands, but Grim kept the connection shut.

I hadn't even realized that was an option—my bonds to my four other mates had been a constant flow, when I was still alive. Painful and confusing a lot of the time, but always open.

I didn't ask him why he shut me out—he would open up to me again when he was ready—but his ability to control our bond made me think of Loki's comments about his youngest son. How he was the one with the greatest gift of magic.

When we made camp underneath a weeping willow late that night and I'd perched Mimir on a log by the fire, I walked over to where Grim was busying himself with sharpening his blades and sat down by his side, close enough that my knee bumped into his.

He looked up at me, the slide of his whetstone pausing as he took me in with unreadable blankness.

"Hey," I said.

He didn't respond, but kept his attention on me.

"I was wondering... all this magic business. Modi taught me a few things, but I'm still not super-skilled. Do you think maybe you could teach me? It'd probably be helpful if I had a bit more control. And knowledge."

Shadow danced in Grim's eyes as he held my gaze for a long second. Then he returned his focus to his blades, resuming the slick slide of stone over metal. "It takes years upon years of study and practice to master the art of magic. Once this is all over... If we are still here, I will teach you then."

I frowned. "I don't expect to master it, but it's not going to do much good to wait until *after* we've stopped Ragnarök. I need all the skill I can scrape together, and as quickly as possible. I know I have the raw power, but that's only going to go so far. You saw how helpless I was against that first troll."

When the word *helpless* left my lips, Grim's arm paused its sliding motion again, his muscles trembling ever so slightly. Something like an echo resonated in our bond, but was gone just as quickly.

"Just the basics," I pressed. "Maybe something to help me not burn out so fast. Though... I'm not opposed to your help in replenishing my energy either."

Grim finally looked back at me, eyebrows raised, and I gave him a grin.

"Only if you want to, of course."

His lips flattened disapprovingly, but I saw the flash of heat in his eyes before he sighed and returned to his work. "Fine."

"Fine, you'll teach me, or fine, you'll... replenish me?"

"I will teach you. The *basics,*" he emphasized. "First lesson: You open yourself too wide when your use your magic. It comes out too unfocused, and you have to use more of it to get enough power behind you. Envision a narrow keyhole. Push your magic through it—laser-focus it."

"Now?" I asked.

"Unless you have something better to do."

I glared, but he was still looking at his daggers. It seemed our mating hadn't killed off the part of his personality that caused him to be a prick when he wanted to be.

"Okay. Fine." I got up and turned my back to the campfire, surveying our surroundings for an impromptu target dummy.

"The rocks by the brambles," Grim said. "Drill a hole through the biggest one. All the way through and no wider than an acorn."

It was a lot more difficult than it sounded. He was right—up until now, I'd pretty much slung my magic at whatever target, hoping the sheer mass of it would do the job. Trying to focus the thrumming power and channel it into a keyhole-sized beam was... difficult.

The boulder had several scorch marks and large chunks missing before I collapsed by the fire two hours later, as exhausted as if I'd run a marathon. But it also had a jagged hole only slightly larger than an acorn running at least halfway through.

Grim, who'd otherwise ignored me, got up and went over to inspect my work.

"You need to be consistent. You let your magic overwhelm you several times—the unevenness shows every time you lost control," he said.

"But I did last a lot longer than I'd normally have," I countered.

"And yet you didn't manage to complete the task. There's still nearly a foot of rock left to drill through. It shouldn't have taken you more than a few minutes."

I blew a raspberry. "You really need to work on your feedback skills. Have you ever heard of positive reinforcement? I'm entirely beat and very proud of myself, and here you are, pooping all over my efforts. Not cool."

Grim moved across the soft grass, coming to a stop by my side. He looked down at me, collapsed on my back underneath the willow tree, eyebrows furrowing. "You spent most of your energy on this?"

"Well... yeah. Mostly. I still have a bit left, but—"

His frown deepened, nostrils pulling up a quarter of an inch. "And what are you planning to do if we are attacked again? Throw rocks? Second lesson, though it really shouldn't need to be said: *Never* leave yourself depleted unless you absolutely have to."

"*You* set the task," I reminded him. I might have gained a softer touch when it came to my brusque new mate, but it was still pretty insulting to be talked to as if I were a complete idiot.

"Clearly I overestimated your abilities. It won't happen again," he snapped.

"You're such a prick." Annoyed as I was, there wasn't any true venom in my words, mostly because I was too tired to argue with him.

Grim gave me a dark look, then began unfastening the straps holding his armor in place.

"What are you doing?" I asked, arching an eyebrow when he threw his chest piece and tunic to the ground next to me, revealing a whole lot of icy skin and rippling abs.

"You need your powers replenished," he said flatly.

"Oh." Despite the rush of nerves awakening in my abdomen at the implication of that statement, I cracked a grin at him. "Well, I'm glad to see you're working on your positive reinforcement skills after all."

Grim only arched an eyebrow at me before he began working on his belt.

"Can you turn her over so I get the head end this time?" Mimir's dry voice cracked through our little camp, jolting my gaze from what Grim's hands were doing back to the prophet. "I think I've had quite my fill of your backside, Lokisson."

"Oh. My God." If the soil underneath me could have

opened up and swallowed me whole, I would have felt nothing but gratitude. I really, *really* needed to stop forgetting that we weren't alone every time my ovaries took over.

Grim, pants open and halfway down his hips, turned around and stalked to the other side of the fire, where he grabbed Mimir by the skull and turned him around to face away from the camp.

"Now, now, I didn't say I didn't want to watch. Just that there is only so much of a man's thrusting buttocks I can take," Mimir protested.

Grim didn't respond. He returned to me and continued to push off his boots and shove his trousers down his thighs, baring his body entirely, save the linen breeches covering his privates.

"Uh, yeah, no," I said, reaching up a hand to stop him when he hooked his thumbs in his breeches. "We are not... doing *that* with an audience. Again."

"Then how do you propose to regain your strength?" Grim asked, as nonplussed as if we were discussing the weather.

"I..." I grimaced and shot a look at the back of Mimir's head. "Maybe I'll recover with some sleep."

Grim only snorted and shoved his underwear down, exposing that mouthwatering cock of his already half-erect. It grew rapidly before my eyes, momentarily distracting my protests.

"You didn't seem to mind an audience that last night in Valhalla," he said, brushing a hand up the length of my thigh before reaching for the waist of my leather pants.

Heat gathered in my cheeks. "I wasn't given much of a choice," I muttered, though truthfully, it wasn't like I'd been particularly bothered. I'd just been so relieved to be back with my mates.

"Then perhaps consider that you don't have much of one now either," he murmured, enough heat lacing through his words to ease the sting of the threat in them.

I lifted my brows. "Oh? Feeling up for a bit of forced ravishment, are we?"

It was meant as a playful taunt, but Grim's hands stilled on my belt, his eyes darting to mine. Shadows flickered in them when he said, so quietly it could have been a whisper, "Without your powers, you are vulnerable. If you will not yield, I... will still do what I must."

"Grim." I forced my tired muscles to contract so I could sit up, propping myself on one elbow and reaching for him with my free hand. I pressed my palm against his chest right where our quiet bond attached below his ribs, his coldness leaching into my skin. "I won't ever make you do that. I promise."

My other mates liked it with an edge of reluctance. I suspected they enjoyed the opportunity to show me their strength and dominance, that my submission was all the sweeter if it came hard won. And, truth be told, I liked that too. But Grim?

He might have all the alpha instincts, and he'd

certainly shown me his dominant side while he rutted me through my heat, but his scars... Those awful memories still haunted him, no matter how much he pretended they didn't.

No, the idea of a reluctant partner did not delight him. That he was telling me he would do it anyway was only proof how fundamentally our mating had rocked him. He would rather break himself apart than leave me defenseless.

I pushed up fully and embraced him, pressing my face into the crook of his neck.

He sat frozen for several long breaths, a statue carved from ice—unsure of how to respond, I realized.

"Hug me," I mumbled, rubbing my nose against his shoulder.

Hesitantly, he obeyed. I hummed a pleased note and skimmed my lips over the muscle that connected his shoulder to his neck.

Grim *trembled* under me, a soft gasp blowing against the top of my head. I smirked and let my tongue flick out to tease that same spot.

My mate responded with a groan, strong arms tightening around my body to the point of pain.

"You feel... so *much,*" he rasped against my scalp. "Every touch of you is... amplified."

I let my hands find his back and trailed one finger down the length of his spine in response. He shuddered again, cool breath huffing out against my ear. His hands found my feathered top, and with a few yanks on straps, he pulled it off me, throwing it to the ground with little care for the invaluable leather. When he closed his arms tight around me again, I was the one to shiver as his icy skin enveloped me from all sides.

Grim released me as if he'd been burned. "I'm… sorry."

I arched my eyebrow at the unexpected apology. "For what?"

In his usual style, he didn't respond—only closed his eyes for a moment. When he opened them again, it took me a second to realize I no longer felt the chill of him radiating out.

Frowning, I put a hand on his chest. No sensation of temperature met me. He'd… magically nullified his natural chill? To not cause me discomfort?

"Don't do that," I said softly, spreading my fingers out over one hard pec. "I want to feel you."

"You're no longer in heat," he countered. "It will be… unpleasant. To mate."

"I like it—your coldness. Nothing feels right here. Even the water is just… nothing. You're the only thing that doesn't feel wrong. It reminds me that I'm not dead. Not fully," I said. I stroked my hand over his chest for emphasis. When my thumb brushed over his nipple in the process, his entire body trembled underneath me, his eyes squeezing shut. A soft moan echoed in the space between us.

With another breath, he opened those mismatched eyes again. They seemed to bore into mine, into my soul, as if he was searching for something. Slowly, coldness radiated against my palm and up through my thighs.

I smiled and rubbed his nipple again, but he was apparently prepared this time, because he only narrowed his eyes in response.

"Is that how you blended into the human world? You would... dim yourself when taking a girl to bed?" I asked. I don't know why the question popped into my head—and I certainly don't know why I asked it right then. The thought of Grim between some nameless, faceless girl's thighs had acid churn in my gut, some of my own desire waning.

"I never did," he said. Something in his tone made me think he'd sensed my idiotic jealousy even through the wall he'd put up between our connection.

I grimaced. "I shouldn't have asked. Sorry. It's none of my business."

Grim's eyes flickered from mine down to my breasts. When he reached for one, I gasped at the coldness of his touch, my nipple puckering into a tight tip.

"I sometimes felt you. When you climaxed. On your own, or with someone," he said, rubbing one thumb over my peaked nipple and drawing another shudder from me. "This... trickle of pleasure. It was the only times I felt the call to copulate. But I never yielded."

I frowned, some of my attention scattering for every cool touch against my achingly tight nipple. I probably should have been embarrassed that he'd felt me in such intimate, private moments, but I wasn't. "Why not? Bjarni and Saga... I'm sure they... enjoyed themselves while they waited for me."

He didn't look up from my breasts, but I still saw the dark flicker passing over his features. And then it clicked. Like it should have before I'd even opened my mouth in the first place.

"Oh, Grim," I whispered, the ache in my heart withering the tendrils of desire his thumb had awakened. I'd had some hazy idea that maybe he'd been like Modi, unwilling to risk offspring, but no. "Of course. I'm so sorry. That was... thoughtless."

"I'm not broken, Annabel." Grim looked up then, and to my surprise his eyes weren't coolly distant like I'd expected, but mildly annoyed. "I don't think of *her* when I'm inside of you."

"How can you not?" Shame made me look away. I'd done what I did because it was the only way, but... "I blackmailed you, just like her."

He snorted and grabbed my other breast with his free hand, pushing both up and out in lewd invitation. "No," he said, and then closed his lips around my unattended nipple.

I drew in a sharp breath, my hands flying to his hair without conscious thought. He flicked his tongue over the tight bud before he sucked, deeply.

My pussy tightened and my clit *sang,* scattering my focus and driving away the clenching guilt from my chest.

"There was no pleasure," he murmured against my breasts. "Only submission."

I slid my fingers down to cradle the back of his head as he suckled, skimming my lips over his scalp.

"I'll kill her," I whispered into his hair. "For what she did to you."

"If I wanted her dead, I would have killed her myself," he said, lifting his head to meet my gaze. "She is my brothers' mother."

"And you don't want to cause them pain," I said, placing a kiss on his forehead. "My noble, kindhearted mate."

He chuffed a laugh, bitterness drawing his mouth into a line. "No one's ever called me *that* before. Calculated, yes. Weak. Miserable. *Grim.* And here you are, little mortal, with your soft human heart, lost in the depths of Hel because I *killed* you... and you're calling me *noble?*"

I flushed. "Yeah, well, I'm not saying I'm pleased about that, but you did it for your brothers. I get it. What matters is that you've realized you were wrong and are helping to rectify it."

The wry smirk slid off his face, his features turning stony. But in his eyes, hunger flared. My pussy clenched on instinct, slickness gathering deep in my core.

Without another word, Grim slid his hands to my hips and shoved me to the ground hard enough to force a huff from my lungs. A yank around my waist ripped my trousers down my thighs past my knees. I tried to sit up to push them all the way off and kick off my boots, but Grim fell on top of me before I could so much as get up on my elbows, settling his hips against mine.

I gasped softly at the chill of his skin pressed against everywhere I was bared, and again—sharper—when he pressed the thick head of his cock against my lower lips.

I stared up at him, up at the simmering darkness in his eyes as he took me in. Then he forced himself inside of me in one hard push, penetrating me all the way to my womb.

I shrieked, my body entirely unprepared for the suddenness of his entry, even though I was wet enough to take him. My pussy shuddered around his girth, stretching to fully accommodate him inside of me. Where his coldness had felt like a blessing during my heat, my body was decidedly more susceptible to it now, muscles contracting hard as my nipples and clit tightened.

It was still delicious, but also... different. More *raw.* Bordering on painful.

"You yield so prettily," Grim rasped. He was panting even as he held perfectly still inside of me, shudders traveling through his body every time my pussy fluttered on his cool length. "So perfectly. You feel it, don't you? How entirely, excruciatingly defenseless you are underneath me. How fully you let me in.

"You may have blackmailed me, Annabel, but you are the one who surrenders when we fuck."

He gave me a slow, full roll of his hips that made me

hiss and cling to his biceps, nails digging in to keep me anchored to reality.

"I could harm you so, so easily. I could make this *hurt.* Make you plead for me to stop. And yet you lay with me so entirely willingly. Eagerly." He bent his head to the side of my neck, drawing in a deep lungful before he brushed his lips against my ear and whispered, "Perhaps it will ease your guilt if I tell you that nothing in the nine worlds feels like your sheath clutching me like your life depends on how deeply I penetrate you."

I groaned out something that could have been an agreement. *Holy* hell, where did he learn to talk dirty? My body lit up like a torch, everywhere he touched me inside and out so very *alive,* as if life itself welled from our entwined bodies.

Grim rolled his hips again, a lazy movement that drew a groan from my throat. "Do you know how many nights I have stroked myself to release, remembering how your scent bloomed around me when you came into my stables that first day? How often I've imagined what it would have felt like if *I* fucked you up against the kitchen counter that first night?

"I've cursed your name for how you make me *want,* mate. So no, taking you is nothing like fucking her." He punctuated his statement with a hard thrust that made me arch and dig my nails deeper into his shoulders. And another.

"Grim!"

"You sing my name so beautifully," he growled into

my ear, his cool breath sending shivers down my neck even as I writhed at the violence of his penetration. "It was given to me to warn of my gruesome nature, yet you make it sound like the gentlest caress. Do you know how badly I ache for you every time it spills from your lips?"

"I ache for you too," I gasped, breaking on a moan when he took another rough stroke in my pussy. "I need you. Oh. *God,* yes! I need you!"

His lips danced over mine, featherlight at first, then deeper. Hungrier. I moaned into Grim's mouth, my breath hitching with every roll of his hips. Every cell in my body was alight with him, every nerve tense and frayed. He was so cold inside of me, but that couldn't extinguish the heat in my core.

Grim let out a strangled groan, and then darkness spilled through our bond and into me.

Heat. Bliss. Mate. Images and words that didn't belong to me tumbled through my mind as Grim released the block on our bond, his thoughts like soothing caresses.

"Yes," I groaned. "Yes, yes. More, baby. *Yes."* I wrapped myself around his presence inside of me, hugged him to my chest and tried to bracket his hips with my legs to pull him tighter still, but my knees were trapped in my trousers.

Grim obeyed me nonetheless. His thrusts came harder, the darkness inside of me swelling as it wrapped around my light, while one hand traveled down my stomach to the apex of my thighs. I keened when he reached my clit, ripping my mouth from his as I threw my head back against the dirt beneath us.

He circled my pulsing nub with rapid, tight movements, as if he knew exactly what I needed, and in response the fire in my core rose through me like a tidal wave.

An image of my face screwed up in pained bliss flickered through our bond. *Can't hold back. Can't. Can't.*

"Do it! Grim, do it!" I shrieked and arched my pelvis up high as every muscle in my body locked up. Release tore through my spine, blinding me to anything but the ecstasy of coming on his pounding cock.

Grim snarled, a savage sound, and slammed his cock all the way to my cervix through clenching muscles protesting the forced stretch. A stretch that quickly became so much more intense when the bottom of his shaft swelled.

"Shit!" I'd asked for it, and even as I clawed at his shoulders and writhed to escape the inevitable, some dark, primal part of my mind thrilled as my pussy lost the battle against his knot and yielded to the stretch.

Grim's groan of pleasure mixed with my pained howl, the thick bulge forcing its way in behind my pelvic bone and locking us together.

My muscles contracted again, forcing a mewl from my throat when the pressure of it pushed hard against my G-spot. I was already coming again when Grim pressed his thumb against my clit, taking my orgasm into the skies.

I cried out his name and heard mine echo through my mind in return. Cool semen bathed my cervix, making my pussy spasm around his knot again. My G-spot shuddered at the renewed pressure, and I seized up in another bone-shattering release spurred by Grim's constant circles on my swollen clit.

Tenderness swarmed my mind, a mixture of my own endorphin-fueled emotions and his, soothing the physical roughness of the knotting. I clung to him, moaning his name as I rode the waves of pained pleasure, my ecstasy-addled thoughts blending into his.

I was halfway to oblivion when another image flickered through my mind. It was of me in my feathered leathers, sitting on a throne of bones, a skull in one hand and a still-beating heart in the other. Behind me, a sentinel half-hidden in shadows stood guard.

Grim.

"W-What was that?" I groaned, the imagery different enough from all the sex-addled thoughts we'd shared it sobered me.

Grim's only response was to press his thumb hard against my clit and rock his hips into mine, and my thoughts scattered to the wind as my body seized with another climax.

By the time sleep finally stole me away, I'd forgotten all about that unsettling image.

14

GRIM

I loved her.

Norn-forced or not, I loved her, and it was a dark, hideous, possessive urge so deeply rooted in the most primal parts of my soul it would be impossible to weed out.

I rubbed absentmindedly at my ribs as I watched Annabel climb over a fallen tree while holding Mimir safely under her left arm. Her backside swayed, drawing my focus from our surroundings. I gritted my teeth, ignoring the stab of desire low in my gut.

Lust. I was starting to understand why the desert religions thought of it as sinful. What my body ached for every time I so much as glanced at my mate was distracting, easily overpowering, and all-consuming. There was nothing good or pure about it, that much was certain. But it wasn't what had the darkness inside of me swelling.

Love.

I almost laughed amidst the bleak horror of it all. There were those among the gods who saw Freya as weak, mild—easily ignored. If they'd ever felt what I did after my soul wove itself with Annabel's, they would cower in fear of the Goddess of Love.

Tendrils snaked through my thoughts, plucking out the memory of my mate holding me tight while she swore she'd kill the one who'd harmed me. Fierce. She was so ruthlessly fierce, even if she submitted eagerly underneath me. *Iron and flesh.*

My magic swelled, pushing at the wall I'd erected between my end of our bond and hers. Keeping it in place was a constant battle—my very soul ached to blend with hers again, but if I yielded, it would truly be the end. Those brief, euphoric moments during my climax where I'd lost control of myself so completely my mind had spilled into hers nearly undid everything I'd ever cared about.

I sent my brothers a thought, steeling my mind against the seething anger flaring from somewhere deep in my primordial makeup.

I'd been prepared for this—for the jealousy, the urge to rip apart the men who meant everything to me, and for the sudden shift to make the omega my primary priority.

I hadn't been prepared to love her.

As if sensing my distress despite my ironclad grip on our connection, Annabel shot a look at me over her shoulder. Her plump lips curved up in a soft smile that made me wonder if Verdandi's web had cursed her with the same feelings as I. No one had ever smiled at me like that before.

I doubted anyone ever would.

"It's not much longer now," Mimir said, drawing our attention. "We will have to ask them for guidance. Respectfully, please. I don't much desire having my eyeballs pecked from my skull."

"*Them?*" Annabel asked as I instinctively laid a hand on the handle of a dagger at the implied threat of what was ahead. "Who?"

"The ravens," Mimir said. "Come to think of it, best let me do the talking. They are tricky beasts."

"Ravens?" Annabel asked. "Like Arni and Magga?"

"Arni and Magga?"

"My father stole two ravens from Odin's rookery, once upon a time, and gifted them to Saga and Bjarni," I explained.

"Who names a raven Eagle?" Mimir muttered. "Yes, plum, like Odin's birds, and not. Every raven flies across the skies, plucking gossip and secrets from the winds. And when they die, they come here, to this place, where they exchange their secrets and find many more."

"So you think they'll know of another way to escape Hel?" Annabel asked, urgency coloring her voice.

"If anyone knows of a way, it will be the ravens," Mimir said.

WE HEARD them long before we saw them.

A low, continuous rumble in the distance grew in volume with every step we took, until gray light filtered through the trees up ahead and the noise was an unbearable, squawky crescendo.

"Such chatter," Mimir shouted over the cacophony. "Something must have excited them."

We broke through the tree line and into a large, barren field. In the center of it a large, dead oak stretching up toward the sky, Hel's inferno of souls swirling in the distance behind it. And on every branch, hundreds upon hundreds of ravens perched, leaving not a single space. On the ground surrounding the ancient trunk, many more thousand black birds sat, chattering and squawking.

I pushed up beside Annabel, ensuring I was a half-step ahead of her when we stepped into the clearing, my right hand resting on the hilt of the dagger on my left hip.

Silence spread like a wave through the ravens. The ones closest to us ruffled their feathers and hissed. When I pushed forward, they reluctantly hopped a few steps backward. Low curses followed our path as the sea of black cleaved in front of us, leaving the way to the oak free.

"Sorry," Annabel kept muttering as we passed raven after raven, and I rolled my eyes at her genuinely apologetic tone. I'd always gotten on well with animals, but ravens? Rats of the skies, as far as I was concerned. Gossiping rats, at that. At least dead ones didn't shit everywhere.

When we finally stopped in front of the barren oak, one of the larger ravens on the top branches flapped its wings and took off, swooping down in a graceful spiral.

"Away!" it squawked, and the sixteen birds on the lowest hanging branch closest to us took off with a fluttering of wings. The large one—undoubtedly their leader—landed where they'd been and peered down at us with its black, beady eyes, focusing first on me, then Annabel, and finally on Mimir in her arms.

"Well, well. A godling, a human, and a prophet. The start of a fine pun, if I am not mistaken." It laughed, a hideous sound. "Is that why you have come? To entertain us?"

I didn't miss the predatory gleam in its eye as it looked us over once more, and I curled my lip in silent warning.

"Alas. We are not here for sport, wise one," Mimir said smoothly. "Not today."

"Pity," the bird said, its attention remaining on Annabel long enough that I put a hand on her shoulder and let a plume of my magic rise up behind her—a reminder that there was no easy prey to be had.

The raven only laughed again, drawing goosebumps down my back. "Oh! The little human is your mate, godling? How deliciously horrible. If you are not here for sport, then I suppose *that* is the reason. She died tragically, and you seek a way to return her to the living?" Its tone was filled with exaggerated sympathy.

Pecking. Always pecking.

"The winds told another story," another bird squeaked from high above—a female, judging by its higher pitch. It took off and glided down to the lower branch, landing effortlessly next to the other raven. "Of a human girl brought to Hel by the son of mist and shadows. Tricked to her death and stalked by the evil male determined to see the job through."

"And how did the wind come up with such tales?" I asked, raising an eyebrow at the female.

She clucked—an amused sound—and turned her head to stare at me. "Oh, *that* little tidbit the winds seem to have picked up by the side of a pond, from a poor water nymph who barely escaped the dark beast with her life. She was trying to save the human girl from her killer, but he interfered before she could."

The water Huldra.

"S-She was trying to *save* me?" Annabel choked by my side.

I'd only hunted for the blasted thing long enough to ensure she wouldn't return before we'd continued on our journey, a decision I now regretted as the female raven lit up with cruel mirth.

"Did he tell you otherwise, dear girl? Ah, a child of Loki with a tongue dipped in poisonous lies. How... predictable."

"We do indeed seek your wisdom for a way out of this realm," Mimir broke in before I could spear the feathered rat with a scathing reply. "It is no secret that if one seeks an impossible answer, the only question must be to a raven."

A cawing echoed from the field around us and up through the mighty oak. Laughter.

"Oh, how he *flatters,*" the female bird cooed, nudging the leader.

"He can flatter as much as he pleases," the male bird said. "There is no escape from Hel, not for the dead, or we would all have left a long time ago. Our answer to you, prophet, is the same as when Frigg herself came to plead for our help: What is dead will remain so. The only way out is on Naglfar, as a bound soldier for the Queen of Death when she sails across the sea to lay siege to the mortal shores—a fate I promise you is far, far worse than remaining here."

"Well, that is the thing... The girl isn't *entirely* dead," Mimir said. "She has eaten an apple from Idunn's garden. She can leave—if we find a way for her to do so before it is too late."

"Ooooh," the female crooned. "How interesting."

"Very interesting," the male agreed. They both studied Annabel as if she were a new and puzzling trinket.

"Is there a way?" Annabel asked. "I need to get back as soon as possible."

Mimir cleared his throat, a wordless reminder to let him do the talking.

"*Needs* to get back, does she?" the leader croaked. "My, my, my. But what will she pay?"

"Pay?" Annabel asked, her voice wavering.

"Whispers are not free, little immortal mortal," the female said. "What will you give in return for a way home?"

"What… What do you want?"

I grimaced. That was about the worst possible thing she could have said to the greedy vultures.

"Ooooh," the female crooned again, echoed by raspy laughter from the tree above. "An eye, my dear."

"Or perhaps a heart," the male supplied.

"A shiny trinket," the female said.

"A magical rose," the male said, cawing a rough laugh.

"You know of a way, then?" Mimir interrupted. "One which does not involve servitude to Hel?"

"We do," the leader said. "But not for free."

"All I have to offer is this." Annabel shifted Mimir to one arm and pulled out a small metallic circle—the ring she'd placed on my finger. I bit the inside of my cheek to avoid voicing a protest. As much as I shuddered at the idea of an item of such power in the ravens' possession, at least she wouldn't be using it on me again if she bargained it here.

"Oooh," the leader of the ravens hummed. "Dwarven magic. Now *that*… that might be worth a whisper." He set off, flapped his wings once, and landed on Annabel's shoulder. His feathers mixed perfectly into those adorning her armor as he leaned forward to study the ring closer. "Give me that ring, human girl, and I will tell you of a way out of Hel."

"Tell us the way first, wise raven," Mimir said before Annabel could comply, "and you will have your trinket."

The leader squawked. "You expect trickery and deceit, old man? I am half in mind to take insult. We have made a bargain with the girl. We will fulfill it."

"And once you have upheld your end, we will ours," Mimir said mildly.

Annabel closed her hand around the ring. "After," she agreed, having apparently wised up to the nature of these cretins at last.

The female raven hissed, and the male tightened its claws on Annabel's shoulder enough to make her grimace, but he relented. "Fine. Whisper first. Then the price. But be warned that you will not leave without payment.

"There is a boat. A small, ancient vessel perched by the sea separating Hel from the lands of the living. It can carry a living being across. *If* they survive the waters."

"No," Annabel said. I could hear the frustration in her voice. "No there is not."

"No?" the female asked, voice sharp. "We offer you a whisper, and you tell us *no?"*

"The boat is gone. Broken. Tell us of another way," Annabel said, her voice turning sharp as well. Commanding.

"We have already traded our secrets, mortal," the leader said, and there was enough danger in his tone that I turned halfway in preparation to smack him off her shoulder and spear him with a dagger, should he decide to attack. "That you don't believe us is not our concern. Now, the ring."

"Unfortunately, the girl speaks the truth," Mimir interjected. "We saw the boat destroyed before our eyes. Our bargain was for a way out of Hel. Broken timber on a stony beach is not a way. Now, please—do you know of another path for us?"

The oak tree whooshed with the rustling of black feathers and hissed curses.

"Trickery," the female on the low branch snarled. "Twisty words. We can *take* your trinket, prophet. And your eyes and tongues and hearts along with it."

"I would advise against attempting that," Mimir said mildly. "The little mortal has an awful lot of magic running through her. And her *mate*... Well, as you know, he is Loki's offspring. It would be much safer for us all if you fulfil our bargain and we simply *give* you what you are owed."

Another whooshing hiss from the tree. And a long, pregnant silence.

"They could ask Hel," a raven from a few branches up called down. "The queen could grant them passage."

"She could. But she never has," the leader cawed. "She would likely claim their souls for the audacity of asking."

"She is your sister. Is she not?" the female asked, turning her focus to me. "Perhaps if *you* asked—"

"No," I bit, not letting her finish her question.

"Ah. No familial bonds, then?" she cooed. "No sense of sibling loyalty? What a *pity*."

I didn't deign to answer.

"Perhaps..." the male raven started, then paused. He looked from Annabel to me. "If the winds spoke true, *you* brought the girl to Hel. *You* ended her life. Yet now, you stand side by side. *Mated.* Tell me, son of Loki... has love touched that frozen heart of yours?"

A pit opened deep in my gut. I didn't move a muscle, even as I sensed Annabel shift beside me. A flutter of *something* touched our bond from her side of the wall I'd erected.

"I am not one of your *whispers*, raven," I snapped. "Find your gossip elsewhere."

The female cawed a throaty laugh. "So *prickly*, this one. So scared of showing his soft, fleshy bits."

The male chuckled along with her. "If it has, prickly one, there may just be a way to undo what you've done to that poor little mate of yours."

"*Oooh*, you mean—?" the female clucked. "Yes. *She* could... If he loves her. She might."

"Have you found love in Hel, Lokisson?" the male cawed, his dark eyes twinkling. "Did you *kill* the only woman in any of the nine worlds who could ever defrost the ice in your chest?"

"Stop mocking him," Annabel snarled, shifting her shoulder and twisting sharply enough to dislodge the raven. He only cackled and gave a lazy flap of his wings, landing safely on the lowest branch next to the female.

Annabel's soft hand slid into mine, clutching tightly. "You don't have to answer that," she said quietly before she turned back to the birds. "If that is the only way that doesn't involve Hel, then fine. Tell us who this 'she' is you mentioned, and where we can find her, and I will give you my ring."

"It might only be a way if he loves you," the female warned, that same cruel gleam in her eyes. "Don't return to us claiming foul play should she be unwilling to aid a man who doesn't love the woman he has claimed."

"If this person is able to help us, I'll convince her. One way or the other," Annabel snapped. "Now tell us."

"So feisty," the female laughed. "Is that the problem, Mistborn? She brings shame to you? Such a bad, willful omega. A stain on any alpha's reputation."

I bared my teeth at the bird, ridiculous urges to defend my mate rushing to the surface. But I managed to keep silent. What the ravens thought of her, or me, was unimportant. Besides, they weren't entirely wrong. As far as subservient omegas went, Annabel was a complete failure.

There was nothing shameful about that.

"Who?" Annabel growled. "And where?"

"So impatient, little human," the male raven cawed. "Very well. You seek the Goddess of Love. She resides in a glade straight west of here, singing such mournful songs the trees around her weep. Follow those tunes, and you will find her."

By my side, Annabel went utterly still. "Freya?" she whispered in abject horror. "Freya is here? In Hel?"

15

ANNABEL

"How did a goddess get kidnapped to *Hel,* and no one knew about it?" I stomped my way through the underbrush, anger fueling my pace. "For fuck's sake, *someone* must have known! Sensed it..."

I trailed off as something dawned on me, and I spun around to face Grim.

"Did *you* know? Is this another part of that grand plan your ex-ally set up to end everything that was ever good?"

Grim only looked at me, his features stony.

"He won't be able to tell you if he did," Mimir reminded me. "The binding spell he is under is iron-clad. And mine too, for that matter."

I bared my teeth and hissed. "Is it that easy? Exiling gods and prophets to Hel, and silencing those who know about it?"

"No," Mimir said. "It is not easy. Very few—"

He broke off on a gargle, as if someone had snapped his windpipe shut. I gave him a concerned look, but the choking fit was over as swiftly as it started.

"Damned spell," he croaked, eyes still watering.

Whoever was behind this was powerful; I already knew that. But if few were powerful enough to kidnap a goddess—or a prophet—to Hel, then at least that narrowed down the list. Too bad I didn't know who might fit those parameters.

"I don't suppose either of you will be able to name everyone who might be strong enough for this bull-shit?" I asked.

"I'm afraid not, plum," Mimir said. "But perhaps Freya can help. We should keep moving. The sooner we get to her, the better."

GRIM DIDN'T SPEAK to me for the rest of our journey through the woods that day. I wondered if he was quietly brooding over what the ravens had said—that he had doomed his own mate to Hel, and that loving me might be the only way to save me. That unbreakable wall separating our bond was proof my newest mate struggled with intimacy and soft emotions. I wondered if he felt regret now. And I wondered if he did—love me, that is.

If he'd even know.

I glanced over my shoulder at the darkhaired alpha. His focus was on scanning our surroundings, but every once in a while I felt his eyes rest on me, heat trailing up my spine in response.

It was easy for me, relatively speaking. I'd been through this four times before, and with Grim—that extra layer of being his soulmate had made it effortless to give in to the tug on my heart from my new bond. I knew what love felt like.

It was a lot less likely that he did.

As if sensing my attention, my broody mate shifted his focus to me. Pleasant warmth spread through my chest when our eyes met, and I gave him a half-smile. It didn't matter if he wasn't there yet. Freya would help us. And hopefully, we could help her in return.

Grim didn't return my smile, but the intensity in his eyes deepened as he took me in for another heartbeat. Then he returned his attention to the woods surrounding us.

I too turned my focus to the path ahead, something akin to relief fluttering in my chest. Soon we would be back in Asgard. Soon the aching hollows in my soul would spring back alive, and together, we would find out who was behind this whole nightmare and put a stop to them.

~

We traveled through the woodlands for three days without coming across weeping trees or goddesses of love.

Every night when we made camp, Grim would light a fire even though it brought us no warmth, and then instruct me to practice refining my powers. Despite his silence during our travels—and his less-than-enthusiastic approach to the role of teacher—once I proclaimed I didn't have it in me to light another branch on fire or drill yet another hole through whatever hapless rock was nearby, he would come to my side, strip me bare, and let me teach him about love. Or *refuel my powers,* as he called it. But I knew, in those intensely intimate minutes when the wall he'd put between us came crashing down and our souls merged, that being with me was anything but an objectionable task to him.

Sometimes he was gentle, sometimes rough, but his mind always, always sang my name with such reverence before his knot forced my mind back to the present, and our souls separated even as our bodies locked together.

Every morning when I woke up, even though Grim was always awake and crouched by the fire, my skin was still chilled from where he'd held me through the night.

On the third day—sometime in the afternoon, as far as I could judge—our journey west came to an abrupt halt as a deep, wide ravine opened up in front of us like a gaping wound.

I peered down the steep cliff. Far, far below, I could make out gray crowns of trees covering the bottom of it, interrupted by large, sharp-looking rock formations. On the other side of the canyon, the woods continued.

"Uh... I don't remember the ravens mentioning anything about a ravine," I pointed out, frowning at Grim as he took in the steep fall.

"They likely wouldn't have thought much of it," Mimir said. "They'd just fly over."

"So we're not lost? Just screwed?" I reined in my frustration and turned to look up and down the deep scar. Neither direction showed where it might close. "I assume there's not some easy magic trick to getting down this side and then up that one?"

"No," Grim said, his eyes narrowing as he too looked first left, then right. "Without a bird's costume, we are not crossing."

I remembered the feathered costumes Freya had given him and Bjarni when we first came to Asgard. They'd sure come in handy now.

"So... we go around," I sighed. "But which way is faster?"

"South," Grim said. "We go south."

"I wouldn't advise that," a hoarse, creaking voice said from somewhere behind us.

I jolted, nearly losing my footing on the edge of the ravine, but Grim grabbed me by the shoulder and yanked me back and behind him. His daggers were in his hands in the blink of an eye.

"Show yourself!" he growled. Darkness welled up around him, partly blocking my view of the forest.

Movement above our heads made all three of us look up. A bird broke free from the trees and glided down to a lower branch a few yards from where we stood. Another followed, landing by the first's side.

Two ravens.

I squinted. They looked... awfully familiar.

"Arni and Magga," Grim said quietly, and without a drop of jubilation at the unexpected reunion.

"Oh my God!" I gasped, pushing past Grim and shoving Mimir into his arms so I could reach my hands out toward the two birds. "It *is* you! Oh, I am so, so sorry for what happened to you. Bjarni told me what Loki did."

"Loki," Magga spat. "That son of a troll."

"One thousand years we served him," Arni said, his voice tinted with bitterness. Not that I could blame him. "And he sends us to Hel."

"Hel," Magga echoed. "By *fire*. Dramatic cunt."

"Is there anything I can do for you?" I asked, biting my lip as the memory of Bjarni's sorrow over their death filled me. He'd want me to help them in any way I could.

"We don't have time for this, Annabel," Grim snapped. "Come now. We must press on."

Arni cawed, turning a black eye to the alpha behind

me. "If you go south, you will be lost in the swamps before nightfall. If it is Freya you seek, north is your path."

"We are here to help *you,* girl," Magga said, sounding entirely not thrilled about it. "We will guide you to the goddess."

"Oh, that's really wo—" I began, but Grim interrupted me.

"At what cost?" he asked, the chill in his voice as cool as his skin. "What's your price?"

"There is no cost, Misborn," Magga hissed.

"But if you can bring us with you when you escape this place, that would be great," Arni added.

"I'm not sure we can," I said softly. "I think there's only a loophole for me because of Idunn's apple. But if there is a way, of course we will."

Grim growled under his breath, but when I glanced at him over my shoulder, he didn't voice a rejection of my promise.

Arni bowed his head in acceptance, then pushed off the branch and launched into the air, circling our heads once. "North, then. To Freya's glade."

"To the weeping goddess so far, so fair," Magga crooned, following him into the skies. "With breasts aplenty and golden hair."

I glanced at Mimir still in Grim's arms. "Breasts aplenty?"

The prophet shot me a grin. "Valhalla's ravens might speak, but no one ever accused them of being poets."

"They always did envy Huginn and Munin their riddles," Grim said. He heaved a sigh and shoved Mimir back into my arms before gesturing at me to follow the ravens. "Saga and Bjarni insisted they deliver their news plainly. They never developed the knack for rhymes or verses."

~

THE TREK NORTH of the ravine took us nearly six hours and involved a lot of scrambling up and down jagged paths, but the ravens led us safely around the canyon and deeper into the forest beyond.

On the second morning after they joined us, Arni landed on my shoulder and stayed there for most of the day, only occasionally taking off into the sky to see how much farther we had to go.

"We should arrive in her glade before nightfall," Arni informed me when he returned to my shoulder sometime after midday.

"Have you visited her before?" I asked. "Here, I mean."

He cawed a bitter laugh. "We have flown past once or twice. Visiting a goddess throwing a temper tantrum was... not entirely appealing, considering what happened the last time a god in a mood got his hands on us."

I grimaced. "Bjarni was so distraught. Still is."

"He's always been a good boy," Arni sighed before

he shot a withering look over his shoulder at Grim, who was bringing up the rear. "Unlike the squalling little darkling his father brought home, rather than drown in the nearest stream like he should have."

"Behave," I said, bopping him gently on the beak. "That's my mate. I don't care that you don't like each other—we're all in this together."

Arni ruffled his feathers with a final look of disdain in Grim's direction. "He didn't want you, you know. He spent years attempting to persuade his brothers not to send for you."

I glanced back at Grim and gave him a half-smile. He was glaring so intensely at the bird on my shoulder I was pretty sure he'd heard most of our conversation. His scowl darkened when Magga swooped down from the sky above our heads to perch on my free shoulder.

"He had his reasons," I said to Arni as I turned my focus back to the path ahead.

"Was it his inability to mount a female?" Magga asked, the innocent air to her voice not entirely managing to hide her malice. "Please do tell us. You would settle a long-standing bet. I have fifty silver marks on his cold blood inhibiting the function of his manhood."

"I keep telling you, they worked fine that time I saw him underneath Madna in the woods," Arni said. "Wasn't much more than a whelp, either. Of course, old age could have taken its toll. Is that it, Misborn? Did you miss an apple one year?"

Before Grim could respond—if he even planned to —I reached up and brushed a finger against both birds' taloned feet, sending a spark of my magic into them.

They both squawked and shot a foot into the air before they managed to unfold their wings for a more dignified incline.

"If you're going to be bitchy, you can find another ride," I told them.

"So sensitive," Arni huffed as Magga shot me a few choice words and swung higher into the sky.

I looked back at Grim, whose face had gone stony. He hadn't known Arni had seen him with her, I realized.

Madna. I hadn't thought to ask her name. It wasn't important—not to me. She wasn't worthy of the effort of asking her name. But to Grim...

I reached through our bond and brushed a gentle touch against the wall he'd placed there, feeling it shudder in response. Without waiting for permission, I paused to let him catch up to me, then grabbed his hand.

His fingers were stiff as I laced mine through them, but he didn't pull away. I gave him a small squeeze he didn't return, but after a few steps he folded his hand around mine. He didn't let go as we continued the journey side by side.

THE FUNNEL CLOUD of souls was fading to the darkness of the sky by the time the trees around us started to change.

It was subtle at first, and it took me a while to notice the droplets trickling down their broad, oaken trunks as we made our way through the woods. At first I thought it might be some sort of sap, and paused for a closer look.

"Tears of the goddess," Mimir murmured as I touched my fingertips to the rough bark, and I remembered what the ravens had said about the woods weeping for Freya.

"We're close," I said, pulling away from the tree to look up at Arni, who'd perched on a branch above us. "How much farther?"

"Just beyond the creek," he said, nodding in the direction of a trickling stream.

"Let's go, then," I said, reaching out for Grim's hand again. "Let's find our way home."

Wordlessly he twined his fingers with mine, and we continued over the shallow creek and through the underbrush.

Gray vegetation gave way to a large clearing soft with moss and grass. And in the center of it, surrounded by a swirl of white flowers, sat the Goddess of Love.

"Freya! I called out, exhaling as relief flooded my cells. We'd made it. We'd found her.

We were going home.

The goddess turned her head in our direction at my

call, and the relief turned leaden in my veins. Her eyes were sunken deep in the sockets, and her golden and bountiful hair now hung gray and limp around her bony, hunched shoulders.

"Annabel. Oh, no," she whispered, and I barely recognized her voice. When I'd first met Freya, she had been brimming with vitality and life. But now, even her voice sounded so… frail. Broken.

I stared in horror at the goddess, at the only one who might have been strong enough to help us find our way home, as her face contorted in anguish and tears streamed from her dulled eyes.

"He killed you too. Oh, everything… everything is lost."

16

GRIM

"Who? *Grim?*" Annabel's voice went from shock to horror. She swiveled on me, pulling her soft hand from mine with a jerk. "*You* killed Freya? And you didn't think to mention it?"

I forced down the wave of anger that my own mate so readily thought the worst of me—I *had* killed *her,* after all. She couldn't be entirely blamed for jumping to conclusions.

"I did no such thing," I said, giving Freya a dark look. I had a good idea who had killed her, though. And why.

"Grim?" the goddess asked, her tears slowing as she took us in. "Why would Grim...?"

Annabel turned back to her, frowning. "It wasn't Grim? Then who?"

Freya shook her head. "I cannot... Cannot tell you. Tell anyone."

Annabel hissed out a breath. Repeatedly. "You have been cursed to silence?"

"I have," Freya said, her voice soft and confused. "I discovered the truth, but he... He took my ability to voice his name. And then he killed me. Why... Why are *you* here? Who killed you, if not he who murdered me?"

Annabel gave me a long side-eye before she crossed the rest of the distance to Freya and kneeled down by her side, placing Mimir cautiously next to her. "It's... a long story. We are trying to find our way back. The ravens said you might be able to help. We've got to get back, to stop Ragnarök."

Freya shook her head and lowered her lashes with a grimace. "There is no escaping Hel, little one. There is nothing left for us but this. And there is no stopping Ragnarök. He has won."

My mate reached up to gently wipe the tears from Freya's sunken face. "I don't believe that," she said. "I am going to stop it. Verdandi wove my thread with my mates' for a reason. *We* are going to stop it. And you're going to help me."

"I used to believe that there was no greater power than love," Freya said, her voice hollow as she looked back up at Annabel. "That in the end, nothing could break it, and it would overcome anything if nurtured enough. Of course I did; I was the Goddess of Love. But he drove a knife through my heart and plucked me from the world. I am dead, little omega. And with me, love will soon die too.

"The Norn who wove your thread with your alphas did so to harness the deepest of devotion one would usually only find in bonds such as yours. But without love, it will never be enough. He is far too powerful a foe."

"Nothing and no one will ever destroy the love I have for my mates," Annabel said quietly. "We *are* strong enough, and we *will* stop him. Three of us defeated Nidhug. Whoever he is, he won't be able to stop the six of us together."

"Have faith, goddess," Mimir said, his voice softer than normal. "All is not lost. Not yet." He shot Annabel a look from underneath bushy eyebrows. "Give us some space, plum. I will speak with her."

Annabel cast another look at the broken goddess, then nodded and got to her feet. With one last, lingering glance over her shoulder, she returned to my side.

"Now what?" she asked, eyes darting to my face. Her gaze slid over my features, taking in my every expression. She was so *aware* of me, as if I were a planet and she my moon—a curious sensation, since she pulled on me like gravity itself. It wouldn't be long until I could no longer fight it—until everything I was would be wrapped around her.

"I suppose we wait," I said, shrugging with a casualness I didn't feel. "Make camp. See if Mimir can make something useful happen."

"You're so rude," she scolded, giving me a stern look. "She was killed. I think it's fair to have a bit of a breakdown."

I chuffed through my nose and walked to a willow tree on the other side of the glade, where I sank into the soft grass beneath it. Hel had sucked all color and life from every inch of this world, but this close to Freya, a kernel of life remained. Perhaps this was not entirely unexpected from the Goddess of Fertility.

I gave Freya's hunched figure a careful study. Did she have enough power left to revive Annabel?

If *he* had plunged a knife through her heart, her death was final—like Annabel's would have been, had my brothers not been doomed if I'd done the same to her. But still...

My gaze fell on the white flowers surrounding her, then on the two ravens jumping from branch to branch on the outskirts of the glade, and finally to my mate. She was clearly eavesdropping on whatever the prophet was saying, despite how inconspicuously she tried to look as she paced.

She was so determined, so utterly willful in her refusal to accept defeat. If the ravens were right, if Freya could give her the means, she would make it happen. If anyone could defy death, it would be her.

I leaned my head back against the willow's trunk

and closed my eyes, wishing I could protect her from what lay ahead.

A FIRM PRESSURE against my shoulder made me blink my eyes open, realization that I'd drifted off jolting adrenaline through my body and rendering me wide awake.

Annabel looked up from where she'd nestled in against my side, a soft smile curving her lips as our eyes met. "I'm sorry. I didn't mean to wake you." She reached up to let a fingertip smooth over my forehead. "I rarely get to see you sleep. You looked troubled. Did you have a bad dream?"

I scoffed, but didn't move away from her touch. "We are in Hel. If we dream, they are unlikely to be pleasant."

"Mmm, I suppose that's a good point." She shifted against my side, rolling up on her knees so she could straddle me. The firm pressure of her groin against mine alerted me to her intentions before I caught her mischievous smile. "You know… it seems like we have the rest of the night. And you haven't made me practice my control since Arni and Magga joined us."

"You want sex?" I asked flatly.

Annabel grimaced and poked my chest. "Way to kill the mood. I was *trying* to flirt with you. I miss you."

"I'm right here," I countered, even if my cock was already rising to the occasion.

Annabel huffed and leaned in close, her breasts pressed firmly against my chest and her breath tickling my throat. "I miss you inside of me, Grim. I miss what it feels like when you lose yourself to me," she whispered. The heat in her voice made memories of exactly that flicker in my brain, and I swallowed a groan as my cock swelled to full size and prodded insistently at what lay above it.

"We are not alone," I reminded her, catching her hips when she ground down against my hardness.

"So?" A genuine frown crossed her features when she pulled back to look at me. "It's not like Mimir hasn't heard us every single time—and watched a few as well. And Freya is the Goddess of Love. You know that whole *thing* with Magni and Saga was her idea."

She was right. I shouldn't mind. It was just sex.

Except sex with Annabel was... It was so much more than physical. When I was inside her, the sheer elation of joining with her stripped me of control, and my every wall came crashing down—and there was nothing I could do to prevent that.

Understanding broke behind my mate's eyes, and her gaze turned soft and sorrowful. "It's not about Freya or Mimir, is it? It's Arni and Magga."

I sneered, even as my innate ice gripped my gut tightly. "They're nothing but flying rats. If you want to be fucked while they watch and *comment,* far be it from me to prevent you living out your exhibitionistic desires." I straightened against the tree trunk and reached for her leather armor, fingers sliding underneath straps to undo the fastenings.

But Annabel reached up to grab at my wrists, pausing my movements. "You don't have to pretend with me, Grim," she said so softly my heart shivered. "I get it. They pecked at you when you were small and vulnerable. I'm not going to ask you to be vulnerable in front of them again."

And with that, she leaned forward again, this time placing a chaste kiss on my lips before she rested her head on my shoulder. Her slow breaths raised goosebumps along my skin, doing nothing for my still-straining cock nestled firmly against her covered groin.

"I didn't know that he saw me with her," I said. I hadn't meant to; the words just slipped out.

Annabel pressed in harder against me. Her hands came up around my neck, stroking through my hair, but she remained quiet.

"I guess he didn't know that it was... unwanted. If he had, he would have tormented me with it. I don't want..." I fell silent, already regretting having opened this door.

But Annabel asked, "What don't you want, Grim?" so softly, I had no choice but to answer.

"I don't want them to see us together, because they will take any softness and pick at it until it's a raw, open wound. It's their nature," I answered

Annabel was silent for a long time, until she finally breathed, "Hold me."

Slowly, somewhat reluctantly, I obeyed. She felt so solid in my arms as I tightened them around her torso. So alive, despite what I'd done to her. But she wasn't. She should have been warm under my palms, and her beautiful, haunting scent should have filled my lungs with every slow breath I drew in against the top of her head.

"I love you," she said, her voice quiet but not weak. She didn't move her head from my shoulder—simply let the words hang in the air around us.

Everything inside of me went still.

"You don't," I said, my voice rougher than expected.

She flicked my earlobe with a finger, but otherwise didn't move. "Yeah. I do. And once you trust me enough to let me in, you'll know I'm telling you the truth."

I expelled a breath that should have been a laugh, but only came out like a hollow bark. "If I truly let you in, believe me, Annabel, you would not love me. What you feel is biology and Fate's manipulation. And that is fine. I am not small and vulnerable any longer. I do not need you to tell me fairytales."

She finally pulled back to look at me, into my eyes. There were shadows in her gaze, but also steel. "You are not unlovable. You are not broken, or *wrong.* The people who should have cared for you let you down. They hurt you. And you did not deserve that, Grim. All you've done that has been dark and awful has been to protect the people you love. You were willing to turn yourself into a literal monster to save your brothers from Ragnarök. However misguided that was, it tells me everything I need to know about your heart. You can keep your shield in place until you feel ready to trust me, but I see you, my mate. And I love you."

It took more effort than it should have to twist my mouth into a wry smile. "That human heart of yours—even in death, it's so *soft.*"

Annabel didn't so much as blink at my mocking tone. She simply leaned in and placed a lingering kiss on my mouth before she rested her head against my shoulder once more, wrapping her arms loosely around the back of my neck.

When I glanced down at her face, her eyes were closed, her expression peaceful. It wasn't long until she was asleep, safely nestled in my arms.

I WOKE up to the sensation of being watched. But instead of alarm bells, a sense of utter peace flowed through my body in languid waves paced to the steady rise and fall of my chest. I cracked my eyelids open, only to stare into a dark mass of messy hair still semi-bound into a long braid.

Annabel. I tightened my arms around the solid form resting on top of me, and sighed when something soft and tender slid into place in my chest as she nuzzled in closer in her sleep.

"Perhaps," a quiet voice said from somewhere close, and I jolted upright, shoving Annabel to the ground behind me as I grabbed for my knives.

Pealing laughter mixed with my mate's sleepy protests, and Freya's sunken face came into focus.

"Relax, little godling," she said, her laughter quieting even though a faint smile remained on her lips. "No one is trying to hurt your mate."

"What's happening?" Annabel grumbled from behind me. She placed a hand on my hip to push herself into a seated position.

"Nothing," I said, irritation sharpening my tone as I shoved my knives back into their sheaths. Freya was sitting cross-legged by our side with Mimir in her lap. She was idly combing her fingers through his coarse hair—a treatment he seemed more than pleased with, judging from his half-closed eyes. "Just a goddess getting her voyeuristic kicks."

Freya laughed again and reached out to pinch my cheek with her free hand. "Such a saucy boy."

"You seem… better," Annabel said, her tone careful.

"Better?" Freya hummed. "I suppose."

"I have managed to convince the goddess that there might be hope after all," Mimir said.

"I am told you are soulmates," she said, her smile brightening ever so slightly. "There is… such powerful magic in a soul connection. And watching you now, wound in spirit and body as you sleep, perhaps… *perhaps* all is not lost.”

I shot Mimir a dark look. “That was not your information to share, prophet.”

“Oh, hush.” Annabel swatted my arm, but the excitement in her voice was palpable. “She is the Goddess of Love. I don’t think we have to fear her using that knowledge against us.”

“Certainly not,” Freya said. “It is the most sacred of connections—two souls uniting as one. It is my deepest duty to protect such a match. Even here, as this… shadow I’ve become.” Her smile faded.

I scoffed. “Even here? You mean the Norns still have their claws in you in Hel?”

Freya shot my mate a bewildered look. “The Norns?”

“Grim believes I only love him because of Verdandi weaving our threads together,” Annabel said patiently. She placed a kiss on my shoulder before resting her chin against it and wrapping her arm around my torso so she could lean against my back. “He’ll get there eventually.”

I bristled at her easy dismissal of what I knew to be the truth, but the firm pressure of her body against mine stopped any true anger from coloring my words when I bit, “Do not patronize me.”

She only kissed my shoulder in response again—much to Mimir’s amusement. I narrowed my eyes at the chuckling prophet.

But Freya looked at me with genuine surprise—and upset. "No. No, absolutely not! The Norns weave their webs as they please, but a soulmate connection is not something even they can create. Verdandi may have woven your threads together, ensuring you met, but no one can force a soul bond—not her, not her sisters, not me. But... it is so exceedingly rare... Are you *certain* that is what you are to each other?"

"I am certain," I said, my voice flat. Annabel nuzzled against the back of my neck—a simple, loving gesture that made my heart ache. I shifted out of her grip and got to my feet. "But how will that help Annabel return to Asgard?"

Freya watched us both carefully, and I had the uncomfortable feeling she was analyzing every movement, every interaction between us.

"To return her to full life... it would take a miracle. And I am in no state to perform such a thing," the goddess said. "But *if* your love is strong enough, true enough... Perhaps... *Perhaps* I can help you."

"And you and Mimir?" Annabel asked. "Will it be enough for you to return with us?" A caw from the tree line made her add, "And Arni and Magga?"

Freya gave her a sad smile. "The prophet is not dead. He is simply... visiting Hel against his wishes. He can leave through the same means as your mate. But those of us whose bodies were struck down and no longer possess a physical manifestation among the living... no. Only the Queen of the Dead would be able to grant us such a gift. And she will not."

"We will find a way to get her to release you, once this is all over," Annabel said, her voice so firm I knew that she genuinely believed she would.

"Isn't there enough resting on your shoulders? Must you be the one to save *everyone*—even after you are expected to stop Ragnarök itself?" I asked.

"We can't very well live in a world without love," Annabel said mildly, completely unruffled by my interjection. "If not me, then who?"

I ground my teeth, biting back my retort that she needed to stop this unholy habit of martyring herself. It was a moot point anyway.

Annabel brushed a hand down my back, clearly taking my silence as compliance, and looked back to Freya. "How do we proceed?"

"I will have to look into your hearts to see if there is enough strength there to draw on. If there is... If the three of us combine our powers, I will attempt to send you through the dimensions and back to Asgard." Freya reached out a hand toward me, palm up. Expectant.

Numb dread clutched at my gut. My *heart*. She wanted to see behind my shields, learn the truth of my devotion.

"We can trust her, Grim," Annabel said quietly from behind me. When I didn't move, she got to her knees, kissed the top of my head, and crawled a few steps around me before she placed her own hand in Freya's.

"You can look into my heart," she said.

Light flared between the two, bright at first, then turning to a soft glow.

Annabel gasped, but before I could reach for her, her lips turned up into a blissful smile and her eyes fluttered closed.

I watched them warily, the darkness in my gut turning acid. This was the last hurdle, the final step before Annabel could return to the living and continue her woven destiny. And for it to happen, I would have to let someone—a goddess of Asgard, no less—in.

There was some poetic balance in it, I supposed. I was the one who'd taken her life. I would have to give some of myself to return it.

It took a long while, but finally Freya released Annabel's hand and they both opened their eyes. But now, as the goddess looked at my mate, some of that divine glow had returned to her eyes, her skin a bit less sallow and sunken.

"Your heart is... so bountiful, omega," she said softly. "A true life-bringer, even in the depths of despair and darkness. Your blessing brings me so much joy, as it will those around you."

"Oh." Annabel returned her smile, even if she looked flustered at the praise. "Thank you?"

Freya chuckled and turned her focus back to me. "Are you ready to save your mate, Grim Lokisson?"

Save my mate. She was as manipulative as her reputation would suggest. I had no doubt she chose her words to stir my alpha instincts to life. Slowly, I got to my feet.

"Very well," I said through gritted teeth. "But... not here. Somewhere private."

"Oh." Freya looked surprised for a split-second, but then smiled and stood as well, pleased she'd gotten her way. "Of course. If that will make it easier for you, young one."

"Do you want me to come?" Annabel asked, already rising onto her knees to follow.

"No," I said, and she fell back down in the grass, eager to make this as comfortable for me as possible. "Please, just... stay here. And keep the flying cretins with you."

"Of course," my mate said softly. She smiled at me, and I pushed away the thread of sadness worming its way through my chest at the knowledge that it would be a very long time before she looked at me like that again.

If ever.

I turned around and stalked out of the glade, into the dark woods surrounding us.

I STOPPED by the side of a small waterfall trickling over mossy stones and waited.

Freya's soft footfall found me soon enough, and I steeled myself and turned around to her.

She gave me a gentle smile, and in it I saw the

echoes of what she used to be before *he* drove his dagger into her heart and ripped her from the world. "There is nothing to fear. Your mate loves you so much. She has nothing but forgiveness and understanding in her heart for your sins."

"She has such a soft nature," I said. "It is perhaps her only real flaw."

"What she feels for you, for all five of you, is no flaw, Lokisson. It is her greatest strength." The goddess stepped closer. "Will you let me into your heart, young one?"

"I wish that you would take no for an answer," I said. "But there is no way around this, is there?"

She shook her head. "No. There is not."

I drew in a deep breath and inclined my head once. "Then do what you must."

Freya placed her hand against my chest, eyelids fluttering closed as a warm sensation spread inward from where she touched me, threading through my flesh and into the cavity behind.

I stood still while she searched my innermost and laid every private thought bare. It was... excruciating. She was gentle, but it was nothing like Annabel's presence within me during those fleeting moments our souls had merged. She belonged there, within me, and I within her. Freya did not, and my powers rose up in defense, dark and violent, only scarcely tethered by the full force of my will.

It took longer than it had with Annabel before Freya withdrew from me.

Her eyes were wide as they met mine, and there was no trace of her gentle smile.

"You have to surrender to her, Grim," she said. "You must. I see your love for her. It is such a bright, burning fire. It is strong enough to banish the darkness in you. I swear it."

I gave her a mirthless smile. "You are wrong; my love for her *is* darkness. But I loved my brothers before I ever did her, and though my mind is being twisted by this... bond, I will always remember my duty to them.

"I will give anything, *have* given everything, to make sure they live through Ragnarök, and that will not change even if fickle biology wills me to sacrifice my previous obligations for her."

"They will live through Ragnarök, and so will billions more, if you surrender," Freya said, desperation tinging her voice even as she strained to keep calm. "With you and the four others by her side, she will be strong enough. You must trust in her."

I pulled my lips up higher, my smile turning into a sneer as I towered above her. "And therein lies the problem, sweet goddess. She requires five mates by her side to stop Ragnarök. Five gods sharing her powers. Her body. Her soul. You are no better than the Norns, twisting their vile webs around free will. You, the Goddess of Love, have created this... festering *thing*, and you dare act as if it were a *gift?*

"When I imagine her with them, when I saw her with them even before I made her mine, all I could think of was to close my hands around the necks of the only two beings I have ever loved and squeeze their lives out.

"But she is mine. She is half of my godsdamn *soul.* I cannot share her. And I *will not* risk harming my own brothers. So no, Freya—I will not be helping you perform your little miracle. I will not send Annabel home. She will stay here. With me. For eternity. *That* is what your precious gift of love has wrought."

Freya opened her mouth as if to speak, but in my face, she saw the truth of the darkness she had encountered in my heart. Naked fear flared in her eyes and she made to turn, to run from me and that darkness she had believed could be conquered if I just *surrendered.*

I felt no joy when I plunged my knife into her heart.

17

ANNABEL

They were gone for a long time, so long that I had started to comb my fingers through Mimir's hair just to have something to do with my hands while we waited.

I didn't know why every nerve in my body was on high alert, but perhaps it was because I knew that Grim feared nothing quite so much as he did opening his heart for judgement. His end of our bond was silent, yet *something* pulled on me, urging me to go to his side. Only knowing that whatever fragile trust was building between us would be shattered if I barged in on the private session between him and Freya kept me from stalking after them.

When he finally emerged from the tree line some forty minutes later, my heart leapt into my throat. I got to my feet and hurried to his side, leaving Mimir in the grass.

"Oh, *finally*. Are you all right?" I asked as I reached for his wrists.

Grim didn't pull away, but he didn't respond either. His face was cast in shadows, his features drawn in severe lines.

"Grim?" I asked, my chest constricting with concern again. "Is something wrong? I…" I zeroed in on the spray of gray liquid on his chest. *Blood?*

"Oh my God! Oh, what happened? Baby, please, are you hurt?" I asked, releasing his wrists to press both my palms against the blood smear. I reached for my magic on pure, panicked instinct and forced it into my mate, forgetting all about his lessons of control and accuracy, because the only thought that filled my head was that if he died, nothing would ever matter again.

"I am not hurt," Grim said, his voice calm, emotionless. He closed his fingers around my wrists, severing the connection between his chest and my magic.

Slowly, his words sank in. The glow around my palms died as I looked up at him, confusion mixing with the panic.

"It is not my blood," he said softly.

"Then whose…?" My voice died as I stared into his darkened eyes. Ice-cold dread crept up along my spine and down my arms. I jerked away, unable to move my gaze from his as I asked, "Freya?"

He didn't respond.

"Freya?" I shouted, still staring at Grim. It was written all over his beautiful face—what he'd done. But

I couldn't believe it. *Wouldn't* believe it. Because... Because it made no sense.

"It is too late, my mate," he said, his voice soft like silk over ice.

"No." I shook my head and took a step away. It couldn't be true. It wasn't. *"No."*

Yet Grim kept silent as he looked at me, the truth staring me in the face in the absence of reassuring words.

I ran out of the glade and into the woods, some dark thread of horror yanking me along the mossy forest floor until I came to a waterfall.

By its side, half-hidden in vegetation, lay a slumped figure.

"Freya!" I cried as I threw myself to her side. My magic welled within me as I brushed my shaking hands over her, searching. She was unresponsive, and when my fingers touched her chest, they came back sticky.

He'd stabbed her in the heart.

"No, no, no! Please, goddess, stay with me," I whispered. I was more conscious of my control as I directed my powers into her wound, searching for her heart.

The goddess spasmed once, and a wet gurgle escaped her throat. Slowly her eyes cracked open, her gaze finding mine.

"Annabel. Stop," she croaked.

"I can't." I had never attempted to heal a damaged heart before, and I gritted my teeth as the broken flesh within knitted together, only to slide back open again, over and over. "Why isn't this working? Please, please, help me!"

I don't know who I was pleading with, but only Freya responded.

"You need to stop." Her voice was so weak—barely a wheezing whisper. "You can't... can't save me."

"I can," I bit, forcing more of my magic into her chest. But her heart still wouldn't stay fused, and I growled in frustration. "You can't die!"

She closed her slim fingers gently around my wrist. "If you keep... trying... your child... will die. Please, Annabel. Stop."

"My child?" I asked, uncomprehending. "I don't—"

"You carry... *his* child," she croaked. "But she is still... only a kernel. She needs your strength to live. I am... I am dying, and even your powers won't stop that. Please. Save your strength. For her."

The glow around my hands faded as I stared at the dying goddess. Her words echoed in my mind, through my chest, but I couldn't take them in. Not now. Tears slid down my cheeks as I grasped her hand in mine.

"You can't die. You are the Goddess of Love! There is no life without you. There is no stopping Ragnarök without you."

"You have to keep trying. Until... Until the very end. I will give you... what I have left. You will need all five of them. If you channel... all your love... Perhaps... Perhaps it will be enough to bring you home."

I wiped at my tears with my free hand, trying to

comprehend what she was saying. "My mates? I can't—Saga, Magni, Bjarni, and Modi can't help me here. And Grim..."

The clutching, horrible darkness squeezed around my lungs, and I fought against the despair threatening to swallow me whole. I had loved him so completely, and it hadn't been enough. He had still done this. He had murdered a goddess to stop me returning to the world of the living so I could defeat Ragnarök.

"Please don't surrender the love you carry in your heart," Freya croaked. "Please, Annabel. If you do, if you cannot find forgiveness... understanding... all will be lost. For eternity. Even if you... cannot find your way home... if you... remain here... with him... if you surrender to the darkness, there will be no more love.... ever again. For your... For your child. Hold on."

Love him? She lay dying, pleading for me to *love* the man who had killed her? Who had betrayed me even after he had claimed half of my soul? Who had betrayed all the nine worlds?

I shook my head, my tears still falling thick and fast, but Freya placed her palm against my chest and rasped, "Call your mates to you. Unite with them all. You *must*, Annabel. There is no other way."

Warmth spread from where she touched me, and then I felt it—a rosy, glowing ember of magic sinking into my flesh and threading through my own golden well deep within.

Freya let out a soft gasp and her eyes glazed over.

"No!" I cried, reaching on instinct for her with my magic again, but before I could connect, a gust of wind swept through the trees and over her still body. Her fingers turned to gray dust in my hand.

"No!" I shouted again, grasping for her face. Her skin disintegrated under my touch—every part of the woman that had once been the embodiment of love turned to ash before my eyes and swept up into the sky in a ribbon of smoke, another soul that would join the siphon churning high above Hel.

I WAS numb for a long time as I knelt by the waterfall, staring at the vegetation still flattened from where Freya had rested.

She was the patron of omegas, she'd once told me. Had been. Behind the numb wall of grief and despair, I wondered what would happen to omegas now.

If it would even matter when Ragnarök swept through the worlds and broke it into particles and darkness.

Grim had done this. My soulmate had done this.

I had found forgiveness after his first betrayal. I'd forgiven him for taking my life because I understood he'd thought it the only chance to save his brothers. He'd ultimately killed me out of love for them, and knowingly doomed himself to a fate worse than death in the process.

But this time?

He knew me now. He knew me so intimately, knew I loved him, knew I'd fight until the very end to stop Ragnarök.

He'd known I relied on him. Trusted him. And in those pleasure-hazy moments when he was inside of me, I'd thought he loved me too. How had he faked that? How had he made me feel so... *whole* when it was all a lie?

I pressed a hand to my aching chest. Gentle warmth touched my fingertips from the remnants of Freya's powers. *Call your mates to you,* she'd said, but even if there had been a way to bring the four from Valhalla to me, Grim had made it clear he would never help me stop Ragnarök.

He had killed the Goddess of Love to prevent her from aiding me.

As I knelt by the water, I finally accepted that my love wasn't strong enough to break through the kind of darkness that lay within Grim's heart.

And so there would be no stopping Ragnarök, and there would be no more joy, no more love—no more anything. Just all-expanding, all-consuming nothingness.

18
ANNABEL

Grim was sitting in the center of the glade when I finally made it back. I wasn't sure how long I'd been staring at the waterfall in a stupor—if it had been minutes or hours.

My alpha looked up when I broke through the tree line, surveying my face.

I didn't so much as glance at Mimir or the ravens perched on a nearby bush as I walked straight to the dark god, my limbs feeling oddly mechanical and disjointed like they didn't fully belong to me.

He opened his mouth as if to speak, but I didn't give him the chance to. Striking more swiftly than I'd thought myself capable of, I backhanded him across the cheek with enough power to send him sprawling in the grass.

"You swine!" I hissed, aiming a kick at his stomach

that made him cough. "You traitorous, murdering *swine!*"

When I raised my leg to kick him again, Grim managed to roll out of the way in time. On my second try, he caught my ankle and held firm.

"Enough," he said more evenly than most men who'd just been slapped and kicked might have.

"Enough?" I snarled, pulling at my leg with all my might. Somewhat to my surprise—and Grim's, judging by his slightly widened eyes—he had to put in effort to keep me in place. "You *killed* her! You killed her so she couldn't help us get back! You betrayed me again! After everything we've shared—I *loved* you, you fucking psychopath! I forgave you. But that wasn't enough, was it?!"

I tugged on my leg again, but Grim held firm, his mouth a tight line and those mismatched eyes swirling with an emotion I didn't care to decipher. I reached for my magic and hurled it at him, giving no thought to conserving my power nor what would happen to my soul if I killed him with the blast.

Grim managed to raise a dark shield around himself in time for my light to part around him in a harmless flash.

I bared my teeth and reached for another ball of energy, but that dark shield wrapped around me and sank deep, containing my magic within me.

"I said *enough,*" Grim repeated, his voice firmer as he released my ankle and got to his feet.

I tried to throw myself at him to strike him again, but invisible bonds pressed my arms in tight against my sides, leaving me completely immobile.

I snarled and spat and strained against his magic cocooning my own, immobilizing it as thoroughly as it did my body, but I wasn't strong enough.

"Enough." Grim said, softer this time, as he closed his thickly muscled arms around me and pulled me back against his cool chest. "If you spend any more of yourself, I will need to join with you to ensure you are not left depleted."

"What's the matter, you don't want to add rape to the list of your crimes?" I snarled, flexing my muscles to try and buck against his grip.

"I would rather not." He brushed one hand from my ribs to my abdomen before anchoring it on my hip. "But if you leave me no choice, I will not hesitate."

A chill lingered on my skin from the path of his hand, even through my leather clothes. Like a ghostly caress against my stomach. And the spark of life within.

Slowly I stopped fighting until I hung limp in his arms. I would kill it if I continued expending my powers past my limits. Freya had been clear on that. *Her.* She'd called my baby *her.*

Grim's baby. Not Bjarni's, not Modi's. Not Saga's. Not Magni's.

Grim's.

I'd not fully taken in what the goddess had told me

before she died—the words themselves, yes, but not the emotional extent of them. The consequences.

I was *pregnant*. I was carrying a daughter. And thanks to her father's treachery, she would be born in Hel. She would never know color, or warmth. Or joy.

"I know you hate me, Annabel," Grim said so softly as tears slid down my cheeks. "You think I betrayed you, but this was the only way. In time, you will come to understand."

"I *think?*" I bit through the tears. "I *think* you betrayed me? You killed Freya. You made sure I will never see my other mates again, you made sure we won't be able to stop Ragnarök. I don't *think* anything, Grim. I *know.*"

"You still don't understand how hopeless your quest was," he murmured. He pressed his nose against the side of my head and rested his lips on the shell of my ear. "The prophecy was a lark. The Norns wove nothing but a web of pointless misery for you, and for that, I am sorry. Because I can never share you, Annabel. Just the thought of them touching you makes me want to kill all four of them. It makes me yearn to slay my own brothers. And that... that I can never let happen.

"I may be wrapped up in this foul web now, but I still remember my duty to Bjarni and Saga. My only goal was for them to live through this, and if they die by my own hand in a fit of jealousy because I cannot control this... *thing* I feel for you... I can't let that happen. I won't. Even if the cost is the end of everything.

"So they will remain alive, the new gods of a new world, and we will be nothing but a faint memory to them once I break their bonds to you. That will be my gift to them.

"And you, Annabel... you will stay here, with me. You can hate me for as long as you need to. I understand. But I will guard you, always. I will protect you, and I will make you a queen. My gift to you."

"Queen?" I whispered. "What do you mean *queen?*"

"Once Hel takes her army of undead to the shores of Midgard, there will be no one left to rule this realm. I will make you its new queen—make sure every creature left here bows to you. That is the only way I can ensure your survival."

"I thought you wanted me dead," I spat. "Once you'd broken my bonds so your brothers don't die with me. What do you care if some undead troll ends my misery? Is it our bond? Do you fear what it'll do to you, now that we are mated? I thought you were happy to die yourself —worse, even."

Grim snorted—not quite a chuckle, but the ghost of his cool breath tickled my ear and made my skin prickle with awareness. Even now, after everything he'd done, that part of me that belonged to him ached for his nearness. I pushed it down with savage fury.

"It is a curious thing, isn't it?" he said. "Even though I know that what I feel for you is wrong—fabricated;

forced on both of us by biology and Fate—I cannot deny it. The thought of you... *dying,* truly and irrevocably... If it came down to it, if I was forced to choose between you and my brothers... I would choose you. There is... *something* in our bond that will not let me risk you, mate, despite my convictions and oaths.

"As Queen of Hel, no one will dare lay a finger on you, and I will watch over you. I cannot offer you happiness, Annabel. That was never my gift. But I can offer you a different path than the one Fate decided for you. In death you will be worshipped, not for what you are, but for the power you'll wield. And you will know true power, and freedom from the strings of the Norns. You can forge your own destiny here. And I will see that you do, my mate."

I hung limply in his arms as his words conjured a memory—a vision I'd seen during one of the times he'd lost himself in me and let me glimpse his mind. A vision of me, sitting on a throne of bones, ruling over a barren world of death and despair.

19

ANNABEL

I didn't have it in me to keep walking. Not when there was nowhere to travel to.

Even if I could make it to Hel without Grim stopping me, even if I could somehow do what none had been able to do before me and convince her to release me from this place, it wouldn't matter. Not without Grim. And he had made it plenty clear that he would never help us stop Ragnarök.

It was... understandable, I supposed, in some sick, fucked up way that made my heart ache and tears sting my eyes as I lay in Freya's glade and stared into the swirling sky. Asking five alphas to share a mate was insanity. How my first four had come to accept it, I wasn't sure—family loyalty at first, perhaps, or obligation. But once they'd claimed me, once they'd felt the true force of that bond between us, I didn't know how they had remained calm as three other men staked their claims on my heart. My soul.

Grim's claim had felt so easy in comparison, so blissfully right. I hadn't even paused to consider that he might not be able to share me. That he would still be hellbent on his original plan to sever my ties to my other mates and bring about the end of the world, even if his motivations to do so had shifted some.

"So this is it? You have given up?"

Mimir's quiet voice made me turn my head to look at the prophet. He sat a few yards from where I'd lain down in the grass after Grim finally decided that I would no longer try to kick his skull in. It had been... I wasn't sure how long it had been. Hours? Days? I didn't remember if the sky had darkened at any point.

"It's what smart people tend to do when there are no other options left," I said.

"We could still go to Hel," he said, hesitance lacing his words. "It is dangerous, foolish even, but—"

I shook my head. "And do what? Beg her to send us back to a world that is doomed to end in horror? We can't stop it without him, and I can't make him help us. You spoke the prophecy yourself—you should know."

Mimir frowned. "Freya... Freya left a spark with you. I can feel it. It is faint, but it is there. She wouldn't have done that if she hadn't thought there was still hope."

I placed a hand over my heart where the goddess had pressed that kernel of magic into me. My other hand skimmed my abdomen at the reminder of what she had said as she did so. "Freya may have had hope, but what she asked is impossible."

Mimir glanced past me, to the tree line. "He is patrolling—we are not within earshot. Tell me, plum. What did the goddess ask of you?"

"She said if I can gather all five of my mates and channel *all my love,* it might be enough to bring us home. But yeah, not exactly doable with four of them on another plane of existence and Grim determined to win Villain of the Year. She said I had to find forgiveness for him, but how am I supposed to forgive something he doesn't even regret? That he has no intentions of rectifying, even if we could somehow get in contact with the others?"

I sighed, letting the sense of defeat and despair swallow me whole as I gently stroked my still-flat belly. "I'm sorry. I know I've let you down. I've let literally everyone down—the entire world, *nine* of them. But I can't fix this. I'm not strong enough."

"You are not strong enough on your own," Mimir said quietly. "You never were. That is why the Norns wove your thread with five powerful godlings."

"Their mistake, then," I said bitterly.

"All this wallowing is highly unattractive, plum," Mimir chided. "What we need is a way to bring your mates to you. Once they are here, we can work on the broody one."

"Oh, yeah, of course. I should have thought of that." I glared at him. "Why don't I just snap my fingers and send for them? Meanwhile, you can work on convincing the man who just killed the Goddess of Love to put on his best smile and get with the program."

Mimir leveled me with an unamused look. "Less sass, plum. More thinking."

I waved a hand at him and turned my head so I could look back up at the sky. "You can think as much as you want, prophet. Let me know how that works out for you."

"*Highly* unattractive," Mimir repeated. I ignored him.

Mimir stayed silent for hours, which suited me just fine. I lay on my back and stared into the sky, letting my mind drift into blessed oblivion.

Occasionally I would hear Grim's soft footfalls draw near. I knew he was checking on me—felt his eyes linger on my prone body, my face. I didn't bother to return his gaze.

At some point I supposed I would have to tell him about my pregnancy. He was the father, after all.

That thought was the only thing that penetrated my numb oblivion, filling me with tendrils of fear. I'd thought I understood his motivations—his heart. I'd felt so safe with him as we lay together, intimately tied in flesh as well as spirit.

But now? This man, who had killed and deceived

and betrayed? What guarantee did I have that he wouldn't harm my child, either in some twisted attempt at protecting me, or out of sheer indifference for the life we had created together?

I rubbed my thumb over my abdomen. It was... funny. I hadn't known about my daughter's existence for more than a few breaths, and she was still hardly more than a couple of cells—a spark, at best. But I loved her. Whatever else Grim was, at least he had given me her, even as he'd rent my soul in two and crushed the last flicker of hope in the world.

But if he hurt her? I wouldn't survive that.

The flapping of wings drew me from my gloomy thoughts, and I looked up at the two ravens circling above me. Arni and Magga had flown off sometime during my fight with Grim—probably so the dark god wouldn't take out his ire on them like his father had. I hadn't seen them since, not that I'd been looking.

"News of Freya's demise is spreading through the realm," Magga said. "Even here, her death ripples through the denizens. Despair and bleakness abound—more so than normal."

"Any news from above?" Mimir asked.

"Nothing," Arni cawed. "Too soon for the recently deceased to bring any whispers of the consequences of her absence with them."

Mimir blew out a breath. "Hel has all days been woefully behind the information curve. It would really be helpful if the queen allowed passage for more than just dead sou..." He trailed off so abruptly my indifference waned enough for me to turn my head in his direction.

The prophet had a faraway expression in his eyes as he stared at Arni.

"What?" I asked.

"Hel does allow passage between the realms for more than just arriving souls," he murmured. "There is *one* way for the dead to leave freely."

I jerked upright as an ember of hope I hadn't known still existed deep within flared to life. "What is it? *How?* Why has no one thought of it before?"

He grimaced. "Because it is not... an ideal solution. If one became a spectral—a ghost... they would be able to walk through the barriers separating our plane of existence from the living. But once passed, that barrier will close for eternity, trapping the soul in the living lands without a body. Eternally lost, and invisible to most."

I blinked. "...Your suggestion is that I return to Asgard as a ghost?"

"Stars above, no!" Mimir furrowed his bushy brows. "You wouldn't have access to your powers, and your mates likely wouldn't be able to speak with you without a medium present, much less use your connection to battle Ragnarök. No, I'm afraid your physical manifestation is entirely necessary."

"So ghostly passage *isn't* going to help us after all?" I clarified, frowning at the prophet, who still looked much too excited for what sounded like completely useless concept.

"It could. If..." He looked at me. "Freya said you needed your five mates with you to free yourself from this place?"

I frowned deeper. "Well... she said I *might* have a *chance* if they were all with me."

"But for that, we need to alert the four above of your whereabouts, and the urgency in joining you," Mimir said, though from the distant expression on his face, I wasn't sure he was talking to me as much as himself.

"Wait, are you suggesting we send a ghost to inform Magni, Modi, Saga, and Bjarni to... what, *kill* themselves?" I croaked.

"Oh, don't be dramatic, plum," Mimir chided. "They are gods. They do not need to die to visit Hel, as proven by your grumpy mate when he brought you here. Leaving can get a tad more complicated, without the right kind of magic—or Hel's blessing—but if you six can channel that power Freya left you and create a path home, we should all be able to leave the same way."

"Should?" I repeated.

"Should." He gave me a mild smile. "It is not an exact science. But I am wagering, if given the choice, your mates would not hesitate to risk being stuck in Hel with you if the alternative is a lifetime apart. Even if the dark Lokisson believes he can sever your bonds to them."

I chewed on my lip as I weighed his words. Every

instinct in me screamed to not even give them the option. As much as I longed for each and every one of them, the thought of dooming them to share my fate in this joyless place filled me with a deep sense of dread.

But they would come; I knew that without a shadow of a doubt. If there was a way, if they knew how, they would come for me.

"All we need now is to find a willing messenger," Mimir said.

"You mean someone who's happy to be stuck for an eternity in some in-between plane?" I asked. "How can we even ask someone to do that? It sounds like... well, an eternity of lonely misery."

"Worse, anyone desperate enough to consider such a fate would be doing it for their own purposes," Mimir mumbled, definitely mostly to himself this time. "There would be no guarantee they would even make the effort to find your godlings once there."

"I'm not sure that classes as *worse,*" I said tartly. He ignored me.

A soft caw drew our attention to Magga. She looked to her brother, who tilted his head and clacked his beak as he returned her stare.

The female ruffled her feathers and cawed again. "We will do it," she said.

I blinked. Twice. "*You?* You... volunteer? To...?" It probably wasn't the politest response, but the shock of her offer made the words spill out before I could stop myself. From what little I knew of the Lokissons' ravens, self-sacrifice wasn't exactly in their nature.

Arni hissed. "It could be said that the place between is a preferable place to Hel for a raven. So many whispers we can gather while few are the wiser of our presence."

"And we can haunt that bastard Loki until his dying breath," Magga added, her eyes gleaming with vicious glee.

Arni bobbed his head in agreement.

"But... won't you be lonely?" I asked.

"We need no one but each other," Magga cawed.

"And the occasional medium to share our whispers," Arni added. "If we cannot return to the living, a spectral presence is far preferable to.... *this*."

"Gorbul is a prick," Magga hissed. "Beady-eyed tyrant."

"Gorbul?" I asked.

"The leader of the ravens here," Arni explained with a sigh. "He only gained speech after entering Hel, but insists he should lead those of us with superior breeding."

"And his mate refuses to make room on the branches," Magga muttered.

I didn't quite know how to respond to that, so I didn't.

"We would be very grateful for your sacrifice," Mimir said instead. "All nine worlds would. If you are certain, I gladly accept your offer."

"We are certain," Arni said with another bob of his head. "We will leave as soon as the transformation is complete."

All three of them looked to me.

I frowned. "Er... *I* don't know how to make someone a ghost, if that's what you're waiting for?"

"Another dead soul needs to call their spirits out of their physical manifestation," Mimir explained patiently. "Come now, before Grim returns. I will guide you."

I hesitated. "Does it... require me to use my magic?"

"Yes," Mimir said. "But not much. You should have plenty left."

I bit my lip, weighing my options. I wasn't too close to being drained, and normally I wouldn't have hesitated, but the little one in my womb needed me to conserve strength. I didn't know how much I could use without hurting her.

"This is our very last shot, Annabel," Mimir said softly.

He was right. I closed my eyes and steadied myself with a deep breath. If there was any possible chance of escaping this place, of not making my child grow up without color and warmth and laughter, then I had to try. I would just have to be cautious.

"Okay. Guide me."

"Touch both of them," Mimir said, "and call on their spirits through your magic."

Both ravens hopped closer, and I placed a hand on each of them and closed my eyes.

My magic swirled up to meet me, and I threaded it through my conscience and opened my mind.

Magga. Arni. Come.

A touch of something mirthful and sharp brushed against my magic, tugging on it. I kept a tight leash on the glow within, using Grim's teachings to keep the flow steady and focused.

"Again, plum. Keep calling them," Mimir said.

Arni. Magga. Come. Come. Come. Be free of this place. Come.

I opened the flow of my magic a little wider. The mirthful presence seemed to amplify.

"What are you doing?" The shout cracked like thunder from somewhere outside my magic. *"Annabel!"*

I would recognize that voice anywhere—Grim.

"Hurry, plum," Mimir urged as cool darkness wrapped around my magic. "Hurry!"

He was going to stop us. I yanked harder on my magic, forced it out as I called for the ravens over and over.

That dark, balmy magic penetrated mine as Grim closed his strong hands around my shoulders, shaking me. "Stop, Annabel—*now!* Stop!"

But he was too late. A ripple of release went through my mind, and I opened my eyes to see the translucent outlines of Magga and Arni rise out of their bodies over Grim's shoulder.

"Too late, Misborn!" Magga cawed triumphantly as they beat their spectral wings up, up, up, invisible winds carrying them into the sky.

But Grim paid them no mind. His eyes were on me, wild and furious. "What did you do?" he snarled.

"It's none of your concern," I rasped. My head felt light, as did my body.

"None of my concern?" he echoed, dark brows drawing down. "You used too much of your power for whatever harebrained scheme you were attempting!"

I had. I'd given up my control at the end to ensure the ravens escaped before Grim could stop me, and I had used more of my power than I'd intended. A flicker of worry wormed its way through my mind as I let a hand rest against my abdomen. I didn't feel anything wrong—but then again, would I? She was still so tiny.

"And *you,*" Grim snarled, pulling me from my worries as he rounded on Mimir. "It's always you, isn't it? Every time she runs, every time she puts herself in danger, it's because of *you*—you and your hopeless attempts at stopping the inevitable. You of all people should know that there is no point in fighting him. And there is no point fighting *me.*

"You have risked her one too many times, prophet. Always weaving your schemes, your plots—giving no thought to the lives of the people you draw in. Is it not enough that you yanked her from her family with your prophecy? You continue to burden her at every step!

Enough. If you refuse to accept defeat, then I will make sure you have no other choice."

Dark power rose around Grim, and my gut lurched with realization.

"No!" I pushed my own floundering magic at him, tried to stop him before he could do any harm, but even at my strongest I was no match for Grim. My light slid off his darkness, leaving not so much as a dent.

Grim jerked his head to me, eyes wide and furious. "Stop! Do *not* give any more of yourself! You know the consequences."

He meant forced sex. Even now, despite his fury, despite what he had done—was still going to do—he didn't want to force me. He was desperate to avoid it.

But violation was not the only consequence of emptying my energy. Not anymore.

Reluctantly, I pulled my magic back from his and placed a trembling hand on his thigh. "Please, Grim. Don't hurt him. Please."

Grim bared his teeth at me, but his magic held still in the air around him. "He is *nothing* to you. *He* is the reason you were pulled into this mess to begin with. Without his prophecy, Loki would never have made his bargain, and you would have been with your family now. And yet you wish to spare him, when he continues to risk your life? Your heart may be soft, Annabel, but I did not think you stupid."

"Without his prophecy, without my Fate woven into its current path, I would still have been your soulmate,"

I said quietly. "There was never any escape for me, even without Ragnarök swallowing the nine worlds. Don't take your anger out on him for still trying to do the right thing, even if you have given up. What I have done to return to Asgard, I have done of my own free will. If you punish him for trying to find a way home, you should punish me as well."

Grim stared at me in silence for several breaths, and the expression on his cold features was... stricken, as if my words cut through his ice and into something soft and vulnerable.

"I would never have come for you," he finally said. "I would have let you live a human life in oblivion."

"Then you would have deprived me of half my soul," I said. "You would have taken what belongs to me for your own selfish reasons."

A grimace cut over his face, and the power around him pulsed and swelled. "*Deprived* you? I would have *gifted* you a lifetime without darkness!" Grim turned back to Mimir with a sharp jerk, nostrils pulled up in rage. "Don't *ever* attempt to help her escape again, and don't so much as *think* about persuading her to use her powers for your nefarious schemes! No amount of her begging will sway me a second time."

Without another look at either of us, Grim swung around and stomped across the clearing, disappearing into the trees again, undoubtedly to stew.

"Such a temper," was all Mimir said, his voice

completely calm, as if he hadn't just been threatened with the very real prospect of annihilation.

I didn't respond. Couldn't—because Grim's eyes still danced in my mind. So anguished. So filled with *regret.* And behind it, behind the darkness, the rage... despair.

He may think himself nothing but darkness and ice, may think our soul connection a curse for me, but there was a glimmer of humanity buried deep. Despite what he'd done, despite his heritage and broken spirit, he despaired at what he believed he had to do—and that it ruined any chance that I may... love him.

Grim craved my love, enough that he had stopped himself from harming Mimir because I'd begged him.

I wasn't sure what to do with this realization. It hadn't been enough for him to push his convictions aside, hadn't been enough to stop him from murdering Freya.

And it wasn't enough for me to forgive what he'd done.

But something in my innermost trembled at that look in his eyes, those jagged edges of my soul calling out for its other half.

20

SAGA

The wind howled as the tempest battering my body did its best to rip me off the mountainside to plummet into the depths below.

It had taken us weeks to get to Verdandi's peak. The only portal to Jotunheim that had shown up on our map had seen us trekking over the Spine through a blizzard so violent I would never have so much as contemplated braving the climb for anything other than our current quest.

Annabel.

The last time Magni and I had made the journey up this mountain, it had been because of her as well—before Ragnarök had truly sunk its claws into Jotunheim and he and I had squabbled like children over their favorite toy.

Purple light flashed high above our heads, sending a

shock of electricity through the air and pulling Bjarni—who had taken up the lead—to a stop.

"Your dad?" he roared over the shrieking gale.

"No," Modi shouted, pointing at the sky. "That is not our father. That... That is the end."

I followed his finger with my eyes and drew in a sharp breath. The thick charcoal clouds that had choked out the sun since the beginning of our journey parted around a purple tear in the cover, and *through* that tear...

"Is that... Jörmungandr?" Magni choked.

"The fabric between the worlds is starting to shred. That is Midgard," Modi said as the giant sea serpent reared up through a violent sea, spraying venom into the sky. I couldn't make out the city its acid fell on through the fissure, but judging by the faint outline of skyscrapers behind the monster, the loss of human life would be significant.

"Press on," I roared, tearing my gaze from the rift between worlds.

We continued up the mountainside until we finally stood in front of Verdandi's obsidian cave carved to resemble a dragon's open maw. Even the howling of the wind could do nothing to drown out the horrendous shriek emitting from its dark throat.

"You're sure she lives down there?" Bjarni shouted. "That thing looks like it's gonna break free from the mountain and take flight any moment."

"It's a cave. Nothing more," I said through gritted

teeth. If I hadn't been down there before, I would have been less convinced.

Modi looked about as skeptical as Bjarni, but they both followed me and Magni as we made our way through the dragon's stone teeth.

The darkness swallowed us after the first two turns, leaving nothing but the eternal howl and a creeping, bone-clattering chill that sank through our clothes and deep into our flesh. It wasn't as aggressive as the icy cold of the mountainside, but it brought a kind of damp, slithering dread that only increased the farther down the dragon's throat we walked. Before we had taken many steps, both Magni and Modi called to their magic to illuminate our path.

Time was an unreliable companion in this place, and I wasn't certain how much passed as we made our way down. It could have been perhaps half an hour, perhaps six when the lack of life became concerning.

"Verdandi!" Magni called. His voice echoed through the cave, up and down through the length of the dragon's throat. Only that infernal howling answered.

"Hell of a time to go on vacation," I growled.

"What if she is not here?" Modi said so quietly I barely heard him over the screeching.

I grimaced. If the Norn wasn't in her cave, then... "She is here. She has to be," I bit. "Onward."

We called the Norn's name over and over as we walked, with nothing but our own echoes answering, and that quiet terror growing stronger the deeper we went.

I will never stop trying, sweetling. Not ever.

"What in Freya's name is that?"

Modi's voice broke through my quiet oath, and I let my gaze follow the glow of light from his hand as he held it out in front of him.

A gossamer veil hung on wooden beams in front of the naked rock blocking our path.

"Looks like it's the end of the road," Bjarni said.

"Or not," Magni murmured as he stepped closer to the veil. "This... Is this a portal? It feels magical, but... odd. I have never seen something like this."

I closed the gap between us, my focus on the fabric. It hung limp from its rafters, but when I was so near I could have reached out to touch it, I too felt a soft, nearly imperceptible hum. It whispered to my subconscious, whispered of *otherness* and forbidden power. The longer I studied it, the more the small hairs on my body stood on end.

"Do you remember," I began slowly, "when the Norn took Annabel? Shortly after, it felt... almost like it did when you tried to take her to Jotunheim without me. As if she was ripped from my reality."

"You think she took her through here?" Magni asked. From the way he clenched his light-free fist to his chest, I knew he remembered it too.

"Where else would she have taken her? The path

has no divergence—this is the only way they could have come," I reasoned.

"So it *is* a portal," Bjarni said. He shouldered past both of us and looked it up and down. "Then what are we waiting for? Come on."

I opened my mouth to caution him against that low, warning hum prickling against my own magic, but I didn't get the chance. My brother lifted his arms to brush the veil aside and stepped through—and smacked right into the stone wall behind it.

"Fuck!" Bjarni rubbed his nose and turned to glare at the portal. "What is wrong with this thing?"

"Perhaps it requires a toll, like the portal that brought us to Asgard," I suggested. I looked closer at the old wood and frowned. There didn't appear to be any runes or symbols carved on them, nor on the surrounding stone.

Modi and Magni followed the path of my eyes, scanning the structure as closely as I, but after more than an hour's scrutiny, none of us had found anything that might help us figure out how to use the damned thing.

"Blast it! How are we supposed to find that cursed Norn if we can't get to her?" Bjarni growled, smacking his palm against the wood hard enough for it to creak in protest.

A small flicker at the edge of my magic made me freeze, eyes trained on Bjarni's large hand. "Do that again."

"Do what?" He frowned, looking from me to the others.

"Hit it," Modi said. "Hard."

Bjarni arched a brow, but gave the beam a slap hard enough to make the veil shake. And again.

The flicker turned to a buzz tainted with… *irritation.*

"Here we go," Magni murmured just as the buzz turned to a physical press against my skin.

Bjarni's next smack against the wood sent a squeal through the old beams and made him stumble back a few steps. The veil whipped wildly before white light flashed, momentarily blinding us all. When we could see again, Verdandi stood in front of the portal.

"*What?*" The Norn hadn't bothered with the more human disguise she'd worn for Annabel, and I suppressed a shudder at the sight of her pointy teeth as she glared at us.

Modi didn't manage to hide his shiver, but he steeled himself and bowed deeply. "Wise one, we are here to seek your aid."

Verdandi tsked and snapped her fingers in his face. "You come banging down my door for *help?* Modi Thorsson, it is the end of all that is. I am *busy!*"

"Please, Verdandi," I said, stepping forward to rescue Modi from the Norn's terrifyingly wide glare. "Our mate is lost, and we don't know where else to turn. Trud Sifsdottir believes you will be able to help us find her."

Verdandi snapped her head around to me. "I know

she is lost! She is gone, and there is no stopping Ragnarök now. So many years I watched over her, so many years I protected her. All for nothing."

"No. It was not for nothing," Magni said, his voice hoarse, but determined. "She is not dead. Not truly. My sister believes she is stuck in Hel, but she cannot be dead or we would be too. Blessed Weaver, you *must* help us find her. It is not too late. Not yet."

"Not too late?" she barked. "Not too late? *Ha!* The sky is literally falling, and everyone—*everyone*—is dying! Go home, godlings, and spend this finite time we have left with those you love. We lost. We all lost."

"You wove our life threads with this mortal," Modi said quietly. "*You* spun our fate. You should know that we will never, ever give up on her—not until the universe implodes into atoms and we cease to exist in this world or the next. So long as she breathes, there is hope, wise one. I will implore you one more time to help us. Do not deny us, sacred being, because there is nothing I will not do to bring my mate back. *Nothing.*"

Verdandi snorted, her neck wrenching unnaturally as she stared him down. "You think to *threaten* me, godling?"

"To be fair, it's Ragnarök and our mate is gone. Even if you snip our threads, you won't bring us more misery than what we already carry," Bjarni rumbled.

"They are right," Magni said. "We have nothing to lose without her, wise one."

Verdandi looked at all of us one at a time. She shook

her head and tossed her hands up, the movement making my stomach clench from the way her elbow joints popped the wrong way as she did.

"Fine. *Fine!* If you wish to see for yourself why I cannot help, by all means, come on through."

Without another look at us, she spun and disappeared back through the veil.

To Bjarni's credit, he didn't even hesitate before he followed her.

The rest of us took a half-second before we followed in his footsteps.

The second I passed through the veil, pressure gripped my ribs and squeezed, and I experienced a moment of blind panic before I smacked my knees into dusty soil, and the sensation of having the life squeezed out of me eased.

I coughed and rubbed at my ribs as I looked around.

My brethren all knelt around me, also gasping for air as they took in our surroundings. We were in a large earthen cave with roots growing through the crumbling walls and high ceiling. Shimmering threads in earthy tones of greens, browns, silver, and gold hung from them, millions of them interwoven in intricate patterns, but there were large gaps between them and piles of what looked like ashes on the ground beneath them.

"Come on!" Verdandi called from deeper in, impatience coloring her sharp voice. She twisted to eye a tangle of what looked like a few thousand threads, sighed heavily, and pulled a pair of golden scissors out from a fold in her clothing. With as much care as a low-grade gardener, she chopped several bunches in a few brutal hacks. They all withered to ash and trickled to the floor in another large pile.

"Tidal wave," she explained at our dumfounded stares, pointing at us with her scissors. "You see what I have to deal with?"

The Norn didn't wait for a response before she swung around and continued stalking through the multitude of threads, snipping off clumps left and right as she walked.

By the time she stopped at a fine tangle of four golden threads, I was pretty sure she had culled a few hundred thousand lives.

"You see the problem?" she asked, voice clipped. She poked one of the golden threads with the tips of her scissors. Magni shuddered, his face taking on a green tinge.

"This is us?" Modi asked, his eyes trained on the strands. They were woven together with knots and braids at different intervals, but toward the bottom they all coiled together, as if swirling around an invisible core. "Where is Anna's thread?"

"And Grim's?" Bjarni added as he too leaned forward to examine them closer.

"That's just it—they are simply *gone*." Verdandi threw her hands into the air again. Her scissors brushed against another of the golden threads in the process, and something *twanged* deep in my gut and in my spine. I croaked before I could steel myself.

My eyes immediately dropped to the floor, my heart lurching, but there was no hint of ashes below our tangle.

"How is that even possible?" Magni asked, his brows knitting into a deep frown. "Where is our mate?"

Verdandi bared her too-many teeth in irritation. "I have no idea! My threads don't just get up and go walking about. The only way out of my cave is if I snip them. But these two just... *poof!* And if there is no thread, I cannot find the soul. I told you—I cannot help you, godlings. Not this time."

I turned to my brethren, trying my best to keep a hold of the fissure of despair threatening to split me apart from the inside. "This changes nothing. She is still out there, somewhere."

"So we still go to Hel," Magni said, his lips pinching as he stared at our web of threads with its missing core. "And we keep searching until we find her."

"Hel is vast, young ones," Verdandi said, and for the first time I could almost make out a drop of empathy in her voice. "If she is truly there, you will not find her in time without knowing her approximate location."

"Perhaps we can help with that."

I jerked upright at the voice creaking right next to me and spun around, but I saw nothing.

"What in Ymir's armpit is *this?!*" Verdandi shrieked

behind me. "No. *No!* I do not care if this is Ragnarök—I will *not* allow pests in my house! Shoo! Psst! Out!"

"Who are you calling pests?" another voice squawked, and though its hollowness rang through the air around us like a bell, I recognized its haughty tone.

"Magga?" I spun around again, trying to catch sight of my old raven companion. "Show yourself!"

"Now where is the fun in that?" the other voice asked.

"Arni!" Bjarni gasped. "You're alive!"

"Well, technically..." Magga muttered.

"They are wayward spirits," Verdandi broke in, disapproval clear on her face as she stared at a point above our heads. "Misplaced souls who have decided to break out of Hel and come wreak havoc with the natural order of things. Your kind is not welcome here. You're disturbing my threads!" She snapped her long, bony fingers in the air.

Perching on a root a couple yards above our heads, two semi-opaque ravens came into view, their matted feathers outlined by a shimmering green.

"Well, that's just petty," Magga huffed.

"You say you can help us?" Modi asked. If he had any reservations about the ghost ravens, he didn't show it. "You come from Hel. Is Annabel Turner there? Do you know where she is being kept?"

Arni looked to Magga, then to us. He set off from the root and swung through the air, landing on Bjarni's shoulder with an echoing caw. Magga followed, but when her claws gripped my shoulder like she had so many times before, I only felt a gentle chill.

"We were sent to you with a message," Arni said.

"From the human girl you so love," Magga added.

"She resides in Hel. She bids you to come to her side." Arni nodded at Modi. "Most urgently."

Bjarni swiveled toward the Norn. "Can you help us get there? Or do we need to get there the old-fashioned way? If the ravens can come back after what Loki did to them, so can we."

She sucked her teeth at my brother and gave Arni a displeased look. "You do not wish to share their fate. An afterlife as a spectral may suit the Masters of Whispers, but it is a miserable existence for any creature who wishes to feel another's touch ever again."

"But can you help me?" Magni insisted. "Because if you cannot..."

He didn't finish the thought, but we all shared it. If she could not, then eternity by Annabel's side in Hel was a far better fate than staying here without her.

The Norn fell silent as she stared at the two ravens, her lips pinched in thought. After some time, she hummed and cocked her head, eyes narrowing.

"*Perhaps*... Perhaps there is a way. Your familiars may be little more than spirit vermin, *but*... they are still souls, of a sort. If there is enough left, mayhaps I can... borrow a connection."

Arni and Magga looked at each other, then at her. *"Borrow a what now?"*

"A connection. If I can reach back to the place you exited Hel, perhaps I can create a portal." Verdandi gave her cave a long look before she turned her attention back to us. "It is not a safe passage, young ones. If the cretins have too little spark left, there is every chance you will all be lost in the in-between for eternity. But I see your devotion to the girl I tied you with. Your determination. Perhaps... *Perhaps* it will be enough to bring her back. Enough to save us all. But it is your choice. I cannot weave this destiny for you."

"There is no choice," I said. "We will go."

"Good." She nodded, and without warning, reached for both Arni and Magga.

They shrieked and flapped their ghostly wings, but Verdandi held firm, her fingers plunging through their semi-opaque bodies and making green sparks fly. Slowly a flickering, obsidian rectangle specked with emerald rose from the cave floor. Up and up it stretched, until it was as tall and wide as a doorway.

Verdandi released her grip on the birds, who both flew back up to the root above our heads, slinging several hollow curses at the Norn.

Verdandi ignored them, her expression grave when she looked at us. "You must be careful on your journey, godlings. Things have shifted. Fates have been rewritten without the guidance of me or my sisters. If you are to succeed in saving us all, there will have to be a sacrifice."

"Whatever sacrifice is needed, it will be given,"

Modi said, voice gruff as he looked at the portal. "You have our eternal gratitude, wise one. You and the birds." Without another look at the cave or our golden life threads, he stepped through the dark portal.

One by one, we followed him.

21

GRIM

Annabel seemed fond of the glade, or as fond as my despondent mate could be of anywhere in Hel.

She didn't speak to me, nor did she smile or seem to listen much when Mimir prattled about some story or other, but she didn't attempt to leave, either.

She spent most of her time lying on the grass and staring into the sky. I had to restrain myself not to lower the wall I'd erected between us to reach through our bond and sense what she was thinking. I had a fairly good idea that I didn't want to know her thoughts, even if my instincts were itching to sate my curiosity.

What good would it do to probe for how to make my mate feel better when I was the reason behind her sadness?

So instead I spent my time patrolling the woods surrounding the glade, ensuring nothing crept up on us. But nothing did. There was no trace of any of the foul creatures that haunted the rest of Hel—only songbirds and small mammals scuttling across the forest floor. It was entirely… peaceful.

Perhaps it would be worth the effort of setting up a more permanent base here until Hel took her army and left, and I could begin my plans to put Annabel on the throne.

I let my gaze sweep over my mate as she sat on the grass with her arms around her knees. My would-be goddess.

She had the strength. It had taken all I had to restrain her after she'd found Freya's body, and she was not even at her full power then. With my help, she would be capable of ruling the underworld. She might not like it, but it would keep her safe.

Until then, I would build her a cottage here, in this glade. Somewhere she would feel more comfortable and secure, with a roof that might break her endless staring at the churning soul siphon high above. As if she sensed my attention, Annabel turned her head and looked at me.

I steeled myself against the fire snapping up my spine as our eyes connected and held her gaze, willing her to speak.

She didn't, unsurprisingly. She just kept staring at me, *through* me, as if she was looking for something in my eyes.

If I hadn't known better, I would have thought she

might be searching for some sign I wasn't the dark monster she now knew me to be.

A pity we both knew there was no such sign to be found.

Annabel shifted on the grass, and I expected her to simply lie back down to continue staring at the sky. Instead she got to her feet, swaying a little as she found her balance.

She was too spent. Weakened. I had told myself she had enough strength still. As I watched her now, struggling to get to her feet, I knew I had been lying to myself.

Lead settled heavily in my gut and I closed my eyes for a moment, letting my inner chill swallow anything and everything. But when I opened them again, Annabel was walking toward me.

"Grim," she said, hesitance lining her voice. "I need... help."

The way she grimaced as she said it, one hand flailing vaguely for demonstration, I didn't have to ask what sort of *help* she had in mind. Eyebrows high on my forehead, I asked, "You come to me willingly?"

Annabel grimaced again. "I suppose that sounds sexier than I'm here because I need an energy boost."

I would have laughed if it wasn't for the relief easing the dread in my gut. At least we would be spared that.

I sucked in a breath through my nose. Unsurprisingly, no touch of desire flavored her pheromones. As happily as she had given herself to me since the troll's cave, I knew she hated me too much to desire me now.

It didn't matter. I was obligated to protect her, and ensuring she was not drained of power was of the highest priority. Before Annabel, sex had been nothing but a transaction, and now it would be again. I would endure that a thousand times over. For her.

She made no move to undress herself, or me. She simply stood in front of me with her gaze locked on my chest, refusing to meet my eyes. That was fine; it would be easier this way.

With mechanical movements, I undid the straps of first her leathers, then my own, until we both stood naked in the silent glade.

"Down," I rasped, clearing my throat to combat the unexpected hoarseness. "Hands and knees."

She darted one look up at me at the command—just a swift glance before she knelt on all fours in front of me. My cock, subdued until now by the awkwardness of the encounter, surged at the sight of her surrender.

I strode around her, coming to a halt between her slightly spread knees. Her pussy sat so prettily between her soft thighs, a thatch of dark hair covering closely sealed lips, calling to me despite her unaroused state.

I knelt down, forcing her stance wider with the pressure of my own knees inside hers, until she went down on her elbows in picture-perfect submission.

I hauled in a ragged breath and placed a hand on her hip, steadying myself as much as her. I *ached* for her

—in body and soul. Memories of being inside her, of losing myself in her cunt and spirit, welled up, and I dug my fingers into her hip to rein myself in.

It wouldn't be like that this time. Or ever again.

Every other time she'd been on her hands and knees, her pussy had been open and slick for me.

Sucking in another breath, I pressed my free palm between her spread thighs, cupping her small sex.

Annabel gasped and shivered when I dipped my middle finger in to press it against her still-hooded clit.

Over and over, I rocked my hand back and forth, stimulating her where she would feel me the most. It didn't take long for faint notes of awakening pussy to hit my nostrils.

I had no control over the growl that escaped me at that scent. Everything in Hel was deprived of sensory stimulation: no warmth, no cold, no color, no smell, except the raw, tantalizing scent of Annabel's sex readying her for penetration. It was little more than the lightest of hints in the air, but it was more than enough.

She mewled in response to my growl, and syrupy slickness seeped into my palm. Even now, even if her heart despised me, her body still craved mine. It was an unexpected comfort.

I raised up higher on my knees and released her hip so I could lean over her with my knuckles on the ground next to her elbow, never stopping the rocking motion of my palm against her nether lips.

She wasn't warm underneath me like she should

have been, but it still felt good to press my chest and abdomen against her back and feel her shiver at the contact. When I dug my teeth gently into her nape, she whimpered, *"Grim,"* so softly it felt like a velvet caress.

"I ache for you," I rasped against her neck before I could stop myself.

Only the hitching of her breath in response to my words let me know she'd even heard me. I gritted my teeth, angry with myself for releasing into the illusion of contentment so swiftly. This was a transaction, a necessary evil. Nothing more.

I slid my middle finger form Annabel's clit to her entrance and dipped it inside, testing her. She gasped, but her sheath yielded easily for my shallow intrusion. Had things been different, I would have continued stimulating her, would have drawn her pleasure out until she was begging for penetration. Memories of our nights together on our way here made my cock jump and my heart ache. My name had spilled freely from her lips then, fevered kisses peppering my skin whenever I let her face me.

This time, she was offering herself out of necessity.

I pushed it down—all of it—and slipped my finger from her pussy to grab for my cock, aligning it.

Annabel's breath hitched again as I pressed my cock head up against her now-splayed lower lips, and her thigh muscles tightened for a second before she spread her knees wider, inviting me in.

There was nothing but darkly throbbing need filling

my head as I pushed into her, spreading that delicate, soft flesh inch after yielding inch.

"Gods!" She was so *tight!* Her flesh was willing and slick, but her body wasn't as open as I had become accustomed to, and she mewled and threw her head back as I slowly sank deep.

"Grim." My name was a plea urging me to be gentle, but it fueled that dark possessiveness, that instinctive response to her that took over my entire being whenever I let myself give in.

"Mate," I groaned, falling on top over her once more as my cock found its home nestled against her cervix. I wrapped an arm around her and held her tight as I steadied us both on my elbow. *Stars above,* she felt... she felt like *life,* like the sun, the moon, the stars—like oxygen and everything I needed to breathe. *"My mate."*

Annabel whimpered and clung to my arm wrapped around her ribs, nails digging in. It hurt her, our joining, but when I gave her a slow thrust, her entire being rippled underneath and around me, and I felt her pleasure shudder through her body and into mine.

"I'm sorry," I rasped against the shell of her ear as I rolled my hips again, giving her more of that slow, agonizing bliss that had her quaking against me.

I was. Sorry that she hurt, sorry that I caused it, sorry that there was no way around it. I forced myself deep into her again, shivering with her at the brutal pleasure cracking up my spine as her cunt squeezed on me. Talons of fire and bliss raked the shield I had put between us, threatening to break it down with each shuddering breath I gasped against my mate's skin. *Gods,* she was *life.* She was life, and I *needed* her, needed to meld with her, be absorbed by her...

Annabel gave another mewl, and then I felt *her* pressing against that shield. A plea for entry.

"No," I grunted, a flicker of awareness bursting through the haze of bliss. "Annabel, no. You don't... Not that. Not this time."

But she was persistent, my mate, and our bond hummed violently in my chest as she brushed against that wall of flimsy will and desperation.

Something wild and uncontrollable rose from my gut—terror and euphoria and dread. I couldn't. Not now. Not when I was this raw and dark and ugly.

"You don't want so see me!" I snarled, giving her pussy a hard thrust that had her choking out a cry, some of the pressure in our bond shifting as her attention was diverted to taking my too-thick cock without the balm of gentleness. Again I took my desperation and despair out between her thighs, and again she cried out, nails scratching at my arm. And again, until her pussy surrendered, and I fucked her mercilessly deep and hard in smooth, fast strokes that had the glade echoing with the wet *thwacks* of our flesh joining and Annabel's broken moans.

Only when I no longer felt her pushing at me through our bond did I relax into the sensation of primal purpose. I groaned and reared up behind her, grabbing her round hips to pull her back on me. Her sheath accepted my presence fully now, and Annabel's cries were no longer tinged with pain as much as carnal delight. She was as lost in the sex as I, and when I released my grip on her right hip and reached down to rub at her clit, she gave in.

Her keening moan of release was followed by her muscles fluttering along my cock, the slick flesh sucking me in. I groaned with her, my hips stuttering to a halt to let her ride out her orgasm.

"Fuck, *Grim!*" she whined, one hand coming back to clasp onto my wrist as I continued to rub her clit, forcing her pussy to milk me through her first climax and straight into another. Before she could try to push me away from her swollen bud, I wrapped my other arm around her torso and pulled her up against my body, distracting her with the new angle of penetration.

Annabel stiffened as my cock head pressed firmly against her cervix, hands flailing back to clasp onto my body in a plea for mercy.

"I'll never hurt you," I rasped into her ear, still rubbing circles on her clit to ease any discomfort of how deep I was in her. "Not like this. Never like this. No matter how deeply you hate me and how much I deserve it, I won't ever... Not like this."

I don't know why those words burst from my lips, but I could do nothing to stop them, nor the conviction tightening my gut somewhere past the fog of desire. Whatever small hurt she endured to open for me was fine—a sliver of pain that felt good for both of us. But to truly harm her, harm my *mate,* with the only act that allowed me a few moments of bliss?

Never. *Never.*

Annabel gasped out something that could have been a word and clung to me for dear life, but I held steady, allowing her body to feel nothing but pleasure. Soon she relaxed in my grip, her pussy easing into another climax. It was softer this time, but it still shot lighting up my spine as her muscles massaged my length, and I groaned and gritted my teeth against the swelling threatening to expand. *Not yet.* I wasn't ready to return to the bleakness of reality. Not yet.

Annabel slumped fully back against my torso, and I eased off her clit and focused on my rough breaths to stave off my knot. If we had been among the living, if her beautiful scent had wafted into my nostrils, I would have had no chance, but Hel's dampeners worked out for me this time.

I was almost in control of myself again when Annabel asked, "Grim?" in a soft and sex-drugged voice.

"Yes?" My own voice was rough and raw.

"I want my final truth."

It took me a moment to get enough blood to my brain to remember what she was talking about. *The bargain.* Three truths for her healing magic. She'd had two, and admitting to both had ripped me apart.

"Now? You want a truth *now?"*

"Yes," she said, determination creating a hard edge to her softness. "Right now."

I spat a curse and clenched my hands into fists, willing my flaring testosterone under control before I surrendered to the urge to pin her in the grass and fuck her into oblivion. "Then *ask.*" There was more threat in my growl than intended, but Annabel was not cowed.

She sucked in a deep breath, and still staring straight ahead, speared on my throbbing cock, she asked, "Is what you feel for me love, Grim? The genuine kind? Or is it... something else? Just... hormones or instincts, or whatever? Something that gets twisted by this... bond we share?"

The genuine kind. I scoffed and opened my mouth to tell her there was nothing *genuine* about that dark, twisting possessiveness that throbbed in my chest where we were connected and threatened my sanity with every second that passed... but no words would leave my throat.

I frowned and tried to force them out. Only a rattle escaped my tight windpipe.

"Grim?" Annabel asked, concerned now. She twisted her neck to look at me, eyes darting to mine.

"You swore to give her three truths, Lokisson," Mimir said from somewhere outside our cocoon of pleasure.

I jerked my head up and saw the prophet sitting several yards from us, face turned away. It seemed

Annabel had had the wherewithal to ensure he wouldn't be watching us fuck before she came to me.

Three truths. The bargain bound me to answer her truthfully. My frown deepened.

Is what you feel for me love? The genuine kind?

What I felt for Annabel was all-consuming and destructive, and I knew into the marrow of my bones that it was anything but *genuine.* It was forced on me by biology and Fate, perverted into something terrible by my own darkness... But when I again tried to tell her as much, the words wouldn't come.

"I..."

I stared down at the soft woman in my arms as ice-cold terror mixed with a sickening realization. Was this...? Was what I felt...? *This* was true love? This unending *need,* this intimate knowledge that I was nothing without her, that I would break myself into atoms for her—it was not some befoulment of nature. It was... genuine.

It wasn't forced on me by a manipulative Norn, wasn't the result of primitive instincts wired into my DNA to ensure procreation.

"You are my soul," I told her, horror lacing my every word as the truth of them speared into me, into that soft, weak place I had always known was still there, but refused to acknowledge. "I... I *love* you. With everything I am."

And what was I? I had killed for my convictions that what I felt for her was a lie. Killed a goddess. Killed *her.*

"Grim," she whispered, but the rushing in my ears drowned her out.

Gods. What had I done?

I gasped at the truth staring back at me across the abyss that opened in the cavity of my chest, next to the muted bond I shared with her.

"Grim!" she repeated, digging her fingers into my arms, and I dazedly realized that I was crushing her to me, clutching at her as if she were my only source of oxygen in the ever-tightening void closing around my mind.

I pushed her away—face-first down into the grass—but my cock was still inside her, and the squeeze of her muscles as she fell forward reawakened the roaring, mindless beast in me. I needed her. I needed her *right now,* or that void would swallow me and never let me go.

Annabel whimpered in protest when I fell on top of her, making her take more of my weight than was comfortable and hilting my cock in her depths once more.

I buried my face in her hair. "I need you. I *need* you, Annabel. Please... *Please!"*

She mewled when I rolled my hips, but it wasn't a sound of protest this time. It was *acceptance.*

Relief blasted through me, and I clung to her small body as I thrust into her, desperate to burn away that black void with her light. My magic burst through the barrier between us as I cried out her name.

She *was* light; light and love and everything warm, everything *good.* I lost myself within her, lost myself to the caress of her soul. I wanted to disappear within her and never emerge.

"Annabel. Annabel. Annabel!"

My knot swelled, yanking me back into myself with the tight burst of pleasure and Annabel's sharp cry as the physicality of our joining overtook us both once more.

I groaned as I came with everything I was, the sensation blissful beyond words. Beyond reason. I was blind to anything but my mate and her tight, fluttering pulses as she cried and coaxed every drop of seed from my body and into her own.

Utter stillness embraced me. Only shivers of phantom pleasure from where I was so intimately joined with my mate hummed underneath the silence. She was still too, underneath me, around me—one perfect moment of nothing but a quiet sensation of being *home.* Whole.

I love you.

It was only a thought—I didn't have the breath to voice it. One simple thread of awareness shared through our still-open bond, pulled from me without my conscious effort.

Annabel shuddered underneath me, and then... then the most awful sob broke from her lips, slicing through my pleasure and right to the marrow of my bones.

"Annabel," I whispered, panic and despair flushing away the last remnants of afterglow. "Don't cry. Please, don't."

My essence flowed through our bond and spilled into her of its own accord, every instinct in me yearning to find the cause of her distress and soothe it. What I found when I melded my soul with hers made shame clutch at my throat and rip at my lungs. She was crying because… I loved her. Because someone who truly loved her had doomed her to this existence, had ripped the last shred of hope from the world and killed a goddess so pure of heart she had begged Annabel to forgive me even as she lay dying.

"I'm sorry," I whispered as something deep in that black pit that was my soul shattered. I had thought I could make her Queen of Hel. I had taken this woman who embodied everything that was life and light, and I had doomed her to death and darkness. "I'm so sorry."

She shook her head, but in our bond I felt her emotions whirl: sorrow, despair, longing, pity. Fear. She *feared* me?

Loathing, I would have understood, but fear? "I won't hurt you. I can't," I rasped, willing her to understand. "Not like that, not… not physically. Not you. Never you."

"I know." Her voice was so tiny it made my heart shudder.

I clutched her closer to me and skimmed my lips over her bared shoulder. "Annabel," I murmured, not knowing what to say, how to put into words what I barely grasped through the horrible realization of what I'd done. "I... I am..." My voice died off as my gaze fell on her right hand sprawled over her lower abdomen.

For a moment, I thought she was simply pressing against where my knot forced her wide to ease some of the discomfort, but no. Her hand would have been lower for that.

Her touch was... so tender. Protective.

I trailed my hand down to brush against hers, and she trembled and held on tighter. Fear shot through our bond in a sharp spike before she willed it away. Yet her arm was stiff as she lay silent underneath me.

"You're... You're with... child?" It came out as a question, but I knew. With a bolt of clarity so bright it nearly blinded me, I knew why she feared me.

Nausea made me jerk up off her. She let out a cry of dismay when I pulled on our tie, and I forced myself to still, resting up on one elbow to stare down at her.

"You think.... You think I might *hurt* your baby?"

She didn't look back at me, but I saw her bite her lip and look down to where her hand still splayed on her soft skin. "Won't you? If it somehow hinders your plans, if there is risk... to me?"

I curled my lip. "I would *never* harm your baby, Annabel, never! I can't—"

My voice snuffed when the obvious hit me. I don't know why the realization wasn't immediate, but as I stared down at her hand, I remembered her heat—and the tantalizing scent of blood and woman a few weeks before that, when her period had come.

Not *her* child. Not Bjarni's or Modi's. Not Saga's. Not Magni's. *Our* child.

She was carrying... *our* child.

Distantly, I found some humor in how concerned I'd been with keeping her safe from those of Hel's creatures who would have gone to great lengths to sire offspring with she who could create life in the realm of death. Yet I had been the monster to impregnate her.

Ignoring her frozen muscles, I placed my hand on top of hers with firm pressure and buried my face in her hair. She carried a spark of *me*, of a man who had proven to her that there was nothing but darkness and horror in his veins.

No wonder she was scared.

We were both silent in the few minutes it took my knot to deflate. I forced my mind into blank nothingness, into that core of ice and mist, because I knew what I had to offer. What I owed her. Even if I couldn't bring myself to move my hand from hers until my knot finally released her.

I pulled out with a low groan, allowing her to sit up and pull her legs underneath her. My semen flowed from her swollen opening.

I forced my gaze to hers. "If you wish to terminate... I will help you. I can ensure it is painless."

Annabel's eyes widened, both hands immediately

fluttering to her abdomen. "What do you mean, *terminate?*"

"If you do not wish to keep... our child." It took everything I had to force those last two words out. "You do not have to. I can... take care of it. Safely."

Annabel stared uncomprehendingly at me for a full second. Then outrage and horror settled across her pretty features. "You are not *touching* this baby!" It was a snarl—fierce and underlined with the promise of violence. "I swear on everything there ever was and ever will be, Grim, if you try to harm her, I don't care what it'll do to me, nor the nine fucking worlds—I'll kill you!"

I drew in a shuddering breath as her words sank in. Her protective posture. The snarl curling her lip. The threat.

"You want to keep...?" I breathed in again. Something felt tight and light in my chest. Painful. "Any child I sire... will be like me."

She stared at me, still uncomprehending and her teeth bared, but uncertainty clouded her gaze. "What do you mean, *be like you?* Of course she will. She's half of you. I don't care if she's cold, or—"

Her voice died mid-sentence, and then grief, understanding, and empathy cracked her face into a pained grimace.

"Oh, Grim. No. No, no, no." She crawled to my side and cupped my face in her hands, those soul deep eyes searching mine. "Whatever you have done, whatever you have chosen to be... no. I do not fear the life we have created together. I want her with everything I am."

I stared at my mate, trying to comprehend that emotion laid bare in her eyes, but it seemed... almost impossible. Because what I saw there was something I never dreamed I could have had. I'd hardly known it existed, until her.

She would have given me a family—a true one. Someplace warm and safe and *mine.* She would have filled my life with love and my dark and fractured soul with peace. I stared at her, and I finally saw what I had not been capable of recognizing before.

Somehow, some way, I would have found the strength to share her with her other mates, because Annabel had enough love to give herself wholly to all of us. Even now, she still loved me. She couldn't help herself, though we both knew that I deserved nothing but her hatred.

But I had ruined everything. There would be no eternity of warmth and happiness—not for me and not for her. Only death and cold, dark regret.

I swallowed hard, trying to encapsulate the agony flaring through my mind and body as the full realization of what I'd done finally set in.

Annabel made a small noise, and then she pressed her soft, naked body against mine, trying to comfort me with her presence.

Even now, after everything I had robbed her of. Even now.

I wrapped my arms around her, loathing myself for accepting comfort that I did not deserve, buried my head in her hair, and clung to the woman I had betrayed so irrevocably.

"I'm sorry," I croaked into her tangled hair. It was only when cool, salty liquid touched my lips, that I realized I was crying. I hadn't cried since I was a child lost and alone with no one to care for my sorrows—not once in a thousand years. But I was now. For the future I had ruined. For the pain I had caused her.

For the love whose loss I hadn't fully understood the consequences of when I plunged my knife into Freya's heart and ripped it from the world for good.

Annabel didn't comment on my tears wetting her hair and cheek. She simply held me and rocked me gently, as if I were small and vulnerable. And in her arms, I allowed myself to be.

The agony took a long while to ease into dull anguish, but by the end, when my tears stopped and I had nothing left but regret and quiet sorrow, I placed one hand against her abdomen and stroked across it with a thumb.

"Her?" I asked, echoing how Annabel had spoken of our unborn child as she warned me of what would happen if I hurt the tiny life.

"Freya called her 'she,'" she replied, unwrapping one arm from my torso so she could place her palm on top of mine. "It's a girl."

A daughter.

I squeezed my eyes shut and pressed my forehead to Annabel's. *My* daughter, who would never know the kiss of the sun. Never know color. Or joy.

"I will give anything to undo what I have done. Anything." My words were quiet, solemn—and not meant for Annabel. She didn't need to hear me speak my regret, not when the bond between us was wide open and my dark essence mingled so entirely with her soft light. My plea was to the Fate I had done everything to break, to the weavers of destiny I had denied.

But it was through Annabel that they answered.

She let out a sharp gasp, her entire body jolting and going rigid in my arms a half-second before I felt it too. Warm, blinding sensation flared to life behind her ribs where only muted pain had been before, ricocheting through our connection and penetrating deep into my consciousness—her other mate bonds.

"They're here!" Annabel gasped, her eyes filling with desperation and hope so wild it took my breath away. "Grim, the others—they're here!"

22

BJARNI

Hel was as miserable as the stories suggested. Everything was gray and dull and dead—which I suppose shouldn't have come as a surprise, seeing as how this was the realm of death and all.

It could have been fire and pitchforks, for all I cared, because the second we stepped through that portal, the place next to my heart that had been so unbearably silent flared to life with a light far greater than any sun, and I knew we had finally found her.

"Hel's tits!" Magni spat by my side as he keeled over with his fist pressed to his chest.

"Maybe don't blaspheme the Queen of Hel in her own realm," Saga suggested, his tone dry despite the hand he was clutching to his own ribs. "She's a prickly bitch—you don't want to summon her attentions."

"Isn't she your sister?" Modi asked. He too was

rubbing at the spot his bond to Annabel had reawakened, but his gaze was on our surroundings, trying to work out the easiest route to follow the unrelenting tug from our mate's end of the connection. "Surely we should seek her out. She should be able to help us get Annabel back safely."

I choked out a laugh at the idea of willingly seeking out Hel. "Not everyone's blessed with sisters like yours, Thorsson. We don't exactly get together to play bridge with Jörmungandr and Fenris, and we're not going to draw Hel's attention anywhere near Annabel."

I shot the dark funnel clouds in the sky a long look. I'd never been to Hel before, but I recognized the soul siphon from stories of old. I shuddered before turning back to the others.

"She's likely too busy, ya know, raising her army of undead to raze the mortal world for family visits, anyway," Saga said, slanting a sardonic look Modi's way. "Maybe if we'd called ahead."

Thor's youngest son shot us both a dark glare, and I was sure his cheeks would have been tinged pink if Hel hadn't washed all color from his features. "Right. Fine. Then let's not waste any time dallying here. I can feel her—if we follow the bond, we should have no trouble finding her."

"Or Grim," Saga murmured, drumming his fingers against his chest.

I frowned as it dawned on me what he meant. I hadn't noticed it at first—the flare from finally feeling

Annabel again had been all-consuming—but right next to that glowing bond, in the same place I felt Saga, Modi, and Magni, a cool, dark shadow rested. Watchful. Reserved.

Grim.

I broke into a wide grin. "Well, whaddaya know? Our baby brother managed to claim our girl all on his own! I wasn't entirely sure if we'd have to give him pointers to get the deed done."

Despite my words, relief—and guilt—filled me. I hadn't had the capacity to worry too much over my brother's fate, not with Annabel missing and every cell of my being focused on how to retrieve her. But he'd been here all along, by her side.

Surprise flickered across both Modi's and Magni's faces as they too realized there was another presence within our connection.

"I heard a rumor that your brother's kind reproduces asexually. Quite a feat for him to claim a hotblooded woman," Magni said, and there was just a drop of malice in his voice as he gave his rib a final, irritated rub. He and Modi were clearly less thrilled than Saga and I at this new addition—probably about as much as Saga had been when he felt Modi claim our girl. They'd get over it fast enough.

"Ha," Saga said, his lips quirking up in a grin to match mine. "He wishes. You should have seen him when Annabel came to our farm and her scent was everywhere."

I chuckled at the memory of Grim's torment as he'd tried to control his body's response to the omega's budding heat—*complete* denial. "I'm sure their courting has been interesting. Let's get moving. Once we are all together again, we'll make him tell us all about it."

"He'll be thrilled to share, no doubt," Saga agreed, his devious smirk faltering as he stared in the direction we all felt Annabel's presence. As much fun as tormenting our younger brother with his new mating experience would be, it drowned in the wave of longing and desperation at being so close to her. There would be time for that and other recounts of what had happened while we'd been apart, but all that mattered for now was reuniting with our mate.

WE RAN through the barren landscape where we'd arrived and into the dense woodland. That bright glow pulled harder at us with every step, urging us forward, to hurry. We obeyed.

We had been running for maybe half a day and were jogging across a gray meadow when Modi rasped, "She's close."

He hadn't needed to voice it, because we all felt it—that overwhelming sense of her presence, as if everything was on the cusp of falling into place. Of finally being right again.

And then there she was, bursting through the trees ahead of us like a wild spirit.

She gave a shriek and sprinted at us, and my heart thumped so hard it sounded like a drum in my ears as the four of us raced to close the gap.

Magni reached her a fraction of an inch before the rest of us. He yanked her into his embrace, but we crowded them, every one of us reaching for her. *Our mate.* She was here.

"Annabel," Saga groaned as he pressed desperate kisses to her shoulders and neck. "Gods, sweetling."

"We feared... We feared you were lost forever," Modi choked as she stroked a hand through his hair and cupped his cheek.

And there it was, that uncurling sense of relief as I muscled my way through my brothers' wide shoulders to clasp onto my small, soft center of existence. I would never have given up on searching for her—never—but we had all feared the worst.

"I've missed you every second of every day," I said as I tugged her against me, forcing the others closer as they refused to release their holds on her. I buried my nose in her messy hair and inhaled deeply, but her beautiful scent didn't fill my nostrils like it should have. Frowning, I pulled back to look at her.

Her usually flushed skin was grayed like the rest of ours, and I missed the rich chocolate of her eyes even as my soul slid into place when I looked into them. She smiled at me, making them crinkle at the corners.

"I missed you too. So much. Every one of you—"

I didn't let her finish the sentence, but she didn't seem to mind my lips covering hers—she kissed me back until my heart sang.

Modi pulled her mouth from mine to claim her for himself, and I gave an irritated growl and dug my fingers into the swell of her hips to ensure he didn't attempt to pull her body from me as well. We were a violent ocean of need and yearning, and Annabel the rocky island caught in our maelstrom. Not that she seemed to mind. She cooed and kissed and touched us all, sobbing, "You came," in between our frantic claimings of her mouth.

"Of course we came," Magni whispered as he rubbed his bearded cheek over her skull. "We'll always come for you, mate. Always."

I rumbled my agreement, but a flutter of sensation finally managed to pull my attention from the fogged bliss of reuniting with my beloved. It was cool and dark—just a muted whisper from the same place my pair bond was attached. It came *through* it—from her. I looked up with a frown and saw Grim hovering a few feet away.

I broke into a wide grin at the sight of him—and then at the head tucked under his arm. "You found Mimir! Brother, you did it!"

The others looked up at my call and toward our youngest brother.

"Grim!" Saga said with a relieved smile. "Congratulations are in order, I believe. And... gratitude. You followed our mate and protected her when we could not."

Grim didn't return our greetings. His face was as carved from stone as he stared at us. When I looked closer, I noticed his fists were clenched tight. I frowned and prodded at the connection I shared with him through Annabel, but got no response.

"Grim," Annabel said, her voice as soft as if she were coaxing a wild animal. She freed one arm and reached out toward him. "Come."

He hesitated, even if I saw the tremble in his muscles to obey his mate's request for his nearness.

"Go to them," the prophet under his arm murmured. "It is the only way to correct your course, grim one."

Grim shot Mimir a glare, then dropped him on the ground none too gently and stalked to us to clasp Annabel's outstretched hand.

A shiver went through all of us—a current of awareness and a sense of... something akin to completion I couldn't quite put my finger on. I didn't need to. I grinned again and released Annabel with one hand to clap Grim on the shoulder.

"It's good to see you too, brother," I said.

He only gave me a dark look, and despite the stony planes of his pale face, the glare in his mismatched eyes raised the small hairs on my body. He was... angry.

I prodded at that connection between us again and

found it still blocked. Where I felt the three other men I shared Annabel with open and flowing through her like a warm current, the place where Grim was supposed to meet us was nothing but that slight sensation of chilly darkness.

"What's the matter with you? Did we drop in at an inopportune time?" I asked, eyebrows raised at my brother's dour face.

"Leave him be, Bjarni," Annabel murmured, reaching up to give my beard a chiding tug before she refocused on Grim. "It's okay, baby. Stay here with me. I need you. I love you. And so do they."

Baby? I opened my mouth to mock my mate's chosen pet name for my surly brother, but—somewhat to my surprise—Modi gave me a shake of his head, his eyes blazing a warning to stay quiet.

I frowned deeper and took in the scene. Magni and Saga were staring intently at Grim, both their eyebrows bunched. Only Annabel still smiled, and it was softer than it'd been just moments ago. Gentler. She didn't take her eyes off Grim as she murmured soothing words of love and devotion.

And Grim... I sucked in a deep breath at the tortured look in his eyes mixed with volatile rage, and a love so intense it echoed deep in my own devotion to Annabel.

It took me several more moments than it seemingly had my brothers, but it finally dawned on me when Grim took a shuddering breath and closed his eyes, reluctantly allowing Annabel to draw him into our circle of twined limbs and bodies.

He was fighting tooth and nail to keep genuine rage in check. Rage that we—his brothers—were touching the woman he considered *his.*

Grim was not happy to see us. And, I suspected as I regarded his stiff shoulders warily, was very much wanting to fight each and every one of us, rather than relax in our midst.

I gave a snort, half of amusement, half of disbelief. *Grim,* of all people, was the one to go primitive idiot over this arrangement? I'd felt that kernel of demented jealousy too—we all had in the beginning—but even Saga and Magni hadn't looked quite as murderous as my darkhaired brother currently did, even with his eyes closed and his face pressed to Annabel's cheek.

Grim, who had tried everything to persuade Saga and me not to send for her in the first place, and who'd been a grouchy prick around her from day one, now pressed himself to her as if she were his only reason for living. Which she was. She was that for all of us.

I shifted and managed to wrap my arm not clutching at Annabel around Grim's shoulders, pulling him in tight against both mine and Modi by my sides, without tugging him away from Annabel.

Mismatched eyes flew open, and a warning snarl rumbled out of his throat.

"Bjarni, don't," Annabel warned. I only gave her a reassuring squeeze in response.

"It gets easier. I promise," I said to my brother, offering nothing but a wry smile in the face of the threat of violence he snarled my way. And then I purred.

"Oh," Annabel breathed, and I turned my head just in time to see her eyelids flutter closed. Our bond hummed blissfully in my chest, and I nuzzled at her hair as she relaxed between us.

Another rumbling purr broke from my side as Modi followed my example. Annabel made a small mewling sound of pleasure, and again when Saga and Magni joined us.

Only Grim remained quiet as we surrounded our mate with the reassuring comfort of our purring embrace. He was a silent, cold presence of darkness in our midst, his anger nearly palpable even if we still couldn't feel him through her bond. But he didn't lash out with either of those nasty daggers he carried, nor his powerful magic. Judging from his enraged expression and the tremor of his tight muscles, that was as much as we could hope for.

I squeezed him tighter to me and purred all the louder, eternally grateful that he was here with us anyway. Our fifth brother.

23

GRIM

I wanted to *kill* them. Every cell in my body throbbed with red-hot fire as the four alphas pawed at my mate, *kissed* her and murmured possessive words of devotion. Only Annabel's unwavering hold on my hand kept me grounded enough to remember my vow: I *would* give anything to undo what I had done—the future I had doomed our daughter to.

Even allowing these men to *touch* her.

The purring... helped. A *little.* As much as I fantasized about ripping Magni's fingers off one by one as he curved them around one of Annabel's breasts, it was as smidge easier to resist with the unwavering rumble vibrating through my body, even if I wasn't its creator. I wasn't even sure if I *could* purr. I'd never had the inclination, not even with Annabel in my arms, but my instincts responded to its promise of peace and comfort.

My brain... not so much.

Annabel, on the other hand, was a blissed-out puddle. She gave me a somewhat dazed smile that pulled on that soft, fragile thing she'd planted in my chest when we mated. *See?* her eyes seemed to say. *You can do this.*

I still hadn't unclenched my fists, and I doubted I would for a very long time. But yes, I… I could do this. For her. If only because it was so obvious that she was truly happy now—that even the moments of joy she had shared with me had been incomplete without them.

I wanted her happy. I could do this. Somehow.

It took well over an hour before the purring softened and then, one by one, quieted.

"We should get back," Saga said, even as he continued to stare at Annabel with a soft, goofy smile that made my fists itch to make contact with his face. "We can continue this when we are safe."

The way he said *this,* and that gleam in his eyes as he said it, made a warning snarl rumble again from my chest.

My brother only gave a me a patient look before he gazed across the meadow.

"Magga and Arni didn't say what you needed from us to get home, sweetling. Do you know the way? Is it close?"

"Oh." Annabel grimaced, and from the flustered look on her face, I suspected she was blushing. "It's… um… We all need to… Freya said I need to, uh, join with all of you. To be strong enough."

Magni broke into a wide grin. "I adore that woman and her take on magic." Then his smile faded. "It is true, then? The Goddess of Love has been taken to Hel? Trud suggested as much, but..."

"We will bring her back with us," Modi said, steel in his voice. "We are not leaving one of our own in this place. And she may be able to help us capture Loki."

Annabel gave me a long look, and some of my fury softened as shame welled from that festering place in my gut. Apparently Arni and Magga hadn't told them everything that had happened here.

"Freya is gone," Annabel said. Even though her voice was soft, every one of her mates jerked their heads to stare at her.

"What do you mean *gone?*" Bjarni asked.

She shook her head and drew a deep breath. "She died, and her soul got sucked into... that thing." She gestured toward the siphon in the sky.

All four alphas hissed.

"No!"

"How?"

"She is the Goddess of Love! She can't be gone!"

I tensed my shoulders, preparing for the weight of their disgust, but Annabel shook her head.

"She is, and nothing we can do will change that. We can only attempt to honor her sacrifice by escaping this damned place so we can stop Ragnarök."

"How did she die?" Bjarni asked.

"I can't talk about that," Annabel said softly, brushing the hand she wasn't holding mine with through his beard. "Please don't ask me to tell you. Not... Not yet."

He nodded and pressed his cheek against her palm, closing his eyes at the sensation of her touch. "As you wish, my sweet one."

"Thank you," she murmured, a small smile tugging on her lips at his obvious tenderness. Bjarni had always been open with his emotions, and that hadn't changed with Annabel's arrival. He loved her so easily and so openly, I wasn't surprised at the devotion in my mate's eyes as she looked at him.

Jealousy seethed like a poison in my veins.

As if she sensed it despite the wall I'd slammed back in place between us, Annabel squeezed my fingers, a silent reminder that she loved me too.

My heart pulsed, and I closed my eyes to control the maelstrom of emotions threatening to tear me open again. I wasn't sure if she refused to talk about what happened to Freya to protect me, or to protect the union she needed between the six of us to have a chance to free herself from Hel. Perhaps it was both. But one day, they would learn the truth of what I'd done—to the goddess and to Annabel.

"So," Saga said, visibly steeling himself against the devastation Freya's death had brought them all. "She told you that to flee from Hel, we need to channel our magic together like we did when we healed Magni?"

Magni huffed and glared at my brother. Bjarni gave me a slanted grin—one I didn't return. He was endlessly amused by the predicament we had found Saga and Magni in when we'd arrived in Freya's hall, locked in a far more intimate embrace than either would have ever voluntarily shared. For me, though, the memory of them sharing my mate so roughly only made the fury resurface.

"Will *someone* tell me what happened?" Modi asked, irritation lacing his words. "It can't be worse than what we *all* did in Valhalla."

"It doesn't matter," Annabel snapped, embarrassment making her tone curt. "I'm sure we don't need to do *that*. But... Well, we all know what she meant by *joining*. It's the only way for me to meld our powers and make us strong enough to face down Hel."

"I'm sorry, pet—I could have sworn you said *face down Hel?*" Magni asked. His eyebrows rose nearly to his hairline. "But you are not insane, so I must have misheard."

"It is the only remaining way," Mimir said.

We all turned to him—we'd entirely forgotten him in the midst of the reunion. He didn't so much as glance at me as he continued. "We have exhausted all other avenues. To save your mate from the depths of Hel, the Queen of Death will have to release her."

"That's why I needed you here," Annabel said as the four of them blinked in stunned silence. "If I am not strong enough, she will just..." She trailed off with a glance at the churning funnel cloud.

A shudder went through the four and echoed through my bones. The thought of Annabel's soul lost to Hel's siphon was sickening.

"Once we are out of this place, I am going to find Loki and murder him," Modi growled.

"Loki isn't behind this," Annabel said, finally ready to divulge the identity of the Betrayer. "It is... someone else. I don't know who, but it's not Loki."

"How can you be so sure, then?" Saga asked with a frown. "He disappeared when you and Grim did. We all assumed he took you when you went to free him."

Annabel glanced at me before she looked to Mimir. "Whoever is behind my kidnapping took Mimir too. Before me. He is under some sort of binding spell, but... It is not Loki, that much they have been able to confirm."

"They?" Bjarni asked.

"He," Annabel corrected with a small grimace. "Right, prophet?"

"I am afraid I cannot provide further detail," Mimir agreed.

"It's not important. Not now," I interjected. "Nothing else matters until we have escaped this place."

Saga gave me a long, evaluating look that I pretended I didn't see before he returned his focus to Annabel. "Right. So if there is but one path, there is no point in arguing or delaying. Do you know of a safe location? I don't want to be surprised by whatever creatures roam these lands while I'm knot-deep in my mate."

"Aren't you romantic?" Annabel grumbled, earning a chuckle from Bjarni.

"Freya's glade is half a day from here. It is... as safe a place as can exist here." It took everything I had to get the words out. The thought of what would have to happen once there filled my veins with acid and my gut with lead. I had no idea how I would survive watching them with her—how *they* would survive. But I had to find a way.

"It will also take us closer to Hel's residence," Mimir agreed. "Very well. Back to Freya's glade."

Modi swooped in and placed a kiss on Annabel's lips. He lingered for a moment, and I saw the heat in his eyes before he turned away to grab Mimir. "Lead the way, prophet."

We fell in behind Thor's youngest son, but before we'd walked many paces, Saga tapped me on the shoulder and jerked his head at me.

I hesitated, my fingers as reluctant to release Annabel's as my heart was to leave her side. But the seriousness in my brother's gaze made me let go and fall back with him. Bjarni immediately swooped in and looped his arm around Annabel's shoulder, crowding her against Magni on her other side.

"What?" I snapped, the view of my mate giggling

between the two alphas doing nothing to ease the churn of jealousy.

"You have been gone for some time, brother. I wish to know all that has happened," he said, a careful note to his voice. "How you came to this place."

"I can only tell you so much," I said, forcing the pounding rage in my temples down. "I too am under a binding spell."

"You… You know who did this to you? Who is behind it?"

I nodded, the threatening swell in my throat from the blasted spell keeping me silent.

Saga was quiet for a long while, and I felt his gaze on me as he mulled over his next question.

"Do we have a chance, brother?" he finally asked, quietly enough that the others wouldn't hear. "I felt the strength of whoever it is. During the trials to pass through to Asgard from Jotunheim, it was… like facing off against the cosmos. I have never seen anything so powerful. I know Annabel is strong, and that the prophecy claims we can, but… I worry."

I closed my eyes to steel myself. No. We did not have a chance; I had made my bargain because I understood as much. But it didn't matter anymore.

"We will succeed," I said quietly. "Because if we don't, Annabel will die. And this place… It is not for her."

Saga nodded, and from the draw of his mouth, I knew he understood both that what we would face was too powerful to overcome, but that we had to do it regardless. For her. "And you? Will you be able to do what must be done?"

I gave him a glare.

"Don't look at me like that. I don't question your strength," he said, raising both hands.

"Then what do you question?"

"Your ability to share her." He nodded toward Annabel. "I don't know what you're doing to your pair bond to keep it muted from us, but you really don't need to. It's written all over your face. You want her for yourself. But this prophecy—we *have* to share her, willingly, or we don't stand a chance."

I gritted my teeth against the reemerging throbbing in my temple. "Willingly? Is that how you share her with the Thorssons?"

Saga chuckled. "Well—now, yes, though perhaps not at first. But there is... peace in surrendering to this fate of ours. A brotherhood. Love. I want that for you, Grim. I know you were never keen on claiming her in the first place. Frankly, I was expecting to have to lock you in a room with her during her heat and just hope your instincts would kick in.

"But you've claimed her now. You know how deep this bond goes. How all-consuming it is. That is what we all share, this unexpected and volatile *thing*. You are not alone with it. We are here with you. The sooner you surrender to our connection, the sooner you'll stop picturing our heads smashed in."

I scoffed. *Surrender.* He had no idea. I *had* surrendered, or I wouldn't just be picturing their heads bashed in and their lifeless corpses littering the ground. I had surrendered everything I was and everything I ever would be, for *her*.

"When did you know you loved her?" he asked softly.

I pressed my lips into a thin line and kept my eyes on Annabel.

"Grim. You have to open up, or this won't work. You can't keep shielding yourself like this. No one is going to make fun of you. We all love her the same," Saga sighed. He clapped a hand on my shoulder and gave it a squeeze that was possibly meant to be comforting.

I jerked away from his touch and swiveled toward him. My brother, the man I had given everything to save —as I looked at him now, every muscle in my body *ached* to grab my daggers and slice his throat open. Judging from his wide-eyed stare, my thoughts were painted clearly on my face.

"No. We do not love her *the same,*" I hissed, low enough not to draw the others' attention. "She is my *soul*, Saga. I do not fear *mockery*. I am not a child. And I do not simply picture your heads smashed in. I am fighting with everything I have not to rip the four of you to shreds. Do I make myself clear? I want you dead. All of you. Every time you touch her, I want to snap you into bloody, broken pieces, because *she* is *mine*.

"Do not *question* me, *brother*. Do not push me. You

do not want to see what I am keeping from you, why I am muting my pair-bond. I will do what I must to save her, but I will not be part of your *brotherhood*. I cannot."

Without another look at my stunned brother, I stalked up ahead, past Magni, Bjarni, and Annabel, then past Modi and Mimir, taking up the lead.

None of them would ever understand. Their love for Annabel was easy and bright. Mine was dark. Possessive. Brutal.

And I had no idea how I was going to survive watching them take her.

24

GRIM

Freya's glade was as quiet and serene as we had left it. The trees surrounding it still wept—a trait that greatly disturbed Bjarni—but no monsters lurked nearby. There was still a mark in the grass where Annabel and I had lain together only hours ago.

I stared at it, remembering everything that had happened between us in that spot. I had sworn I would give anything to undo what I had done. Fate had taken me up on my bargain. I was going to get through this, even if it broke me.

"I love you," Annabel said softly.

I turned around to face her, and was greeted with her beautiful face and the barest hint of a smile. She trailed her hand up my chest and cupped my cheek. "It'll be okay. I promise."

Silently I pressed my cheek into her palm. There was no point in answering.

"Come," she said, taking my hand. I let her, but when I looked up, I saw her four other alphas standing a few yards away. Watching us. Waiting. For her.

Dark ice clutched at my lungs. My fingers tightened around hers as I stood frozen to the spot. *Willingly.* I was supposed to give her to them *willingly*? My mate. *Mine.*

I wasn't in control of the low snarl that rumbled out of my throat.

"Grim," Annabel whispered. She moved closer to me, pressing herself tight against my body as her eyes sought mine. "You can do this, baby. For our daughter."

Our daughter. Our little spark of life who would never see the sun if I didn't go through with this.

I let my free hand slide over Annabel's abdomen before I drew in a breath and nodded. It was as much acceptance as I could muster, but it was enough.

Annabel pressed a kiss to my chest and pulled away. Without releasing her grip on my hand, she turned back around and led me to the others.

"We're ready," she said, giving Bjarni a chuckle when he lit up in a wide grin filled with easy excitement and just a touch of heat.

"It's been *weeks,*" my brother huffed at Annabel's amusement. "If you didn't want me desperate, you shouldn't have gotten yourself kidnapped, sweetie."

"Man has a point," Magni added as he sauntered a step closer. "Even in Hel you make my body yearn, pet."

"Take it slow," Saga warned. He was the only one of them who was looking at me rather than our mate, and he wasn't trying to hide the fact that he was evaluating me, gauging the probability of me making good on my threats.

"If we can share her nicely, so can he," Modi said, impatience coloring his voice. "No one went slow the last time we did this."

"You and Bjarni weren't exactly *nice* about anything at the beginning," Annabel reminded him, her tone sharp. "And neither were Saga and Magni. Give him some space."

"He's had weeks by your side," Magni protested. "*Weeks.* You don't know how bad it's been, Annabel. I wanted to claw through my own chest every single second of every single day—we all did. I want to tell you how much we've missed you, but that word simply isn't enough to explain..." He trailed off with a grimace as he touched his ribs.

Annabel took a step forward and placed the hand she didn't have clutched in mine against his chest.

"I do know," she said. "When it looked like I would never be able to return, I couldn't bear the thought of never seeing you again. I need you too, Magni. I'm aching for you. But we need to take care of each other, and right now, Grim is struggling. So please, be gentle with him."

I swallowed a growl and returned Magni's irritated glare. I didn't need any of them to be *gentle* with me. I needed him to get his hands off my mate.

Annabel patted Magni's chest, drawing his attention from me back to her. She raised up on her tiptoes and planted a kiss on his lips that he quickly returned, humming with pleasure.

Anger churned in my gut at the sight of them, but before I could lose myself in it, Annabel pulled on my hand, urging me closer.

Hesitantly I obeyed, until I pressed up against her back.

"Closer, Grim," Annabel groaned between kisses. "I need you closer."

I obliged her—I could never deny her my body—and she hummed a happy note as the curve of her ass pressed tight against me and I buried my head in her hair. My hands slipped from hers to her hips, anchoring us both with my grip.

This felt... better. My fury still roiled under the surface, hot and bitter, but Annabel's closeness kept it in check.

I breathed in against the side of her neck and wished I could smell her before I rubbed my nose along the tendon there, drawing goosebumps along her skin.

Annabel moaned into Magni's mouth and moved her hips against me, drawing my attention to my already rock-hard dick. How did she *do* this? How did she make me yearn to be inside her even when she was surrounded by other alphas?

I pushed my contemplations aside and allowed myself to drown in the pulse of desire—forced my mind to focus on nothing but the feeling of my mate against my body and how much I needed her to sate me.

Soft footfalls drew nearer, and through my haze of ever-growing lust, I sensed the others surround us. Hands reached out, touched her, brushed against me in a soothing caress before someone pulled her armor off, letting her breasts spill free.

I drew my hands up from her hips to grab them both, groaning against Annabel's neck at the soft sensation of them filling my palms.

In front of her, Magni bent and wrapped his lips around one of her nipples, drawing a shuddering gasp from Annabel.

I snarled, fury rising through the haze at the fact he thought I was offering him her breasts, but Annabel reached back to clutch at my hip, returning my attention to her.

"It feels... feels good, baby," she moaned. "You want the other?"

"*All* of you is mine," I reminded her roughly, earning me a warning growl from someone else—Modi, it sounded like.

"The lady asked you to suck on her tits. If you don't, brother, I will," Bjarni rasped by my side.

"Please, Grim," Annabel urged, arching back against me. "I need you to suck me."

I grunted at the plea—somehow I suspected she

knew I could never deny her when she begged me so sweetly. I shifted, moving to her front where Magni was still playing with her left breast, seemingly oblivious to my presence. I bent my head next to his and latched on to her right nipple.

"Ooh, *Grim!*" Annabel gasped. She laced her fingers through my hair and tightened, clutching me to her breast as if she feared I would let go.

I sucked her nipple deeper into my mouth and earned another gasp from my mate. Nothing felt like this. Sucking and licking her tight nipples was an intensely sexual sensation, heightened by Annabel's audible pleasure, but there was something else too—something primal that lulled my darkness and soothed my anger with every pull. I pushed the thought away, disinclined to pursue the origins of that warm sensation of comfort and safety I found at her breast.

Bjarni stepped up behind her, pulling her tight to his body and nuzzling at her neck with a low rumble.

Annabel whimpered and clutched harder at me and Magni, but when I let my fingers slide down to the apex of her thighs to give her more stimulation, I brushed over Bjarni's hands deftly undoing her pants. I growled a low threat at his uninvited presence.

"We can fight over who gets first taste of her pussy later," Bjarni said mildly, not pausing as he opened her pants and yanked them down over her hips. "Help me bare her."

"I've got her," Modi said. He stepped between me

and Magni and knelt, then looked up at Annabel. There was worship in his eyes as he slowly pulled her pants all the way down her legs and off. It made me feel... uneasy to see an old enemy so open, and I refocused my attention back on the plump breast in my mouth, teasing the tip of its pert nipple with my tongue.

My mate moaned sweetly, her eyes flickering to mine. The hazy glow of desire in them was achingly familiar by now, and I forgot about the others and held her gaze as I sucked her hard.

Annabel squeezed her eyes shut and groaned, digging her fingers into my scalp, only to yank savagely the next second when her eyes flew back open and she let out a keening wail.

"Fuck! *Modi!*" she cried, her gaze moving down. A fine tremor played across her features before she threw her head back against Bjarni's chest. "Yes! Yes! More!"

I pulled back from her head and looked down at what had caught her attention so thoroughly. Modi was still kneeling between her thighs, his mouth now firmly pressed to her small sex. From the hollowing of his cheeks, I could only assume he was giving her clit as much attention as I had been her nipple.

Something hot and uncomfortable crept up through my chest as I watched Thor's son pleasure my mate—some ungodly mix of seething jealousy, scalding desire, and deep, dark despair.

I had never pleasured her like that. I'd wanted to when she was in heat, and the scent of it had overwhelmed my senses and begged me to bury my mouth between her thighs until her flavor filled me. But I hadn't.

I didn't think of *her* much, when I was with Annabel. Sex with my mate was nothing like it had been when it was forced upon me by someone I despised. I loved every second of being entangled with my mate. Even the terrifying intimacy when the pleasure of it overwhelmed my inner resistance and our souls merged felt like nothing else ever could. And yet that one thing, that one way of giving her pleasure, I hadn't undertaken.

I stumbled back a few steps as I stared at Modi licking and sucking at Annabel's clit so thoroughly, she seemed to be incapable of coherent thought while she writhed between the three alphas. The hand that had held me tight to her breast now clutched at Modi's hair, urging him deeper, and *he*... His eyes were closed, and sheer revelry was written across the planes of his face. He loved it just as much as she did, that much was clear.

A hand clasped onto my shoulder, making me jolt and snap my head around to glare at Saga.

My brother didn't release his grip, despite my bared teeth. He only gave me a long, searching look, as if he understood that *something* about watching Annabel ride Modi's tongue made my lungs tighten, a pit of despair opening in my gut.

"Lay her down," he said to the others, moving his attention back to them and Annabel in their midst.

They moved as one, easily shifting her down onto the grass. Bjarni knelt by her head, stroking her face while freeing his cock with his other hand. Magni was still busy with her left breast and Modi sprawled on the grass between her thighs, clutching at them as he licked the full length of her slit before refocusing on her clit. I couldn't take my eyes off him, couldn't shut out his groans of pleasure as our mate ground against him with increasingly frantic gasps.

"That's my girl," Bjarni rumbled as he petted her hair and stroked his thick cock. He grabbed her arm and pulled her resistant hand from Magni's head to his own bobbing erection. "Let it come."

Annabel wrapped her hand around him seemingly on instinct. Her movements on his cock were jerky and erratic, most of her focus still on Modi's tongue, but Bjarni still hissed with pleasure.

"Gods, yes!" He arched and wrapped one hand around hers, guiding her movements over his pulsing flesh. With the other, he reached for Magni. Thor's bastard looked up at my brother's touch, but instead of pulling away like I had half-expected, or even snarling out a warning, Magni threaded his fingers through Bjarni's and held on tight.

"I'm... I'm...!" Annabel's voice, high-pitched and desperate, broke on a moan as her body arced into a tight bow. I sensed the wave of pleasure roaring through her as it crashed against the barrier in our bond.

She collapsed back onto the grass with a sated sigh

and smiled down at Modi. He gave her a few more licks before he returned her gaze with a grin.

“Missed you, Anna,” he murmured, voice raw from his own pent-up desire.

“I missed you too,” she whispered, her smile fading as she stroked the hand not wrapped around Bjarni through his hair, as if she were sharing that moment only with him.

My gut clenched as the dark thing in me welled up. All I saw was another man between my mate’s thighs. In my mate’s heart.

“Snap out of it!” Saga hissed. He shook my shoulder hard, and I realized the darkness was welling out of me in a threatening cloud of power. I was seconds from surrounding Modi with it and squeezing until he was gone.

But if I did that, if I killed him, Annabel would die too.

Growling with the effort, I pulled my magic back inside of me. It thrashed against my restraint, volatile and furious, and I tightened my grip on it, willing it into submission—even if every cell in my body ached to unleash it on the alphas who dared touch my Annabel.

Saga gave me another long look. Then he shifted his grip from my shoulder to my hand and yanked me forward a few steps.

“Get up, Thorsson. It’s our turn to make her moan,” he said.

Modi gave him a frustrated look over his shoulder. "You can do that after I'm done."

"Don't be greedy," Magni chided, nudging him with a knee.

Modi bared his teeth at his brother, but Annabel stroked her hand down his face to cup his chin, regaining his focus. "I will need you just as much later as I do now. I will never stop needing you, Modi."

It dawned on me then, through my own seething jealousy and darkness, that I wasn't the only one struggling with this. Only Modi didn't so much as attempt to hide the vulnerability in his eyes as he sought Annabel's gaze, searching for the truth in her words. He sighed softly as he found it and bent his head to place a final kiss to her nether lips before he pushed off the ground, relinquishing his place between her splayed thighs.

"Come," Saga said to me. He pulled me forward, leading me to that sacred space.

I stared down at Annabel's glistening sex. Even though I couldn't scent her arousal, it was evident in the slick sheen clinging to her puffy lips, in her soft gasps as Magni returned his focus to her breast, and in the tremble running the length of her legs as Saga knelt by her waist. He brushed his hand through her dark thatch of pubic hair before he pinched the hood of her clit and pulled it back, fully exposing her already swollen nub.

"Come, brother. Your mate needs you too," he said, his voice soft—cajoling.

I fell to my knees as if someone had snipped the thin thread keeping me upright. The darkness rushed in my ears, drowning out everything but my own ragged breathing and the too-fast beat of my pulse. Instincts pounded at my brain, every alpha cell in my body desperate to bury my mouth there and force that bared little clit of hers to climax. I wanted to—I wanted to so badly it hurt—but I sat frozen, incapable of doing what my mate needed me to do.

"Grim."

Annabel's voice broke through the rushing in my ears. I jerked my head up, catching her gaze. She sat up, ignoring the growls of annoyance from Bjarni and Magni, and cupped my face with both hands, ensuring I saw nothing but her.

"You don't have to do that, Grim. I need *you.* You pleasure me in so many ways. This does not have to be one of them."

She understood; I knew that as I read the sorrow in her eyes. I hadn't been explicit about this part, about what had happened when I had been made to bed my stepmother, but I didn't need to.

I bared my teeth around a snarl. It had been a thousand years and she *still* took from me. From Annabel.

No. *No.* I would not let her do this, would not let her ruin how I pleasured my mate.

I grabbed Annabel by the shoulders and pushed her back down on her back before I refocused on her eager pussy.

Saga reached down again and pulled her hood up once more, baring her clit. But instead of waiting for me, he bent to give her a flick of his own tongue.

"Ah, shit!" Annabel jumped and tensed at the teasing caress, and her clit throbbed in response.

Saga rolled his eyes up to meet mine. There was a challenge in them, egging me on, but also...

I frowned at him as it dawned on me—he thought I didn't know how to do it. He was trying to *help* me.

"I don't need a guide," I growled at him. He only lifted his eyebrows and waited, and I huffed, then bent to swipe my tongue over Annabel's exposed sex.

My mate jumped again and hissed. One hand fluttered down to rest on my head, but despite the tremor in her muscles, she didn't yank me closer.

I let the tip of my tongue draw a light circle around her clit and was rewarded with a throaty moan. Gods, if only I could have smelled her. My head throbbed and my dick ached. The rushing in my ears was back, but there was no hesitance left. This was Annabel, my mate, and I wanted to devour her.

I opened my mouth and dug my tongue between her folds, sucking her in until she writhed for me and chanted my name over and over.

I pulled back, wanting to see her face, but as I did, Saga dove down to replace my tongue on her clit.

"Saga!" Annabel whimpered, shifting her grip from my hair to his. Her other hand was once again preoccupied with Bjarni's thick cock.

I glared down at my brother. As if he sensed my anger, he looked up at me and shot me a provoking grin before tilting his head to the side, offering me space without moving away.

I stared down at him until he turned his attention back to Annabel's pussy, licking teasingly on the right side of her clit and leaving the left for me.

"Please... Please!" Annabel gasped. I wasn't sure if she was begging me or him, but the sound of her pleas pulled me down to her center—to that part of her that had brought me to my knees.

When I swiped my tongue along the left side of her clit, she whimpered and tensed, tugging harshly at my scalp. The pressure was gone the next second, and from the way Bjarni expelled a breath, I knew her fingers were now wrapped around his cock. Ignoring him—ignoring everyone but *her*—I focused on the little pleasure bud under my tongue.

I didn't need her hand in my hair to guide me. It was easy to read her writhing, easy to follow the squirm of her hips to lick her just how she needed it. I didn't care that my efforts made my tongue dance with Saga's, only growling warnings at him when he became too greedy and encroached on my territory—I only cared that this was my mate, my *home,* and every cell in my body throbbed with need to show her how much I loved her.

"Please suck me, please! Suck me!" Annabel's plea held an edge of desperation, one I knew well. I released my grip on her hips to shove Saga away, ignoring his snarled protest, and finally wrapped my lips around her pert little clit. And then I sucked it.

Annabel keened and bucked hard, but I re-anchored myself on her hips and suckled her like I had her breasts so many times before. Finally she arched for me, practically levitating, and froze.

I barely heard her through the rushing of blood in my ears. My mouth filled with her climax, smearing my lips and chin, and even though it lacked her beautiful scent, it still went straight to my dick, making me ache to bury myself between her quivering thighs.

But I couldn't. Not yet. I had to give her this first.

Sucking ever gentler, I stayed on her clit as Annabel writhed and came for me, and when the longing to be inside her became too great, I thrust to fingers into her fluttering sheath and curved them after that secret spot inside.

My mate's wail took on another tone, and she ground herself against my face as I forced her into a second climax. Only when her body's spasms had eased into gentle trembles did I back off her swollen bud and slip my fingers from her wet inners, lifting up to look at her. *My mate.*

Her gaze was hazy with exhaustion as it met mine, but that curve of a smile gracing her soft lips made my heart tremble. *Gratitude.* Gratitude and love were in that curve.

I didn't break eye contact as I raised fully onto my

knees, grabbed her left leg to slide it over my hip, and drove myself inside of her.

Annabel gasped and tensed, her eyelids fluttering shut for a second at the strain of taking me. But when she opened her eyes again, nothing but love and desire shone back at me.

"Who gave you permission to go first, Lokisson?" Modi growled from somewhere outside the haze of bliss shuddering through me at Annabel's slick embrace.

"Don't fight. Please. Don't fight," Annabel gasped, her words turning to a moan as I gently pulled myself halfway out of her, making her pussy cling to my girth. "I'm… I'm here for all of you. *Oh*. I promise. Oh, *God!*"

"I'll remind you of that," he said, a richer note to his growl this time as he took her hand and wrapped her fingers around his thick, throbbing cock. "Because I have every intention of catching up on every night we've missed, Anna."

"Yes," she whimpered, and I wasn't sure if it was in response to him, or to the slide of my cock filling her to the brim once more. I didn't much care either way.

I barreled into her, losing the will to stay gentle, and groaned with her every time I hammered home. Pleasure fizzled up my spine, down my thighs, and deep into my pelvis, and I knew I would forever lose myself here, watching her come undone while she clutched Bjarni's and Modi's dicks, with Saga and Magni sucking her nipples and heightening the pleasure I was stoking.

A soft caress against the wall in our bond made me

shudder, the rough rhythm of my hips stuttering at the intimate touch. I knew what she wanted, but even through the pleasurable haze of sex, even through my instincts roaring to unite myself with her in every way possible, I resisted.

"Please, Grim," Annabel moaned. "I need you. I need you… everywhere. Inside me. Please."

I bared my teeth and growled a curse in response, never slowing my thrusts even as my inner barrier threatened to give way. How could she do this? How could her pleas make me fall to my knees and surrender myself in every way?

"I don't… want—"

My panted protest died on a grunt as her muscles squeezed me.

"You're safe," she gasped, blunt teeth digging into her pillowy lower lip. "You're safe with us, Grim. I promise. Please. I need you. I need all of you."

She felt too good. I sensed it—that instinctive urge to give in. The overwhelming roil of my essence pressing against that wall, desperate to unite with her. Every slick thrust pushed me closer, no matter how hard I tried to hold back.

But if I let go, if I gave in… *they* would be there. Her other mates. I would open myself as fully to them as I would her, and I couldn't…

A strong hand clasped around my forearm, jerking my attention from Annabel's eyes.

Saga looked up at me, his mouth still close to her

wet and swollen nipple. There was heat in his eyes, but also… love.

"It's okay, Grim," he rasped, his voice hoarse with pent-up need. "Let go. We've got you, brother. We always will. Let go."

My brothers. The men I had given everything for—the only ones who had ever mattered to me before Annabel. I'd wanted to kill them for their claim on my mate—still did, despite the roar of the mating high—but somehow having them here with me… For these few breaths, it felt… okay.

I flashed my eyes to the Thorssons, my lip curling at their presence. Not okay.

But Annabel was happy with them, comfortable. Loved them. And… so did my brothers, unfathomable as it was to me.

If they trusted them, so could I. I had no other choice.

When I looked back to Annabel, she released her grip on Modi and Bjarni—much to their displeasure—and sat halfway up, dislodging Magni and Saga.

The glade erupted in angry alpha growls, but my mate only had eyes for me. She reached up and wrapped her arms around my neck, guiding me down on top of her.

"I need you, baby," she whispered in my ear, voice raw and maddening. "Make me come, Grim. Don't worry about the rest of it. Just give me your knot and make me come."

There was no way for me to deny her.

With a hiss, I buried my face in her neck—and gave her exactly what she'd asked for.

Having her this close, begging for me to force her wide and make it hurt, ensured it only took a few dozen hard thrusts for my knot to swell. Annabel's panting breaths turned to whines as I ground the ever-growing bump through her straining lips, forcing her wider and wider. She dug her nails into my back, her teeth marking my shoulder, but she wrapped her legs around my hamstrings and clung tight, relishing the painful stretch.

When I pushed my knot past her pelvic bone, we both came. My groan of release drowned in Annabel's high-pitched scream—a scream that muted to a dull throb as my essence rushed through our bond, broke down the wall between us, and flooded into her consciousness, melding my soul with my mate's.

Her warm, golden glow rose to greet me, swirling around my darkness and pulling me close.

"Annabel," I groaned, blind to anything but the pleasure of her fluttering pussy and the sweet embrace of her soul. *"My Annabel."*

As always, her essence was like a warm caress—like the sun breaking through the clouds after a long winter—and I lost myself in her.

And then I felt *them.*

They were... curious, but restrained as they touched

us—our bodies and minds. I shuddered at the foreign sensation, and Annabel held me tighter.

"Stay. Please, stay," she whispered. "I need you. *We* need you."

I didn't have the strength to deny her, even if that dark, icy part of me recoiled at being so intimately bared. But this was it; this was what she needed. This was what the curse of our twined fates would always have led to.

Too exhausted to fight anymore, I lay on top of my mate, my knot buried in her depths and my face pressed into her hair—and I let them in.

They saw everything. Every weakness, every bitter, petty thought. Every wound. And every dark deed.

Grim.

My name was a sorrowful whisper in my mind. It came from Bjarni; I knew that from the warm, bright blue shimmer in my consciousness as my deceit was laid bare. But no anger followed—not even from the Thorssons—because they saw too the overwhelming devotion and desperation that had forced me to align myself against them.

They understood. And they forgave me.

I shook in Annabel's arms as they watched my complete and utter capitulation brought on by the love for her that I had tried and failed to fight. Only warmth and amused empathy met me from the four men who had surrendered their own hearts.

And when they saw the moment I realized my mate

—*our* mate—was pregnant, saw my gut-wrenching understanding that I had sparked a life, and the agony of knowing that I had doomed my daughter to the same darkness that had swallowed me whole...

"Ha! A daughter!"

"You're pregnant, pet?"

"You're giving us a baby girl, sweetie?"

"Truly? Even here, the Fates have blessed us? Anna, this is wonderful!"

They drew away, the four of them, pulling from the intimacy of our union as their excitement echoed in the glade. Several palms clapped my shoulders, even as they focused their words on Annabel.

Her daughter. Fathered by me, yes, but... they saw her as theirs too. *Ours.*

I blinked my eyes open, too dazed to speak as my mate smiled up at me before her gaze darted to the alphas surrounding us, pure joy crinkling the corners of her eyes.

The connection between us was still wide open, and her gratitude and love swelled around me. I felt them too, through her—not as clearly as before, not as intimately, but I felt them.

Mine. They were all mine. The understanding was crystal-clear and shocked me to my core.

I should have been furious. Should have fought tooth and nail to lay claim to what was mine—*my* mate and *my* child—but I wasn't. Because *they*... they belonged to me too.

I kept waiting for my alpha instincts to kick in, but the primitive part of me was... soothed. Content. Safe in his pack.

My family.

Annabel's gaze flicked back to mine as if she'd heard that thought through our bond. Perhaps she had. She placed a hand against my chest, over my heart, and whispered, "You were the final piece. You complete us."

The spark came of its own accord, a dark kernel pulled from the very depths of my being, glowing faintly as it passed through our bond and into Annabel to light up her eyes from within.

"What—?" Her voice died as she moved her hand from my chest to her own.

"A part of me," I murmured, placing my fingers above hers. "Forever yours."

"I feel you in me," she whispered, eyes wide. "Your power. I can..."

She tugged on something, and my magic answered, hers to command as much as I was.

Hesitantly she released her grip on it, letting it retreat back into me.

"This is how we can beat Hel. This is how we stop Ragnarök," she said. "It's why the Norns wove us together." She looked up at the others. "I need you to do that too. Right now."

Saga lifted his eyebrows. "Oh, you do, do you?"

"Someone should teach that demanding little girl some manners," Magni drawled. The heat in his voice was unmistakable, and it dawned on me that they all had yet to sate their desires the way I had. The thought of them taking her had infuriated me before, but now it seemed almost... natural that I share my mate with my brothers—old as well as new.

Annabel huffed. "It's always about sex with you lot. I'm telling you I figured out how to save the nine goddamn worlds, and you just want to get laid?"

"Yes. Yes, we do," Bjarni said matter-of-factly. He looked at me. "How's that knot coming?"

"If Grim gave you his kernel after a climax, it would seem plausible that we would require similar circumstances to give you ours," Modi said. "After all, I know of no spell to make it happen, and I suspect if one did exist, Mimir or Verdandi would have provided it."

Annabel quirked a brow at the redhead. He only smiled in return.

"Fine," she sighed, sounding nothing like the wanton woman who had writhed between the five of us only moments ago. "If you insist."

"That's the spirit," Magni chuckled.

"Poor Annabel, having to spread her legs for all her alphas, one after the other, until we've had our fill," Saga said. He reached for her and stroked a couple of fingers over her cheek. "How ever will you get through this, hmm?"

"It's a good thing our mate likes her cunt sore and used," Magni purred. "And her pleasure forced."

"I do not!" Annabel lied, the indignation in her

voice almost enough to block out the glazed look of mounting desire at their taunts.

"Your knot?" Bjarni asked again, impatience lacing each syllable. "If you need help, the thunder god's sons know a handy trick."

Saga snorted and lifted his chin at Modi, who was shifting to move around Annabel's still-prone body. "I wouldn't. He's not as mild-mannered as the rest of us."

I gave Modi a withering stare that made him settle by Annabel's side with a grimace before I returned my focus to my mate. She reached up to brush a hand along my cheek and asked, "Are you good?"

I only managed a hum in response. I didn't have the words for anything else.

"Good," she said, giving me a soft smile that turned mischievous at the corners. "How *is* your knot coming, baby? Because the last time we did this, there were some very... *intriguing* suggestions on how to settle one quickly."

I quirked an eyebrow at the decidedly wicked smirk on her lips, but before she could clarify, Saga said, "I'm not shoving a finger up my brother's ass, sweetling. I can't fuck you if I'm dead."

"I didn't know you were a scaredy-cat," Annabel huffed as she stuck out her plump lower lip in a pout, earning a chuckle from him.

"Hmm," Modi hummed as he eyed me up. "I suppose it's good you have far braver mates, then."

I blinked as he moved around me, the implication of

his words slow to set in. So slow it wasn't until I felt his hand on my lower back that I realized what he had planned.

Shock rocked through my body, alpha instincts flaring in a heartbeat. I snarled and whipped my head around, baring my teeth at the male who sought to penetrate me. He only flashed me a knowing grin, popped his middle finger between his lips, and sucked it lewdly.

I snarled again, but instead of reaching for him to tear his head off—like I *should* have wanted to—I only clutched Annabel's shoulders. Because despite the alpha instincts roaring at the unnaturalness of getting *penetrated,* that new emotion in my gut, that sense of family and belonging and home, whispered of something more. Something I didn't understand, even as I turned my gaze back to Annabel's and held my body perfectly still, waiting.

Modi brushed his hand from my lower back to my ass, spreading me none too gently. And then the wet touch of his finger rubbed across my exposed anus, making my entire body shudder and another snarl rip from my throat.

But my eyes stayed locked in Annabel's, and I drank in the look of excitement on her pretty face and her fast, shallow breaths as she waited with me.

When he slipped his fingers into me, it was like nothing I'd ever experienced. The stretch was small but entirely alien and wrong, yet so... so *right*. I threw my head back and hissed a curse as Modi shoved in deeper, angling the tips of his fingers against a too-tender spot.

"No!" I roared, the alpha in me finally breaking through, but it was too late.

Modi pressed down and rubbed that spot hard—and the deepest release of my life grabbed me by the throat and choked off my roar until it was a long, drawn-out wail. I came so hard I shook, clutching onto Annabel as if she were the only thing that could anchor my soul through the onslaught of sensation.

"Fuck, Grim…!" my mate mewled underneath me, and for a horrifying moment I thought I was hurting her—but the flutter of her pussy on my cock told me the truth. I rocked mindlessly against her, groaning like a wounded beast until I had nothing left to give. Modi slipped his finger from my ass, leaving me trembling and not entirely sure what I had just let happen.

He had once been my sworn enemy.

No one spoke as I slowly eased off Annabel. My knot had retracted completely, and both my mind and my nerves were raw with the overload of sensation that had washed over me since we'd returned to the glade—but my cock was still hard and made Annabel squirm as I pulled out of her.

"Well. I guess no one's gonna to crack any more jokes about how Magni and I *mended fences,"* Saga said, interrupting the silence. He looked from me to Modi, then down between Annabel's still-splayed legs where my abundant release flowed. "Though from the looks of it, it's a more pleasurable alternative to your little lightning trick."

"I will never not crack jokes about the two of your milking each other's knots," Bjarni rumbled. He reached for Annabel's hand and brought it back to his still-throbbing dick. Obligingly, she wrapped her fingers around it.

"*I* didn't milk anything," Magni growled. "I was entirely incapacitated. *He* molested *me*."

"You're welcome for saving your ungrateful ass," Saga said, his attention more on Annabel's slow movements over Bjarni's dick than either Thorsson. He shifted languidly, moving to her hip, ensuring their focus was on the argument rather than his intentions.

"Will *someone* explain what happened between the two of you?" Modi asked, frustration lacing his words as he turned to Magni—giving Saga the in he needed. "Enough with the hints!"

My eldest brother moved quickly, grabbing Annabel by her hip and rolling her toward himself and away from me and Modi. She squeaked and laughed—and then groaned deeply when he seated his cock to the hilt in her still-open pussy.

Modi's head snapped to them, eyes widening with outrage. "You thieving bastard! You have no honor!"

"None," Saga moaned, eyes closed with reverence as he shuddered in Annabel's embrace. "Not when... it comes to this. *Fuck,* sweetling. I've missed you."

"I've missed you too," she said, voice dying on a

whine when he rolled his hips, filling her anew. She let go of Bjarni and wrapped her arms around Saga's shoulders, clutching him to her. "So, so much. Oh, Saga… Yes. Please, *yes.*"

Bjarni grimaced at the loss of her touch, but didn't try to force her hand back. We all felt Saga pulse through our connection with Annabel—his yearning, his relief, and his desperation. I finally understood then why Annabel had been so adamant that I couldn't break their bonds to her without irrevocably damaging them. No matter what I had been told, no matter the power needed to destroy something as eternal as a mate bond, I saw the foolishness of my convictions as Saga gave himself to our woman. He would love her until the end of time itself, and no spell would ever change that.

We all watched in silence as my brother coupled with our mate—heard his gasped whispers of love and felt his eternal gratitude that she was back in his arms. That she hadn't been lost to him like he had feared in the darkest parts of his mind while they had searched for her.

He laid himself bare—not only to her, but to us as well, allowing himself to be as vulnerable as I had been in her embrace. Memories fluttered through our connection, some muddled, some clear. Every weakness, every fear was laid out for us as his defenses drowned in the pleasure of making love to his mate once more.

I wasn't conscious of moving. I only realized I had when my palm connected with his shoulder and my darkness wove through the bond, through Annabel, and into Saga, soothing his raw soul like they had done for me. The others joined me, and when Saga gasped out in pleasure and allowed his tie to swell into place, we felt his climax like a storm crashing through our connection.

Annabel's whine as she took his knot, and her subsequent cry of completion, sent ripples through that blasted bond, chasing Saga's pleasure. I groaned through gritted teeth at my cock's responding throb, tightening my grip on Saga's shoulder to stem the urge to rip him off and mount her again.

Even through the onslaught of four other alphas' desires, Saga only had a mind for Annabel. He groaned softly as he rocked his hips into her, ensuring his knot kept her trembling in one, long climax, and peppered her neck and jawline with kisses and sweet words of devotion.

And then it came, a fleck of flint traveling through their connection from him and into her, glowing softly as it settled within Annabel's soul. It lit up her eyes from within until, some long moments later, her body finally stilled underneath his and peace flooded our bond.

"Thank you," she croaked.

Saga smiled gently at her. "For you, I would give everything."

"I know," she murmured, turning her head to rub her forehead against his arm. "As I would for you."

"I know," he echoed. "My fierce little mate."

They lay in silence for some long moments, and despite our combined urgency to have her, none of us interrupted their quiet afterglow.

Until somewhere in the region of twenty minutes had passed and Magni had seemingly run out of patience. He got to his feet and asked, "Finger or lightning?"

Saga finally looked up to give him a nasty glare. But instead of threatening violence, he growled, "Finger."

Magni grinned—with more than an edge of maliciousness to the curve of his mouth. "My *pleasure.*"

Saga snarled at the emphasis on pleasure—a sound that only deepened when Magni knelt behind him and reached down.

I didn't see the moment of penetration, but Saga's hissed, "*Fuck!*" and the stuttering of his hips made it plenty obvious.

"Want a cum like your brother's?" Magni asked, that evil note to his voice mirroring the smirk on his face.

"Don't you fucking dare!" Saga snarled, twisting his head to glare at Magni over his shoulder. "*Stop!* Gods, stop, you fucking bast—!"

The rest of his sentence died on a long, deep groan as his eyes rolled back in his skull and his entire body quivered.

The echo of his release shuddered through us all.

Magni only pulled his hand away once Saga had stilled completely. The moment he withdrew, my brother collapsed in a boneless heap on top of Annabel.

"Godsdammit," he muttered breathlessly. "You're going to regret that, Thorsson."

"Don't care," Magni said. "Get off her. You can have your revenge later."

"I will," Saga growled, only managing to muster an edge of a threat through the aftermath of his orgasm. He placed a kiss on Annabel's lips, then managed to push himself off her body and roll onto his back on the grass by her side. He made no move to get up as Magni crawled in between Annabel's still-splayed legs.

"I've missed you, pet," the redhead murmured, a hoarseness to his voice that wasn't only from sexual urgency. "Every second of every day."

"Don't cry," Annabel whispered. "I'm right here, Magni. You found me in time." She cupped his face with both hands, and I saw the single tear trailing down his cheek as he closed his eyes to savor her touch. "I'm right here, my love."

Magni groaned and bent for her lips. He kissed her slowly at first, savoring every brush of her mouth over his, until the need for her turned too painful to resist. When he buried his cock inside her, his groan of pleasure shuddered through their bond and deep into all of us.

I closed my eyes at the reverence vibrating through that bond—at the relief and wonder he felt now that he was finally reunited with his mate. He'd been lost without her. His pain flowed freely through our connection, followed by images of him sobbing on his knees at night, pleading to the stars above to return her to him.

Claiming her was the first time he had ever felt like he truly belonged. She was his home, much like she was mine—his center—the only one who could drive away the agony of a life lived feeling unwanted. Unloved.

Magni didn't hold back any of his painful scars as he made love to our mate. For me, I dimly realized—he wanted me specifically to see, because he wanted me to know he understood, and that I wasn't alone with my festering wounds carved from the darkness of a past not too dissimilar to his.

Home. This was home. My safe place.

I pressed my palm to his shoulder, allowing some of my cool darkness to flow through Annabel and into him, soothing the echo of that raw pain.

Magni grunted in response, amusement and gratitude filtering back to me—from him and his brother.

Modi's pain still tinged our connection, even as Magni refocused on the pleasure of mating. He had watched his brother's mistreatment and been powerless to stop it, and that old ache still festered. Seeing Magni like this, surrounded by love, by his true family, went a long way to soothe it.

Annabel's moaning turned sharp, pulling my focus

from the Thorssons to her just as Magni pushed his knot through her pelvis and roared his release.

His kernel was blue-flecked green and came eagerly on the rush of his climax, embedding itself deep within Annabel even as she was still writhing on his knot. It illuminated her, that blue-green light glowing through her eyes for several long seconds until the two of them collapsed, panting and spent.

"I will love you through the end of the world and beyond, woman," Magni said softly. He found the strength to lift onto his elbows and planted a couple of gentle kisses on Annabel's lips, smiling as she didn't manage more than an exhausted groan in response. "You can have every ounce of my power, so long as you let me remain by your side."

"By her side is fine. But if you remain *inside* of her for much longer, you're going to experience what the Lokissons have already," Modi growled, shattering the peaceful moment. One look at him made it plenty obvious that watching Annabel come again had pushed his patience over the edge for good.

Magni chuffed through his nose. "Relax, will you? I'm still seeding her."

"I don't care," Modi said, and from the roughened sound of his voice it was clear he was telling the truth. "I want her. *Now.*"

Magni bared his teeth at his brother's aggression, but he didn't have the fire to follow through, thanks to the clamp of Annabel's pussy. "Fine. But I'll take the lightning. Keep your fingers out of my asshole."

Modi didn't respond—he just knelt behind the pair and reached forward. Lightning flashed, and Magni jerked hard and spat out a string of curses. Another flash of lightning had him howling and rolling off Annabel. When he glared at his brother, there was murder in his eyes, but Modi paid him no mind. He sank down on top of our prone mate with a shudder.

"Anna," he murmured, lifting one of her legs over his hips to ease her onto his cock. She gasped at the immediate penetration, but Modi was gentler than the rest of us had been. He pushed into her inch by slow inch, rubbing small circles on her clit with his free hand to ease the sensation of his entry. Only when he was fully seated within her did he leave her sensitive bud to reach for her face instead.

"I waited a lifetime for you, my mate. Don't ever leave me again."

"I won't," she said, pushing her chin into his palm, eyes closed. "Never again."

Modi's pain came slower to us than Magni's. He was hesitant, but he didn't fight it in the end. There was such shame in his relationship to his family—in his love for a mother who had hated his brother, and his worship of a father who might not have deserved it.

But the deepest scar for Modi was still fresh and pink and smarting at the edges. He hadn't thought Annabel loved him—still found it hard to truly believe, even though he himself had fully surrendered to the Fate that had been woven for him. He saw himself as an outsider in our little group—someone expendable.

Annabel's essence flared as that particular thought filtered through. Fury filled our bond—fury and a love so intense it made Modi's hips stutter mid-thrust.

"You *still* believe this nonsense?" she growled. "How can you still think such things? You are mine, Modi. *Mine.*"

She pushed at his shoulders, and he let her roll them over, leaving Annabel on top. She straightened her back, placed her palms flat on his pecs, and stared down at him.

"What will it take for you to hear me, mate?" she asked. "Just the thought of you gone, of our connection permanently silenced... It makes me want to die. You are not expendable. You are *mine.*"

With that last, growled word, Annabel rolled her hips, letting her pussy rise along the proud column of his flesh embedded within her. Her lower lips clung to him, showing the rim of his head bulging through the thin flesh before she sank back down with a moan.

"Mine!" she repeated. She dug her nails into his chest, but Modi seemed too far gone to feel it. His eyes were half-hooded and filled with worship and desire, and though we all felt his simmering alpha instincts fighting against letting his female put him in such a submissive position, he let her ride.

Annabel loved it. It may have started as an urge to

show her troubled mate that she wanted him, but there was no hiding the rush of elation weaving through our bond. She moaned shamelessly as she rode him—a wild warrior queen taking what she wanted from the men who worshipped her.

A goddess.

The word flickered through my mind and settled in my chest as I watched her rise and fall on that thick cock, and I doubted even Freya could have mastered five alphas the way our mate did now.

Her pussy still clung tightly to Modi's hard flesh, though the shine on the rigid pole left the unmistakable proof that our mate was an omega and built to take us. *All* of us.

My own cock throbbed painfully at the sight of their joining, more than eager to return to those hallowed depths, and I gritted my teeth to resist the building urgency in my abdomen. Even if I somehow managed to hold back until Modi was done, it would come to a fight if I tried to have her again before Bjarni took his turn to reunite with her.

I was halfway through planning how to overpower my battle-hardened brother and somehow keep him restrained while I took Annabel again when my mate let out a particularly deep moan, and a memory struck me. I'd seen her straddling a man once before. In Freya's Hall, she'd been astride Magni when Bjarni and I arrived—but she hadn't been alone.

I narrowed my eyes as my plan veered down

another path. Modi had asked about that incident—perhaps he'd like a demonstration instead?

And if not, he would have to accept it as payment for how he'd gone about releasing my knot.

I moved behind Annabel to kneel between Modi's sprawled legs. She chirped happily when I reached around her to grab her breasts, another moan spilling from her lips as I rolled her pert little nipples between my fingers and bent my head to lick at her neck.

"You are the only woman who could do this, mate," I murmured hoarsely in her ear as I let one hand slip from her breast to her clit. She eagerly spread her thighs to let me rub it. "Bring five gods to their knees and make them worship you in their surrender. Do you feel powerful, Annabel? Because you are. Let me worship you like you deserve to be, mate. Please."

Annabel's response was an unintelligible, but enthusiastic groan, and I hid a smile against the side of her neck as she leaned back into me.

"So eager, little goddess," I whispered against the shell of her ear. I stroked my hand not busy on her clit down to anchor on her hip. "Be strong for me now."

I pushed her forward with the bulk of my torso, making her lean over and rest on top of Modi, stilling her movements on him, and released her clit to reach for my throbbing cock.

Neither of them seemed to clock on to my intentions before I guided the tip of my erection to the root of their joining and pressed forward.

"Shit, that's cold!" Modi hissed as our members touched.

Annabel jerked hard and whipped her head around to stare at me over her shoulder. "What are you—no! Nope! Absolutely n—*nnngh!*"

Her protests died on a drawn-out groan, every muscle in her body tensing as I managed to wedge my head into her already stuffed opening.

Everything was pressure, heat... ecstasy. I felt Modi through the bond, the pleasure roaring through his veins as violently as it tore through my own body, and in between us... *Annabel.*

She sobbed, her entire body trembling with the effort of taking us both as her pussy slowly, reluctantly adjusted to the harsh stretch. Her fists were tight and clutching onto the grass, knuckles white, and I knew there was more than an edge of pain for her.

I mumbled soothing words of encouragement into her ear and reached down to gently stroke her clit while I held still and waited for her body to adjust.

"What... in Odin's name... are you doing, Lokisson?" Modi panted between gritted teeth. He was clutching at Annabel's hips—whether to ensure she didn't try to move off us, or to anchor himself, I didn't know.

"Mating my woman," I rasped. "Showing you how your brother *bonded* with mine."

Modi's eyes widened even as he swallowed a groan at an involuntary spasm traveling up the length of Annabel's sheath, transplanting into the both of us. I didn't give him time to protest. Slowly, agonizingly, I pushed my hips forward and drove my cock home.

Annabel's wail drowned in Modi's roar as I rubbed along his meaty dick until I was finally fully seated within my mate. She seized hard, and I hugged her tight and tried to soothe her, but only ragged grunts escaped my throat. My vision swam, turning Annabel's messy hair into ribbons of bronze and white, and all I could sense was how tight her pussy clutched me, how hot Modi's cock felt against mine, and how completely the sensation of both took my breath away. My heart pounded in my ears, and my soul was a swirling vortex of pleasure and *him,* with Annabel as our center.

I moved on instinct alone, pulling halfway out and drawing howls from both Annabel and Modi. But when I forced my way back up inside again, Modi pulled halfway out, drawing a shudder from my body at the slick sensation of his cock moving against mine. He pushed in, and I drew back, again and again, the seesaw rhythm building between us as naturally as drawing breath, even as our mate screamed and cursed our names right up until she came so hard it hurt.

Modi swore too and stilled as her muscles rippled and clamped down, forcing us to pause while she cried out, ecstasy crashing through our bond.

It lasted almost a full minute before she collapsed on Modi's chest in a boneless heap.

He looked up at me, locking his gaze on mine for a

short moment before heat tinged his cheeks. "She's had enough. Pull out."

Saga snorted. "She can take plenty more cock than that, Thorsson. Or are you not enjoying the experience as much as your brother did?"

"I didn't *enjoy* anything!" Magni protested. "You forced it on me!"

"Ha! You looked to enjoy it plenty when we arrived. I remember a spectacular amount of cum when Saga milked your knot dry," Bjarni said.

I didn't hear Magni's reply—I tuned them all out as I stared back at Modi. "*You* can pull out, if you've had enough." I didn't wait for him to respond before I gave Annabel another thrust.

Modi hissed and Annabel whimpered, but she wasn't as painfully tight after her climax, and pleasure crawled through my nerves and into our bond. I only managed one more stroke before Modi joined me, once more taking up the seesaw rhythm that had us both groaning.

It took a while for Annabel to give in. She was still fighting us through her second orgasm and halfway to her third, cursing and clawing in between sobs and mewls of pleasure, but we both felt the truth in our bond. Despite her resistance, her omega instincts had her pussy gushing and pleasure throbbing down our connection with every rough push through her trembling channel.

But somewhere between orgasms, her threats of murder and mutilation shifted to pleas for more.

"You surrender so prettily," Modi growled. "My perfect little omega whore."

I might have been furious at another male using such language for my mate, but Annabel's response was a moaned, *"Yes,"* followed by a ripple along the sheath of her pussy that made it plenty obvious she didn't mind. In fact, every growled vulgarity edged her closer to another climax—and both of us along with her, thanks to the rhythmic pulses of her slick muscles around our cocks.

"Look at you, omega—so desperate for sex you allow two alphas to open your little cunt horribly wide. Is this what you would have been, had Fate allowed it? Nothing but a whore for alpha cock, bending over to be violated in exchange for pleasure?" Modi hissed against her ear as he thrust up hard, rubbing his cock deliciously against the both of us.

I groaned along with Annabel, and then cussed when her pussy clamped tight and she reared up against me.

Mindlessly I reached between us to rub her clit through her orgasm, but the shuddering release was too much to bear. I felt my own knot start to swell just as Modi hissed, "Shit! I'm gonna—"

It took everything I had to pull out, leaving her spasming pussy to be plugged by her other mate. He fucked up into her hard a few more times, then forced his knot past her pelvic bone with a roar of release.

Her responding cry undid me. Trembling, I rested one hand on her thigh and jerked my cock roughly once, twice—

My groan mixed with Annabel's and Modi's climax, that all-consuming rush of ecstasy swirling through our connection and deep into my soul.

I slumped by Modi's side, sliding my hand from Annabel's thigh, up her hip, and to her shoulder as I shivered through the final echoes of orgasm.

Modi's kernel came in the afterglow. Deep blue and glowing, it rose from him and sank into our mate as she lay unconscious on his chest. I wasn't sure exactly when she'd passed out, but the realization shot a jab of fear through my haze.

I forced myself up on an elbow and brushed her hair from her eyes. "Annabel?"

"She is not hurt," Modi murmured. He petted her scalp and smiled gently when she made a soft sound in response, despite her unconscious state. "Just exhausted. Our mate is tougher than she looks."

Our mate.

"She is," I whispered. "Tough enough to bring five gods to their knees."

"Five gods—and Ragnarök itself," he agreed.

25

ANNABEL

You know how they say you know you're not dead if something hurts? Yeah, that's a load of bullshit. Turns out, you very much *can* feel pain even when you're dead, as my vagina bore testament to it the moment consciousness returned.

"You guys *really* need to stop doing that," I croaked into whoever's chest I was lying on.

It was Bjarni's, it turned out, his deep laughed rumbling underneath me and into my bones. His lips skimmed my forehead as he hugged me gently. "You don't mean that."

"I really, *really* do," I grumbled. "God, it feels like I've been run over by a horny bull."

"Wrong pantheon," Modi hummed from somewhere behind me. He rested a large, warm hand against my lower back, and I sighed at the immediate relaxation in my sore muscles. They were all so wonderfully warm. I'd relished Grim's chill in the sensory deprivation of Hel, but the other four had retained their natural body heat. Perks of not actually being dead, I guessed.

I forced my neck muscles into action and twisted my head to look at Modi. He sat cross-legged by Bjarni's shoulder, still gloriously naked from when he'd been inside me. I wasn't entirely sure how long I'd been out, but it couldn't have been too long, or the sticky mess I felt clinging to my lower lips would have dried up. "Are you okay?"

He smiled, a soft touch to his lips as he moved his hand from my back to my cheek. "Yeah. I'm okay, Anna. More than okay."

I felt the truth of his words in the pleasured hum in my chest where his warm bond hooked. There was no more doubt there, no more fear—just deep, eternal devotion.

Motion to his side caught my attention, and I locked eyes with Grim. There was concern in his gaze as he looked me over. "Are *you* all right?"

I quirked an eyebrow at him. "You didn't seem all that concerned about that before."

He frowned, and a spark of guilt fluttered through our connection.

Groaning with the effort, I reached an arm out and smiled when my fingers interlocked with Grim's. "I'm fine. Sore, but fine."

I was going to say more—voice my astonishment at

how thoroughly he'd gotten on board with the whole sharing aspect—but one look into his mismatched eyes and I knew it wasn't the right time. It was still so new to him, my wounded mate, and I was just grateful that he had allowed himself to let go.

I squeezed his hand with what little strength I could muster and sent a wave of gratitude through our bond.

"Does that mean you're done resting, then?" Bjarni asked.

I chuffed a weak laugh. "Not even close. I'm going to sleep for at least twenty-four hours, or however long it takes my poor vagina to reshape itself."

"Hmm," the blond Viking rumbled. His muscles bunched underneath me as he leaned up on one elbow to rub his nose along my scalp. "I'm afraid I can't wait that long, sweetie. You and your vagina are gonna have to rally."

I groaned and rolled my eyes back to meet his. "You're kidding me? You didn't...?

"While you were unconscious?" he asked, eyebrows high on his forehead. "You think that little of me?"

There was just an edge of genuine hurt to his voice, even if he tried to play it off as humor.

Which was fair enough. I grimaced and released Grim to stroke a soothing hand over Bjarni's pecs. "Of course not. I'm sorry—I'm just... so exhausted."

"That's okay," he hummed, instantly mollified. "You just lie back and enjoy it, hmm?"

I whined, perhaps not the most articulate of

protests, but the only thing I could manage as Bjarni gently rolled me off his chest and onto the flattened grass, shifting his massive body to rest between my thighs.

My blond mate chuckled at my pathetic whimper. "Can't very well save the nine worlds without your last mate's powers," he chided before he pushed himself down to lay flat on his stomach.

Despite the exhausted state of my core, my pussy gave a small twinge when his plans dawned on me.

"How very selfless of you," I said. What should have been sarcasm died on a long groan as he pushed his mouth to my slit and dove his tongue in to tease my still-swollen and tender clit.

Despite my well-worn muscles' aching protests, it didn't take Bjarni long to bring me back to a simmer. Soon I was panting his name and moving my hips in restless waves against his skilled mouth, a rising orgasm battling the tissues too overstimulated to allow an easy surrender.

But Bjarni was not one to be defeated—not on the battlefield, and not atop me. When I grasped at his hair and whined for him to stop, he only clasped his huge hands around my thighs and sucked hard on my clit, trapping it in vacuum.

"Bjarni!" I shrieked, thrashing in his grip as I bucked for freedom. *"No, no, n*—unnnnhhhhhooly *shit!"*

My body seized hard as pleasure burst through me, forcing every nerve to spark. I shrieked and sobbed at the agony of it, but there was no stopping the thundering wave crashing through my flesh and into my mind until there was nothing left but hazy bliss and my own, panting breaths.

Bjarni eased off my clit and kissed my mons. "Feeling better?" he rumbled, the edge of raw desire unmistakable in his tone as he crawled on hands and knees over my splayed form.

I could only manage a guttural grunt in response. If I'd been more with it, I might have attempted to close my legs to avoid what I knew came next, but my brain was foggy and light—and even if I'd been aware enough to try to move my limbs, there was no way my body would have been capable.

"Good." He rose onto his knees and hiked one of my legs over his hip, opening me for his girth. With his free hand, he fisted his cock and pressed it against my opening.

I groaned again. It was meant as a protest, but just then Bjarni looked up from my nether region, catching my gaze. There was so much love there. So much longing. He had feared me lost too, and though he had remained strong for the others, it had nearly broken him. *My sweet one.*

"Bjarni," I said softly.

He pushed into me. Slowly. Gently. I still bit down on my lip to hold back a cry of denial as his thick cock stretched me so, so wide. I was open from Modi and Grim, but my tissues were worn and tender, and despite the obvious care Bjarni put into penetrating me, it still hurt.

But when he bottomed out with a moan and fell over me, the ache of taking him faded to the background. His eyes were hazy with desire and filled with wonder as he let them sweep over my face, as if trying to commemorate every detail.

"I love you too," I whispered.

"I know," he murmured, offering me a smile that had my toes curling. "And I'm gonna show you how much I love *you,* mate."

I clung to his shoulders and wrapped my legs around his waist as my gentlest mate took me slow and deep. I felt the urge to go harder vibrate through him and into my innermost, but he kept himself in check. He may have had a gentle nature, but he was still every inch an alpha, and I heard the song for conquest and domination echo through his blood as he filled me again and again, never losing control.

"It's okay," I gasped as my pussy took him to the hilt once more, the last remnants of pain disappearing behind my own rising desire for completion. "You can take me harder. I can handle it."

Bjarni chuffed something between a laugh and a groan against the side of my neck where he'd buried his face. Slowly he pushed up on his hands so he could peer down at me. The wildness in his eyes made me swallow thickly.

"You want it like that, mate? Rough? Does your pussy need to feel how desperate I am for you?"

"I... *you* need more. It's okay," I stammered. His words and that look in his eyes made my nipples tighten and my core clench on his hard cock. Immediate regret had me flinching as aching muscles panged. Yes, a part of me did want him to show me how much he'd missed me—but it would hurt. There were no two ways about it.

He groaned at the involuntary flex of my pussy and gritted his teeth. "I need *you,* Annabel. I need your love, your happiness—and I need that sweet little cunt of yours to take me until you scream my name and cream on my cock. If you need it to hurt, I'll make it hurt. But all *I* need is you, and until you beg me for more, that's all I'm taking."

"Bjarni," I murmured, blinking away a few stray tears as I clutched him tighter. I loved my other mates—loved them so much it hurt—but Bjarni... he was so easy. There was no doubt in our bond as he made love to me, no pain, and no trauma. Just deep, warm devotion and the ecstasy of reuniting.

He opened his heart and soul to me as he filled my body with aching bliss, and there was nothing but happiness and gratitude over a core of battle-hardened steel.

I relaxed underneath him and wound my fingers in his long hair, surrendering.

Bjarni let out a low moan and bent his head to my

exposed throat. He dug his teeth into my flesh and thrust in deep, making me cry out and tighten my legs around his hips in an effort to contain the sensation.

"Gods, Annabel," he groaned. And then he took what he needed.

Slow as he may have paced it, I could do nothing but cling to his strong body as he rode me toward that jagged, inevitable cliff with each powerful thrust. Growling richly, he bit at my neck until I was panting, then reached between us to circle my swollen clit. It was my undoing.

"Shit! More, Bjarni. Give me more!" I whimpered as the zing of stimulation went straight to my brain, melting any grasp of the consequences in the process. "More, more—God, make me *come!*"

The next second, Bjarni's thick cock barreled through my core so hard I saw stars.

"F-*Fuck!*"

My howl drowned in the lewd and unending slurps of my pussy as my gentle mate rose onto his hands for leverage and *fucked* me.

His thrusts fell hard and fast between my splayed thighs, his grunts of pleasure a steady rhythm underscoring my wails as I clawed at his back and writhed and *came.* My climax roared up from my pelvis in an overpowering wave, shattering my grasp on reality as pleasure ripped through my every nerve ending. I cried out his name and arched into him, frozen in that brutal torrent of bliss.

Bjarni gave me no respite. Growling with the effort, he forced his cock through my desperately clinging pussy, eternally pounding his own need deep into me. It was too much, too hard. Too relentless.

I sobbed through my orgasm and straight into another—and another. My body ached and my pussy trembled with exhaustion, but there was no stopping the alpha on top of me, not now that he had finally unleashed himself. All I could do was take his cock until he had no more left to give.

I don't know how many times I came underneath my alpha before *finally*, I felt that unmistakable bump catch against the mouth of my weary pussy. *His knot.*

Usually the pain of taking it had me writhing to escape, but this time I felt nothing but gratitude as Bjarni pushed the horrible thing through my straining lips and hooked it in place with a shout.

His kernel of power came on the rush of semen bathing my womb. Gray-blue and shimmering, it penetrated my soul while my pussy's contractions on his member forced me through one final, shuddering climax.

The moment that glowing ember clicked into place, I felt my entire soul light up in a flash of gold. Power rushed through my body and sank into my bones, even as my muscles gave in to exhaustion and I collapsed underneath Bjarni in a puddle of endorphins.

"I love you, Annabel," my mate whispered against the shell of my ear. His muscles trembled against my skin as his cock released the final drops of his essence deep within me, and he groaned and rubbed his cheek against mine.

I didn't have enough strength left to tell him I loved him too, but that golden light trickled out of me and into him, swaddling him in every tender feeling I had.

He smiled softly, kissed my lips, and grasped my limp body, rolling us over so I could lie on his chest, the thickness of his knot still locking me to his lower body.

"Rest, little goddess," my mate said. The rumble of his voice vibrated through his chest and into mine, soothing me as thoroughly as the sensation of his thick arms wrapped around my naked body. "When you wake, we will show Hel that nothing and no one gets between an omega and her destiny."

26

ANNABEL

I woke to the soft rumble of male voices, too groggy to make out the words. It took me a little while to realize that the disorientation came from being wrapped in a warm cocoon. It had been so long since I'd felt anything but Grim's chilly touch that Bjarni's body heat threw off my senses.

Reluctantly, I cracked my eyelids open. Judging by the gray light, it was barely dawn, and Bjarni was out cold on his back underneath me, snoring faintly. On his left, Magni was curled up with an arm slung over my lower back, and on his right, Modi...

I blinked as I realized Modi was resting with his head in the crook of Bjarni's arm, even if his leg was wrapped over mine. It seemed everyone had gotten awfully close during yesterday's events.

Speaking of getting close... I grimaced as my numb lower parts twanged when I tried to shift and it became evident that I was still straddling Bjarni's half-erect cock.

Irritated, I poked my blond mate in the chest.

He cracked an eye and gave me a sleepy, "Hmm?"

"You're still in me," I hissed quietly so as to not disturb my sleeping mates.

"Mm," he agreed, eyelid sliding closed again.

"Bjarni! Pull out."

"Don't wanna," he murmured. "Missed you."

"I missed you too, but if you don't get out of me in three seconds max, I'm gonna ask Magni to zap your balls," I threatened.

Bjarni cracked both eyelids this time to give me a reproachful stare. "That's harsh."

"Bjarni."

Sighing, he shifted his hips, and I bit down on my lip to stifle a whimper as he slowly slid out of my hypersensitive channel. He pulled free with an audible pop and a groan from me as my opening panged at the sensation of suddenly being empty.

Bjarni made an unhappy sound at the loss, pulled his arm free from Modi, and hugged me tighter to his body before he closed his eyes again and went back to sleep.

I flexed my pelvic muscles experimentally, grimacing at the deep, responding ache from my worn body. Someone was absolutely going to be carrying me today. Really, it was the least they could do after that stunt Modi and Grim pulled.

"...could have come to us. You know that. Or I thought you did."

Saga's low voice pulled me from my self-pity, and I craned my neck to follow the sound. He was sitting with Grim a few yards away, far enough that their voices wouldn't disturb us, but still close enough that I could make out their words.

"She is your mother," Grim said softly.

My heart skipped a beat as I realized what they were talking about, what had been laid bare when Grim opened his soul to me yesterday—to me, and to them.

"You think I'd choose her over you? After what she did? Grim..." Saga was clearly struggling to stay quiet through the awakening of his temper. "All those times we made you visit her as adults, all those times we teased you about not wanting to go... Gods, brother. I will never forgive myself. And I will never forgive *her*."

"I... wasn't sure you would have believed I didn't want it. You saw me... with her. That first time." Grim's voice was quiet, but steady. I reached for him through our bond and found the connection open. He responded with a tendril of darkness—a caress against my innermost, promising me that he was okay.

"That means nothing. I would have known that even then. I told you, my first rut, I nearly fucked a mountain troll. Bjarni rutted a dwarf. He wasn't even certain she was female before he had her legs spread." Saga reached out and grabbed Grim by the shoulder.

"Once this is over, I will make sure she pays for what she did."

"Annabel has already promised to murder her," Grim said, soft amusement in his voice.

Saga snorted. "I bet she has. She's got a nasty temper, that one. And a bit of a protective streak."

"I don't need either of you to kill for me," Grim said, his amusement fading. "It was a long time ago, and I have done... much that might make me deserving of worse, since."

Saga was quiet for a long time before he said, "That part... was difficult to see clearly. It was... muddled. I don't understand who could persuade you to betray us. I saw... *something* in your memories. Some... entity."

"I am still under a silencing spell. I cannot tell you who, only that he showed me the worst of my fears made flesh. I still thought I could fight against Annabel—this pull she has on me—that I could choose my own fate, even if it meant the end of everything. It was better than you and Bjarni dying." He scrubbed his face with both hands. "I never thought we could have... this. Even if we can't stop Ragnarök, even if it is all for nothing... I wish I had been brave enough to give myself to her sooner."

Saga squeezed his shoulder. "It's a lot to ask—sharing her. I fought against it too, before I understood the truth of our connection. Of course, I didn't fuck off to Hel in the process..."

Grim snorted and lowered his hands with a sigh. "I have done unforgivable things."

Saga watched him for a moment, then shook his head. "You may have fought against the Norns' web, but I think perhaps this was the only way you could surrender to Annabel. You had to feel for yourself what this bond means. No amount of telling you could have explained what it's like.

"So no, brother—what you have done is not unforgivable. Not for us. Not after showing us..." Saga hesitated, his brows drawing into a frown. "Not after baring yourself to us like you did. You took her from us—to Hel, of all places—and I should want to strangle you for it... but I don't. I understand why you did what you did."

Grim exhaled a deep breath and glanced back at me. "How can one little human do this? Unite enemies and offer redemption where there should be none?"

Saga chuffed a quiet laugh and followed his gaze back to mine. He gave me a soft smile. "I'd suggest it's that magic pussy of hers, but I don't want to piss her off. I've been apart from it for too long to risk her withholding it."

I gave him a glare that only made his mouth hike into a broader grin. Even Grim chuckled. He breathed deeply again and clasped his hand to Saga's shoulder in quiet thanks. Then he looked back to me.

"We should wake the others. If Hel leaves with her army before we reach her, we will be stuck here."

~

MAGNI CARRIED me bridal-style as we made our way from Freya's glade and deep into the woodlands. He spent most of the time looking between my abdomen and face, a look of wonder and happiness on his handsome features that pulled at my heart. The joy of our reunion was palpable in all my bonds, and it relaxed every tightly wound nerve in my body.

I was finally home. Even here, in the middle of Hel. I was home, and no task was too great when I was surrounded by my mates. Not even persuading Hel to let us leave the realm of the dead.

Sometime during the middle of the day, Saga insisted on swapping Mimir's head for me, and Magni shifted me into his arms as he picked up the unusually quiet prophet. Mimir had been treated to a first-class seat to our debauched reunion—something I only discovered when Magni pulled me from Bjarni's embrace and into his own that morning, and I saw Mimir's head sitting not too far away, facing where we had spent the night.

But unlike when he'd watched Grim and me, he didn't comment on what he'd undoubtedly witnessed, and he spent the day humming to himself as we made our way toward the swirling vortex of souls darkening the gray sky.

We saw none of Hel's creatures on our journey, and I was starting to suspect that it was thanks to the presence of the five battle-hardened alpha gods making up my escort. Grim had been a formidable enough opponent for even a mountain troll—as peaceful as I felt while in their midst, I doubted even the most nightmarish of Hel's denizens would be keen to tangle with four more.

MY PEACEFUL STATE lasted until evening.

Saga sat me down on a fallen tree trunk to go with Magni and Grim to find firewood. Even though it would provide us no warmth, a fire would still ward off some of the nocturnal horrors—and as Bjarni said, it just felt wrong to make camp without one.

I hadn't sat on my tree trunk for more than twenty seconds before Modi scooped me up, stole my seat, and placed me in his lap.

"Hello, you," I said, and then hummed when he gave me a soft, lingering kiss. "How are you holding up?"

The corners of his eyes crinkled as he took me in. "You are asking how *I* am doing, when *you* are the one who has been complaining of being sore all day?"

I swatted his chest. "I can worry about my mates, even after they savage me like a pack of horny wolves. But... I know things were still... raw with us before I left. New. That you struggled a bit. How...?"

He scoffed and tugged lightly on my braid. "I am fine, Anna. You being gone..." He swallowed, and for a moment, raw pain flickered in his eyes before he composed himself. "Being ripped open from the inside out has a way of putting things into perspective. Especially sharing it with the others. Like Grim learned yesterday, I too discovered that there is a special bond between all of us. It helped me through these past weeks of searching for you, and it opened my eyes to the truth of our union. You and I would not be whole without them, as they would not be complete without me."

Silently I bumped my head against his. He stroked down my back in response and breathed deeply against my hair, scenting me, even if there was no smell to be found.

"But I have missed you... so terribly," he murmured, voice gruff. "I need some time with you. Just you."

I grimaced and pulled back to look at him, one eyebrow raised. His lap was turning distinctly pokey, giving a pretty clear indication what he meant by needing "some time" with me. "Look, I missed you too —all of you. But I'm *human,* remember? I'm quite sure my lady parts are going to fall off if you guys don't slow down a bit."

"Actually..." Mimir's voice sounded from where Magni had sat him down before heading out to look for firewood. "After your mates offered you their powers, you are not... quite human. More of a demigod, if we are to get technical."

I blinked and stared at him. "I'm sorry... are you saying I'm a *god?*"

"*Demi*god," he emphasized. "They imbued you with their combined essences, and they changed your DNA in the process. It was... quite spectacular to watch. Even in my long life, I have never seen the creation of a demigod before. I did not realize Freya would have known of such magic, if she even knew that was the outcome of her instructions to you."

So that was why he had been uncharacteristically quiet about our reunion—he'd been... awed? I shook my head and tried to come to grips with what he'd said.

A demigod. *I* was a demigod?

"What... What does a demigod do? I mean... How am I different?" I asked.

"Well, for starters, plum, you should easily be able to handle your mates' amorous attentions," Mimir said evenly. "Your body will be tougher—not quite as strong as a god's, but able to withstand much more than a human's. And your lifespan will be longer—if we get out of Hel, of course. Even without Idunn's apples, you would probably live three, five hundred years. Give or take."

I opened my mouth, to say what I wasn't entirely sure, but Bjarni broke in with a happy, "Excellent!" He straddled the tree trunk Modi and I were sitting on and reached out to cup my cheek. "If we start now, we might be halfway done before the others get back."

I glared at his smiling face. Of-fucking-course the

only thing he cared about when hearing, *"hey, your mate's a demigod!"* would be the part where he didn't have to worry about breaking me with too much sex.

"Did you miss the part where y'all had to *carry* me around all day because I'm still hurting from last night?"

He shrugged and leaned in to steal a kiss. "It's like sparring. In the beginning, you hurt, but the more you do it, the more your body gets used to the strain. Eventually it's no longer painful."

"Or," I said, pulling back from his kiss to continue glaring, "it's like kicking a god in the balls. He's a god, so he'll probably be fine, but he'd still very much like to avoid it."

Bjarni heaved a sigh. "Again with the testicle threats. We just want to pleasure you, sweetie. We *need* to."

"He is right," Modi said quietly. "I need this, Anna. I need you."

I leveled my glare at him, but the earnestness in his eyes made me bite the inside of my cheek as I reconsidered. They were all plenty capable of forcing their will when it came to sex, but they weren't. Not this time.

Bjarni curved his strong hands over my lower belly. "We'll be gentle," he murmured. "Please, little goddess. We need to worship you."

Goddammit. "Fine. *Fine.* Fuck's sakes." I leveled them both a glare for good measure and folded my arms over my chest. "At least turn Mimir around this time."

"There is really no need, plum; I've seen you intimate a great many times," Mimir protested. "One more won't matter."

I glared at the talking head. "For a bodiless man, you're a real pervert."

"I am merely academically interested," he said mildly. "Mating habits have always fascinated me. Of course, when I was still *intact,* so to speak, I did occasionally indulge past scholarly interests."

I gave my alphas a pleading look.

"On it," Bjarni chuckled as he got up from the trunk and turned to the prophet. "Sorry, old man. If we make it out of here, I'll find you a nice whorehouse to vacation in, hmm?"

Mimir sighed. "I guess that's better than nothing. But I have rarely seen an omega who enjoyed her knottings as thoroughly as your mate."

I choked out a sound of protest as blood filled my cheeks, but Modi wrapped his fingers around my chin and pulled my focus back to him. The smolder in his eyes made tendrils of awareness crawl up my spine, the embarrassment of Mimir's observations fading into the background.

Some three hours later, as I was falling asleep on Grim's chest, surrounded by my four other, sated mates, I had the thought that maybe the prophet hadn't been entirely wrong.

27

ANNABEL

I had expected Hel's residence to be a dark fortress—some shadowy counterpoint to the gilded halls of Valhalla and guarded by nightmarish creatures.

Instead what we found at the epicenter of the maelstrom of souls was a cauldron the size of a small house, sitting in the middle of a barren field scattered with broken skeletons. There was no sign of life—or unlife, as it were—anywhere, except from the eternal pouring of souls into the cauldron.

"Where is she?" I asked, frowning as we stopped at the edge of the field. "Where is her throne?"

Grim glanced at me—the only acknowledgement he made that I knew of her throne, thanks to his plans for my ascension he had accidentally shared with me while we made love that one time. "She resides inside."

"Inside?" I asked. "You mean...?"

"Inside the cauldron, yes," Mimir answered. "She draws her powers from it."

"Then that is where we too will go," Modi said. He tightened his grip on the pommel of his sword and stared at the cauldron. "And one way or another, we will convince the Queen of the Dead to release our mate."

Bones crunched underneath our feet as we made our way across the lifeless field. I hadn't been able to see how the skeletons lay intermingled in layers upon layers from the edge, but it made for an unsteady surface as we worked our way across it.

My mates, of course, seemed unhindered by the marrow-laden terrain—probably a benefit of being full gods, I thought bitterly as I yet again got my foot stuck in a gap and nearly faceplanted onto a broken femur.

Saga caught me by the neckline of my armor and pulled me back upright. "I wish you would let one of us carry you, sweetling," he said for the umpteenth time.

"Yes, well, the plan is to intimidate Hel with all my newfound power. I doubt that'll go particularly well if I have to be carried into her home like an overgrown toddler," I bit, more irritated with my own inability to find my footing than my mate's continued desire to baby me at every turn.

"The girl is correct," Mimir joined in. "She is prophesized to stop the unstoppable. Best she make an entrance worthy of a hero, if you wish for Hel to listen."

"Hel will listen," Magni said, a quiet note to his voice that made the hairs on the back of my neck stand on end. "We will make sure of that."

Mimir rolled his eyes. When they met mine, he muttered, *"Alphas."*

I cracked a smile at him. "*You* spoke the prophecy that included *five* of them. You could have picked, I don't know, just *one* nice, genteel beta god instead."

Three furious growls echoed from the group of men around me—from Saga, Modi, and Magni. Grim only leveled me with an icy stare. Bjarni pinched my ass —hard.

"I'm *kidding.* God. Learn to take a joke," I huffed, though I didn't *hate* that they got worked up at the thought of being replaced.

"I simply speak what I see," Mimir said mildly. "I never pick."

"You can take your chosen mates up with the Norns later, if you must," Modi said, and the dark look he gave me before he refocused on the cauldron ahead suggested I better make it abundantly clear later that I was, indeed, kidding, or he'd make sure to remind me why I didn't want a beta husband. "This is not a social call. There is no time for shenanigans."

Shenanigans. I bit my lip and shot him a fond look. He might have looked like a hunky twenty-something, but he occasionally acted like an old man. I wouldn't have been too shocked if he occasionally shook his fist at rambunctious youths ruining his lawn.

Modi, seemingly sensing my gaze on him, shot me a firm look. "Eyes front, Anna. Focus."

"Yes, *Dad,*" I sighed, but I did obey. My mate was in commander-mode now, and it was in my best interest to fall in line.

"I suspect he prefers 'Daddy,'" Bjarni mumbled by my side, drawing a guffaw from Saga.

Modi gave him a glare over his shoulder that could have turned a lesser man to stone. "Do *not* encourage her. Not another word out of any of you! You do realize that if we fail at this mission, she is stuck here forever? I will not allow that. Do you understand me? Now *focus.*"

Bjarni raised his eyebrows at me when Modi whipped back around, taking the lead, but he wisely chose not to respond.

"Sounds like you're lucky Daddy didn't threaten to turn the car around," Saga muttered as he closed in on my other side.

Modi pretended not to hear him.

It didn't take many yards before any amusement left us one by one. As we moved closer to the cauldron, the souls flowing into it from high above became distinguishable. I saw faces in there. Washed of color and twisted in fear, each soul sucked into the black depths of that cauldron emitted a wail that could only be heard because we were so close, and there were so many of them.

It hadn't dawned on me until then what death was truly like. Curious, perhaps, for a woman stuck in the

Realm of Death for weeks, but where I had felt the embrace of this gray nightmare suck any and all joy from the moment I had stepped foot in this place, I hadn't experienced… this.

I stared at the souls disappearing into the cauldron. These were regular humans, just… people who'd died, and this was the afterlife that awaited them.

"What does she do to them once they're in there?" I asked quietly.

"She drains their spark and leaves them empty husks she can command. They become her army," Mimir said.

"Their spark?"

"The kernel in your soul that makes you *you*," he explained. "Your will, your personality… that spark that only you possess."

I swallowed thickly. "No one deserves that. These souls… They were *people.* Their only crime is that they died."

A cool hand clasped my shoulder, squeezing gently. "She is the Queen of Hel. She decides the fate of every soul who enters her realm," Grim said with a measure of kindness in his voice likely brought on by the ache in our bond. "We are here to gain your freedom, mate, so we can bring an end to Ragnarök. This is not our fight, and if we attempt it, we might lose everything."

"He is right," Mimir broke in. "Defeating Hel is not your destiny, plum. Do not deviate from the path the Norns have woven for you. Too much is at stake."

I gritted my teeth and looked back up at the wailing souls. The terror on those pale faces jabbed deep into my gut. So much for eternal peace. "It's not right," I whispered.

"No. It's not," Magni agreed softly. He wove the fingers not clutching his weapon through my own. "But neither is Ragnarök. You are the only one who can stop all nine worlds from ceasing to exist, pet—the *only* one. Are you willing to risk the end of everything to right this wrong?"

I breathed deeply and slowly shook my head. They were right. If I died here, I would doom every living soul to this fate. Or worse.

The responsibility hadn't sunk in before now. Not fully. I had been too focused on the aching matebonds and my instinctive and overwhelming fear of losing the five men who were tied to my soul. I hadn't truly taken in that if I failed, if I didn't live up to the fate bestowed upon me by the Norns, I would be responsible for the death of everything.

Warm hands rubbed circles against my back. I let out an explosive breath as my field of vision narrowed to pinpricks, then slowly expanded again, the weight of our mission settling in my chest. There was only one goal. Nothing else could matter. Not yet.

"Let's go." Modi's voice was still a command, but there was a softer quality to it as he gave me a nod.

I kept my power close as we walked the final yards to the ominous black vessel, and when the lamentations became loud enough to pierce my heart, I hardened it until the tears pricking my eyes dried.

Only one goal.

Modi climbed the side of the cauldron with ease, followed by Grim, who practically scaled it like a cat. They both reached a hand down, and Bjarni propped me up on his shoulders so they could grab me under the armpits and haul me up.

The rim of the iron vessel was plenty large enough to stand on, but I crouched between Grim and Modi and clung to the edge as I carefully peered down.

I don't know what I'd expected to see—perhaps a skeleton queen perched on a throne with her maw open so she could swallow the incoming souls. What I saw, however, was nothing but swirling, silvery threads against a background of inky darkness, absorbing each soul as they plummeted through it.

"Who knew Níðhöggr's well could look downright cozy? Y'know, by comparison," Bjarni said as he pulled himself up next to Grim and gazed into the cauldron.

Modi made a noise of agreement.

"Well, I'm sure our sister will have as warm a welcome for us as the dragon did for you. Let's go," Saga said as he and Magni joined us.

With a deep breath, he swung both legs over the inside edge—and dropped into the cauldron.

28

GRIM

Braziers offering a cold, blue-tinged light cleaved a path through the darkness ahead of us. High above, the unfortunate souls circled before floating in a steady stream above the path and beyond. I couldn't see what lay ahead, but I knew. I felt her.

"I guess follow the souls to find Hel?" Annabel asked. She was holding Mimir's head, and the way she was clutching it, he might as well have been a favorite teddy bear.

An old memory of watching her as a child with her much-loved bear tight in her arms made me reach out to place a hand on her lower back, reminding her that she was not alone.

"Yes," Mimir confirmed. "The souls will lead us to her throne room."

Modi took the lead again. Thor's son had been

changed by his connection to Annabel as thoroughly as the rest of us, but it seemed even she couldn't erase his innate leanings to playing the commanding hero—a gift he'd inherited from his father, I suspected.

The rest of us encircled Annabel and followed close behind, weapons drawn.

Hel's halls were quiet, save for the wails from the souls above. They were faint, but constant, and gave the impression of a wind blowing through a forest. We followed them down the wide corridor and through several darkened passageways as quiet as the barren field above, until we finally entered a grand chamber deep within the bowels of Hel's palace.

And there she sat, our sister, on her throne of bones with her dark, gray-streaked hair adorned by a single iron band.

She was as pale as I, but where my skin was icy, hers was ashen, the sickly hue underlined by the snow white, gossamer dress draped over her gaunt figure. Behind her, the souls of the dead swirled slowly, as if waiting their turn to be drained by the Queen of Hel.

"What a pleasant surprise, brothers," our sister said, her obsidian eyes sweeping over our little group.

By my side, Annabel cringed. I pressed my hand firmer against her, lending her my strength. Hel's voice cracked like a whip—even for a god, it was hard to withstand.

"And you brought company," Hel continued. "Welcome to my humble abode, Thorssons. I wonder—does your daddy know where you are? I don't think he would be too pleased, hmm?"

She smiled at Modi, revealing a set of too-sharp teeth. "But then again, I hear he is already so very unhappy with you both. Something about mating a whore?"

I controlled the burst of anger flaring in my gut, knowing I had to keep my head cool. Unfortunately, neither Bjarni nor Magni managed to contain their snarls.

Hel clicked her tongue and refocused on Bjarni. "Oh, no, baby brother. Don't tell me *those* rumors are true as well? You *do* share a mate with our father's enemies? How... embarrassing."

"You know very well that your brothers share a mate with the Thorssons, witch," Mimir broke in. "Spare us the games. We are here with a purpose."

Hel shifted her gaze to him, arching one eyebrow high. "Prophet. I did hear you were spending some time in my lands. How courteous of you to stop by. And you are here with a purpose, you say? Intriguing as always, but I'm afraid you have caught me at a bad time. Places to be, worlds to devastate... You know how it goes. Ragnarök is all fun and games, but the *planning.* Everything runs on such a tight schedule."

"This won't take much of your time, *sister,*" I said. "We are here to request that you release our mate. Then we will be on our way, and you can return to your plans."

Hel flicked her eyes to me, then to Annabel, where they lingered long enough that my muscles strained with the desire to step between them.

The queen's lips twitched up into a surprised smile before she looked back to me. "*You* wish to return the human to the living? Did you not kill her yourself, my sweet brother?"

I clenched my teeth against the wave of shame at her words. Regret would not help me now. "It was a mistake. A horrible mistake. And now she must be returned to where she belongs—to the world of the living."

Hel tutted and shifted her focus back to Annabel. A look of mild disdain crossed her harrowed features. "Mistake or no, the girl is dead. No mortal leaves my realm once they have set foot here. No exception was made for Frigg's son, and none will be made for your mate."

"Well... the girl is not *entirely* dead," Mimir said. "Her physical body was not killed before she came through to this plane, and as it happens, she has eaten of Idunn's tree. It is possible to return her to the living world without encountering any, ah, *unpleasant* side-effects."

Hel tilted her head as she looked more intently at Annabel. Slowly, her lip curved up in another half-smile. "I see," she said at length. "More lives than a cat, hmm? No wonder he was so adamant she die."

Cold dread closed around my lungs. *He* had allied with her too. Of course he had.

"He?" Modi demanded. "You know the identity of he who has brought Ragnarök to our doorstep?"

"Naturally," Hel said as she gave me a meaningful smirk. "Our goals do align, after all. He gets his revenge, and I… I finally get to leave."

Bjarni blinked. "What do you mean you get to leave? You're the queen of this damned place. Leave whenever you bloody want."

Hel pursed her lips. "Why do you think I never stopped by for family dinners, baby brother? I am bound here until Naglfar sets sail on Ragnarök's winds. Unnumbered years I have resided here, trapped just as tragically as the souls I rule over. *Waiting*. So no, I am afraid that I will not be helping the woman prophesized to prevent Ragnarök's arrival escape her tomb."

"We could help you change your mind," Magni growled as he grabbed the pommel of his sword. "I suspect you would quickly come to appreciate your current position if you were to experience the funnel of souls for yourself."

I gritted my teeth and gave a sharp yank through my connection to Annabel to get the redheaded moron to shut up. All five of them cringed at the brutal jerk on their innermost.

In front of us, Hel's smile turned sharp and dangerous. She leaned forward to rest an elbow on the arm of her throne and her chin against a couple of fingers. "Do you think, Thorsson? Who knows—perhaps a warrior godling waving a sword around *is* enough to send the Queen of Death to her own grave. Care to step closer and quench my curiosity?"

I stepped forward quick enough to yank Magni back by his shoulder. The absolute idiot was bristling and ready to prove himself—against the Goddess of Death. I'd always taken him for the slightly smarter of Thor's sons. Apparently, I'd been wrong.

I gave him a withering stare before I stepped forward in his place. "I am the one who caused my mate's untimely death. I am the one who will pay any price for her release. If it is a bargain you require, sister, I will give you my life in exchange for hers."

Annabel's blind panic at my offer hit me like a cold punch to the gut, but she didn't speak, didn't beg me to recant. She only stood there, silent.

Good.

Hel eyed me, an evaluating look, as if she were weighing up the worth of my soul compared to Annabel's. "An interesting proposal, my brother of Mist and Shadows. How thoroughly a spell Fate must have woven for you to switch your allegiance yet again. I was told you were *most eager* to betray your brethren and murder the woman destined to be yours. I trust that they know the full extent of your deception, hmm?"

"We do. Your barbs will find no purchase here," Annabel said, sharp and clear and uncowed. I turned around in horror just in time to see her place Mimir's head in Bjarni's arms and step forward. Spine straight and shoulders back, she strode past me and continued all the way to the foot of Hel's throne. Shimmering tendrils of power licked along her ankles and rose around her like a billowing cape—an amalgamation of hers and ours.

"As it is my fate we are here to discuss, you will do so with me, Your Majesty," Annabel said. She gave Hel a tiny dip of her head, then stared straight into those void-like eyes that had swallowed countless souls.

Everything in me clenched with abject terror, but when Modi gasped, *"Anna!"* and made to storm after her, I held him back. I had the same, instinctive urge to throw myself between our mate and the danger in front of her, but I also knew that doing so would ruin Annabel's chances. She was right; this was *her* fate, and she was the woman destined to stop the end of the world, not us. Hiding behind us would win her no respect from this goddess.

"Well, well," Hel all but purred as she took in the power gently curling around Annabel. "Now I see why he was so keen for you to die. I admit—the idea that a mere human might stand against the tides of destruction had me... doubtful as to the truth of this prophecy of yours. But *you,* little soul... you are far more interesting than you seem at first glance, aren't you? Look how you have tamed their power and brought it to heel —just as efficiently as it appears you have the males themselves."

"I wish to leave this place," Annabel said. "Tell me what you want in exchange for returning me to the world of the living."

Hel tutted and shook her head. "All I want, little soul, is for Ragnarök to ravage its way through all nine worlds so I can walk free once more. I am afraid there is no bargain you can offer that will tempt me to release you. Your mere existence is a threat to my own desires, and that pretty power you wield only amplifies my need to keep you here."

She shot a glance at me, Saga, and Bjarni. "But out of, ah, *familial obligation,* I shall not send you to my soul siphon unless you leave me no other choice. That is as much as I can do for you, *sister.*"

Annabel was quiet for a little while. Then, without looking at us, she said, "I believe if we speak privately, you will change your mind."

The knot of terror in my gut clenched tighter. *No! You cannot be alone with her!*

The thought I sent through our bond was more instinctive than a conscious choice, but it was echoed in Saga's snarl.

A soft touch through our connection was all the response I got—a gentle promise that she would be okay. To trust her.

It took all I had to obey. By my side, Modi was shaking with the urge to retrieve her, but he too managed to remain stalwart.

We had to trust that she was strong enough to execute whatever plan she had in mind.

Hel watched our mate with a sugar-sweet smile and eyes as calculating as a serpent eying its next meal. "Ooh, how *intriguing.* I am almost tempted to oblige you."

Annabel stretched out a hand toward her, palm up. "Then come. I will make it worth your while—*sister*."

Hel's eyes flashed and her smile widened once more. Locking her gaze on Annabel's, she placed her own, bony hand in hers and rose from her throne. She was taller than our mate, but thinner, looking both frail and eternally dangerous as she stared down at the woman I loved with everything I was.

Without another word—without a single glance in our direction—the Queen of Death led our mate from the throne room and into the darkness beyond.

29

ANNABEL

Loki had sired many a monster. As Hel led me from the throne room and into another dark hall, I was reminded that the goddess beside me had less likeness to a divine creature like Freya, and more to the giant sea serpent we had seen as we flew across the Atlantic.

On each side of the large room and stretching as far into the darkness as I could see, glass cages lined the space. Each one contained a faintly glowing, spectral entity. I didn't need to ask what they were—I felt it into the marrow of my bones: souls from the siphon, waiting for Hel to break them.

"Tell me then, little soul: What do you wish to discuss out of earshot of all those big, strong men of yours?" The goddess turned to me, that sardonic smile still dancing on her lips as she took me in.

"Your return to the world of the living," I said, deliberately not looking at the caged souls all around us. "I suspect there is a reason you have been trapped down here for so long."

Her smile turned sharper. "They fear me, of course. Wield a little death magic, and suddenly you're banished to this place. But I am soon to be free. And they will pay."

It took everything I had not to shrink from the dark fire in her eyes as she relished the thought of revenge on the gods who had trapped her here. "And have you given much thought to *what* you will be returning to?"

Hel raised her eyebrows at me, daring me to continue.

"You have been trapped here, in the land of the dead, for millennia. I have only been here a few weeks, and what I miss the most is color, the scents... Life. But after Ragnarök... as I understand it, there will be nothing. No colors, no chirping birds, no warmth of companionship—just darkness and misery." I cocked my head. "Isn't that what you are trying to leave behind?"

"There will be life, after it is all over," she said. "A new beginning."

I lifted my brows. "Oh? I believe someone told me about that... Something about a few gods surviving? And two humans? Two of every animal? And which prophecy is this from again?"

Hel hesitated, and I could have sworn a look of uncertainty flashed in her eyes, but it was gone just as swiftly as it arrived. "It has been known for as long as we have expected Ragnarök."

"Mmm. But there isn't actually a prophecy that explains what happens after the end, is there? Just assumptions made by scared gods wanting to reassure themselves that everything is going to be okay—that their inability to protect the nine worlds won't mean the end of everything."

I turned away from her, forcing my instincts screaming not to turn my back on a monster to calm, and walked to one of the rows of glass cages. "You know what this theory of what comes after reminds me of? The Christian faith. They have a whole two-people-populated-the-Earth thing going. And something-something two of each animal surviving a global extinction.

"There is no silver lining to Ragnarök, Hel. There is *nothing.* Whatever stories the gods have spun, there is no basis for it. No prophecies, no promise. Nothing. Your freedom will be spent in an eternity far bleaker than your current prison."

She was silent for a long moment. Then the whisper of gossamer fabric on stone approached where I stood, drawing up close behind me.

"You speak with such *confidence,* little soul." Her tone was somewhere between a purr and a sneer. "What are you but a human thrust into a game dictated by powers stronger than you?"

I squared my shoulders at her derisive words, but

didn't look away from the glowing soul in the cage before us twisting in search of a way out. "I am the one prophesized to stop this madness. Do you truly think if life came after Ragnarök, if it was a new beginning rather than the end of everything, that Fate would have thrust me into this mess in some desperate effort to stop it? If it is truly meant to be, why am I here?"

"You make... interesting points, sister," Hel said after another lengthy pause. She placed her bony hand on the glass between us and the soul. The air inside the cage shimmered, and the soul let out a gasp as it seized—only to shatter into a thousand pieces. They fell to the floor with the soft chiming of silver bells, an iridescent smoke slipped through the glass and into Hel.

I stared at the now-empty cage, willing the tears blurring my vision to dry. This was too important; I couldn't falter now.

"But interesting as they might be, I would rather walk in darkness up there than be trapped *here*. Even a realm as vast as the underworld gets... *tedious* after a few millennia." The goddess turned from the glass and strode farther into the grand hall beyond.

I steeled myself before following her. "Then let me suggest an alternative."

She looked at me over her shoulder, eyebrows lifting again. "An alternative? My, you *are* an intriguing little creature, aren't you? No wonder my brothers are so smitten. They may be our father's most banal offspring, but even they have the zest for the macabre he passes on to all of us."

I ignored her comment, even though I was *quite sure* it was some sort of a dig. "Let me stop Ragnarök. Free me, and don't come to Midgard with your army of undead. In return, I will find a way to free you once we have stopped it. You will walk in the world of the living again—in the *true* world of the living. You will see color, feel the warmth of the sun on your skin, and experience what life truly is like."

Her lips curled into that dangerous smile again. "Even if that were something I desired, I doubt you would be able to find a way where I have failed. Intriguing or no, you *are* only a human."

"Human-*ish,*" I said with a nonchalance I didn't feel. "I have captured the God of Mischief, defeated Nidhug, and I will stop Ragnarök. If you agree to this bargain, I *will* find a way to free you. I promise."

"The promise of a desperate woman," Hel mused. She turned from me and walked to another cage, dark eyes hooded as she regarded the soul within. "Willing to lie, beg, and steal for her freedom."

"I will swear a blood oath," I said despite the twang of fear in my gut. "And I will give you anything you desire."

Hel skimmed her fingers down the glass between us and the unfortunate soul within. The air shimmered lightly, but no shattering followed. "Anything I desire?" The purr was back in her voice. "And if that is a life?"

I had known this would be a likely outcome. That was why I had requested to speak with her alone. My mates would never allow me to bargain my life, but this was the Goddess of Death. Her price was expected.

"Then I would give it." My voice didn't falter. For that, I was grateful. "But only *my* life—you will have to find a way to spare my mates death upon our bonds being severed."

And she would have to spare my daughter too. It took everything I had not to press a hand to my abdomen. But if my choice was to let my child grow up without a mother, or to let the world she would live in get swallowed by darkness and doom... then it was not difficult to pick.

The goddess kept her eyes on the cage, but I saw her smile hike up higher. "Hmm. You really are eager, little soul. I am pleased—you passed my test. If you will trade your own life, I deem your commitment worthy of a bargain."

Her test? A thread of relief wormed its way through my chest, even as I braced for the other shoe to drop. If she didn't want my life, then what?

She finally turned to me then, dark eyes glowing, and clasped a bony hand around my wrist with strength far greater than her frail physique would suggest her capable of. "I want the spark within you, Annabel Turner. My brothers can keep you—call it a wedding gift, if you like. But if you want me to release you, if you want me to remain here with my armies while you fight Ragnarök… then you will give me your spark."

I frowned. "My magic? What…"

I trailed off. It was a stupid question. Hadn't I shown her my power as I stepped up to her throne? Warned her of its strength? Told her how I defeated both Nidhug and her father? There were a great many things a goddess as dangerous as Hel could use my magic for.

But what she didn't know was that my true strength came from my mates. Without them, my magic was far less extraordinary. Far less dangerous in the wrong hands.

It was a part of me, yes—something that had offered me strength when I'd thought I had none—and the thought of giving it up was painful. But not nearly as painful as giving my own life, and I had been willing to offer that.

"I will need it to stop Ragnarök," I said slowly. "But… after. If that is what you want, I will give it freely."

"Then we have an agreement." Hel closed her eyes. Black plumes of power rose around her and swept through me, coaxing out my own magic. "Swear to me that you will free me from the underworld and allow me to walk wherever I please. Swear to me that in nineteen years, you will willingly surrender the spark you carry today to my servitude. Swear this, and you will be the first soul I free from my realm. Swear this, and I will not ravage the world of the living with my armies."

Something about her wording caught me off-guard, but the power of her magic tangling with mine and the monumental importance of this moment made me push the nagging notion away.

"I swear it," I said.

My power stuttered in my veins, as if something yanked on it before the spell released its grip on me, and I stumbled a step forward, my gaze sweeping up over the glass and the soul inside.

Her mouth was open in a silent scream, pale eyes wide with abject horror.

I recognized her instantly.

"Such a sweet present my brother sent me," Hel purred by my side. She released my wrist and pressed her fingertips to the glass. "The Goddess of Love, tragically murdered by the man she tried to help. Love can be treacherous."

"Freya," I whispered, the tears I had managed to keep at bay for the other soul now trickling down my cheeks. I placed my hand against the glass in a futile hope to shield her from the dark goddess by my side.

"She is easy to love, isn't she?" Hel mused. "So kind-hearted, so beautiful... Who doesn't love *Love*?"

"Please let her go," I whispered. "The world won't be right without love in it. Without *her*."

Hel clicked her tongue. "I have already agreed to let you go, and now you ask for more? Greed doesn't become you, sister."

"Please," I repeated. "She is innocent. She—"

"I don't care who is innocent and who is guilty," Hel snapped, her voice cracking like a whip through the hall. "They all come to me, every last soul not destined for Asgard—the good, the wicked, the unremarkable... Their bodies nourish the lands above, but their souls feed the powers of this realm."

"Do you even know what a world without love will be like?" I asked. "It will be exactly like here—dead. Miserable. Is that what you wish to escape to?"

Hel chuffed. "I care little for love. But if you do, perhaps you should be the one to take this soul within you, hmm? If you cannot bear the thought of a world without love, I will grant you the chance to return it... after a fashion."

I blinked. Surely, she couldn't mean... "W-What?"

"Devour her," Hel said, the glow in her eyes turning vicious. "Take her soul and make it yours."

"No!" I jerked back from the prison, horror clawing at my throat. "Never! I could never do that!"

"What a pity." Hel stroked her fingers along the glass. The air around Freya shimmered threateningly. "I think, if given the choice, our pretty goddess would prefer her final resting place to be within someone who believes in love. What say you, Freya? Who would you rather be eaten by? Me, or your protégé?"

The silvery soul within the prison twisted, her large eyes sliding from Hel to me. The naked plea in them was undeniable.

I swallowed thickly. Could I do it? Could I... *devour* a

soul? The thought alone was so repulsive it made my stomach lurch, but between me and Hel...

Was I the merciful option?

The grim determination on Freya's spectral features told me the answer.

"Okay." Shaking despite my best efforts to appear strong, I placed my hand back on the glass. "I'll do it."

Hel pressed her fingertips lightly against my nape. "Good girl."

I cringed at her touch, but managed to remain still, eyes locked on Freya's.

The air around her vibrated more rapidly, blurring the edges of her already hazy outline. "I'm sorry," I whispered through my tears. "I'm so, so sorry."

"Take her," Hel hissed. "Now."

Light ripped out from the center Freya's spectral form, shattering her. The pieces fell to the floor with the softest twinkle, a faint whisper of a melody, as the Goddess of Love ceased to exist.

A ribbon of white glided through the glass and into my mouth and nostrils. It tasted like summer rain and green leaves, and the first flowers of spring.

I swallowed on instinct, and then she was *in* me. I felt her sliding through my veins, filling me up not with horror, but with quiet sorrow, and the lightest touch of... gratitude.

She settled low in my abdomen, curling protectively around the still-invisible child growing there.

"See? It is not so bad, is it?" Hel purred. "Mayhaps you will even develop a taste for it."

I glared at her through the tears still trickling down my face. "No. You have not turned me into a monster with this little ploy of yours. Now, are you ready to live up to your end of the bargain? Or do you have more games to play?"

Hel chuckled. "So *feisty,* little soul. Yes, you may take your mates and go fight the hordes of Ragnarök. But don't forget: If you don't fulfil your end of the bargain, you will die. And then your soul and your mates' will return to this place—to me."

30

ANNABEL

The second I stepped through the doors leading back into the throne room, a pair of strong arms closed around me.

"Are you hurt? Is the baby hurt?" Modi demanded as a cool hand slid to my abdomen, dark, cautious power gently probing.

"I'm fine. We're both fine," I said.

"We felt you," Magni rasped, the hoarseness in his voice betraying their terror for those moments we had been apart.

Freya? Grim inquired through our bond. *I feel her... within you? How?*

"I will explain later," I murmured before turning back to Hel. She was leaning against the door frame, watching me surrounded by my worried mates with a sardonic slant to her lips.

"We will be leaving now," I told her.

"I suppose you will," she said, giving me a mocking bow before she reached out a hand. Dark magic plumed from her fingertips and over the combined shields Magni, Modi, Grim, and Saga raised around us. But the Death Goddess' power wasn't aimed at us. It hit the floor a few yards past us and fizzed before rising into a large rectangle hovering vertically in the air. Nothing but blackness could be seen through its center.

"Enjoy your freedom, little soul," Hel said as she inspected her nails. "And don't forget—should you not fulfil your end of our agreement..."

"I will fulfill it," I said, turning to the rectangle. "Come. It's time to leave this place."

But my mates hesitated. Grim glanced from the rectangle to me. "What did you promise her, Annabel?"

"I will tell you later," I said, jerking on his and Bjarni's hands to get them to move forward with me. "Let's go. We've got an Armageddon to stop."

"Nothing is worth losing you over," Bjarni said simply. "What did you bargain, sweetie?"

I drew in a deep breath. "You won't lose me; I promise. But may I remind you that as long as we remain here, I'm dead?"

That did the trick. They moved as one, taking me with them toward the rectangular portal. The inky darkness inside it swirled as we approached, leaching out of the frame.

"Is it safe?" Magni muttered, his head tilted toward Grim.

My cold mate reached out with his magic, letting it slide over the void-like surface. After a moment, he nodded. "It will lead us to Asgard."

"Did you think I would deceive you, brother?" Hel taunted. "How very... hurtful."

No one answered her as we stepped through the portal and darkness consumed us.

THE SUCKING, pulling sensation of the portal released me without warning, and I stumbled onto a cushiony surface. Booming crashes rang in my ears, and disorientation rippled through me. There were so many *colors.* Brightest was the emerald green underneath my knees and palms, and it took me several seconds to realize we'd landed on soft grass.

Grass. I breathed in and the lush scent of it filled my nostrils, tinged with smoke, and something else I couldn't quite put my finger on. I inhaled again, filling my lungs.

Alive. I was alive.

"Pet? Are you okay?" Magni's worried face popped into my field of vision. *Magni's face*—with his beautiful, bright green eyes and his deep-red mane. I laughed at his sheer beauty, at how *vibrant* he was, and grasped his beard so I could plant a kiss on his unprepared mouth.

He tasted so sweet. Sensual. I shivered against him

and hummed with delight as he wrapped me in his strong arms and deepened our kiss.

"As much as properly celebrating our mate's return to the living seems like a great idea, perhaps this is not the time or place," Saga drawled. "We need to regroup and figure out our next steps—and fast."

Reluctantly I pulled my lips from Magni's to look up at my blond mate. He nodded at the horizon over his shoulder, and I finally noticed the smokey haze on a background of orange and red. At first I thought it was a sunset, but the light was different, and that deep, thrumming *noise* jarred my eardrums.

"Surtr's horde must have arrived while we were in Hel," Bjarni said just as lightning flashed. I followed where it struck, and gaped at the sight that met my still-overwhelmed eyes.

We were on a hill in the rolling, lush countryside of Asgard. Valhalla gleamed golden on the mountainside to the west, and to the east, where a mighty wall stretched, winged figures darkened the sky. On the ground, through a great tear in the barrier, warriors battled. I couldn't make out the individual people from this distance, but the screams and explosions suddenly made sense.

"This is... This is the final battle?" I whispered. "The gods' last stand against Ragnarök?"

"Yes," Modi said, and from the tension in his voice and the pang of guilt in our bond, I knew what he was thinking. His father was down there—the destiny he'd thought was his until I came along.

Saga clapped a hand on his shoulder. "Dying in battle might be a glorious fate, but saving Asgard and the eight other realms is preferable—even for a son of Thor, hmm?"

Modi gave him a faint, mirthless smile. "Any more *precise* ideas on how we do that?"

"We start within Valhalla's walls," Mimir said. I hadn't noticed him under Bjarni's arm until then. His face was drawn in far more serious lines than I'd become accustomed to, even in the depths of Hel.

"Valhalla?" Modi frowned at him. "What good can come from us going there? If we are to stop Ragnarök—"

"We start with Valhalla," Grim said, voice firm and lips flattened into a tight line. "We need to."

"Then we go to Valhalla," I said, pushing to my feet. The explosion of color all around us and the multitude of scents was still disorienting, but I forced my mind to focus. I had done the impossible—I had united enemies with love, I had escaped Hel, and I had defeated a *literal dragon*. It was time to end this.

Grim looked at me for a long moment, turmoil evident in his amber and ice-blue eyes. Fear, I realized; he was scared.

We can do this. We will *do this,* I sent through our bond. I was met with dark, impenetrable silence so similar to the shield he had erected between us after we'd first mated that it took me a moment to realize that it was not the same.

I blinked and prodded it again. It felt alien and... wrong. It wasn't Grim blocking me. It was... something else. Some*one* else.

"The Betrayer," I whispered, more to myself than to him. "He is there. To stop Ragnarök, we have to stop him first."

Another flash of lightning from the wall made me look to Bjarni. I saw the same understanding in his eyes that penetrated my own muddled thoughts. If the Betrayer was in Valhalla, it couldn't be Thor.

A thread of relief wormed its way through my chest. Magni and Modi loved their father, despite his flaws and questionable parenting. Having the man who instilled their sense of morals betray them so thoroughly would have been awful.

"Then we go to Valhalla," Modi echoed, his hand landing on the pommel of his sword. "And we kill him."

Grim swallowed thickly, but nodded once before he fell into step beside me. "To Valhalla," he said in a whiskey rasp.

I placed a hand on his arm. "We will defeat him," I said softly. "I promise."

He looked at me then, and the devotion in his eyes took my breath away.

"If we don't, Annabel, I want you to know that I will never regret choosing you. Only that it took me so long to do so."

I bit my lip to stop my stupid heart from making me burst into tears. "We will. We have a daughter who needs us to."

His gaze dipped to my abdomen for a long second. When he looked back up again, some of the fear in his gaze had been replaced by raw determination. He only ghosted a hand down my lower back in before refocusing on the road—and the golden palace looming high on the mountain ahead.

31

ANNABEL

The winding path up the mountain was utterly silent as we made our way to Valhalla's gates. Not a single soul met us, and this high up, even the battle for Asgard could no longer be heard. Not so much as a crack of thunder broke the eerie stillness.

"I guess everyone's busy fighting," Saga said as he looked over the edge of the path and down onto the battlefield in the distance.

"Without Níðhöggr and Hel's forces, it shouldn't be this evenly matched," Modi said, a deep frown forming on his forehead as he stopped to watch the battle as well. "Why *aren't* Hel's forces here?"

"It was part of the bargain I made," I said. "She will not join the battle."

They all turned to stare at me. But if I'd hoped for admiration or praise, I'd have been sorely disappointed.

"What did you promise her, Annabel?" Magni asked, his teeth clenched and a distinctly *no-more-stalling* note to his deep rumble.

I sighed. "What I had to. I promised to find a way to free her, and in exchange, she swore to keep her army from joining the battle."

Saga drew in a sharp breath. Magni's jaw clenched.

"And if you fail?" Modi asked softly. "What price will she exact then?"

"I won't," I said. "*We* won't."

"Annabel. What is her price?" Grim asked, his voice firm.

"My life," I said, already shaking my head when all five of my mates growled, nostrils flaring and eyes widening. "It won't come to that. I swear to you, I will find a way to free her."

"The other gods will never allow it!" Magni snarled, his green eyes sparking with anger and fear. "They sealed her down there eons ago, and they did so for a reason. *No one* wants the Goddess of Death roaming freely through the lands, and the only way to release her is if they *all* willingly undo the magic that binds her. There is *no* other way!"

I reached out and stroked a hand through his beard. "Then we will convince them. But there is no point worrying about it until we have stopped Ragnarök. Let's keep going."

He pushed his cheek into my touch more on instinct

than agreement, judging by the glare he leveled me with. "If I lose you..."

"You won't," I promised again. "I would never do that to you. To any of you."

"And what bargain did you make with our sister to be released yourself?" Saga asked, his voice silken, but with a dangerous undertone. They were all pissed at me. "If you already offered your life to keep her forces at bay?"

"My magic," I said. "But not yet. In nineteen years, she will claim it."

They all frowned, a shared look of puzzlement crossing their handsome faces. "Why then?"

I shrugged. "I don't know. And I don't much care. She can have it. All I care about is that we get through this together."

Saga's gaze softened—I knew why. Of all my mates, he understood how much discovering my powers and finding my own strength had meant to me.

"Let's go," I repeated. "You can yell at me about my choices later."

"We will," Bjarni rumbled. He clasped a hand to my shoulder and nodded up the path toward Valhalla. "All right, then. Let's go knock this Betrayer's skull in."

We all resumed our journey up the mountain, save Modi, who lingered for a moment longer, surveying the battlefield. When he caught up with us, he said, "It's not just Hel and Níðhöggr who are missing. So is the Fenris wolf."

"He will make his way here once he has run across Midgard and spread darkness and terror," Magni said.

I remembered what Bjarni and Modi had told me about Ragnarök, and what Loki's giant wolf-monster and sea serpent offspring would do to the human world, and swallowed thickly. Even if we won, even if we stopped the end of the nine worlds, how much would be left of mine?

"Maybe we should go there," I suggested. "If we can stop Fenris and that huge serpent—"

"No." Mimir's voice was gentle. "If you travel to Midgard, plum, we will lose."

"Will my family survive?" It hurt to force the question out of my too-tight throat.

"No one but the Norns can tell you that, and even they may not be able to see through the darkness of Ragnarök. All we know for sure is if we do not win, they will die, along with everyone else."

He was right. All I could do was believe that by the end of this, I would get to see my parents again.

The enormous wolves that had guarded Valhalla's entrance upon my first arrival were still sitting on either side of the gates. When we approached, they stood up, ears flattening along their skulls and teeth bared.

"Whoa," Modi called, reaching both hands forward, palms up. "You know me, you daft beast. Let us enter."

He barely managed to pull his fingers back in time before sharp teeth snapped the air where they'd been seconds before.

"Let me," Bjarni said as he shouldered his way past the frowning redhead. "You don't have the right touch with animals. Or omegas."

Both Modi and I glared at his broad back, but he ignored us as he focused on the snarling wolf.

"Shh, shh. Be calm, little buddy," Bjarni cooed. He knelt down just out of the chained canine's reach. "We may be somewhat Jotunn-y, but we aren't like those nasty buggers trying to break the wall down. We aren't gonna hurt you."

The wolf's only response was to lunge for his face. Its growl choking off on a howl when the chain dug into its windpipe and black magic pulled it back in place.

"You won't talk sense into this beast. It's been touched by darkness," Grim said. He reached out a hand, and the other wolf was dragged back to the opposite side of the gate and held in place too. "Come. We should make haste."

Bjarni shot the two animals a displeased look, but got to his feet. "It ain't right to do that to innocent beasts," he grumbled.

My sweet one. When it came down to it, Bjarni was much happier on the farm, tending to their sheep and cooking food for his family than he was mixed up in a mythic Armageddon. I wondered if their farm would still be there, if we survived. If it would be waiting for us, or if it would be buried under ice and devastation.

I frowned. Would Magni and Modi be happy settling down there? We hadn't exactly had time to discuss what would come after.

As we entered Valhalla's wide doors, I pushed the thoughts away. Planning for a future that might not be there was a luxury I couldn't afford to get distracted by.

The great hall was dark. Only faint, gray light from the open gates behind us and the windows high above lit the abandoned long tables and benches. No fires blazed in the many braziers and hearths. No raucous laughter or bawdy songs filled the air.

Memories of my weeks in gray, sensory-deprived Hel made me clutch Bjarni's hand. His warmth leached into my skin, and I breathed a sigh of relief as Modi's bright-red hair came into my field of vision as he took up the lead. No matter what came next, at least I would face it with them.

My mates closed in around me as we walked, blocking my view of the darkened hall. One after the other, they drew their weapons, as if the silence set their instincts on edge as much as it did mine. There was something... *wrong* about it, like the great halls were never meant to lay in silence.

"What the—?" Modi stopped so suddenly I smacked right into his back, nose-first.

"Trud?" he called, disbelief coloring his voice.

"What are you doing here?" Magni asked, his brow locked in a deep frown. He took a few steps forward, leaving me with enough of a gap to see what was going on.

In front of us, maybe a hundred yards away, a slim figure sat on the throne on the dais where Odin had cast judgement on my mates, and later Loki. Long, blonde hair spilled over her shoulders, and on her head perched a golden crown.

It was Trud, Modi and Magni's sister.

She regarded them with a blank stare, but didn't speak.

"Trud," Modi repeated, "get down from there. It isn't safe." He made to take a step forward, but stopped himself, not wanting to leave me exposed. I frowned. He thought his sister a potential threat?

"Trud?" I called. "Are you all right?"

Her blue eyes moved over the alphas until they landed on me. "Sister," she said softly. "They got you out. And now you have come to fulfil your prophecy?"

"Yes."

I didn't get to say anything else before Mimir murmured, "Magni, step back. Protect the omega."

I lifted my eyebrows at the prophet. "Against what? She's their *sister.* She's been helping them."

Magni, however, stepped back and to the side without hesitation, shielding me with the bulk of his body.

Trud laughed, a pealing sound that echoed through the hall and raised goosebumps along my arms. "Brother! You believe the old goat when he suggests *I* would hurt your pretty mate? She's right—I'm your baby sister! You used to bring me pretty trinkets and let me ride on your back, remember? I'm just a sweet, soft, harmless little girl."

"Shit," Saga swore behind me. He clasped a hand to my shoulder, and I felt his magic weave through mine, pulling on it until a shimmering shield rose around our little group. "She's the one."

"No. This can't be," Modi said softly, and the heartbreak in his voice made me reach forward and place a palm against his back for support. "Trud, this can't be. You cannot be the Betrayer."

"Why? Because I'm a woman? Because my heart is too soft to let me act when Asgard lays forgotten, and we are too busy quibbling amongst ourselves to do anything about it?"

She rose from the throne and pointed at us—at Mimir. "Ragnarök has been foretold for thousands of years. Who are you to decide it needs to be stopped? You, and those Norn cunts scrambling to prevent the inevitable. But this has to happen, prophet. The nine worlds will fall so that a new dawn can rise from the ashes—a dawn where no one will ever again forget who owns their fealty."

"Trud," Modi whispered. The devastation in that one word tore at my heart, and I squeezed my eyes shut against the pain radiating through my bonds to both him and Magni.

"This makes no sense," I said, more to myself than to any of my mates. I glanced at Grim. My darkhaired mate had his jaw set and soft lips pulled into a thin line—but his focus wasn't on Trud. He was scanning the walls of the great hall, mismatched eyes searching, *searching...*

"She isn't the Betrayer!" I said. "She's a distraction."

Trud's lovely face twisted into a nasty smile. "Oh? You don't think me strong enough, *sister?*"

She raised her hand, and a wave of light slammed against my shield hard enough to make me stagger.

"*Shit,* when did she get so strong?" Saga spat, and I felt more of his magic flow into me to support the barrier between us and the mad goddess.

"I don't need help. Not yet," I murmured to him as I gently pushed away his offered power. "Focus your strength on the fight ahead."

It was true. My magic swelled within me like a great, untamed beast eager to rise to the challenge. It had always felt powerful to me, but now, after uniting with all five of my mates, it was something else. Something *more.*

I looked at Trud. "Borrowed power or not, you do not have the strength to stop us. And whoever is pulling your strings knows this, sister of my mates. Don't make us hurt you to get to him."

Something dark and alien flashed in her clear blue eyes.

"Watch out!" Modi snarled just as another blast of power zinged through the air and slammed into my shield.

But it was different this time. It wasn't a wave of light. It crashed into my magic and ripped at it like a vicious dog, tearing at the fabric of my very being with strength that seemed to come from the core of the universe.

I screamed and dropped to the stone floor, every nerve in my body singed from the unexpected blast.

But my shield held.

Above me, my mates roared as one. Fury ripped through our bonds, and I felt the bloodlust descend. Lightning cracked through Valhalla and slammed into the dais up ahead, twice in quick succession.

I looked up and saw Saga, Modi, Bjarni, and Magni running at the dais where black scorch marks surrounded Trud.

She laughed as if she were delighted that her own brothers had attempted to kill her in retaliation. I cursed softly and slung my shield out to wrap around my four berserking mates.

Cool hands gripped underneath my arms and hauled me to my feet. "You have to harden off the connection through your magic to your core," Grim said, "or he will use it as a connector and tear you apart from the inside."

I looked at him and saw the battle lust dancing in his eyes as he stared at the fight in front of us. But he didn't give in—he'd managed to control his instincts to tear apart the goddess who'd attacked his mate because he didn't want to leave me unguarded.

"Is she in control of herself? Or is the Betrayer making her do this? Oh, *fuck!*"

The last bit I hissed out as Trud hurled another wave of that awful power against my shield protecting Magni, and it ricocheted through my magic and into my core. I managed to stay on my feet this time, but not without clutching Grim's arm for support.

"It doesn't matter," Grim growled. "She's going to kill us if we let her. We can't afford anything less than lethal strikes. Now *focus.*" His words were followed by a rush of cool, soothing power trickling through my veins and finding its way to my innermost.

Like this, his voice echoed through my mind.

Dark tendrils wove around my golden light as he showed me how to harden the connection between myself and the magic within. I followed his lead, and the next blast that hit my shield around Bjarni only sent an unpleasant tingling sensation through my bones.

A rumble of thunder pulled my attention back to Modi. His teeth were gritted, his muscles bunched as he swung his sword at his sister with one hand while slinging lightning at her with the other. There was nothing but murderous intent in my redheaded mate's eyes, but I knew what this would cost him—him and Magni.

I thought of the wolves guarding Valhalla's gates and Bjarni's complaint of what had been done to them to make them mindlessly attack. I also remembered my first meeting with Trud. Her genuine delight at my presence in her brother's life, her gentleness and understanding of my nature and destiny. The kindness I had felt radiate from her.

This wasn't her. Her attempts at killing her own brothers couldn't be her free will. And it did matter.

"We have to find out how he is controlling her!" I shouted. None of the four men on the dais heard me—they only had senses for the fight in front of them. They worked together, darting in with blades and magic, intent on finding a way through the destructive power pouring out of the blonde goddess.

But Grim heard me.

"Annabel, it doesn't matter!" he growled. "We don't have time."

"That's Modi and Magni's sister," I hissed at him. "How would you feel if you were forced to kill your brothers when there was another way? She hasn't betrayed us—someone is forcing her to do this. We will *make* time."

Grim bared his teeth, frustration etched in every feature of his coldly handsome face, but I saw the surrender in his eyes as my words sank in. With a growl, he whipped back around to take in the fight. Moments later, his dark magic floated through the air and encircled Trud.

"There is... something," he said through gritted teeth. "He is blocking me. I can't see."

I didn't pause to think. I clutched Grim's arm harder and sent a thread of my magic into him. It split my focus from my shields, and I clenched my jaw and forced my protections firmer, but Grim had already latched on to my offering. He grabbed the thread of golden light and forced himself at Trud once more.

I saw it this time—the dark, horrible entity latched onto the young goddess as Grim surrounded her with our combined power. Like thorns, it bit into her skull and seeped through the brightness that had once been her gentle spirit.

A flash of pain, followed by roar pulled my mind back into myself just in time to see Saga stumble a few steps before he renewed his attack on Trud. Blood seeped from a gash in his thigh.

I had let my shield around him drop, too distracted with Grim's attempts at uncovering how Trud was being controlled to keep all five of my protective barriers as solid as they needed to be.

Cursing my own stupidity, I strengthened my shields and held.

"There is... a sigil. Or an idol. He is using... something. She is too strong-willed to be controlled with a simple command," Grim gasped by my side. From the strain in his voice, it was clear that even with the help of my magic, this wasn't an easy task.

"The crown!" Mimir called from the floor where he'd been dropped before my mates rushed at the dais. "It has his touch."

Grim swore under his breath, then shouted, "Break her crown! Break her fucking crown, you idiots!"

Bjarni reacted instantly. Just as Magni grasped her arm and sent a shock of lightning through her shields, Bjarni rolled across the platform to get behind her and shot up, his heavy sword aimed at her head. The weapon struck Trud's golden crown, and the impact rang through the great hall.

She shrieked and whipped around, lips pulled back and eyes wild as she focused her full ire on Bjarni.

I strengthened his shield just in time. The force of her attack was enough to make me stumble and grit my teeth against the aftershock, but my blond mate was unscathed. He struck again at her head, but it was Modi who connected with the golden metal from behind her. He hit her so hard that had she not been enveloped in magic, he would have cleaved her skull in two.

The power of his strike knocked the crown clean off her head and sent it flying across the dais past Bjarni.

Trud screamed and seized into a tight arc, her back bowing unnaturally.

Bjarni cursed and jumped after the golden circlet. He reached it before it tumbled off the edge and stomped his foot on the delicate metal, snapping in in two.

Trud's scream broke as instantly as the powerful magic encircling her, and she collapsed onto the wooden platform in a heap.

Snarling, Modi raised his sword and swung.

"No!" My cry broke through the hall and I reached for him—for all of them—through our bonds. All four of them jerked backwards as if pulled by physical ropes.

"It was the crown!" I shouted, already running toward them as fast as my feet would carry me. "Don't hurt her. She is innocent."

I saw the battle lust fade from their eyes, and the horror set in in Modi's and Magni's as they turned back to their sister.

"Trud?" Modi whispered hoarsely, though he kept his sword lifted, ready to strike.

She only groaned softly in response.

I climbed the stairs to the dais two steps at a time and threw myself by Trud's side before Saga could stop me.

"Hey. Hey, you're okay," I said as I let my fingers explore her face and skull with gentle touches. "You're gonna be okay."

She was bone-white and winced when I grazed the area where that cursed crown had sat. I let my magic spill out and found the festering wounds below her skin left behind by its thorny grip. It took more power than it should have to erase the ghostly talons from her flesh, but when it was done, Trud's eyes fluttered open and she looked at me without a hint of malice.

"I'm sorry," she croaked. "I'm so sorry."

Behind me, Magni and Modi breathed deeply, and I felt their relief flutter through our connection.

Modi knelt by my side and cupped his sister's face. "What happened to you? Gods, I... I nearly killed you, Trud!"

"I figured out... who betrayed us. But he found me before I could..." She coughed and rolled her eyes back to me. "You saved me. I was trying to kill all of you, and you saved me. Gods, if I... if I had succeeded..."

"It wasn't you," I said, gently stroking her hair out of her face. "Who did this to you, Trud? Who is behind this?"

A *caw* broke through the great hall, silencing Trud before she could so much as part her lips.

We all jerked in the direction of the sound just as a large raven swept through the doorway behind the abandoned throne and landed on one of its armrests. Its mirror image followed, perching on the opposite arm with another caw.

"Huginn and Munin?" Bjarni said, his voice pitching higher with surprise.

"Indeed," a deep voice rumbled from past the shadowed doorway. "I have tried in so many ways to divert you younglings from this tragic course you have chosen. I have put in your path so many obstacles that you have persistently, petulantly climbed over just to meet your inevitable end at my hands."

The shadows parted, and a tall figure stepped through. He was swathed in gray robes, matching his long gray hair and beard. The staff in his hand glowed softly as he paused next to his throne and looked at us one after the other with his singular eye.

Then Odin sighed and shook his head. "You have left me with no choice. The ravens are here to bear witness to the final moments of Ragnarök. Die well, young ones."

32

GRIM

"I don't... I don't understand." The devastation in Modi's voice was graver than when he had seen his sister on that throne. He stared at Odin, and the sorrow in his eyes suggested that he did understand, even though he didn't want to.

"You are the god-king. You... You are the first among us. Your job is to protect us. To protect all the nine worlds. Yet *you* are the Betrayer? *You* have brought about Ragnarök? Why? Why could you possibly want to see the end of all there is?"

"Because deep down, he is a petty, petulant child," Mimir's voice rang from the hall behind us. "And because the humans have forgotten about him, he wants them to suffer."

I felt it too—the spell that had kept me silent since my meeting with Asgard's ruler so many weeks ago no longer bound my mind, silencing any words that may give away the Betrayer's identity. Now that Odin had revealed himself, its magic was null.

Judging by the vitriol in Mimir's voice, he had been pleased to find his tongue unrestrained.

Odin clucked his tongue. "Come now, old friend. I do not expect you to be charitable in your account of events, but at least be fair. All of this is hardly for my benefit. It is for theirs."

"I'm sorry—*theirs?* As in the humans?" Annabel cut in. Sick terror clenched at my gut, and I threw myself up the stairs to put my body between her and the most powerful god that had ever existed. All four of her other mates beat me to it—the moment the brash words were out of her mouth, they encircled her in a tight wall of muscle and blades.

Annabel ignored them. "You are saying that their complete annihilation is *in their best interest?*"

Odin raised his eyebrows as he looked at Modi. "I see you have yet to find a way to muzzle the girl."

"My mate does not require a muzzle," Modi spat, anger rising in the wake of his devastation. "And certainly not when speaking to you."

"Ah, yes. Your *mate.*" Odin shook his head. "I was saddened to find that you abandoned your principles in favor of this nonsense prophecy, grandson. Thor was ever so... *angry.* The humiliation of *both* his sons sharing a *human* woman with Loki's spawn... *tsk.* I'm sure some of those poor Jotunns out there are taking the brunt of his fury, but perhaps you should be thankful he won't make it through Ragnarök."

Odin turned his one-eyed gaze to me. "And I see my grandsons are not the only ones to disappoint. Do they know what you have done? Did you whisper all your dark secrets to that human girl while you rutted her like a primitive beast?"

"I told her everything," I said softly, "and she still loves me. You won't win, god-king. She is too strong, even for you."

Odin rolled his eye. "I had such high hopes for you. Such power, such talent... Such darkness. And yet I find you here with the rest of Mimir's sheep, desperately pleading for mercy."

"No one's pleading for anything, old man," Magni growled. "We are here to stop you."

"Oh, it is much too late for that." Odin waved a hand in the direction of the battle. "Surtr's army will win and lay waste to Asgard. Midgard will be swallowed by acid and darkness, and there will be nothing left but a clump of clay for me to mold into something new. Something *better.* Nothing you can do will prevent my plans for coming to fruition. Ragnarök was foretold long before any of you were born."

"I can't help but notice that Fenris is nowhere to be seen," Saga said. "I do believe that big old wolf had some role to play, according to the prophecies... What was it again? Something, something... killing you? Funny how he seems to be missing from the battlefield.

You wouldn't happen to know what happened to him, would you, seeing as you are just going along with Ragnarök as it was foretold?"

Odin gave him a thin smile. "Your furry brother sadly got detained. But worry not—Jörmungandr and Hel can destroy Midgard without him."

"Perhaps you have noticed that Fenris isn't the only one who is missing," I said. "Or have you been too busy hiding to see that no undead armies have arrived here or in Midgard?"

For the first time, Odin frowned. "You have delayed Hel?"

"We have stopped Hel," Annabel said. "As we will stop you. I will not allow you to destroy my world for this… this temper tantrum. I can't believe that all this time, it was you, the supposed *god-king* breaking apart the existence of all there ever was because… because people don't believe in you anymore. How utterly pathetic."

The disgust in Annabel's voice was unmistakable, and that innate terror in my gut tightened into an icy clump. I reached for her with my magic as Odin's nostrils drew up, encapsulating her with my essence just in time.

Power struck against my grip on her, cracking it like an egg and fracturing her own shield. She stumbled backward and into Bjarni's grip with a gasp.

"*Enough,* you insolent whelp," Odin snarled, and around him the shadows lengthened. "You cannot comprehend the powers at play, prophecy be damned! You are nothing but a writhing worm in the dirt, an annoyance under my shoe. You speak of divine needs? To *me?* You dare stand before me with your stolen power, brandishing condemnation because a talking head and an insane weaver have told you that you have the *right?*"

Another crack of the god-king's terrible magic blazed through the air and into Annabel's hastily rebuilt shield. I felt it like a kick to the gut, and nearly bent over double when she went flying off the dais with a shriek, taking Bjarni with her.

"Annabel!"

I don't know who bellowed her name—it could have been any or all of us.

She lay sprawled on Bjarni's chest, his thickly muscled body wrapped protectively around her, and the wave of relief that went through me came as much from the connection I shared with her other men as it did me.

Assured that she was unharmed, Modi, Saga, and Magni swung around to the god-king with mirrored snarls, intent on retribution, but I jumped down from the platform and made my way to Annabel and Bjarni in two steps. As much as my instincts were roaring at me to end the fool who'd dared attack my woman, as much as fear and fury made me itch to throw myself at his throat, I knew where my place was.

I had not believed Annabel when she'd insisted she

could win—not at first—because I'd known our adversary: *Odin*, first among all gods, with power so great I had known of none who could rival it.

She'd opened my eyes in the end, and shown me a kind of strength I hadn't known existed. She'd shown me a sliver of a chance, and I had grabbed onto it with both hands because there was no other choice. But it was only a sliver, and Annabel was still new to her powers.

Too new, a voice whispered at the back of my mind. Memories of my rudimentary magic teachings on our journey through Hel made me grit my teeth and wish I could have trained her from a young age. If I had, maybe we would have had more than that sliver to cling to.

If I hadn't been so scared of what she was to me, I could have insisted she be brought to us earlier. I could have hardened her mind for this. I could have protected her better. But there was no point in wishing for what could have been, and no time left for regrets.

I grabbed Annabel's hand and pulled her off Bjarni's chest and onto her feet. "Don't give him a chance to get another hit like that in!" I barked and wrapped my free hand around her nape. "You *always* hold that shield in place, no matter the force of a strike. Draw from us when you need to, but do *not* let him in."

She nodded shakily, but her gaze hardened as she stared at our enemy. His focus was on the three alphas circling him, and Annabel recognized the threat.

I felt a tug on my innermost, and then the hazy bliss of her consciousness spilling into mine. She rippled through my mind, making me shudder, and then I felt *them.* Like those blurry hours of pleasure in Hel, they became part of me, and I a part of them. I felt the strain of their muscles as they swung their weapons as if it were my own arms carrying through—felt Bjarni get up from the floor and join the fray—and I felt *her* burning through us all, making us stronger, faster, *better.*

I gritted my teeth and anchored myself, willing my focus to remain on my own task. But by the stars, she was so *strong.* My golden goddess; she was our muse, our conductor, and I saw the dismay in Odin's eye as he fielded my brothers' attacks with far less ease than he had expected. He had thought us barely an annoyance—just bothersome enough to attempt to rid himself of us before we could come together, become *this*—but he had not expected a true threat.

I remembered his words as he'd swayed me to his cause. He had told me how this insignificant human girl would never be strong enough to prevent the inevitable, how my worry that I would murder my own brothers in a jealous rage was the only outcome if I surrendered to Mimir's prophecy. I had believed him, because he had seen every fear I carried and spun them so perfectly that there had seemed to be no other option than to betray them all.

It was only now, as Annabel lit up like a beacon in

the darkened hall, that he finally understood there was nothing insignificant about her.

I had two seconds' worth of pride. Then Odin's lips pulled up in a feral snarl, and my entire being seized with horror as he lifted his staff and sent out a shockwave, blasting the four alphas around him and Trud's slumped, half-unconscious body off the dais in a scattered heap.

"Brace, Anna, brace! *Brace!*" I roared, wrapping my magic around her in a protective cocoon and steeling it with every scrap of my willpower.

The impact from Odin's next strike made me drop to my knees and vomit bile. Annabel shrieked somewhere past the ringing in my ears, and I crawled toward her, pulled by instinct to make sure she was unharmed. Golden light encapsulated me, followed by soft fingers darting over my face.

"I'm okay," I croaked, because *she* was okay, and that was all that mattered. "You have to take more. Don't be afraid—take what you need, Annabel, and end this."

"No more playing the defensive," she whispered, but despite her decisive words, there was a tremble in her voice.

"You know she can't win," Odin said, his voice nearly gentle. He walked down the stairs, his staff still lifted to keep the others pinned to the floor.

"What happened to you, Grim?" he asked as he stopped perhaps ten yards from us. Every muscle in my body tensed in preparation for another strike, and

Annabel's magic thickened around me and the others, but Odin simply cocked his head.

"You were so determined you would never mate the girl, and were—dare I say—eager to take her life, but then I find you here, in my home, nothing but another dumb alpha enthralled by omega cunt—throwing away your own life as well as your brothers'. I thought you would give anything for them to live? That was our bargain, I believe."

"What happened is that I opened my eyes," I spat. "Annabel, *now.*"

I felt the yank on my magic as my mate pulled power from all of us, sending a ball of pure, golden energy right at Odin.

He waved his hand, clearly expecting for it to dissipate, but the light didn't so much as flicker before it impacted with the god-king.

And for the first time in perhaps millennia, Odin *flinched.*

The force of Annabel's magic was so strong he was forced to yield ground to keep from getting knocked off his feet. He braced with a leg behind him, his ravens screeching, and stared at us with an expression of utter disbelief and *rage.*

I wet my lips. That Annabel had affected him at all was quite the feat, but whatever damage she'd done was limited. A ruby trail trickled from one of Odin's nostrils, bathing his mouth in red, and though part of me reveled in the fact that my mate had essentially backhanded the most powerful of gods, another part dreaded what might come next.

All in all, she had him pegged—Odin was, at heart, a bully. Perhaps he had not always been this way, but eons of watching his followers turn from him had planted a bitter seed in his brain. This betrayal was the fruit that seed had bore, all rooted in a desire not just for power, but for recognition.

Annabel's magic might not have been enough to destroy him, but it now threatened to shatter the illusion of omnipotence he had worked so hard to maintain—the same illusion upon whose altar he'd been willing to sacrifice the nine worlds.

Looking at him now, I knew exactly the kind of person he was. He was my mother, beating a child to make herself feel powerful while proclaiming it was for my own good. He was my stepmother, so eager to have the upper hand over someone—anyone—she'd rape a vulnerable teenager. He was my father, so concerned with his own schemes and pride that everyone around him became little more than cannon fodder.

Odin was every god and Jotunn and creature I'd ever met who was so small and sick inside they needed to gain power through fear, rather than love. I'd almost become that person myself; only Annabel's patience, devotion, and courage had saved me. I no longer needed the walls I'd once built around myself to keep others at bay. I no longer saw compassion as a weakness, no longer believed a façade of perfect control was worth killing for.

But Odin didn't know her love. He hadn't known *any* kind of love in ages. This—Ragnarök, his ability to destroy and reshape our universe—was all he had.

So when he turned from us, staff still raised, I knew it wasn't a retreat. He had to preserve his legacy and future. He had to destroy his opposition so completely whatever survived the apocalypse would immortalize it in hushed tales and epic song.

And to do that, he had to make an example out of Annabel.

"I have given much to get where I am," he mused as she struggled to summon another fount of magic. "You've heard the stories, no doubt—how I learned magic; how I plucked out my own eye. None of this was handed to me. That's the trouble with you younglings. You want it all just as badly as those who came before you..."

My heart shuddered so hard it nearly stopped. Odin was standing over Magni, gazing down into the young god's face not with anger, nor disappointment, nor contempt—but with complete and utter apathy writ upon his face.

"...but what are you willing to sacrifice to get it?"

"No!" I shouted, intending to lunge at the god-king's exposed back, but my muscles failed me. I dropped to my hands and knees, clutching at my chest as if I could somehow reach the void within where my magic ought to be. Annabel had drawn from me so much, the well was all but dry. I could barely stand, let alone wield my daggers against the All-Father, even as a slow and terrible smile began to spread across his face.

"What are you doing?" Annabel demanded. Her mounting panic sizzled through our bond, compounding my own and joining with cacophony of fear and fury emanating from the rest of her mates. "Stop!"

"I am teaching this brave new world a lesson," Odin replied as she frantically tried to siphon just a little more magic from me. But I was tapped; if I gave her any more of myself, it would have to come from my very soul.

Odin turned his head from Magni then, regarding his ravens. "Bear witness—the goddess of love is dead, and so too shall be the last vestiges of her power." And then to me, he added, "Your matebond has doomed you. It has become a weapon in my hand. Were it not for your foolish attachments, I would have to stand against all of you, but now... well, why kill all of you when just one will do?"

Annabel paled. My brothers roared, cursing and spitting as they tried in vain to out-muscle the magic holding them to the ground. Modi cried out, doing his best to reach for his sibling, but even his terror could not overpower Odin's will.

"Brother...!" he gritted, straining against his bonds with all he had.

It wasn't enough.

Magni seethed, teeth bared, and he hissed through them at his grandfather, "You're... a coward... killing me... on my back..."

Odin only smiled. "Oh, my boy. All your days, I've tried to teach you the benefit of working smarter, not harder. But you never did heed a word I said."

He raised his staff higher, a cold white light spiraling around it, creeping along its length where it culminated near Odin's clenched fist. There it blazed, casting out the shadows from the room, replacing them with a luminescence so blinding that to behold it was to stare into the sun.

Annabel shielded her eyes, voice trembling when she said, "I can't let him do this, Grim. I'm sorry. Please understand..."

And all at once, I did. I understood completely. For the first time, without doubt, or fear, or shame, I knew what I had to do.

She began to rise just as Odin aimed one last barb at me: "I told you it was a weakness."

Without warning I grabbed Annabel's cloak, using it to pull myself up at the same time I pushed her down, back to the floor and some semblance of safety. She grabbed for me, screaming my name, but it was too late. I'd made my choice.

I wished I could tell her it would all be okay, but there was no time, and no way for me to know for sure. This half-baked plan that had struck me sure as lightning was little more than a desperate gamble, but it was all we had—all I had left to give.

A leap of faith; all I could do was hope I wouldn't crash and burn, or I'd leave Annabel and the others in the same dire straits Magni's death would bring about.

But if I didn't intervene, that fate was assured. And so I rolled the dice, slammed shut my connection to my mate, and drew upon the remnants of magic in the wellspring of my soul.

It was just enough for me to meld into what few shadows lingered in the great hall, transporting me instantaneously from Annabel's side and into the path of Odin's killing blow.

"Grim!" she screamed, and not just her, but my brothers too, a chorus of anguish that nearly drowned out the howl of magic as it struck me head-on and divided my atoms.

33

ANNABEL

"Grim!"

The force of my scream shredded my vocal chords, but I barely felt it. My agony originated elsewhere—from a deep, soft place in my chest where one of my matebonds had stretched taut, then snapped.

This can't be happening. After everything...

But it was. The flare of Odin's magic had died, swallowed by Grim's dark, and in its wake had left behind only his body collapsed against Magni's. He was so, so still.

The clash of competing magic was enough to dissipate the bonds holding the others down, and enough to send Odin reeling. He staggered back, away from my mates as I rushed toward them, tears blinding me.

"Grim!"

I fell to my knees beside him, brushing his hair from

his face as Magni tried to summon the strength to push himself up. But he was feeling it too, the same excruciating hollowness where Grim had once belonged—and still did.

I cupped his pale face in my hands. "What did you do? *What did you do?!*"

There was no light in his eyes, no spark to illuminate their fire and ice. Amber had turned to flat, tarnished copper, and the blue I once so adored had gone a dark, lifeless gray that reminded me of everything I'd hated about Hel.

"Don't do this to me," I implored him, shaking him and hoping against all hope to get a rise. "Don't you dare leave me, Grim Lokisson!"

Sobbing, I fumbled for one of his hands and pressed it hard against my womb.

"Don't you dare leave *her.*"

"Annabel…" Magni began, my name falling broken from his lips. I could feel his concern not just for Grim and my grief, but for the lingering threat still in the room.

But then Grim moved, fingers twitching against my armor, and all my attention was on him once more.

"You idiot," I hiccupped, covering his hand with both of mine. "Why did you do it? After all we've been through, how could you?"

"I'm sorry," he rasped, lips ashen, gaze unfocused—and yet he was still here, still alive, anchored to me by our hands pressed against our unborn daughter. "There... wasn't time... for anything else..."

Violently I shook my head. "It's not fair. I can't do this without you. *We* can't do this without you. I don't *want* to!"

His touch had always been cold, but with each passing second, it was becoming frigid. Magni placed his hand on my shoulder, only highlighting Grim's lack of heat. His face was bloodless, his once-pale skin now white, save for the bruises that still lingered around his eyes. He was still here with me for the moment, but gods... he looked like a corpse.

"I'm... still with you," he said, though his voice had grown more distant, devoid of its usual power. "Always... here..."

Beneath my hands, he moved his own, a weak spasm heading up the midline of my body, toward my chest, where it stopped over my heart.

"Here, Annabel," he whispered again, tapping his fingers for emphasis, but just barely. "I'm right... here..."

"Brother!" Bjarni breathed, falling to his knees on Grim's opposite side. He too was weak, body ravaged by Odin's magic, yet he'd managed to cross the distance to be at his brother's side as he... as he...

Died.

Saga came next, limping beside Modi, each supporting the other as they stared at Grim's withering form. There was pain writ across my dying mate's features despite how slack they had become—a pain which was reflected in the expressions of the four other males gathered around us.

"Please stay," I begged him, taking his hand once more and kissing the tips of his fingers like I could breathe life back into him with love alone. "Please... I can't do this alone..."

"You're not... alone," he told me, struggling to get the words out between spasms that wracked his lithe, muscular frame. "You'll never... be alone... again... I made sure..." His teeth chattered in the wake of an awful bodily contortion. "Now go... You have... a destiny..."

"Not without you!" I shouted, willing him to understand at last how important, how *vital*, he was to me, to us, and to all of this. But Grim just touched my chest again in the same place he had before.

"I'm here... Here..."

A rattle sounded from deep in his throat, and I wailed as Magni grabbed me, pulling me from Grim's seizing form. Bjarni made a sound I'd never heard him make before, small and helpless, as he lay his head on his brother's chest and held him as he convulsed.

I buried my face in Magni's shoulder as he shushed me, stroking my hair with a trembling hand, but I derived no comfort from his touch. I knew only pain; pain, and a bottomless grief that was slowly, steadily morphing into a murderous rage.

"She... She won't..." Grim was whispering to Bjarni.

"She won't... go to Hel... this time... Our matebond is... broken..."

"Please, brother," Bjarni answered, tears tracking down his handsome face—a face that never should have known this kind of sorrow. "Save your strength. We'll find a way to—"

But Grim wasn't listening. In this godsforsaken place, surrounded by his mates and family, Grim Lokisson stopped breathing.

The sound that ripped from my chest was foreign even to my ears. I'd never known I could make a sound like that, so full of torment and despair. But it came again, a bitter torrent so powerful it made my teeth hurt.

Magni held me, as much for comfort as to keep me from launching myself at Odin, who had at last regained some semblance of composure and was stalking toward us from across the room.

"It did not have to be this way," he said, almost sounding sorry. "You could have stayed with him in Hel—eked out an eternity for you and your soulmate in the land of the dead. The rest could have joined you, and you would have spent all your days together. If only you had given up this ridiculous prophecy..."

The bastard should have read the room. All four of our heads turned to him at once, a slow, synchronized prelude to the wrath brimming within us all. Beyond our grief, beyond our despair, was a righteous fury yearning to be set free. And in my chest, my magic was expanding, more potent than ever, fueled by a desire to ensure Grim's sacrifice would mean something.

One day I'd tell our daughter about what he did and how it saved us all. And to make sure that happened, I had to do as he'd bid.

I had to embrace my destiny.

I didn't realize I was glowing until the light emanating from me began to play on Odin's face, making his ravens shuffle uneasily on his shoulders. I rose without help and felt Magni do the same behind me, then come to stand beside the rest of my mates, flanking me—waiting for me to lead the charge.

"You called our love a *weakness*," I hissed, my magic flaring, filling me from head to toe. "But it was the only thing that could have spared you a hideously painful death."

"You bore me," he easily replied, raising his staff to issue a blast of magic.

But as it tore toward us, I merely lifted my hand, turning the ball of energy into a harmless spray of primrose.

Odin stared, his weathered brow knotting as he murmured, "Freya...?"

Maybe—it was entirely possible, given I'd consumed her only recently—but this burgeoning power within me felt darker than that.

I used it to shield my mates as they charged the Betrayer, teeth bared and weapons raised to end this battle once and for all.

We should have known it wouldn't be so easy.

Odin engaged with staff and magic, blocking the downward sweep of blades, his body more agile than it had any right to be at his age. But every time he attacked in kind, my shields absorbed the blow, mocking him with its very simple message.

You will never touch one of my mates again.

My men were a symphony, each of them perfectly in tune with the others as they danced around Odin in a lethal ballet. Magni and Modi wound under and through blasts from the god-king's staff, graceful as twin serpents, while Saga and Bjarni were always there to fend off a vicious jab or a swipe, holding their ground to give the Thorssons the openings they needed to strike at the old man.

Yet despite our efforts, all we could engineer was a stalemate—and that was when Odin decided to up the ante once more.

"Enough of this!" he spat, and making a wide circle with his staff, he slammed it into the floor.

Reality yawned wide, and with a sickening *tug*, my mates and I found ourselves on a new battlefield.

The one raging at Asgard's gates.

"Hold the line!" someone shouted over the din of the fray. It was Heimdall, Guardian of the Bifrost, desperately trying to keep the Jotunn horde at bay. "Brace yourselves, and—push!"

Asgard's soldiers readied their shields, gold glittering in the tattered sunlight streaming through the smoke. And then they shoved forward, into the Jotunns, in a clash of armor and flesh that muddied the air with clouds of dirt.

"Annabel!"

It was Mimir; he was lying in the path of the battle, just barely able to avoid being trampled by both sides as he rolled this way and that with what little power he possessed to do so. My magic came to me instantly, surrounding me so that when I sprinted for him, it knocked the other combatants out of the way, allowing me to plow through them like a bulldozer.

I snatched the prophet up just as Saga grabbed my arm and yelled, "Look!"

There beyond the roiling smoke and dirt stood the god-king Odin. The All Father. The Betrayer.

All the way on the other *fucking* side of the battle.

"How do we get to him?" Modi asked. A moment later, he was distracted by an incoming Jotunn and forced to fell it with his blade.

"I don't know," I admitted, desperately scanning for an easy way across. "Can you cut us a path?"

"I..." Magni hesitated, looking first to his brother, then Saga and Bjarni before he said, "No. Not before Asgard is overrun."

"Leave that to me," someone else chimed in.

Someone with a voice like thunder.

I whipped my head in its direction. There, pulling his hammer out of a Jotunn's pulpy skull, stood Thor himself, drenched in sweat and blood and wearing a grin as wide as the gulf between us and his father.

Modi stared at him. "You'll help us?" he asked, utterly disbelieving. Even Magni didn't seem convinced. "Why?"

Thor snorted and hefted his hammer onto his shoulder. "Can't a father apologize for being an asshole to his sons?"

"No," the Thorssons answered in unison, to which the god of thunder rolled his eyes.

"All right, then—let's just say a little birdie told me things might not be quite what they seem." He turned partly away from us, jutting his chin at the tangle of bodies fighting for survival. "Well, make that *two* little birdies..."

"Arni and Magga?" Bjarni breathed, his eyes wide. Then he cracked a smile, shouting to the heavens, "*Arni and Magga!*"

Thor chuckled, returning his hammer to his filthy, blood-caked hands. "Come on, lads—and lady—let's save the nine worlds."

With a mighty swing, he brought his weapon down onto the earth, and from the thick clouds above, bolts of lightning raced to do the same.

The storm he'd conjured was indiscriminate. Bodies flew through the air, Jotunn and Asgardian alike thrown from our path as Thor cut a swath toward where Odin stood. Screams of terror and pain mingled with deafening crashes of thunder, and as we followed our divine escort toward our enemy, Odin's eyes narrowed.

"You seem to be down a man," Thor observed. "Where's the Mistborn?"

I shut my eyes. If I talked about Grim now, I wasn't sure I'd be able to see this through.

"Ah," Thor said after a time. "My condolences. You'll be wanting to strike the killing blow, then, milady?"

I met his gaze. "I don't care which of us kills that scheming bastard, as long as it's me or one of my mates."

The thunder god nodded. "Fair enough. We're almost there. Get ready to—"

A bone-quaking roar cut him off. We stopped, eyes on the gates of Asgard, as the Jotunn locked in combat suddenly disengaged and turned as one.

"Shit," Saga muttered. "That can't be good."

The Jotunns' next cry went up as a howl, and Thor's eyes widened. "No... He wouldn't..."

Whatever Thor was talking about, I was certain Odin *would.* But Mimir filled in the blanks. "He's given the Jotunn the power of the berserker."

And he'd aimed them straight at us.

The Asgardians at the gates stood dumbfounded as the Jotunns on the front lines abandoned their assault, instead barreling in our direction, using clubs, swords, axes, and their bare hands to heave any obstacles—including their brethren—out of their way. They moved as a pack, like the wolves Odin had claimed as creatures of his dominion, and Thor cursed before calling out to the contingent around him.

"Asgardians, to me! *Now!*"

Asgard's soldiers were quick to obey, though it was hardly an easy feat; the Jotunns who hadn't received Odin's gift were still fighting, leaving us caught between two fronts.

"Stay behind my shields," I told them, raising a barrier in a wide semicircle centered on Thor. "Fight only when you must. Our priority is getting to those gates."

"Right," Thor said with a wry smile. "Well, you heard the lady. Keep your asses behind her shield!"

I focused with everything I had to ensure the barrier I'd erected would survive impact with the Jotunns bearing down on us like wild animals. Grim had taught me to channel my reserves, to always give my attention only to the task at hand. Now more than ever, I needed to heed his lessons.

The first berserker crashed against my magic, and I grimaced. This wouldn't be easy, not with so many of them dead-set on breaching the shield, but the power within me didn't so much as flicker. It burned like a furnace, unwavering in the face of the onslaught, and Thor and his soldiers pushed our line forward, into the thick of the battle.

But we were moving too slow. Even with a full-fledged god on our side, the sheer number of Jotunn berserkers kept us from advancing at a pace that would make any difference. Asgard was on the verge of falling even after Odin diverted some of the Jotunn forces to deal with us. There was no way we'd make it to him in time to change destiny—not like this.

Sweat beaded on, then dripped down my brow. I had plenty of magic left in me, but forcing it into this shape, for this purpose, was wearing me down, and the nagging fear that I would burn myself out and kill the baby inside me was fucking with my ability to concentrate.

"We can't go on this way," Magni snarled as he fended off a berserker who'd made it around the side of our shield. "Can you put your magic on the offensive?"

I shook my head. "No—not now. I've put too much into this shield. And there's too many of them. If I drop it, they'll tear us apart."

"What about a distraction?" Bjarni suggested. He was back-to-back with Saga, ensuring they could keep an eye on both sides of the battlefield. "One of us could break off, draw their attention. I vote for one of the Thorssons."

"We are *not* separating," I bit through gritted teeth. "No more sacrifices. No more heroics. We are in this *together*. Understand?"

No way in Hel was I losing anyone else.

Suddenly Thor stopped, and I nearly crashed into him, but at the last moment I avoided the collision at the expense of my focus. Our shield flickered and I held my breath, working to stabilize it once more, but something had changed. I could feel it. The air was different, charged with something both familiar and beyond definition—not electric, but close.

Magic. Someone had brought magic—and a whole lot of it—onto the battlefield.

"Well, you wanted a distraction," Mimir said dryly, and I looked up to see the very last thing I'd expected.

Flanking both sides of the conflict between the Jotunns and soldiers of Asgard was another force entirely. They were poised on the high ground, an army of beings with pale skin, dark eyes, and magic humming in their bright blue veins.

"Mistborn," Thor murmured, tone heavy with confusion and awe. "But what are they doing here?"

That question was answered a moment later when their general pushed through their ranks on one side. I could sense his smirk all the way from here.

Loki. Fucking *Loki* had led the Mistborn here—as well as a contingent of trolls.

"Holy shit," Saga said just as his father lifted a horn to his lips and blew.

The sound rolled over the battlefield like a tidal wave, penetrating the very marrow of my bones. It seemed to slip through me, to physically move between my cells, rearranging them to allow itself passage as it echoed throughout all nine worlds.

"He stole that from Heimdall," Bjarni said into my ear.

For once, I didn't care where the hell Loki had

stolen his latest toy from. All I cared about was that he was using it to help us win. It didn't even matter why, so long as he did it.

As the Mistborn charged down upon the enemy Jotunns from either side, bringing with them the trolls as both siege weapons and heavy artillery, it finally gave us the leg up we needed.

"Go!" Thor shouted over the din. My mates and I obeyed, sprinting for the gates of Asgard as the thunder god and his soldiers covered our flight.

The earth shook with the impact of the trolls' great-clubs, and with the pounding footfalls of the Mistborns' charge. Rocks and soil and other detritus rained down on us in sudden bursts, and it was all I could do to try to anticipate where it might land so I could redirect our shield.

My alphas were in their glory at last, cutting through any stragglers foolish enough to think us easy prey. We were not only blazing a trail through Ragnarök; we were leaving a wake of blood, heralding Odin's fall.

But that didn't mean the god-king wasn't still dangerous. As we neared, he raised his hands, not to command the forces around him, but to drain them of any magic, any power, residing in their blood.

For all his talk of my *borrowed magic*, it seemed he had no qualms about outright stealing some of his own. But Mimir voiced the greater threat.

"If he regains his strength, we're doomed!"

I wasn't going to let that happen. I might not have been able to save Grim, or Freya, or even my parents, but I could sure as hell save everyone else. All I had to do was—

Here, Grim had told me with his dying breaths, touching my chest. *I'm here...*

I skidded to a halt, dropping our shield. My mates stopped beside me, weapons drawn and stained with viscera. Together we gazed up at Odin, the source of so much misery, so much death, so much needless destruction.

He thought he'd won. He thought he'd weakened us by destroying Grim. But there was still a piece of my Mistborn mate inside me, one he'd given to me in Freya's glade when we'd finally reunited with the others.

"I love you," I said, calling upon that last vestige of him now.

His magic burned cold in my chest, dark tendrils wrapping around my own golden light, not to overcome it, but to help it along. It bolstered me, strengthened me, embraced me from within, caressing me like I wished its owner could do just one more time.

As Odin took his sweet time gathering power, mine was at the ready, eager to serve. I let it free, hurling at him all my hate, all my rage, all my grief and sorrow.

When Odin fell at the gates of Asgard, it was to a wolf composed entirely of magic both light and dark—just like the original prophecy had predicted.

Only the world didn't end. The skies cleared. The horns grew silent. The Jotunn hordes fled, save for the Mistborn, who held their spears and swords above their heads to signal their triumph.

We did it. After so much loss and so long a journey—we'd won. And Grim had been there too, in the end, though now...

Now he was gone. That last bit of him, the magic he'd gifted me, had dissipated along with Odin's life. It was over, both the battle and any lingering connection I had to him.

As the survivors of Ragnarök celebrated, I fell to my knees in the dirt, hid my face in my arms, and sobbed.

34

ANNABEL

I was only vaguely aware of the cheers erupting across the battlefield. Adrenaline still thrummed in my veins, but I couldn't take in any of the euphoria spreading among the einherjar and Valkyries as Surtr's army fled, the rift between Asgard and the human world healing in a ripple of golden light.

With every pulse of my heart, the ache of loss penetrated deeper now that I had no purpose left. I had done my duty. I had fulfilled my destiny.

And I had lost part of my soul in the process.

"We should go back. To Valhalla," Modi said softly. His warm hand closed around my shoulder. "Grim gave his life for every other living being. We owe him a vigil."

"We owe him a lot more than that," Bjarni rumbled, the grief in his voice echoing through my own anguished heart.

Saga drew in a deep breath through his nose, visibly

steeling himself before he sheathed his sword and turned to me. Gently, he pulled me up into his arms and hugged me tight to his body still caked in Jotunn blood. "Come, Annabel. We need to give him this final honor."

We left the battlefield amidst cheers, but it felt like they came from somewhere far away—like they weren't part of the dark, numb world we walked through.

Grim, Grim. Come back to me, baby. Please come back.

The walk up the path leading to Valhalla was a blur, and I don't think I could have made it on my own. Saga carried me in his arms, like a lost child, and Bjarni, Modi and Magni surrounded us in a tight circle. They were the reason I had to find a way to continue on. Them and the life I carried. *His daughter.* He had given his life for us; I could not let that be for nothing. I wouldn't.

I pressed my hand firmly against my abdomen as we crossed through Valhalla's ports and began the long journey through the quiet hall.

"Trud?" Magni mumbled, his quiet voice cutting through the silence and jerking my gaze up. Ahead, in the middle of the destruction left behind from our first fight with Odin, Modi and Magni's blonde sister sat hunched over a crumpled figure on the floor.

I opened my mouth, but nothing but a hollow sob came out. *Grim.* Seeing his body hit me with grief all over again, and something fragile inside of me *broke.*

I ran. I tripped over the scattered debris and slipped on the floor, but it barely slowed me down. The second

I was by his side, I fell to my knees—and dissolved into tears.

"Grim. Grim, my love. My soul. Please come back to me. *Please!*"

I bent over him and let the weight of everything that had happened press me into his chest. He was so, so cold. My beautiful, haunted soulmate. My fifth. I had only known the true him so briefly. It wasn't fair. He had lived in darkness and pain for a millennium, and I was supposed to be the one to finally show him what true happiness was like.

"Oh, baby, I'm so sorry," I sobbed. "So, so sorry."

"Don't... cry."

I stilled at the hoarse whisper, my insides flicking from a painful, agonizing mess to numb stillness. My shuddering breath sounded like a thunderstorm in my ears as I slowly, so slowly turned my head.

My eyes slid over his wide chest, up the column of his throat, and finally to his face.

He was as pale as ever, but his eyes... His eyes were open—barely more than cracks, but enough that the pale blue and glowing amber of his irises were visible. He... He was alive?

"Grim!" I cried, relief combusting in my chest so hard I burst into another bout of tears.

He only groaned weakly in response.

A warm hand touched my cheek. "He will live, my sister. But he is very weak. Be gentle."

I didn't look at Trud—I couldn't take my eyes off

Grim's face, not even when Bjarni and Saga fell to their knees on his other side and gripped his hand and arm.

"Brother," Saga choked. "We thought we'd lost you."

"How did he survive?" Modi asked. He and Magni knelt on each side of me. I was grateful for the pressure of their bodies, because my head felt too light and my muscles were quickly losing the battle against the flood of emotion.

"I don't know," Trud said quietly. "His matebond was broken. He was dead."

"You are... my soul," Grim rasped. His hand twitched as if he was trying to raise it, but he couldn't manage. "He... He did not... break... that bond. I... felt you. Found... Found my way back. To you."

"The soulmate connection," I whispered. "It called you back?"

He groaned a confirmation.

"Thank you," I whispered, though I didn't know who I was thanking—Grim himself, perhaps. With a deep breath, I pulled myself together and focused inward.

My magic came slowly, like mud being pulled through too-narrow tubes. Magni grabbed me from my left, and I felt his power flow into me, supporting mine. A moment later, Modi joined him. Their magic was almost as depleted as mine, but their support was enough for my golden light to enter Grim's body.

Two more hands clasped onto me, and Saga's magic joined mine while Bjarni offered his fortitude.

There was little damage to Grim's body, but I still filled him with our essence, willing our combined magic to give him strength.

After a few long moments, Grim wrapped his chilly fingers around my wrist with little more strength than a newborn kitten. "Stop, Annabel. That's... That's enough."

My vision swam when I opened my eyes again, but Grim looked... not well, but better.

"He needs time," Trud said. "Time and care. But he will heal."

"He will have all the time and care in the world," Magni rumbled. He kissed my shoulder and clapped a hand on Grim's thigh. "Thank you, brother."

"Thank you," Saga echoed. Then Bjarni. Then Modi. Then me.

"We did it," I said softly. The relief of Grim's survival numbed any joy that should have filled those words. "We killed Odin. We stopped Ragnarök."

"Of course you did," Grim whispered. When I clutched his hand, he tightened his fingers around mine ever so slightly. "You are Annabel Turner. Nothing will stop you."

I choked out a sob and lifted his knuckles to my lips. Four pairs of arms closed around us both, encapsulating us in warmth and light.

We made it. We'd survived.

"There you are!" a loud, male voice boomed from somewhere outside my safe cocoon. "You are the heroes of Asgard! You can't just run off after such a glorious battle!"

"They are the heroes of all nine realms, Dad," Trud said. When I peeked out from my shelter of bulky arms and shoulders, I saw the thunder god standing a few yards from Grim's sprawled body, Mimir's head tugged under one arm. Behind him, more filed in. I caught a glimpse of Loki before he was lost in a sea of Valkyrie wings.

"Heroes of the nine realms they are, indeed," a tall, darkhaired woman said. She stepped forward past Thor and looked down at us with an inscrutable expression. "You saved us all. Where we failed, you succeeded. I thought no one would have the strength to kill my husband. I am glad I was wrong."

Husband?

"Thank you, Frigg," Modi said, and despite the absolute formality in his voice, I felt a flicker of wariness in our bond.

Frigg. Odin's wife. I recalled Mimir's stories about the now-dead god-king. He had occasionally mentioned his wife.

"And you, Frigg? Did you know of Odin's deceit?" A stern-looking man missing one arm took up stance by Thor's side.

She turned to them. "We have not shared chambers for centuries, let alone secrets. I fought the Jotunn hordes by your side, Tyr."

"The god-king acted alone." Mimir's voice broke

through the throng, pulling everyone's attention from the queen.

"Odin included no one in his plans—at least no one he didn't curse to silence. Please, my old friends; we do not have time to bicker. We find ourselves without a king, our walls broken, and Midgard suffering from the ravaging of Ragnarök's harbingers. The Goddess of Love is dead.

"What we need is to come together and rebuild. We cannot abandon the humans now that their belief in the old ways has been forced alive. We cannot allow Freya's death to tear every realm apart with war and strife."

"Freya is dead?" someone gasped from the crowd. Murmurs of sorrow rose and broke like waves through the gathering. "What will we do without her?"

"The loss of Freya cuts deeply, but we have another Goddess of Love." Trud stood, the gentle billowing of her powers masking her stumble as she found her feet. She looked down at me and gave me a soft smile. "This woman stopped Ragnarök in its tracks—and killed the god-king himself—all through the power of her love for five sons of Asgard. Look at her—sense her power for yourselves. She is one of us."

"A mortal?" Frigg asked, brow furrowing as she stared at me. I was too exhausted to flinch under her unnerving gaze. "You wish to make a mortal a goddess of Asgard?"

"Mortal-*ish,*" Mimir said. "Thor's daughter is right.

The essence of Freya lives within this child of Midgard. She may have been born among humans, but she is a mortal no more."

Frigg stepped toward me, and with a graceful swoop, bent to hold out her hand.

"May I?" she asked.

Reluctantly, I released Grim's hand to take hers.

Power washed through me. It wasn't rough or dominating, but it wasn't gentle. It filled me up and searched out every part of my inner self. Then, just as swiftly, it eased back out of me.

"Truly a wonder," Frigg murmured. Her eyes crinkled at the corners as she rose again and turned to crowd. "They speak true. The Savior of Asgard carries a kernel of Freya herself. With her aid, we will get through this."

"About that..." I grimaced as I straightened between my mates. "There is a small matter that needs to be dealt with before I can help you."

"Oh?" Frigg turned back around to me.

"Speak, child," the one-armed man said. "We are in your debt. Whatever you need, we will provide."

I really hoped he was right.

"To escape Hel, I had to make a bargain with the Queen of Death," I said, steeling myself against the murmurs that erupted anew. "If I do not find a way of letting her walk freely among the realms, she will claim my soul. And without my soul... Freya's kernel will die too."

"What? Let Hel go *free?*" Thor blustered. "Do you know how dangerous she is?"

"Is she more dangerous than a world without a Goddess of Love?" Trud asked.

"We stopped Ragnarök, Father," Magni reminded him. "We did what no other god could. If you do not let Hel go free, we will all die with our mate. Is that the legacy you wish for your bloodline?"

Thor huffed and clenched his hands by his sides. "Of course not! But... this is *Hel* we're talking about."

"It would appear we have little choice," Frigg said. She cast me a long look, then nodded once. "We will fulfill your bargain, little one. On the condition that you serve in Freya's place."

"I—I will." It came out as a stutter, because as I looked around the shattered hall of Valhalla, at the gods of myth who all as one nodded their acceptance of me and the five men who had given everything to get me through this, it finally sank in.

"I told you I would make you a goddess," Grim rasped.

"Holy fuck, I'll be... a *goddess?*" I whispered, low enough that only my mates heard me.

"You always were," Bjarni murmured. He skimmed a hand through my hair, and I leaned against him. "Our golden goddess, born from steel and blood and love."

Low in my abdomen, where she was curled safely around my yet-unborn daughter, Freya's soul hummed in agreement.

EPILOGUE

Grim

"Who's the cutest little princess? It's you! Yes, it's you!"

I rolled my eyes at Bjarni peppering our daughter's face with kisses in between cooing nonsense praise she was still much too young to understand.

But Astrid gurgled happily in response, her tiny fingers clinging to my brother's blond beard as if he were the most delightful thing she had ever experienced in her short life.

Annabel had assured me that three months was far too young for her to have picked a favorite.

"If you want time with the baby, you're gonna have

to be forceful about it," Magni said. He was sprawled on the other end of the large sofa, watching Bjarni babytalk at Astrid with measured patience. "He's been hogging her for two hours straight."

"Papa Magni is just cranky because he was on night duty," Bjarni cooed without shifting his focus off our daughter. "Yes, he is. And someone had a blowout, didn't they? Yes, they did! Who's my big girl?"

"For Frigg's sake, you are melting her tiny brain cells," I growled, stepping forward to rescue my child.

Bjarni reluctantly let me scoop her out of his arms, but Astrid clung to his beard with more strength than a baby had any right to. He winced and reached up to gently untangle her fingers from the strands.

"She's gonna be a warrior, this one," he said, giving her a loving smile when she squawked at being separated from definitely-not-her-favorite-parent and flailed to reach for him.

"Just like her mother," Magni agreed with a grin. "She's about as demanding as well."

"Don't let Annabel hear you say that," Bjarni chuckled. "She's been prickly all day—threatened Magga that she'd re-murder her. I had to send her out to help Saga and Modi with the fences to blow off some steam."

"What did Saga and Modi do to warrant such harsh punishment?" I quipped, though most of my focus was on Astrid. She finally stopped reaching for Bjarni and turned her attention to me. As always, her usually so easy smile faded as she looked up at me, her light-blue eyes getting a serious look that she should have been much too young to produce.

Annabel, afraid I would be hurt by my daughter's lack of easy giggles around me, had told me babies didn't truly laugh until they were older, and that she was probably just mesmerized by my "gorgeous eyes." I appreciated the sentiment, but I was reasonably certain that she was wrong on this one. I felt the touch of Astrid's consciousness when she looked at me like this—with intense concentration, as if she were trying to puzzle out how on Earth she could have been born to *me.*

I didn't take offense. I was also a little stunned that *I* had sired a tiny person this perfect.

"Punishment? What could be sweeter bliss than spending an afternoon in the company of our lovely mate?" Bjarni asked, amusement dripping from every word. "So what if the lazy bastards refused to give me a hand with the sheep this morning? That would never stop me from ensuring they have help with their chores."

"Especially not if that help comes in the shape of a cranky goddess deeply committed to her non-stop bitching?" Magni asked, eyebrows arched.

"I think you mean a *divine goddess* whose voice is always a blessing—even when it's used to curse you into the ground," Bjarni replied with a grin.

I tore my gaze from Astrid's, a frown knitting my eyebrows. "Is she all right?"

I hadn't seen Annabel since I'd snuck out of bed that morning to tend to the horses. Not all of our animals had made it through Ragnarök, but I'd been relieved to find Draugr and twenty more of our flock still alive when we returned to our farm in Iceland. It had been a short discussion. The Thorsson brothers had been keener on staying in Asgard, but Annabel wanted to raise Astrid in the human world. Once Modi and Magni tasted Bjarni's hot chocolate with marshmallows, they'd decided they could be happy in Midgard.

Bjarni and Magni exchanged a glance.

"Yeah. She's fine," my brother said, but that slight hesitance in his voice tipped me off.

I narrowed my eyes at him. "What is it?"

"Well, it's been three months since she birthed the little one," Magni said, his voice almost *too* casual. "And you know how irritable she gets around *that* time."

That time. I stiffened as I glanced from him to Bjarni —who only shot me a wry smile.

"You think her heat is coming?" Tension coiled in my gut, reaching down my thighs and up my abdomen. It had been twelve months since we'd managed to stop Ragnarök—a full year since Odin shattered my matebond.

My family had nursed me back to full health, but no matter how many times I made love to Annabel, no matter how full my heart was when I fell asleep in the big bed Saga and Magni had crafted to accommodate us all, I was never complete. Not fully. My soul still reached for where my connection to Annabel had been, and I ached. I missed it. I missed *her*, even as she lay in my arms at night.

In my darker moments, I even missed *them*. I would never admit that out loud, of course, but I envied the connectedness they all shared—which had been mine for such a brief moment.

If Annabel was finally coming into heat, that meant I would be able to claim her again. Reestablish our bond.

Bjarni shrugged, and my stare turned harder. I had long since gotten over my fury at sharing her, but a heat was something different. Any alpha who smelled his omega in that state tended to lose his mind, and if any of my brethren tried to get between me and her before I got my mark on her neck, there would be blood.

Before I could snarl a threat, the door banged open and practically blew a snow-covered Annabel inside.

"Hel's tits!" she snarled. "How is it that we nearly fucking died to end Ragnarök, and it's *still* snowing this badly?"

"It's called 'winter by the Arctic Circle,'" Saga, who'd followed her in, said. He unwound his own scarf, revealing a tired set to his mouth before he reached for the cranky woman and began unbundling her from her many layers of clothes. "And could you please, *please* not blaspheme the Queen of the Dead? She might actually hear you, now that she's roaming around the lands of the living."

"I've got eighteen years until she gets a claim on my magic. *I* freed her. If she's insulted by anything I say, I invite her to come tell me in person," Annabel huffed. She spotted Astrid in my arms and made a beeline toward us, plucking the baby from me with a markedly gentler coo.

"Someone's feisty," Magni chuckled.

"You have *no* idea," Saga grumbled, eyeballing our mate.

"Why don't you all just screw off?" Annabel's harsh words were somewhat softened by the smile still plastered on her lips as she rocked our daughter.

Bjarni and Magni seemed to have a point. I took a step closer to Annabel, slipped an arm around her waist, and bent to breathe her in.

"What the actual fuck are you doing?" Annabel growled. Before I could pull away, she bit my shoulder, making me yank my arm back with a hiss. She gave each of us a glare. "I am *not* in the mood to be manhandled. Not today."

We all watched her stomp off to the bedroom, Astrid safely tucked against her chest.

But dramatic exit or not, I knew what I'd smelled. I'd recognize that scent anywhere, even if it was still in the very first stages.

"Her heat is coming," I said to no one in particular.

There was a small pause. Then Saga said, "You should go to her."

I looked at him, eyebrows raised.

"Did you expect a fight?" he asked, lips quirking in a small smile. "When she is ready, bring us Astrid. We will join you once we feel your bond reignite."

I swallowed, my throat tightening as the others nodded their agreement. My brothers. Whether in soul or blood, it didn't matter—they were my family.

"Thank you," I said softly.

"Sure thing," Bjarni said. "But hurry up. Our generosity only goes so far, hmm?"

Fair. I shook my head and turned back to follow Annabel into the master bedroom.

Just as I slipped into the hallway, I heard Magni ask, "Where's Modi?"

"He'll be in soon," Saga said. "He's still not great with sheep handling. Slagathor got into the feed, and he tried to grab her. He's currently nursing his balls in the barn. Might be a day or so before he's ready to join in."

Bjarni's rumbling laughter trailed me down the hall.

I didn't knock as I pushed the door to the bedroom open, and Annabel gave me an irritated look when I stepped fully inside.

She was naked from the waist up and nursing our daughter, which was likely why I didn't get a scolding.

I climbed into bed, folding my legs under me to sit at the foot. Nothing calmed me like watching Annabel feed Astrid. The others were more inclined to butt in and insist on smearing nipple cream and burping the baby, but I could watch the two of them together for hours—and often did. It was also the reason I got kicked out of nursing sessions a lot less frequently than my four brothers.

"Don't just sit there and stare," Annabel grumbled. "I'm *so* hot. Come cool me down while I feed this insatiable beastling you impregnated me with."

I knelt up to shrug out of my shirt and crawled to her, slipping under the covers so I could wrap my arm around Annabel's torso. Her skin was scorching against mine, and she let out a hum of relief and nuzzled in closer to rest her head on my shoulder.

"Ooh, that's better."

Astrid cracked her eyes open to see what had her food source jostling, and shot me a grumpy glare before she pressed her face back into her nipple of choice.

"The nurse says it's just trapped gas when she does that," Annabel said, but the delicate frown marring her forehead hinted that she too had some doubts.

I reached out to rub between Annabel's eyebrows with my free hand. "I am used to the females I love glaring at me. It doesn't faze me, mate."

Annabel gave me a scowl that pulled a rumble of laughter from my chest. I leaned in and stole a kiss from her before I looked back to Astrid. She had my dark hair and pale complexion, but her already pretty features suggested she would grow up to be as beautiful as her mother.

"You are such a good mother," I said quietly without taking my eyes off our baby. "That gentle heart of yours... I always thought it a weakness, but it is not. It is your greatest strength. And I am... so honored that I am the sire of your first child."

Annabel pressed her lips to my shoulder before she looked up at me. In her eyes, I saw that all-consuming love I had never known before her reflected back at me. My breath hitched in my chest, and I leaned in again to kiss her. My nostrils filled with her slowly blooming scent, and I lost myself to the undertow of everything that was *her:* my Annabel.

She groaned into my mouth and kissed me back with mounting urgency, small gasps of air brushing against my lips as she let her tongue slip between them.

A sharp cry pulled us apart with a jerk.

I looked down at Astrid, who wailed with fury at being ignored.

"Sorry, baby," Annabel cooed. She deftly shifted Astrid to her other breast and reclined against the headboard with a small groan. "Seriously, how is it this hot when there's a damn blizzard rolling in? Is there some other mythological doomsday coming y'all have forgotten to tell me about?"

I shifted my weight to my hip so I could lean more firmly against her and brush my hand over her forehead. "There are no more mythological doomsdays."

She leaned into me with a soft moan, eyelids fluttering at the contact. She nuzzled in close again, lips skimming over my shoulder, encouraging me to pet and stroke her face and body with small noises.

It wasn't until I leaned in to kiss the side of her neck and she let out an involuntary moan that she clocked on.

With a suddenness that made Astrid squeak in protest, Annabel jerked back and stared at me, wide-eyed. "Oh my God! It's a damn heat, isn't it? I'm in *heat?*"

The accusatory note to her voice didn't go unnoticed.

"You are," I agreed.

She looked from me to the baby in her arms and sighed. "If any of you get me pregnant again, we're going to talk to your dad about how he managed to give birth that one time. I know it was to an eight-legged foal, but I'm willing to risk it."

My only response was to kiss her forehead.

After a little while, Annabel said, "When... When we go through it, will you...?"

"Will I what?" I asked, even though I knew. The soft tremble in her voice betrayed her vulnerability, even if she refused to look at me.

"Will you claim me? I know you didn't want to when we first..." She sucked in a deep breath. "If it is not something you want, then you don't have to. I love you, with or without that bond."

My little mate. She knew how I'd struggled with the

intimacy our connection brought—with being laid bare for her.

I grabbed her chin between my thumb and index finger and gently turned her face to me. Her lovely, chocolate eyes met mine, and my heart shuddered in response to the question written in them.

"There is nothing I want more in this world than to mark you as mine," I said quietly. "You were born to be mine, Annabel. My soul was forged for yours. I do not fear you, my mate. Not anymore. Never again. You have given me everything. *Everything.* So yes, tonight I will claim you again. And then me and my brethren will pleasure you until you are sated and full, and our souls are wound together forevermore. *That* is what I want."

A pretty blush spread on Annabel's already heated cheeks, but she said, "I want that too, Grim."

I pecked her lips and glanced down at the still-nursing baby on her breast. "She does eat a lot."

Annabel chuckled and leaned her head against mine, a contented sigh escaping her as she too looked at our daughter. "She'll sleep eventually. And then, Grim Lokisson—then you and the others are going to show me how a Goddess of Love should be worshipped."

And we did.

WHAT'S NEXT ON YOUR TBR LIST?

He is everything she fears – She is everything he needs.

On the run from the demon hell-bent on possessing her, Selma Lehmann finds herself in the hands of a far more dangerous enemy.

Lord Protector Kain is ruthlessly handsome, brutally savage—and exactly the fate she's feared since the day she learned what kind of creatures hunt her from the shadows.
They call her a Breeder, and there's only one thing a demon Lord could want from her... But if she's ever going to reclaim her freedom, she will have to trust the monster who swears to protect her from his own kind.

Kain never wanted a mate—only pain awaits a demon foolish enough to give his heart to a human.
When tantalizing Selma lands in his lap, he knows his duty is to put her to auction and return his focus to the war threatening to bring his entire race to its knees.
Yet every instinct in his body roars to make her his, and he will have to choose. His heart—or her soul?

DEMON'S MARK

ALSO BY NORA ASH

THE OMEGA PROPHECY

Ragnarök Rising

Weaving Fate

Betraying Destiny

DEMON'S MARK

Branded

Demon's Mark

Prince of Demons*

ALPHA TIES

Alpha

Feral

ANCIENT BLOOD

Origin

Wicked Soul

Debt of Bones*

DARKNESS

Into the Darkness

Hidden in Darkness

Shades of Darkness

Fires in the Darkness

MADE & BROKEN

Dangerous

Monster

Trouble

CPSIA information can be obtained
at www.ICGtesting.com
Printed in the USA
LVHW091751120522
718583LV00007B/664

9 781913 924058